Jo Silva is the author  *the World Detective* Cornwall, and also writes historical and contemporary fiction under the name, Melanie Hudson.

BB bookbub.com/authors/jo-silva

THE WRECKER'S CURSE

The Edge of the World Detective Agency

JO SILVA

One More Chapter
a division of HarperCollins*Publishers* Ltd
1 London Bridge Street
London SE1 9GF
www.harpercollins.co.uk
HarperCollins*Publishers*
Macken House, 39/40 Mayor Street Upper,
Dublin 1, D01 C9W8

This paperback edition 2023
1
First published in Great Britain in ebook format
by HarperCollins*Publishers* 2023

A catalogue record of this book is available from the British Library
ISBN: 978-0-00-862281-7

This novel is entirely a work of fiction. The names, characters and
incidents portrayed in it are the work of the author's imagination. Any
resemblance to actual persons, living or dead, events or localities is
entirely coincidental.

Printed and bound in the UK using 100% Renewable Electricity
by CPI Group (UK) Ltd

Dedicated to Emily and Adrian Clark –

'If I really don't like somebody, I kill him…'

Deep Water – by Patricia Highsmith

Prologue

Night-time, and the scene is set to perfection. A fox barks from the direction of Pengelly Lane, while a woman stands atop Logan Rock, encouraging her long velvet cape to billow in the breeze. With her arms outstretched and head thrown back, she beckons a low-lying sea mist ashore to join the party. A murder of crows (not so named for nothing) takes flight from deep within Sam Penhale's wood (that'll be the fox, no doubt) and somewhere in the distance a badger digs his razor-sharp claws into the spleen of a cornered rat while his friend, the barn owl, happily disembowels yet another small, screeching, writhing, defenceless animal, eating it alive until its heroic little heart finally beats out its last teeny-tiny pulse...

And the meek shall inherit the earth, they say. Of course, they will.

The wrecker's lantern (the torch from an iPhone 11, bought for an absolute steal from eBay last week) is especially bright and clear as it swings above the mist, encouraging the prize – Jack Crowlas – away from Penberth Cove and along the coastal path towards his destination, Logan Rock. The rock is a majestic headland that thrusts itself into the Atlantic Ocean, like the prow of a Cornish ship, and is drenched in local legend such as pirates, smugglers, wreckers, giants and, of course, Poldark.

Proper job!

The wrecker watches on as Jack Crowlas – all credit for his perseverance – stumbles along the coastal path at a pace, drawn in by the light, his right hand acting as a navigational aid, reaching out to touch sharp, wet granite rocks as he edges along the path. The stumbling is on account of him feeling quite queasy by now, and most probably dizzy, what with being drugged.

Silly Jack.

If only he'd pause for a moment, if only he'd halt to rest his back against the rocks and have a bit of a think, he would realise that his eyesight is not all that it should be, and that his mouth is excessively dry. He would also realise that the exotic image of the figure he sees holding the lantern ahead of him – a mash-up of Little Red Riding Hood and a minotaur, with an exotic bird of paradise swooping figures of eight around its head – is not the purveyor of all his wildest hopes and dreams, but the exact opposite. In fact, not Little Red Riding Hood at all, but a wolf, and a wolf very definitely wearing sheep's clothing.

But never mind that now. It's time to dance, and dance to music he knows well – 'Enter Sandman' Metallica.

But this is brilliant! He's dancing on the footpath. And

why not? What a promise he's had.

It's a promise that will finally satisfy Jack's ultimate fantasy, and it will be handed to him – no doubt he can barely believe it – on a plate, the lucky devil.

The rasping voice rings out in the darkness, speaking just three little words.

'Are ee ready, Jack Crowlas?' (OK, five little words).

'Oh, I be ready!' comes the reply.

And like an overly excited dog, with his mouth gaping open and his green eyes wide – so wide, in fact, that the whites are now almost completely obscured by the pupils – Jack Crowlas, transforming himself into a trusting child, raises his arms to the heavens and reaches upwards, and with his prize in sight, he begins the final clamber to the top of the rock...

Which is when a huge slab of cold metal slaps him across the head and within a moment he is falling (falling, falling), the ridiculous muscles in his arms now powerless as he claws into the night, the realisation dawning as he looks up that he's been in a trance – a stupid, idiotic trance; that he's been duped – or doped, rather. And when the final words of magic, 'Siri, enable torch,' ring out into the darkness and the lantern is relit, the mask slowly slips away, leading him to yell just a few (profound, one might say) little words into the damp night air:

'I'll kill you, you crazy psychopath!'

A splash echoes across the clifftops.

The wrecker smiles the smile of sweet revenge and turns for home.

'Kill *me*, Jack Crowlas? I don't think so.'

Chapter One

DONNA

'Just before sunrise, on a rocky outcrop by the art deco lido in Penzance, Donna Nightshade – known as "Deadly" to her mates – sits alone in a powder-blue VW campervan and waits. Her focus is soft as she gazes towards St Michael's Mount. Her middle fingers and thumbs are softly touching in a meditative trance, and as the first sliver of golden light breaks out above the horizon and the sun's golden fingers reach out to tap an electric dance on the lapping tide, a sleek line of heavenly stillness steps out of the camper, stretches towards the stars, slips off her surfer's robe, and falls, like a sharp dart of feline perfection, into the shimmering yet icy sea.

'Fifteen minutes, that's all it takes for Deadly to swim to the end of the rocks and back again, the first shock of cold offering an electric bolt of endorphins that no drug has ever matched. And it is that feeling of complete physical presence within her own body that Deadly craves now. It is a euphoria as necessary as the rhythmic breath of life, which is why every morning, rain or shine, Donna Nightshade puts on her distinctive swimming costume, with tongues of flaming fire licking from naval to throat, and as she dives into the mirror sea, she shatters her demons, and baptises herself in the deep, whispering waters so inexorably entwined with her dark, ancestral past...'

My sister puts down the newspaper and glances up, looking anxious.

'What a heap of crap!' I say, referring to the garbage she's just read out. 'I don't swim every morning, and how can I gaze at something if my focus is soft? That journo is trying too hard with his writing. Fact!'

I'm standing at my workbench in a large but crumbling Victorian glasshouse in the walled garden of my ancestral home, Penberth. Penberth is a thirteenth-century manor house (with tenth-century battlements) that nestles in an idyllic valley that runs down to a tiny private fishing cove just to the west of Penzance, where pirates (like us) come from.

My younger (and only) sister, Lamorna, is sitting on the opposite side of the workbench and is reading aloud from the local newspaper. With a hand-tied bouquet of home-grown 'meadow mix' in my left hand and a bright-orange dahlia varietal called Mrs Eileen (a good do-er apparently – lucky Mrs Eileen!) in my right, I put aside my rising temper for a moment and concentrate on the bouquet. I thread five long stems of Mrs Eileen into the bunch and then, bouquet complete, I tie them off with raffia, place the flowers in a metal bucket on the bench and reach across to take the *Penzance Packet* out of my sister's hands.

My eyes run over the article while Lamorna returns to playing the harp (Cornish and handily lap-sized). She's playing 'Secret Love Song' by Little Mix in a soft, understated, angelic way, which isn't surprising, because that's Lamorna in a nutshell – soft, understated, angelic. She can play the fiddle, too, and the guitar and the piano (Lamorna didn't bother with school), which means that her dedication to providing a musical accompaniment to all aspects of my life is thorough. She has a song (and instrument) to match my every mood, every thought, every event and it's *really* annoying, but what can you do? She means well. Back to the article.

'"The sun's golden fingers"?' I say. 'Who the hell writes that way? It's the local rag not the year nine literature prize!' I tap the table hard with my right forefinger. 'That journalist is going down in my book. In fact... Ruby? Ruby!' I look up to the rafters of the glasshouse where our pet macaw usually hangs out. There she is. 'Find Donna's book!' I say. 'There's a good girl. Find Donna's book!'

'Sod off!' squawks Ruby.

Lamorna stops playing. Her hands rest on the harp strings. She looks at me. To be fair, the moment is worthy of the dramatic pause.

'Your book?' she repeats quietly, her eyes swimming with several complex emotions. 'You mean your actual book?'

I return to the bunch of flowers and start to fiddle. 'Yes.'

'Isn't that a little... severe?'

'Ruby? Ruby!' I shout again, not answering Lamorna, who has returned to her harp and is now playing 'Pity

Party' by Melanie Martinez. (She's trying to tell me, not so subtly, that I'm being a bit precious.)

Ruby lands on my shoulder. 'Hello, poppet,' I say. 'Where's my book?' She flaps her feathers, which is Ruby's version of a shrug. 'Find Donna's book,' I say, batting her off my shoulder. 'Go on, lazy bones, find Donna's book!'

An avian eyeroll later, Ruby takes off.

About Ruby.

Ruby is a macaw, which is a long-tailed bird of paradise with a big beak – not to be confused with a common or garden parrot. She has a bright-red body, a plume of multi-coloured feathers, and is totally cool. Her beak is hooked and the colouring around her right eye is black and (by some wonderful quirk of nature) perfectly formed into the shape of a patch, which is handy, given our family history. The moment I stumbled across Ruby on a pre-loved website I was hooked, which was good news for Ruby because, with a dirty cackle of a laugh, a foul mouth, and the bad-ass attitude of a Hollywood diva, she wasn't going to be rehomed easily. The previous owner was an old lady in Plymouth who boozed it up every night down the dockyard and whose drinking buddies taught Ruby some colourful language. Always on the lookout for a marketing ploy (Penberth Manor has never paid its way) I at once introduced Ruby to social media – or rather, I introduced social media to Ruby. She's trending on Twitter this week (#whosaprettygirlthen) and has fifty-thousand followers. But all that notoriety does make Ruby rather difficult to live with, and the only way to keep her reined in is to threaten to put her in my book – which I would never do, but she doesn't know that – and anyhow, it's always best to let everyone, including macaws, think that your mental health is slightly 'on the edge'. (It saves the bother of being arsed about later.)

About my book…

The first-born woman of every generation of the Nightshade family is named Belladonna Nightshade and subsequently known as Donna or 'Deadly' and it's lucky because Nightshades seem predisposed to give birth to females. Thanks to our own interpretation of primogeniture, which favours women, each Donna Nightshade is also the heir to the Penberth throne – *moi aussi*. We share the surname 'Nightshade' with a poisonous plant from the *Solanaceae* family, a plant more commonly known as deadly nightshade. Its Latin name, which I prefer, is *Atropa Belladonna* and it runs rampant in a wild patch behind the glasshouse at Penberth. (As an interesting aside, Belladonna also means 'beautiful lady' in Italian, which is nice.) With a lineage that dates to Agincourt and a family history that includes more than a little swashbuckling and derring-do, there have been quite a few Deadly Nightshades over the years; I'm Deadly Nightshade XIII (lucky for some). My Aunty Donna was the last woman in charge, but I didn't have to wait for her to die to get my hands on Penberth because she's presently indisposed… and by that, I mean that she's in prison on Bodmin Moor on account of being certified insane. It's not a high security prison, although she's not allowed to leave. What happened was that poor old Aunty Donna took her name too literally in her younger days and got into more than a bit of bother with a man called Jack Crowlas – in fact, she married him and subsequently tried to kill him – but unlike other Nightshades before her, she wasn't good enough at covering up her tracks.

I took on the mantle of monarch when I turned eighteen, being the oldest daughter of the next generation of Nightshade women, although not the actual daughter of the previous Deadly (the one in prison) as she has no children. My own mother (dead) was a younger sister to the last Deadly (the one who's in prison). I do have another aunt – Kerensa – who hasn't bothered having children (*'My pelvic floor is too precious, Darling'*) and is Aunt Deadly's identical twin. She's an absolute pussycat. Kerensa lives here in the family manor with Lamorna and me, and we also have Uncle Jago living with us too (real name: Mardon Lucius Nightshade V) who is named after a saint from Wales and whose name means either mad, fortunate, or lucky, depending on which site you go to on the internet. But we just call him Jago.

Every Belladonna Nightshade buys herself a book – a journal, if you like – on the day she assumes command; mine has a nice Liberty print cover. It's an important document in which we are expected to chronicle the events of our lives for future generations to ponder over and, presumably, learn from. This habit began with the very first Belladonna Nightshade, who was the grand dame of the brood and revered by the rest of us as a goddess. This journal is the place where secrets are kept, and helpful hints and tips are passed on. I am, therefore, duty bound to write down the name of any person declared a sworn enemy to the family. The name of the perpetrator is written down on the back page (if there's room) and a line is drawn through the name – preferably in blood, but these days a red Sharpie will do. Strange things tend to befall those who are unfortunate enough to go down in 'the book' – and they really do, honest to God, it's weird. But maybe it's not so surprising because in going down in the book they automatically receive 'ye wrecker's curse', also known as, 'ye curse of the deadliest of all ye black pyrates'.

We're such a pleasant family.

The book works on suggestion – a bit like voodoo but without a shaky rattle or a witch doctor – and although no one outside the Nightshade family has ever clapped eyes on the book, the local population choose not to get on the wrong side of us just in case. (The Cornish do love a bit of legend.)

But back to the glasshouse where Ruby is looking for the aforementioned book. The elephant still lingers in the room (the newspaper article), and I lean across the table to grab it. Lamorna, who is the gently running brook to my Niagara Falls, continues playing the harp.

'It doesn't even make sense,' I say, scanning the page with the speed and unsettledness of a victim of atropine poisoning. 'And he might as well have sent up an aircraft over Penzance trailing a banner with "Deadly is a druggie!" written on it.'

'*Was* a druggie,' my sister corrects, stilling the strings on the harp again.

I assess a photograph (of me, practically naked) that takes up most of the page.

'I just knew that journalist was a weasel,' I say, narrowing my eyes. 'He had one of those weaselly faces, you know?'

Lamorna shuffles on her stool.

'I thought he looked quite attractive when I saw him,' she offers. 'Not that he'd float my boat, obviously.'

She puts fingers to strings again and moves on to Ariana Grande's 'Dangerous Woman'.

I grab a dustpan and start to tidy my workbench but pause with the brush halfway across the table.

'What do you mean, "when *I* saw him"?' (My sister doesn't often venture much beyond the manor, except to skip along the coastal path when she's out searching for wildflowers, rare choughs, unusual moths, sea pixies... that kind of thing).

Lamorna progresses from a shuffle to a shrug. Her sweet, pale heart-shaped face is framed by a mass of copper curls. She stops playing.

'He was down by the cove the other day. You were in town. I'm sure it was him. Fairly ripped surfer type. Nice hair.'

I snort. Ripped? Hardly. Decent pins. But ripped? No way.

'What did he want?'

'No idea.'

'Did you have a go at him?'

'What for?'

Lamorna can be so hazy sometimes. 'Trespass, obviously! Did you tell him the cove is private land?'

Lamorna is doing her usual thing of concentrating more

on her harp than her conversation. 'He was out for a walk along the coastal path and just happened to wander up the valley a little way. No harm done. It was nothing.'

I grab the cuttings bin from the back of the greenhouse and brush the debris from the table into it.

'Journalists, dear one, are never out for a purposeless wander. Never.'

Lamorna glances up. 'I thought you said he wasn't a proper journalist?'

She isn't being sarcastic. Lamorna takes everything literally. It's a spectrum type thing, which is why she's as cool as all hell.

I return the bin to where it belongs, sit down, rest my head on one hand, and pick up the newspaper with the other. I examine the image and decide that I look... well, good. Sexy, even. But no, this is wrong. I'm regretting meeting him at the Penzance lido now... and why on earth did I wear a swimming costume?

Lamorna quiets the harp once more (this is how we live our lives – conversation, music, conversation, music – rinse and repeat) and just as a negotiator might carefully lean forwards to remove a gun from the fingers of a rampaging psychopath, she reaches across the table and takes the newspaper from me while smiling her understanding at my frustration. I have no idea how she understands me so well. Surely, she's too young and innocent to reach into the horror show that often rampages through my mind.

'I think we should frame it,' she says, smiling at the photo. 'He caught you just right.'

My expression is unaltered. I am impervious to flattery.

'And what was it he called you again?' Lamorna runs an eye down the column by tracing a finger down the text. 'A... wait a minute... here it is: a "sleek line of heavenly stillness" and a "sharp dart of feline perfection".' She glances up. A ghost of something bordering on flattered amusement flashes across my lips. I button it up, quickly.

'That's as may be,' I say, 'but it was supposed to be a simple interview for the spotlight feature to drum up business. Not a bloody criminal profile.' I take a deep breath. 'I'm going to regret this, but you'd better read on. Forewarned is forearmed, as they say...'

Ruby swoops by and throws my book onto the bench just as Lamorna begins the next paragraph.

'She approaches me in her swimsuit, a towel thrown over her left shoulder, her right hand outstretched in greeting. The body art on her right thigh draws me in. I'm helpless, fascinated – a scuppered ship heading towards a wrecker's lantern. We sit together at a table by the lido, and I wait while Donna squeezes the water from her long gypsy hair. That's when I see the electronic tag on her ankle, an accessory that speaks of a rebellious past. It is covered by a delicate braid of leather, as though she keeps it there as an echo, a need to re-live the pain of her own (and her ancestors') shackled past.'

Lamorna dares to glance up again. My nostrils are flaring like a tethered dragon. She reads on.

'But we're here to talk about her new venture, not the past, she reminds me, because Donna Nightshade has just launched a new business – the Edge of the World Detective Agency – an enterprise that sets her firmly in history as

Penzance's very first private eye – or *pirate eye*, as I point out.'

Lamorna breaks off and glances up again.

'Pirate eye?' she repeats. 'I *love* that. We should go with *that* as a logo, not the other thing.'

She waits for my response. None comes.

'It's not too late,' she presses. 'I could draw a fab picture? You'd be the pirate, obviously, but instead of an eye patch, you'd have a magnifying glass, and a tricorn hat, just like a pirate Sherlock Hol—'

'Forget it!'

She returns to the article.

'The new business will run alongside all the other Nightshade enterprises, one of which is the "Pirate Experience", which is run from the Nightshade family boat – a sloop moored in Penzance Harbour. Donna is also CEO of a flower farm and floristry service, both run by the whole family – aunt, sister, and uncle – and orchestrated from their business HQ, the family home, Penberth Manor, which is hidden in its very own picturesque valley near Lamorna Cove. The valley runs to the only private fishing cove on that stretch of coast and has been in the Nightshade family for hundreds of years.

'The Nightshades also run a small theatre company that performs regularly at the Minack amphitheatre. Isn't it a little unusual, I ask her, this decision to merge floristry with detective work? Not at all, Donna is quick to answer, her elbow on the table, her chin resting on the back of her hand. "Florists," she explains, "are the keepers of many secrets. The seemingly innocuous handwritten messages written on those little cards hint at all kinds of shenanigans. Flowers are, after all, messengers of the heart, and if crime is linked to emotion… well, Cornwall is rife. Oxford, Midsomer, and Shetland can't have all the fun, you know!" She laughs. "Passion, grief, loss, love, agony, secrets, and lies – it's all here, hidden in just a few simple words on a card and stuffed into a bunch of flowers. I'm hoping to pick up quite a few detective agency clients as a direct link to my flower deliveries. Cornwall is a county that is proud of its colourful and passionate history and remains crammed to the rafters with dodgy characters and illicit goings-on, especially around Penzance. Yes, there are a few more pasty and charity shops here nowadays, but it's pretty much remained true to its roguish past."'

Charity shops? Roguish past?

The locals will kill me!

I am outraged. I turn to another bucket sitting on the table and grab the initial makings of my next order. I grab my snips, and with the nimble fingers of a surgeon working against the clock, quickly strip a rose stem of its thorns while muttering, 'He's painted me as a complete tit!'

Chapter Two

DONNA

A woman in her fifties floats into the greenhouse to break the mood. She is a woman with the grace and poise of an expensive cat, despite wearing a lollipop lady Dayglo coat over yoga gear. (Note for the non-British: a lollipop lady is someone who willingly throws themselves into the path of oncoming traffic and represents an iconic British institution designed to help school children cross the road safely. Every morning in Britain, thousands of women – and the very occasional bearded man – loiter near primary schools holding metal 'stop' signs in the shape of a lollipop, before walking defiantly out into the middle of a busy road during rush hour. With a menacing glance at the driver, she will shove her 'stop' sign in front of a speeding car, and with a saccharine smile to the adorable school children waiting patiently on the pavement, she beckons them to cross the road.) It's a role Aunt Kerensa was not necessarily born to play, but she gets by.

About Kerensa...

Kerensa is a genuine yogi, as opposed to some woman in her forties who orders a yoga DVD and finds herself with her leg stuck behind her head being carted into Accident and Emergency. I have never joined any of Kerensa's popular Ashtanga yoga classes, even though her brand of yoga is regarded as the most rigorous form to practise and would therefore usually appeal. No. I do a kick boxing class twice a week instead, because when the shit hits the fan, as it invariably will for a woman, adopting a tree pose might be restful but it will be bugger all use against an assailant who grabs you from behind in a dark alley – or a lit one, for that matter. And as for the downward dog... my eyes water just thinking of the vulnerability associated with that particular pose.

Lamorna returns to her harp while Kerensa rests her lollipop stick against the back wall of the glasshouse. She removes her sou'wester hat which allows a long mass of soft curls the colour of New Zealand's finest manuka honey (those bees work so hard) to trickle over her shoulders. She shakes the rain from her coat while nodding in the direction of the newspaper.

'You're taking centre stage in every newsagent's in town, darling.' Her deep voice is full of sexy breath. Ruby goes into attack mode and starts strafing Kerensa. They have a love-hate relationship, those two. Kerensa bats her off – rather aggressively for a yogi – but I let it go. 'But you do realise that half the county will have ejaculated over that image by lunchtime?'

My head drops into my hands.

'Only half?' interjects Lamorna, snorting. 'Let's be honest, if she weren't my own sister, *I'd* do her!'

Kerensa frowns. 'Don't say *do*, Lamorna, dear,' she chides, hanging her coat on a peg. 'Say *have sex*, or at the very worst *make love to* but never say *do*. It's every bit as crass as *shag* or *screw*.' Kerensa turns to me and nods to my bouquet. 'Are these the flowers for June Baker?'

'Yes. And have you seen my knife, by the way? I've lost it.'

'Your knife?'

'The one Aunty Donna gave me. It has my name on it.'

'No, I've no idea where it is. No idea at all.'

Kerensa picks up the previously made bouquet and fiddles with a dahlia. 'Are these the ones we're sending from Old Man Bosullow?'

I put down a camellia branch and pick up a couple of sprigs of fern. 'Yes. Why?'

Kerensa hovers by my right shoulder. 'Then you'll need to put the last of the sweet peas in there, too.' (It's been a great year for our sweet peas, and even now, in September, there are still a few left from a late sowing.)

'Won't the colour clash horribly with the dahlias?' I ask.

Kerensa floats through the glasshouse and nips outside, dashing through the rain. She returns with a shake of her head and a handful of sweet peas, cut long on the stem. 'But according to the lore of love—'

'The lore of love, my arse,' I say.

'—According to the lore of love,' she repeats, 'they bring an abundance of luck and blissful pleasure.' She raises her voice a little to be heard from the far end of the glasshouse. 'And Old Man Bosullow needs all the help he can get, poor dear. He's desperate for a sh—' Kerensa floats back towards me holding the sweet peas. Lamorna stills the harp and glances up.

'…A good time?' finishes Kerensa.

I hold the pale-pink sweet peas against the bright colours of the tied bouquet and scrunch up my nose. The candyfloss pink clashes dreadfully with Mrs Eileen. Kerensa sighs.

'You're right,' she says, perching on the stool next to me. 'I'll make a separate little bouquet. We'll call it a special offer. The effect will be the same.'

Ruby jumps onto the table and offers me a sprig of gypsophila to add to the sweet peas before taking up her own perch on the peg where Kerensa's coat hangs.

'Don't shit on my coat, Ruby,' says Kerensa, turning to look at her. 'There's a dear.'

Kerensa titivates the sweet-pea posy and notices my book on the table. She looks at Lamorna. I can't see her face but I know she'll have adopted an expression of troubled concern. Lamorna offers a microscopic nod towards the newspaper while simultaneously arriving at the final bars of 'Dangerous Woman'. I throw a ball of twine across the bench at my sister. It bounces off her head.

'You were reading,' I say.

Lamorna swaps harp for newspaper.

'But if Donna is hoping to find mystery and intrigue lurking in the Penzance underworld, she need look no further than her own family's notorious past – a past infamous for its wreckers, smugglers, and thieves.

'"The first thing you need to know about me is that I come from a long line of pirates," she says, before falling silent and throwing me the seductive smile of a temptress. When I ask what the second thing I need to know is, she leans forward, her gaze as steady as a rock and says, "When the first thing to know about me is that I come from a long line of pirates, there's absolutely no need to know anything else."

Well, quite.

'But when considering the notion of a Nightshade taking on the role of detective, I can't help but conjure the phrase, "poacher-turned-gamekeeper". I say this and she laughs.

'"They do say, set a thief to catch a thief," she says, her eyes glistening. "But I hope to show that my generation of Nightshades has more in common with Robin Hood than Blackbeard. We aim only to do good work in the community these days."

'That may be so, but this latest venture is a serious departure from the past, and at thirty-something (she would not reveal her age) Donna "Deadly" Nightshade is already a true Penzance legend, with rumour and gossip abounding regarding her teenage exploits – exploits that cement her place in local history every bit as firmly as the likes of Cut-throat John and Black-hand Bill.

'When I ask what the local detective sergeant – her childhood sweetheart, Joseph Enys – thinks of her new venture, a flash of something ineffable crosses Donna's face. "Didn't he arrest you on Newlyn Green years ago," I ask, "leading you to spend considerable time at Her Majesty's pleasure? And didn't his great-great-great-grandfather, the local magistrate at the time, arrest your own great-great-great-grandfather at the Admiral Benbow pub, subjecting him to the hangman's noose?"

Deadly throws back her head and laughs.

'I can assure you that no one from that particular family has ever kicked any Nightshade arse!'

'I was going to correct her by saying that, in fact, by sending her to prison in her late teens, Joseph Enys had done exactly that, but whatever the case, if Deadly knows what DS Enys really does think of having a new private eye on his beat, she doesn't say, but there is, I note (at the thought of the detective sergeant) a faraway look on her face and a trace of… is it regret? Affection? Love, even?'

'Stop!' I screech. 'Read that last bit again.'

'Which bit?'

Which bit?

Lamorna glances up at Kerensa, aware that, in the whole article, this is the bit that will truly grip my shit.

'But there is, I note (at the thought of the detective sergeant) a faraway look across her face and a trace of… is it regret? Affection? Love, even?'

'That's it!' I jump off the bench and cross to a set of pine drawers. Ruby, always one to enjoy a good fracas, jumps onto my shoulder and eggs me on, squawking. A terracotta pot acts as a pen holder, and I take a red Sharpie from a collection before opening a drawer to rummage through an assortment of crap until I find a ruler. With pen and ruler in hand, I return to the bench and open my book at the last page. I nod towards the newspaper. 'Carry on…'

'As the interview draws to a close, I ask about the

Penberth Players, a local amateur theatre company that is about to stage a performance of a play written by Donna herself called *Sleeping Dogs Lie*. I confirm that the players are all close friends of Donnas and ask if they are her merry band of men, perhaps? She laughs and says, "Yes, I suppose they are. We're all very close."

'She stands then. The meeting is over. I can't help but glance at the distinctive tattoo on her thigh. She places her foot on the chair and flexes.

"Want a proper look?" she asks.

I do and I am undone.

The tattoo depicts a stem of purple flowers running from knee to hip, the last tendril disappearing into the inner thigh, behind the line of the swimsuit. Body art of a beautiful flower seems fitting for a florist, but then I look deeper and see that the stem weaves its way around a silver cutlass and speaks of a different kind of life entirely, a life that is light years away from the serene idyll of the flower farm at Penberth Manor. For a moment I think I notice something else, too, something hidden deep beneath the cutlass – a scar perhaps. Donna notices the angle of my enquiring head and removes her tanned, toned leg from view. The show is over, and I know as she slips on her shorts, vest top, and flip flops, that this is a woman who will fascinate me long after the interview is over. Who is she, this Deadly Nightshade? This woman who hides behind layer after layer of legend and is clearly caught up in her own tangled sense of self?

As she turns to leave, I quickly ask what motivates her. What motivates a woman to run a flower farm, a tourist ship, a theatre company, and now a detective agency amongst other things (such as singing jazz and soul music at the Star Inn, Newlyn). Without a moment's pause, she says, 'Penberth.' And as I stare across the pale blue waters of the lido, with the bitter taste of espresso lingering in my mouth, I remember that still waters run deep and think of Donna's right thigh – that tattoo, that flower. I quickly google the etymology of the plant and find that deadly nightshade is a chameleon of many uses – it is a plant that can be used either to kill or to cure. It simply depends on how you choose to handle it.

'Words and photograph, Jase Clarkson.'

The glasshouse is silent now, the rain having petered out. Silent except for the scratch of the pen as I write out the name, Jase Clarkson, in my book. Even Ruby knows it's best to keep schtum. Lamorna and Kerensa look on while, very neatly, I draw a line through his name in red.

Tis done.

My fingers begin to tap out a rhythmic drum beat on the bench. Lamorna takes the newspaper to the compost bin and shreds it. (First rule of composting: shred. Things rot quicker that way – cabbages, flowers, dead bodies...). She doesn't return to the bench but crosses to a baby grand piano at the far end of the glasshouse – it's a roomy old place (built by an Edwardian Deadly). She lifts the lid, cracks her fingers (Lamorna's only annoying habit), and begins to play the introduction to 'The Fear', Lily Allen.

Kerensa turns to me with a newly created posy in her hand. A petal falls off – I did say that the sweet peas were past their best. 'He obviously has the biggest crush on you,' she says. 'What's he like?'

I open my mouth. Words are spoken but they aren't mine. Lamorna speaks over the piano to answer for me.

'Hot,' she says, before adding, 'And Donna's type… If he hadn't been subject to the wrecker's curse, obviously.' Lamorna allows herself an amused smile and returns to concentrating on the music.

Kerensa sighs and pops her posy in the bucket of water.

'Well, I hope you haven't been a little hasty putting him in your book,' she says. 'You could have had some rare old fun with a man like that, I should think.'

The woman is deranged.

'Fun?' I add a few sprigs of rosemary to my bouquet as additional filler. The whole arrangement looks like it's had a fight with a bramble hedge, but it is an odd day and I've been distracted.

'Yes, darling, fun.'

Lamorna has moved onto the classic Lily Allen line, *'And I don't know what's right and what's real, anymore…'* while I reach up and stretch.

'Anyhow,' I conclude, 'it doesn't matter how stunning he is; he's called Jase.'

Lamorna stops playing.

'So?' both women say together.

I take the bouquet back. They wait for an explanation as I add three stems of Michaelmas daisies.

'Isn't it obvious?' I eventually explain. 'No woman should ever have to scream out the name "Jase" in the height of passion. It's up there with Des, or Peter, or Harold.'

'Now you're just naming serial killers,' says Kerensa, before adding, 'It wouldn't be a problem for me – the name. I stopped shouting out the name of my lovers ages ago, right after my'—she pauses and looks up at the rafters, thinking—'tenth, no, eleventh, sexual partner.'

I look at Lamorna, whose hands hover above the keys. We both wait for an explanation.

'Why?' we ask in unison.

Kerensa takes the dizzy posy of sweet peas out of the bucket, holds it to her nose, and takes a deep breath. The petals scatter like confetti.

'Because my eleventh lover was José...' Kerensa's eyes betray the fact that her mind has taken a quick stroll down memory lane, which is a pleasant lane by the looks of things, paved with gold, and erotica. 'What a difference a single vowel and an accent on the E can make! Now *there's* a name to be shouted out in bed! His lovemaking had the majesty of the bullfight mixed with the spiritualty of the Catholic church. Amazing. But I suppose I'm always worried that I might shout out José's name by mistake – my mind does tend to drift back to him to get me in the zone sometimes, so to speak.'

I nod my understanding.

My sister pipes up. 'What happened to him, Aunty Kerensa? To José?'

Kerensa sighs the sigh of a person recalling a beautiful memory. She shrugs. 'He moved on, as is the right way of things. Some men should be shared liberally, I think. Never

look back in anger, girls, never look back in anger.' She pops
the posy back in the bucket. 'Not if the sex is *that* good, at
least.'

Lamorna and I make eye contact before Lamorna grabs
her guitar, joins us at the bench, and hits the intro to 'Don't
Look Back in Anger' by Oasis.

Kerensa and I sing along to the line, '*So, Sally can wait,
she knows it's too late…*' etc.

'Well, it's stopped raining,' says Kerensa, rendition
complete. 'I think I'll head up to the dahlia field and do a
spot of deadheading.' She pauses to kiss me on the head.
'Stop thinking about the article, Donna.'

'I'm not.'

'You are,' she says. 'You're clenching your jaw. Such a
bad habit, darling. It's ageing, and you'll get all kinds of
problems with your neck.'

I relax my jaw and smile. She strokes my hair and adds,
'For what it's worth, I think that was a fabulous write-up.'
She nods towards my book. 'And I'm sure that your Great-
Great-Great-Great-Great-Grandma Donna (that might not
be enough "greats", but you know what I mean) would be
very proud of you.' She grabs a trug and a pair of
secateurs and heads towards the door. Ruby, having
sensed my body relax, decamps to Lamorna's shoulder
and perches on the left strap of her dungarees. Kerensa
pauses by the door.

'But… perhaps let's make sure Uncle Jago doesn't catch
sight of it – the article.' She turns the door handle. 'Or he'll
be taking the blunderbuss off the wall again to chase after
this Jase fellow, and that thing is such a pig to clean.'

'Good!' I shout. 'I wish he would! This family is becoming far too "live and let live" for my liking.'

Kerensa wafts a final angelic smile our way before turning to step out of the glasshouse, which is when a hulk of a man wider than he is tall, with a hoop in his left ear and wearing a pair of 1980s-cut faded jeans and a heavy-metal-inspired T-shirt steps in.

A fraction of a second later, Kerensa has dropped the trug and her hands are around his throat.

Oh great! Uncle Jack is back.

Chapter Three

A woman stands in front of an altar with her hands in a prayer position and gazes upwards at a big gold cross. The heavy doors of the Church of All Saints, Penberth, are slammed and bolted, and robes are abandoned on the cold, stone floor. On the altar sit what seem to be offerings of a vicar's dog collar and a photograph of a naked woman. She bows her head.

'Dear Lord,' begins the woman, which is as good a start as any. 'I am the way, and the truth, and the life. I know that you are the all-seeing omniscient one and so you alone know what I have become. I have veered from the path of goodliness, godliness, and of righteousness, and damnation and regret are to be my burden. Can you ever forgive me?'

A trapped bird flutters in the rafters suddenly. The woman takes this as a sign that He will ... or maybe He will not, forgive her. It's always so difficult to decide with signs. She drops her hands from the prayer position, picks up the photo, and reverses from the altar to take a seat on a pew.

Like a motorist that can't help but glance at the car crash on the other side of the road, the woman looks at the photograph before lifting her head to look through blurry eyes at the stained-glass window above the altar. God is bearing down on her, and if she's not mistaken, he's started to grimace (well, as much as any man with a beard, white robes, a kind smile, and Jesus sandals can bear down and grimace) and she knows that she's just about as deep in the proverbial poo as any woman can be. She also knows that this stained-glass image of the big man is nonsense – God is love, after all, not a middle-aged white man holding a lamb in one hand and a cherub in the other. But still. He seems to have taken on more of a glower over the past few days, and really, who can blame Him?

Her hands rush to the prayer position again. 'I promise, one way or another, dear Lord, I will do your will, and that wicked man – that *wicked*, *evil* man – will get exactly what he deserves.'

She drops to her knees. 'Bloody hell that floor's hard,' she says, before grabbing a prayer kneeler and slipping it under her knees.

The hands go up again – let's call it an occupational habit – and she shouts out, in full ecclesiastical glory: 'And I say unto him … Jack Crowlas, *May the Lord strike you with Egyptian boils and with tumours, scabs, and itch for which you find no cure.*'

(It is probably the biblical passage quoted least frequently back to the Almighty on a day-to-day basis, but right now, it's all the woman's got.)

Chapter Four

DONNA

I prise Kerensa off Uncle Jack and rest her against the whitewashed wall that constitutes the back of the glasshouse. Jack reeks of the 1980s – stale beer, fags and Paco Rabanne (the more discerning nose would probably pick up a whiff of Newlyn fish market, too). The aroma visibly follows him as he approaches the bench, something with which he is all too familiar.

He's back, then. Jack Crowlas. Uncle Jack. The man who would be king. I've seen neither hide nor hair of Jack for many years, not since Lamorna was tiny.

Lamorna and Ruby pick up on the tension and I realise that they are probably wondering who this man is. Lamorna puts down her guitar and takes up the Cornish harp again while Ruby carries out a quick feather ruffle.

'If it isn't little Donna Nightshade,' says Jack, ignoring Kerensa completely and glancing around with obvious disdain, his nostrils flaring. 'All grown up and out of prison.'

He takes up a position at the head of the workbench and leans backwards against a display stand of exotic plants. The stand wobbles as lots of obvious metaphors flow into my mind – bad pennies, shit on my shoe, an ill wind…

'Hello, Jack. It's been a while,' I say.

Lamorna plucks out the opening bars of 'Scarborough Fair', very slowly and with great feeling. She somehow manages to convey an aura of… is it… menace? Yes, it is, and that's not easy with a tune as innocuous as 'Scarborough Fair'.

'I've had a few things to do,' he says, 'but decided it was finally time to come back to the old homestead.' Jack flexes his arms and looks at his biceps, one then the other, which is quite unnecessary but he's obviously proud of them. He leans forward and places his hands on the table, his jaw tight. I think of advising him to relax his jaw but sod it. Why offer this idiot any advice? 'This place is rightly mine, after all,' he adds.

I'm about to tell him to sling his hook and that he'll have to take us to court if he wants one sniff of my manor, but then he takes a business card out of his jeans pocket and places it on the table in front of me. I see that it's my business card for my new private detective business. He taps on the card.

'Picked this up at The Wink'—that's a pub—'and it's funny because I'd just been thinking to myself, I wonder what my little Donna Nightshade is doing with herself these days? Then I sees this card… which is very handy. Very handy indeed.'

He sniffs and walks around the table, grabbing a stool

before sitting down next to me like he's just rocked up at an American bar.

He leans in. His breath is rank. He lowers his voice.

'Somebody's after me,' he says. 'And *you're* gonna find out who.'

'Whom,' corrects Lamorna, glancing up.

I look beyond Jack and notice the family motto that's written in Latin on a piece of wood hanging lopsidedly from one nail above the door frame: *Suum Cuique*. It translates as, 'May all get their due', and I remember that I'm not eighteen anymore; I'm thirty-something, and frankly, Jack Crowlas (whose own mother, God rest her soul, hated him) can take a running jump off a (preferably) very high cliff.

'I'm not interested, Jack,' I say. 'Find some other mug to sort your life out for you.'

I turn away and start to rise from my stool. It's a mistake. I should have continued to stare him down because I would have won, no question. As a teenager I had regular staring competitions with my Border collie, Schooner, and I never lost – and it's not easy to outstare the type of dog that has literally been bred to win staring competitions with sheep.

He grabs my arm, forcing me to sit down again, then he glances at Ruby and Lamorna, before releasing my arm with a smirk. Lamorna has moved on to 'Spanish Dance No.1' from *La Vida Breve* – fast, dangerous, exciting. He runs the back of a finger up my thigh, tracing my tattoo, or rather, the scar underneath it – he of all people knows about the scar – stopping at the hem of my shorts. He leans in and whispers, 'Little miss high and mighty, ain't ya?' I notice Lamorna's left eyebrow rise infinitesimally.

(As an interesting aside, I am yet to meet anyone who can raise their right eyebrow independently from their left).

'You and that flat-chested bitch'—a nod in Kerensa's direction—'are still the whores you ever were and you'll damn well do as you're told.'

Kerensa steps towards us, lollipop stick in hand, and thrusts the word STOP in front of Jack. But Jack Crowlas is no timid motorist. He grabs her arm, rips the sign out of her shaking hands, and throws it across the floor. It lands with a satisfactory clank. He glances up at Ruby who is still in the rafters and is being *unbelievably* quiet, before reaching for an avocado that sits in a bowl of vegetables Lamorna was supposed to prepare for lunch half an hour ago, and asks, 'Did you know avocadoes are poisonous to parrots?'

'She's a macaw,' says Lamorna, her fingers still tickling the strings.

'What?'

'Ruby is a macaw, not a parrot. There's a difference.'

Jack turns to me. I think Lamorna disquiets him. 'And you remember what happens if you don't do *exactly* as I say, don't you, Queen Bee?' He nods in Ruby's direction, smirks again, and whispers two little words in my ear. 'Woof, woof?'

I won't give him the satisfaction of a gulp.

'Fine. I'll help you,' I say. 'But I don't want to talk about it here. I've got a gig at The Star later. We can chat before that.'

He winks. (Winking men are *the* worst!) 'Good girl,' he

says, and relaxes his jaw. Turning his attention towards Lamorna, with a sickening smile he says, 'And what's your name?'

Lamorna stops playing and stares at him, deadpan. Her Titian hair is cascading over her shoulders and her head is matching the left strap of her dungarees by tipping to one side. Ruby has also jumped onto Lamorna's shoulder and tipped her head to accommodate Lamorna. They stare at Jack for what seems like forever, then Lamorna lifts her left arse cheek, and farts.

About Lamorna…

The moment Lamorna breathed her first breath, my mother breathed her last. Weeping silent tears at the loss of my worshipped mother, Lilias, I looked down at Lamorna in the incubator – tubes coming out of her nose, cannulas attached to her tiny hands, a monitor beating out the rapid pulse of her premature heart – and I vowed to keep my little sister safe, because from the very first moment I looked at her, I knew there was something different, something special, about Lamorna. Indeed, for the first two days of her life, I knew with absolute certainty that Lamorna's soul hadn't yet entered her body, that there was a vacantness within the incubator still – a pod without a seed – and even though the baby's heart was beating, her soul – or whatever else that thing is that makes a body a conscious being – wasn't there yet. My mother and my sister had clearly met somewhere betwixt and between those two things we call life and death, just to have their moment.

On the third day, dozing by the incubator, I drifted into a fitful sleep and my unconscious mind connected with my mother's spirit. She was holding a baby wrapped in the family shawl. She handed the baby over to me, kissed me on the cheek and said, 'Lamorna.' When I woke and looked into the incubator, Lamorna opened her eyes, and I knew that she had finally arrived. Although I was only eighteen years old at the time, I felt ready to take on the task of caring for a child – it coincided with my ascension to the throne of Nightshade, after all, so I was feeling older than my years as it was. Yes, I ended up in the clink for a while shortly afterwards, but I've been sister and mother to Lamorna ever since my release. I always knew she was a special, unusual, gifted child – a child who could nail a major global issue in a single sentence and yet found the touch of clothes on her skin irritating; a child who would happily live her life completely naked and open and free, if only the rest of the world would do that too. Truth is, Lamorna doesn't always understand when she's in danger, so I act as a permanent human shield. Like now.

'My name?' she repeats. 'I'll tell you mine, if you tell me yours.' Her fingers return to the harp strings. ('Sonata No.2: Allegro'.) I lean back on the stool so that Jack cannot see my face and shake my head in Lamorna's direction because a) Lamorna doesn't speak that way and b) it's not a wise decision to dick around with Jack Crowlas.

Jack laughs and steps around the workbench to stand next to Lamorna. I begin to wonder how long it would take me to run to the library, grab the blunderbuss off the wall (mess or no mess), load the thing, and shoot Jack right out of the greenhouse and into kingdom come.

Too long.

He visibly eyes Lamorna (urghhh!) and raises an eyebrow – his left one, see! – and now I'm picturing my cutlass. I could run him through in a moment, but it's on the wall next to the blunderbuss. I'm just imagining running florist wire around his throat when he holds out a hand in Lamorna's direction.

'Jack Crowlas, at your pleasure, ma'am.'

Lamorna takes his stumpy paw, holds it briefly rather than shakes it, and stares at him, more intensely now, taking him in.

'Lamorna Nightshade,' she says.

Jack turns to me and laughs. A full belly laugh. I feel sick, properly sick.

'Bugger me!' he says. 'If it isn't the babe in arms, all grown up!' He cups Lamorna's chin in his hand and raises her face up to his (there's really no need to do this as she is at his height sitting on the stool but, as my mother used to say, Jack never did quite get over the fact that he started growing out rather than up when he hit thirteen). Ruby, now on the right page, lunges at his hand with vicious pecks. Jack swipes out and poor Ruby lands with a thud on the workbench. I reach out to Ruby as she pushes herself onto her knees (OK, feet), but the glance she flashes me says, *I'm fine, don't give him the satisfaction.* If I'm not mistaken there's also a flash of something with a hint of revenge about her eyes, too.

Lamorna slips off her stool and walks to the dresser drawer where she takes out a printed sheet of paper. She hands it to Jack.

'These are the daily rates for the Edge of the World

Detective Agency, Mr Crowlas,' she says. 'Terms & Conditions are written quite clearly on the back. I suggest you glance over them before deciding whether to engage my sister's services.'

Jack guffaws, throws the paper on the table, and steps back, knocking over a stool, which is left rolling on the floor. He turns to face me as he opens the glasshouse door.

'The Star, later. And don't forget...' He nods towards Ruby, or maybe even Lamorna – I can't be sure. 'Woof, woof!' The scrunch across the gravel confirms that he's gone.

What. A. Cock.

Kerensa puts down the lollipop stick, picks up the stool, and drops down next to me. Her posture has gone to rat shit for the first time in a decade.

'Well!' is the only word she manages.

As for Lamorna? She returns to her harp, her deft hands flying across the strings to the sound of 'Tocata and Fugue in B Minor' (fast, feverish, intense, with a hint of excitement and danger, too). There is an expression on her elfin face that I can't quite fathom. Ruby is more straightforward and sums up my feelings exactly by jumping onto the door frame and screeching out her favourite maritime word after Jack as he exits the garden.

'Anchor!' she squawks.

You got that right, Ruby. You got that right.

Chapter Five

With a fresh cup of street-trader coffee in one hand, a buff file in the other, and an almond croissant hanging from his mouth in a paper bag, Detective Sergeant Joseph Enys of the Penzance constabulary closes the door to his office with an elbow shove and returns to his desk. An aspidistra claws for breath in a corner and fishing rods line a wall in a space that would be light and airy if only the council would ever pay for the windows to be cleaned. He sits down on a chair that was designed to be ergonomically beneficial but has never been levered into quite the perfect position and stares at two pictures sitting on his desk. Both pictures are of Donna Nightshade. It's not unusual for Joe to start his day seeing pictures of Donna, but they're usually in his mind, and are images of a vibrant teenager smiling up at him, invariably wearing a bikini and sitting on his boat, as she used to do a long time ago, before he got put into her book. Not that he knows for certain that he's in there, but come on, he put her in prison – actually put the cuffs on – and others have gone into her book for far less than that.

With the croissant hovering an inch from his mouth, he shakes his head and sighs. One photo of Donna is the shot from the newspaper article; the other was left on his desk by his sergeant, having been handed in by the editor of the local rag this morning. In the photo from the editor (taken last evening, apparently) Donna is sitting in a dark corner of The Star Inn, Newlyn, (to be fair, all the corners of The Star are dark) talking to a thick-set man called Jack Crowlas.

The bane of Joe's life is back in town.

Just brilliant.

His phone rings. Joe looks at the screen. It's the editor of the *Penzance Packet*, Bill Smiley. He lets it ring out. He's got a newspaper article from yesterday's rag to read, a pastry to eat, and, Bill is on his naughty list. Joe shakes his head in disdain while reading the article. A flash of a memory of Donna at primary school crosses his mind. It's a memory of her dragging Billy Jacobs across Mousehole harbour by his hair and throwing him into the sea because he'd mimicked her uncle who was – is – in his eccentricity, an easy target. Just the week before, Uncle Jago, known locally as The Captain, had been found brandishing a blunderbuss from his vantage point on the roof of the Admiral Benbow pub while on the lookout for the Royal Navy Police.

Joe reaches a part in the article about Donna's 'faraway look'. Really? A faraway look? For him? Nah. He smiles all the same.

The phone rings. It's Bill again and it's a video call. Joe hates video calls.

'Wasson,' says Bill. (*Wasson* is what the Cornish say to each other in greeting. It's a bit like the English *Hi* and American *What's up?*)

'Been to Warrens then?' asks Joe. (Warrens is one of the many pasty shops in town.)

Bill swallows, looks at the pasty, and laughs.

'Correct. You should be a detective. How did you guess?' Bill is a bit breathless. (He's always a bit breathless, being on the large side of massive, but if you will insist on eating a Cornish pasty first thing in the morning...)

Joe taps his nose. 'It's all in the crimping,' he says. It's not. He saw Bill's assistant coming out of there half an hour ago.

Bill puts down the pasty and wipes his mouth. It's flaky pastry and there are flakes everywhere. 'I take it you've seen the photo of Donna and Jack,' he says. 'Any comment, Detective?'

'No comment,' says Joe. 'Best not to overthink it, Bill.'

Bill pushes on. He's sniffing out a juicy story and he's not going to let Joe mask the scent.

'Jack's been around for a couple of weeks apparently but kept it low-key. Sailed straight into Newlyn I heard.'

'Bill Bolitho's boat brought him in,' says Joe.

'No flies on you. Is that why the harbour – and every other cove and inlet in West Penwith – was crawling with police last night?'

No point lying. 'Yep.'

'Drugs tip-off?'

'Yep.'

'Any joy?'

Joe picks up his coffee to hide his humiliated face.

Bill lets out a long whistle. 'Big boss lady up Truro must be seriously pissed off. That amount of policing doesn't come cheap.'

Pissed off? She's raging. But Joe goes with, 'That would be a correct assumption, yes.'

'Not to worry, my friend, because I've got a cracker of a tip for you because guess who—'

Joe cuts Bill short. He's got no time for gossip because there's something more important he wants to talk about. 'We'll get to that later,' says Joe. 'First, I want you to tell me about the bullshit you printed about Donna yesterday.'

Joe refuses to call Donna 'Deadly', because as far as Joe is concerned, if you call someone a rose they will bloom, and if you call them a weed they will wither and look a bit naff, and anyway, Donna isn't deadly, not at all, not these days. (A leopard with funny-shaped spots runs across his imagination.)

Bill laughs. It's a nervous laugh.

'What? The PR article?' Bill's voice is two octaves higher now. 'It's what she *wanted*, Joe. A bit of PR, that's all it was. You know Deadly, always on the lookout for publicity.'

'PR my arse! I'm just so...' He glances at the photo again. 'To be honest, I don't know what I am.' He does really. He's angry as hell. 'I'm just so... disappointed, Bill.'

Bill looks at his pasty. He's inspecting a juicy but steaming-hot piece of meat. 'No harm done. Won't happen again.' He takes a bite and seems to regret it, judging by the look on his face.

'And this bloke…' Joe scans the page for the name of the journalist. 'Jase Clarkson? Who is he?'

'Ex Fleet Street,' answers Bill, before cooling his mouth down with a swig of Coke. 'I had a spot of trouble chasing down his references, but he's a decent hack so I'm not going to push it.'

'Why's he here?'

'Slower life, bit of surfing, the usual story for all the up-country folk who run away. No doubt he'll go back to the old smoke after his first winter down here. They usually do. He's missing Uber Eats already, apparently.'

Joe closes the newspaper. Donna stares seductively at him from the page. He turns the paper over.

'The article is sexist, defamatory rubbish. And Clarkson is bad news. Rein him in.'

Bill, only a few streets away in his office on Chapel Street (best street in England as it's got that perfect balance of ye olde worlde charm and yet is also just a little bit edgy) shakes his head and sighs. (There's a lot of sighing going on in Penzance concerning Donna since *that photo* went out yesterday.)

'Your loyalty does you proud, mate,' says Bill, 'but honestly, she wouldn't piss on you if you were on fire.' He throws in a snort. 'In fact, she'd throw petrol on the flames and dance around your burning grave! You're in her book, you know that?'

Joe looks at the photo once more. He doesn't necessarily see the sexy woman walking out of the water smiling into the rising sun, or the suggestive tattoo. He sees the tomboy he once knew, his best friend at school, his hero, his old confidante, back in the day, before...

Joe turns over the newspaper a final time while Bill moves on to natter about his latest big catch – some sort of steroid-fed sea bass (it'll be bullshit – Bill's never been a great angler) – and glances longingly out of the dirty window, past the harbour and out across Mounts Bay, and wonders if Donna can truly pull off being a private detective. After all (and as Joe knows more than most) she will have to understand why the most ordinary people do the most batshit crazy things. He shakes his head in bemused wonder. Even now, after years on the force, Joe still can't work people out. He decided quite some time ago that all humanity is just nuts.

But then, he thinks with a smile – with Bill still waffling on about some night-fishing he has planned off the headland at St Ives – that maybe, just maybe, the one person in Penzance who might fathom everyone out is Donna Nightshade. Joe smiles again, as he always does at the thought of her, and is suddenly overcome with a feeling that everything will probably be all right, and just as a ray of sunshine forces its way through the windows and forms a halo above the other picture of Donna sitting on his desk, Joe's mind is once again filled with doubt... and jealousy... and fear – oh, and regret (it's complicated).

'Anyway, Bill. Must get on.' Joe returns his attention to the croissant. 'I've a cold coffee to drink, a drugs ring on the loose, and an inbox full of crap.'

'But we haven't even talked about the reason I rang.

About Deadly and Jack Crowlas. You must be gutted he's back. Any statement, Detective?'

Joe finally takes a bite of his croissant. Bill can wait. He swallows. 'If Donna wants to have a drink with a relation, it has nothing to do with me.'

'Have a drink? But that's what I wanted to tell you. The whole pub heard her threaten to kill him, man!'

Joe picks up his phone. It's time to swipe Bill away. 'What else do you know, Bill? Because I really must—'

'Rumours.'

Joe takes a sip of his coffee. He gleaned it for free from Skinny Pete, a man familiar with the wrong side of the law until Joe offered him a sturdy bridge across which to clamber his way back over to the right side. He now runs a coffee shop out of a converted horsebox on the promenade. There are times still when the hint of manure hits the lips.

'Rumours? Come back to me when you've got something more concrete.'

'They're decent ones, so hear me out.'

Joe leans back in his chair. He must get around to adjusting it properly. 'Go on.'

'Some say he's back for good – Jack is – and that he's planning on getting a gang back together.'

'It won't last.'

'You say that, but he's moved into his mother's old place.'

'In Newlyn? It's not fit for man nor beast – so it'll suit him just fine, actually.'

'But Joe! He's planning on taking over at Penberth. Been telling people that it's his rightful family home…'

Joe's body tenses. He tries to relax by twisting his neck and wobbling his jaw.

'The whole thing's got people talking. Remembering.'

'Remembering what?' asks Joe, although he knows perfectly well.

'The reign of terror! It's like Voldemort's come home and he's rounding up his Death Eaters, and there's word going around that your Donna is one of them.'

'Donna? A Death Eater? Nah.'

'You've seen the photo? It was taken last night. They look *very* cosy.'

'You just said that she threatened to kill him. You don't cosy up to someone you're going to kill. It's nothing, Bill. Tell them – these 'people' – to keep their imaginations in check. Jack Crowlas is a has-been, and if he even thinks about stepping a toe out of line this time, I'll have him in cuffs quicker than you can say... well, I'm not sure what, but anyway, if there's noth—'

'Jase Clarkson says he's seen Jack down Penberth way and—'

'Jase Clarkson is a player.'

'You've never even met the man.'

'I don't need to. Anyone who is referred to by both their names – forename and surname – in general conversation is always an arsehole. Jack Crowlas. Jase Clarkson...' *Bill Smiley*, he thinks but doesn't say. 'They're all chipped from the same block, trust me.'

'That's as may be, but Jase Clarkso— Jase,' Bill corrects himself, 'has been sniffing around down that neck of the woods and—'

'What neck of the woods?'

'Penberth. Lamorna Cove. Basically, the whole of West Penwith – Donna's patch – and is coming up with some interesting stuff. You ought to speak to him.'

'He's just trying to suck up to you.'

'Trying to prove himself, yes.' Bill begins to speak in a whisper. 'And yes, he's an annoying little shit, but if Jack is up to his old tricks again…'

'What? Drugs? Smuggling?'

'And the rest. And if it's kids that he starts recruiting, like last time…?'

Joe takes another bite of his croissant. 'You make him sound like Fagin.'

'Fagin? He's worse than any Fagin. But get this: word is, there's somebody out to get him. Proper out for him too. He's rattled. Jase has made inroads with one of his old gang in Newlyn, and word is that Jack is scared. He's been getting threatening notes.'

'What kind of notes?'

'Plain, old-fashioned notes. Paper ones. Delivered to the door.'

Joe sighs. 'Listen, Bill. No one sends notes anymore. They WhatsApp. And also, Jack Crowlas, scared?' Joe can't see it. 'If someone's out to get him, it won't be a local man. More likely some oligarch gang leader who Jack double crossed while he's been away. Anyway, let's hope somebody does wipe him out. That man is not welcome on my manor – or, for that matter, on Donna's.'

Joe's mind flashes back twenty years to an image of Donna's tanned, happy face staring up at him; to a time when they were just a couple of sixteen-year-old kids sailing in Mounts Bay, laughing and playing, promising each other the world, like Bing Crosby and Grace Kelly in *High Society* but without all the singling on Joe's part, although Donna was always singing away. Oh, he remembered that one time – it was so funny – when she—

'Anyway, I can see you're busy,' says Bill. 'So I'll leave you to it. Are you going to the Minack tonight?'

'What for?'

'What for? To see Donna's new play! Or are you still in her bad books?'

Joe laughs. It's a soft, uncertain laugh. He shakes his head.

'Bad books? I don't think Donna would mind if I pitched up in plain clothes and sat at the back. She wouldn't even notice I was there. It's the uniform and the siren she can't stand.'

Bill snorts. 'Then think again, shipmate! You sent her to prison, remember?'

'I didn't send her to prison, Bill. A judge did that. I just arrested her.'

'S'as good as. But look at her now! You did her a favour, Joe.'

'That was the idea.'

'Does Deadly see it that way?'

'She's called Donna, and I have no idea. So anyway, if that's all…'

'I'm covering it for the paper.'

'What?'

'The play at the Minack. You know she wrote it herself?'

He didn't, but he's not surprised.

'It's a closed room, murder-mystery-in-a-country-house-type-thing. Sounds bonkers to me, but knowing Deadly – Donna, sorry – it'll be a good craic. Something about a dead dog.'

A dead dog? This piques Joe's interest. Donna lost her own dog several years ago. It was a gorgeous little thing. The moment Donna lost that dog everything changed – she went completely feral. It marked the moment that Donna Nightshade went to the bad and she had never owned a dog since – a bloody parrot, yes, but a dog? No. But then, the poor animal had died in such a tragic—

'I don't suppose you know what happens to the dog?' asks Joe. 'In the play.'

Bill opens his desk drawer. 'Just a minute, I've got the flyer with the blurb on somewhere in here. Ah, here we go. "Celebrated crime writer, Mimi Fox, has had one rule her entire writing career – to never kill a dog in a story because her readers would simply not accept it. Then, one day, in a cruel quirk of fate, her own dog is murdered and Mimi, taking on the investigation, becomes entwined in a murder mystery that will outstrip anything she has ever imagined before." Shame you're not coming. She's got loads of pyrotechnics in it, too.'

Joe smiles. It's a loving smile. Of course she has. It's a Nightshade production. It's bound to be wild.

'Why do you still look out for Donna after all these years?' Bill's voice is softer now. Joe can tell it's an off the record type of a question, but it's not one he'll ever answer, not with the absolute truth – if there is such a thing (and Joe is beginning to believe that there isn't).

Joe stands without answering, the coffee long forgotten. He grabs his jacket off the back of the chair to indicate that the conversation is over.

'I just do,' he says.

'Out of interest,' says Bill, 'what do people call *me* when they talk about me?'

'Call you?'

'You know… just plain Bill, or…?'

Ah. Poor Bill. He's taken Joe's comment to heart.

'Don't worry. You're just plain old Bill,' he lies, throwing on his jacket. 'What about me?'

Bill starts to fiddle with a cat's cradle.

'You?' he asks. 'Well, you're Joe Enys. The copper. Always have been.'

Joe pauses. His jacket half-on, half-off.

'Joe Enys? Both names. Not just Joe?'

Bill looks into the phone and shrugs. 'But everyone thinks the world of you mate, obviously.'

That's enough. Joe does what he should have done ten minutes ago and swipes Bill away. The screen goes black. His desk sergeant, Demelza Braithwaite (late twenties, blonde, nice woman – incomer, despite the name; parents originally from Yorkshire but were obsessed with the Poldark books so they gave their only daughter a Cornish name and moved to Mousehole when she was little, which is a good job, as they'd never be able to afford to buy a house there now), grabs his attention from the outer office.

'Note for you, boss,' she says, rushing over and handing

him an envelope. 'Thought you'd want to look at it straight away.'

Sir. If you search a certain 'animal' at the Minack Theatre on the opening night of the Nightshade play – after the play, that is most important – you will find a significant stash of cocaine on that person (or drugs of some description). Can't say more. Anon

Joe can't help but laugh.

'How did it arrive?'

'You won't believe it.'

'Try me.'

'By pigeon – or possibly parrot – straight into the lap of PC Trago.'

'Here? At the station?'

'Yes. He was having a sneaky ciggy in the yard.'

Joe stuffs the note in his pocket and heads out into the sunshine. He's got a ticket for a show to buy, after all.

Chapter Six

DONNA

It's three in the afternoon and I'm at the Minack Theatre, a magnificent amphitheatre overlooking the Atlantic Ocean just around the coast from Penberth. Ruby is on my shoulder and she's shivering. I told her not to come but she suffers terribly from FOMO, so what can you do. Today is one of those September days where the weather is trying to fool itself into believing that it's still summer, but the breeze, eager to crack on with denuding the trees, knows otherwise.

My jean-covered backside is perched on a stone seat at the front of the amphitheatre. The ocean is the main player on our stage – or behind our stage, more precisely – and I'm taking a moment to stare across Porthcurno beach towards Logan Rock, beyond Porthcurno beach, and have a think. I take a bobble out of my jeans pocket and pull my hair into a knot before cocking my head into the wind to blow all the anxiety away – far, far away. Why do we let others affect us so? It's a silly habit, really, considering we're all so transient.

Nothing – absolutely nothing – I do in life will be of concern to anyone in years to come, so why do I get so bogged down with mundanity when I'm clearly so insignificant? Basically, why do I care?

It's a rhetorical question because I know what the answer is: it's because of love, that's why we care.

It's thanks to love that all the nice people in the world become vulnerable to the machinations and general dickaboutery of others – others who love less, others who think less, others who care less. The more we love the more we experience hurt and it's best, I find, not to love too much at all. Also, at a grass roots level, the more I love, the more others will suffer now that Jack is back – it's his weird thing with me. Which is why I have a very small and very select group of friends.

Talking of friends, they will all be here in a minute – the players. It's the final dress rehearsal for *Sleeping Dogs Lie*, my latest crime thriller, which is a tongue-in-cheek parody with shockingly sinister overtones. *Sleeping Dogs Lie* is scheduled for a 'one night only' performance in a few hours' time here at the Minack (the stage manager is an old school mate) and the doors open at seven. I began to write plays while serving at Her Majesty's pleasure a few years ago – adapt and overcome, as they say.

Lamorna is here too. She's been behaving oddly all day and has taken to carrying a cutlass around with her (we have lots of interesting antique weaponry hanging on the walls at Penberth). When I asked her why, she said, 'Oh, no reason. I suppose if anything it's because it's the right accessory for my outfit today.' Right now, she's playing the violin, which is why I can hear her rather than see her as she's sitting in the orchestra pit, which is a sturdy tent that's a permanent fixture stage right. The violin is connected to an amplifier and at the moment she's playing the frenetic masterpiece, 'Summer Presto'. The sound is incredible. I imagine her hair as wildfire as she dips and sways to the music. Musician and bow will be moving in unison to the energy and confusion of the piece. No one can arrange music like my sister – except, perhaps, Uncle Jago, who taught her everything she knows.

Fact is, I'm confused, and Lamorna knows it – hence the music. She knows I'm wondering what to do about Jack and she's trying to give me strength. It's working.

About Jack...

Jack Crowlas is Aunty Donna's husband; they met when she was nineteen. Aunty Donna is twenty-three years older than me. She's in prison for attempted murder (of Jack, who else) and for losing her marbles. It's one of those friendlier types of prison for the certifiably insane, so it's not too bad. In Jack's eyes, Penberth and all that goes with it should have gone to him when his wife went gaga and tried to slit his throat (to be perfectly accurate, she tried to slit his throat before she went certifiably gaga), but thanks to the very first Belladonna Nightshade, who kicked quite a bit of pantaloon-covered arse in her day, the estate is handed down the female line if the present incumbent dies or is declared unfit to rule the roost (aka goes mad) – she was so ahead of her time, the original Deadly. Except that isn't the end of the story, not for Jack. I took to the helm when my mother died in childbirth (which is coincidentally when

Aunty Donna tried to kill him) and he continued to lord it around like he owned the place – and owned me, too. Subsequently, in my late teens my life was a mess. He ruled me. He wrecked me. And then finally, after one dodgy deal too far, he threw me under the proverbial bus and legged it. I took some of the rap for the whole kit and kaboodle of his dodgy affairs (mainly smuggling) and he got away free. I thought he'd legged it forever, but now he's back and wants to be lord of the manor. Over my dead body. God only knows what delights Aunty Donna saw in him back along. Maybe she was bonkers even then?

My meeting with Jack at The Star last night was short. I have been given three tasks:

One. I'm to find the man (or woman, I suggested, which was met with mirth) who's after him because someone has been sending him threatening notes, apparently.

Two. I'm to hand Penberth back into his steel claw grasp by Christmas.

Dream on!

Three. I'm to meet a man called Aeolus Jones (which is the oddest blending of Greek and Welsh I ever saw) at Porthleven Harbour in a few days' time to arrange some kind of dodgy drop at Penberth. A drop of what, I have no idea, but it won't be a crate of rainbow shitting unicorns, that's for sure. I don't want to do it. I'm clean as a whistle now. Almost.

Four (four? I thought it was three. My mistake). I'm to provide him with a watertight alibi for 7pm tonight because he's 'got a job on'.

That's it. Those are my tasks. Just like the old days.

I said no to him once before, of course. I called his bluff. It was a mistake. Massive. And I now have a hole in my heart the shape of a dog. Jack Crowlas is a nasty man, and he is very definitely the sort of psychopath who follows through on his promises.

But what to do?

Ruby nuzzles into my neck while Lamorna reaches her Vivaldi crescendo. The wind is gaining momentum. I look towards Logan Rock and take a very deep breath. It must end, this living in fear of a bully who manipulates me through tapping into my weakness – love. The music stops. Lamorna appears from the music tent, cutlass in hand. She crosses the stage and takes a perch on a stone seat behind me. She's wearing baggy yoga trousers, flipflops, and a jumper that has a winking fox on the front (so much for the matching cutlass). I feel her arms wrap tightly around my shoulders.

'Time for action?' she asks.

I kiss her arm. 'Time for action,' I say.

Ruby circles overhead and we sit in silence, waiting for the players to arrive.

Chapter Seven

DONNA

The first to arrive for rehearsal is Skinny Pete. He's fortyish, and despite the drug abuse of previous years and the occasional bit of pot after an evening's surf (oh, and the magic mushrooms he sprinkles into his savoury croissants now and again – special customers only) he's wearing well. Pete isn't that skinny anymore, or really called Pete. He picked up that tag because at his skinniest he looked exactly like the actor who played Skinny Pete in *Breaking Bad*, especially when he was wearing his trademark woollen hat, as he is now.

No one ever auditions for a part in one of my plays. It's a closed theatre group and I write specific parts tailored to each player's strengths and deliver the scripts a few weeks before. Secrecy is vital. In *Sleeping Dogs Lie*, Skinny Pete is playing an ex-drug-user-turned-good who owns a coffee van on the promenade in Penzance. (OK, so there is a blatant element of the 'based on a true story' about this play). Pete usually plays the guy everyone expects to have committed the crime/murder/theft but hasn't, and that's based purely on the fact that he has the wiry look of a psychotic villain about him, and that kind of preconceived opinionising is hard to shake. So, I don't shake it, as a rule. I use it to my advantage. There was this one play where Pete really was the murderer, the ending of which absolutely no one saw coming, and the fact that no one guessed Pete was the murderer gobsmacked me because – come on – the play was called *When Skinny Got Fat*, and the dead man was called Fat Justin. I was going for obvious but sardonic comic elegance in that play, but the audience thought that Pete couldn't possibly be the murderer because it was just too obvious to be true. Rather than applaud my beautiful simplicity, the audience were annoyed by the obviousness of it. They felt duped (which is kind of the point with that kind of thing, surely?). I explained that I had wanted to create not so much a whodunit, but a *why*dunit, and hoped to show the complex and yet simple workings inside the mind of a murderer and how it could transpire that someone (Skinny Pete) could be pushed to commit the ultimate crime and yet be forgiven for it, and I had hoped to do all this by writing a thought-provoking play of masterly craftswomanship. But nobody gave two shits about the inner workings of the murderer's mind, or the craftswomanship. They just wanted to be led down numerous garden paths until, right at the end, the gates to the truth (big iron ones, preferably gothic) opened to reveal the identity of the murderer with either a 'Well I never' surprise gasp, or a 'Hello? I guessed that five minutes in!'. But the gates never opened. It was

Skinny Pete who did it, just like I said it was in the title.
The end.

It didn't review well.

Skinny Pete's long legs descend the steep stone steps of
the amphitheatre with the awkwardness of an unsteady
baby gazelle who has decided to have a go at walking down
an up-escalator. We fist bump but the greeting seems half-
hearted on Pete's behalf.

'Wasson,' I say.

'Wasson.' He doesn't stop to chat but carries on walking
in the direction of a wooden cabin that is the performers'
changing room. Pete isn't the sort of guy who believes in
conversation for conversation's sake, and a fist bump says
much more than words could ever convey, but still, there
are fist bumps and fist bumps. I let it go.

The next of my players starts slinking her way silently
down the steps – Cat.

Cat is not proper Cornish but somehow, she kind of
edged her way into the group via the local vicar, who found
her homeless and penniless one night in the middle aisle at
Lidl. She told us that she earned her name over the course
of her childhood because her mother would often lock her
out at night, which led to her roaming the streets or else
slinking into a neighbour's home, drinking their milk, and
curling up to sleep on their sofa. I have no idea what her
real first name is; she's never seemed to want to divulge it,
but things are on the up for Cat these days. She has a home
(an old fisherman's hut of ours overlooking the cobbles at
Penberth Cove, which is sooo London chic) and a job
working the night shift at Lidl – she was hanging out there

anywhere so, as I said to the manager, she might as well be earning money while she roams. It's surprising then, that Cat has a face like thunder today. Yes, she's more than a bit rough round the edges in manners and grace, but her chin-length blonde hair looks like rat shit, which is not like Cat, who usually nails the 'just got out of bed but still rocking the beach-wave' look.

'All right, bird?' says Cat with a sniff. (She's talking to me, not Ruby. *Bird* is what Cornish women sometimes call each other and Cat's adopted the local patois.)

'All right. *You* all right?' I ask, while throwing in a microscopic eyebrow raise (the left one, obviously).

Cat shrugs. 'Yeah, all right. Is Pete here?'

'Why?'

Cat throws me a nasty glance – that's new.

'Why do you always think everything is your business, Donna?' she says. 'Anyway, this gonna take long? Only I've got somewhere I need to be before my shift starts.'

I want to say, 'You can't rush genius,' but go with, 'I'm waiting for Gabby and Jago to arrive and then we'll crack on.'

Cat slinks towards the dressing room. I call after her.

'I've got a flower delivery in Newlyn this afternoon,' I say. 'I could meet you for a coffee later?'

'Nah, you're all right,' she shouts, still walking.

Well. That's me kissed off.

As Cat exits stage left, I look up to see an athletic forty-something woman leaping down the amphitheatre steps, two at a time, while ripping off a dog collar. She jumps onto the stage.

It's Gabrielle.

Gabby.

Jones.

The vicar. The one who introduced me to Cat.

I came across Gabby during my spell as a prison inmate a few years ago. Gabby popped in once a week to offer spiritual guidance along with the occasional cigarette (she plays a mean game of poker, too). Gabby said that on first noticing me across the prison exercise yard she stopped in her tracks because a nimbus – an actual nimbus – hovered gloriously above my head in a perfect glowing circle, and she was sober when she told me so it must be true. From that point on, Gabby refused to believe that I was anything other than an angel, even if I *was* banged up for smuggling, aiding a drug dealer, and a touch of knife crime. It was a turning point for me, though, no question. When someone believes in you – truly believes – it can spark the beginning of believing in yourself. After all, call someone a rose, and it will bloom etc…

Anyhow, we kept in touch and after I was released Gabby pitched up out of the blue at my manor (that sounds like I'm a Cockney villain, but I mean my actual manor house, Penberth) saying that she was desperate for a change. As luck would have it, the vicarship (is that a word?) at the little church at Penberth had just become vacant. Uncle Jago spoke to a couple of old boys he knew from his days of sitting in the House of Lords (he doesn't bother with that 'archaic, mind-bogglingly stupid and elitist nonsense' anymore) but nevertheless still managed to wangle it with an archbishop (he had dirt on him, I believe) for Gabby to get the gig at Penberth church and live at the vicarage permanently. I invited Gabby to join the players after her first harvest festival and she has been ensconced within the fold of the Nightshade Players ever since.

'Wasson?' I say.

'Wasson,' she replies.

'Final rehearsal, then,' she states, not that I need, or want, reminding. She nods in the direction of the music tent. 'Lamorna sounds better than ever.'

Lamorna has seamlessly transitioned from 'I Can't Make You Love Me' to Gabby's favourite hymn, 'Lord of the Dance', which is Gabby's go-to uplifting hymn on a Sunday. Gabby always becomes particularly animated when reaching the line, *I danced on a Friday when the world turned black; it's hard to dance with the devil on your back.* I've always had an inkling that there's a darker side to Gabby, which only adds to her appeal, frankly.

'I can't believe it's come around so quickly,' she says. 'Everyone here?'

'Two missing,' I say.

Gabby rolls up her dog collar and places it into her trouser pocket. 'The Captain and Kerensa?'

'Wasn't that a pop duo in the 70s?' I joke.

Gabby shrugs. She'd normally laugh at my daft quips.

'Climate change protest,' I explain. 'Kerensa has set up a netted compound in the car park at Sainsburys. She's encouraging people to take all the plastic off their shopping as they exit the store and dump it in the compound, then she's going to leave the whole lot for Sainsburys to sort out.'

'That's not like her. She's usually so... demure.'

'I know. The world's gone mad.'

'Much media interest?'

'Tons.'

I take my iPhone out of my back pocket and scroll through Twitter.

'She's just tweeted to say the BBC are there and that #stickyourplasticupyourarse is trending on Twitter.'

'And Uncle Jago?'

'Down in a minute, I should think. He'll be distracted by his new pigs.'

Gabby's head drops. 'Not new ones? I thought he said never again when the last batch got trailered away. It was awful. They squealed like they were being taken away from their mother.'

'Which they were,' I say.

Gabby signs a cross over her heart.

'It's tragic,' I agree, 'but he just can't resist the lure of the piglet, poor old soul. He knows the rules, though. No pets at Penberth. If he fattens 'em, he flattens 'em – that's the rule.'

Gabby glances up the amphitheatre steps to see a flash of red winging its way towards us.

'Except for Ruby,' she says.

'Except for Ruby. Although Ruby isn't a pet. She's more of an employee.'

Ruby turns with a hairpin swish and lands on my shoulder. My phone pings and I see two text messages from Uncle Jago. The first reads:

Down dreckly. Late out of bed due to lock-in at the Admiral.
Also, need to feed the piglets.

I look up at Gabby. 'Yep. He's with the pigs.'

The second text is also from Jago and is a little less bland.

Intruder alert! A damn journo has just pitched up. Annoying
arsehole. Says his name is Jase and that you're expecting him.
Wants to do an early review to drum up business. Don't trust
him! His eyes are too close together. Sent him down to you (the
long way). Blunderbuss at the ready. PS Tell the others I stink of
pig shit.

'Everything all right?' asks Gabby.

'Perfect,' I say. 'Except…' I pause. 'He's back, Gabby.'

'Who is?'

'JC.'

Gabby pirouettes on the stage. 'Oh, I always knew he'd come back. I just knew it! Two billion Christians couldn't be wrong. Oh, Donna. Everything will be OK now, just you wait and see – the oceans, the climate, my hair…'

I see the misunderstanding and throw my arms around my friend. 'Sorry, my lovely. I meant my Uncle Jack. Jack Crowlas. But the real JC will pitch up one day, I'm sure of it.' (I'm not.)

Gabby's expression is… flat. There is no expression.

'I met him at The Star last night,' I say.

'You met him?'

'I had no choice. He thinks someone's out to get him,

and to be honest, with any luck, they will. Someone's been pestering him with threatening notes. But whoever it is, I pity them, because when Jack finds out – and he *will* find out, that's for sure – he'll bloody kill them.'

The door to the dressing room clicks open. Pete and Cat spill out, faces like thunder, dressed for the show. Gabby grabs my arm. 'I'm worried,' she says.

'For me? Don't be.' I pick up the script from a seat on the front row. 'I can't do anything about him until this play is done and dusted, but I'll sort it all out after that, once and for all. He won't get the better of me this time, Gabby. No way.'

Lamorna kicks into the final chorus and Uncle Jago appears, all puffed out, carrying a blunderbuss and smelling of pig poo.

'All will be well,' he says, guessing the mood and patting me on the head. 'This time, all will be well.'

'I really hope so, Uncle,' I say. 'I really do hope so.'

Chapter Eight

It was 2am earlier that morning when Jack's stubby fingers fumbled to get the key in the door of his terraced cottage in the centre of the harbour village of Newlyn. The cottage is of the two-up two-down cobbled street variety, which is the type of house that once upon a time had a genuine fisherman living inside and reeked of blood, sweat and gutted herring. Not so much anymore. The Cornish coast is littered with these houses, but they are now the boltholes of second homers known locally as *Londoners* and have the faint waft of a bergamot and geranium candle drifting out of a cracked window into the street, but only when the plantation shutters are open. Jack's house isn't like that. It's a shithole.

He dropped the key on the pavement, picked it up, glanced down the dimly lit street, then finally turned the key before darting into the house and locking (and bolting) the crumbling door behind him. He dropped to his haunches with his back to the door and tried to still his shaking hands while wondering how on earth he had survived the horror show that had just unfurled on Logan Rock. He was right after all: someone really was after him. He didn't get a proper look at the face, what with the swinging torch from the iPhone, but surely it must have been someone drenched to the bone in evil up on that rock, like a mangy kitten taunting a defenceless mouse. He should never have believed that cock and bull story from the Nightshade girl in the pub about the priceless ruby and the offer of sex... He'd let himself slip, let his guard down for a bit of skirt – he'd have to watch that. Was it one of the new gang up on that rock? Possibly, but why? No, it was most likely some link to Lithuania... Maybe that Russian cartel he'd duped? He needed to think – and to strip himself of his dripping wet clothes.

There was a bread oven in the recess of the inglenook fireplace that Jack used as a safe. He took out an envelope, which was full of handwritten notes. Sets of numbers were written on the notes, written to look like code but he knew what they represented. He darted upstairs, knowing that he would find a well-thumbed Bible in a bedside drawer, a Bible that he had been forced to learn as a child, while being smacked with a cane if he quoted it wrongly by his mother.

About Jack...

Jack's mum had a dog when she was younger and the bitch had got caught by the local shag-about-town-mongrel, leaving Jack's mum lumbered with a litter of puppies. The dog accepted all the puppies onto her teats except one, whom she kept abandoning behind the bins in the backyard. Jack's mum had felt sorry for the abandoned puppy and so trickled cow's milk down its throat until it grew strong. Eventually the same pup turned around and bit Jack's mum on the arse – and subsequently bit everyone else's arse on the street – and it dawned on Jack's mum that the bitch mother had known instinctively that this dog was a bad pup. It was ironic, therefore, that she felt the same about her own pup, Jack. He was a bad 'un – and she'd known it from the minute he had been 'untimely ripped' – only it was against the law to leave a human pup behind the bins, so she fed him anyway, not with mother's milk, but with the Bible. It didn't help.

Bible in hand, he ran down the stairs, closed the tatty curtains as well as he could as they weren't exactly hanging well, and after stripping off his clothes down to his unflattering Y-front underpants, he kicked his way across the detritus of old pizza boxes, plastic curry containers, and beer bottles, flopped down on a threadbare sagging sofa and, still shaking with cold and fear, took a note out of the envelope at random.

H 9:22

H – that must mean the Epistle to the Hebrews, but which passage? He flicked through the pages of the New Testament with wild fingers until he found…

> *9:22 And almost all things are by the law purged with blood; and without shedding of blood is no remission.*

His nostrils started to flair. How dare they play him at

his own game? His mother's Bible was littered with folded corners marking her favourite passages, which were usually the fiery ones quoted to him throughout his childhood. He flicked through them for inspiration, and with a rush of blood and confidence, he scrambled to the door and after faffing for a moment with the key and the bolt, his eyesight and coordination not being quite what they should be tonight, he flung the door open and yelled, '*But I will forewarn you whom ye shall fear: Fear him, which after he hath killed hath power to cast into hell; yea, I say unto you, Fear him. FEAR HIM!*' With his rocking horse nostrils now flaring and his inflated biceps burning, he continued to yell, 'And I shall be revenged, do you hear? Revenged!'

A dog barked his annoyance on the next street and Jack tottered back inside in his underpants, leaving the door wide open this time. He selected another number, and with a rush of blood to the brain fired out a text:

Get me that dog suit. We're on.

Chapter Nine

As clandestine venues for an illegal drop go, the middle aisle at Lidl seems like an unlikely place, but it is in exactly the most benign, unlikely places that the most successful clandestine drops tend to happen. As is the case at Lidl, where the workers are simply too easygoing to give two shits about what anyone else might be up to. Which is why one person (Pete. It's Skinny Pete) is rooting around with his arse in the air, deep inside a large dumper basket of fleecy slippers, looking for a pair of size sevens, which is odd as Pete is a UK size ten. To his left is a large stack of inflatable Jacuzzis ('When it's gone, it's gone') and to his right is a pile of baking appliances like the ones used in *Bake Off*, which have been selling like... well, hot cakes. He has been told to stuff a 'package' inside a size seven slipper (the left one). With shaking hands, he takes a last glance up and down the aisle, slips a small, padded envelope out of his jacket pocket, and stuffs it in the slipper. He looks up and is surprised to see a familiar face handing money over to a furtive-looking store manager by the door. The store manager hands over a naked mannequin, which is subsequently tucked awkwardly under the woman's arm.

Ask no questions, Pete. You've got your own shit to worry about, he thinks, before legging it out of Lidl with an inflatable jacuzzi under one arm and bottle of cider under the other.

Chapter Ten

DONNA

The rehearsal went just about as badly as it's possible for a last rehearsal to go, and now, just a few hours later, it's here, the moment of the actual performance. I feel sick. This is the stuff that naked dreams are made of. Even so, the sun has set, and the theatre is cosseted in a subtle orange glow. The sea, the perfect backdrop, is behaving herself and looking truly fantastic, all dressed up in her best bib and tucker.

I wish I could say the same for the rest of the cast.

I look through a crack in the dressing room door as the first members of the audience find their seats. Uncle Jago was weird during the rehearsal and was distracted to the extent of fluffing his part, which is a difficult thing to do considering that all he has to do is don a dog suit and perform a non-speaking, walk-on role that lasts for about a minute. All but Lamorna seemed edgy, and Kerensa didn't even pitch up to support us, which wasn't the end of the world because she refuses to be a player, stating that, life is a big enough performance without creating even more drama. Also, she's got a full schedule of online yoga classes on Zoom with clients in Australia tonight, which I'm a bit disappointed about because, come on, she's my aunty, and who wouldn't cancel everything to see a Donna Nightshade production?

Not Kerensa, obviously.

All I can hope as we approach curtain-up is that the encouraging pep talk I gave the players earlier ('That was absolute crap! Get a grip, you bunch of absolute wastrels!') has brought them all up to snuff.

Lamorna is in the orchestra tent and is playing Cornish folk songs on the harp to settle the audience. Before the show starts, she will play 'Trelawny', which is the Cornish anthem – anyone who's anyone sings along to 'Trelawny'. I feel a sudden sense of calm when I see her silhouette backlit by the tent lantern lights, her arms running up and down the strings like she's tickling a trout: my sister is with me, my uncle is with me, and all will be well. The theatre is full, which is just bloody typical as we've never managed a full house before, not even close. Deep in my soul I was hoping that a storm would blow in and Poseidon would appear with his mighty fork (is it a fork?), which would mean that sadly, with much regret, we would have to cancel the show ('full refunds' and so on). But no. The stubborn sea and sky have refused to make more of the previous swell, and one way or another, the show will go on. Which is why, dressed as an angel – an avenging angel, to be completely accurate – with outlandishly large wings spreading out from my shoulders and a nimbus above my head (I'm the narrator –

it makes sense eventually), I nod towards my mate from school, Louise Thomas, the stage manager for the Minack who's watching from the lighting control balcony, and on cue, she dulls the lighting and the audience quietens.

I feel sick.

Chapter Eleven

The first person in the audience I clap eyes on as I step out onto the stage is Joe Enys. He's the copper who sent me to prison many years ago. That roguish hack, Bill Smiley, is sitting to one side of him and another copper, Demelza, is sitting to his left. Joe must think I'm smiling at him personally (as if!) because he's smiling back like it's 2002. I puff out my wings and begin my narration just as a giant dog comes bounding down the steps from the top of the amphitheatre, weaving his way through the audience. It's Uncle Jago's moment of glory. Right on cue, the dog collapses into his kennel, having been brutally murdered in a way that would make most Greek tragedies look tame, and I close the door on the kennel (a large bolster wood affair) moving on to open the play in a way that, I admit, may have been 'adapted' slightly from Shakespeare...

'In fair Penzance, where we find our scene, an old wound spurts forth from new, and ancient ties and grievances make beautiful minds bend crooked, and Death's dagger blade is unseen...'

Two hours later and it's all gone off surprisingly well. The audience has been in stitches, sometimes intentionally but mostly not – hey ho, a laugh's a laugh. In-between my narrator slots I couldn't help but stand in the wings and watch Joe. I admit, it was pleasant to see his face lit by the glow of the stage, but it also seemed lit from within by something else too. Could it be... the glow of happiness? Has he fallen in love again? With Demelza? (No!) Or is he just a bit hot under the collar? There's no time to ponder, because fireworks complete, it's time for the rug-pulling showstopper finale. Skinny Pete rips open the kennel door to free the dog, who is now an angel (it's symbolic), which is the cue for Jago to come running out wearing a halo and skip around the stage before disappearing up the steps through the audience – to heaven. I can't see inside the kennel from where I'm standing, but no dog has come running out and when Pete improvises to glance inside the kennel, he steps back with a hand to his mouth. A woman's scream is the only sound that rings out through the theatre, and it's a sound that represents perfectly the faces of a gobsmacked audience.

A wave of fear rises within me.

Jago.

I cross the stage and look inside. A dog is indeed dead on the floor. There is a knife in his neck – which is a new twist that is not in any of my actor notes – so I'm guessing that this is no play acting. Blood is splattered on the kennel walls and has pooled across the floor, which is a great visual aid to the drama, but Louise isn't going to be happy with me because it'll be a nightmare to scrub off. My immediate reaction is relief – happiness, even – because it's not Jago in the dog suit at all. It's Jack Crowlas, and he's lying on the kennel floor exactly like a dead human, rather than like a dead dog, which, from a production point of view, is disappointing. By the colour of his face, I'd say he's definitely dead, especially given that the dog collar is wrapped so tightly around his neck that his face is cobalt blue, although that could be the theatre lights, but the knife in his neck kind of seals the deal on the murder front. A child's toy is lying on top of him. It's Thomas the Tank Engine.

Shit.

A million questions rush to mind but there's no time for answers now because I've an audience staring on in horror, a vicar who is crouching next to the body while wailing, and a reputation as a playwright and production manager that needs to be managed.

I smile, close the door of the kennel and nod up to Louise again (whose mouth is gaping) to indicate the need to throw on the big lights, or at least turn off the blue ones. I grab Pete's hand just as Joe Enys starts making his way to the stage. That's all I need! The newspaper hack looks like he's orgasmic and takes out his notebook while Demelza looks on like it's the best day of her life and has taken out her phone.

The other players are waiting in the wings, unsure as to what's going on. I hold out my hands and encourage them onto the stage, smiling. Lamorna, who has completed her finale ensemble of 'Lord of the Dance', stands by the door of the music tent waiting to be invited onto the stage. As we all join hands and begin to bow, someone high up in the gods begins to slow clap. It's Jase Clarkson. I hear sarcasm in the resonance of his clapping, but it doesn't matter because, completely hoodwinked and more than a little confused, the rest of the audience is beginning to laugh and clap also – a slow clap of relief with growing momentum. We all turn, as rehearsed, towards the music tent, which is when Lamorna steps out to the loudest applause of all. I've never seen her look so happy.

With our final bow complete, the audience begins to disperse. My eyes meet Joe's; he doesn't look so radiant anymore. The only word to describe his expression as he crosses the stage towards me is sad.

He opens the kennel door and steps inside.

I hear a siren in the distance.

Here we go again.

Chapter Twelve

DONNA

I'm sitting in the dark in a seat in the gods at the top of the amphitheatre wrapped in a foil blanket, watching on as the scene continues to unfold on stage. I'm no longer the main player in this production but just another spellbound member of the audience. The rest of the gang are all in the dressing room being supervised (guarded) by a female officer while waiting to be questioned. Cat is chain smoking Benson & Hedges and Pete looks like a startled rabbit in headlights. As for Gabby? She's gone to pieces entirely. So much for pastoral care in times of crisis.

I've already been questioned, and by Demelza rather than Joe, which miffed me a bit because surely, I'm the main suspect. It seems that every officer serving in West Cornwall police has descended on the theatre, which isn't very many as the force has been cut to the bone over the past few years, but no doubt social media is alive by now with comments and zoomed-in photographs of dead Jack. Scene of Crime have arrived from Truro and have erected a white tent around the kennel.

Certain obvious but frankly bizarre questions remain unanswered, like, why on earth had Jack Crowlas (of all people) taken Jago's part in the play? Where *is* Jago? Was the killer out to kill Jack, or did they intend to kill Jago and Jack copped it by mistake? The biggest question of all, though, the one I just can't fathom, is: how the hell was it done? I have no answers to these questions, and I told Demelza that, too.

She didn't believe me.

None of the policemen seem to have noticed that I'm looking on, except for Joe, who has glanced my way a couple of times, throwing me an indecipherable expression. Detective Chief Inspector Jenny Penworthy from Truro Police (nice woman; driven, but nice) has just arrived. She shakes hands with Joe, and I see her do a little dance and hear her say, 'Ding dong, the witch is dead,' which I think is proper cool for a copper, but someone really ought to tell her that the whole point of an amphitheatre is that sound carries from the stage. I'm hearing a whole bunch of things that probably should be 'for police ears only'.

Someone takes a seat in the dark behind me while I'm trying to listen in. I turn around to look. It's Louise, the stage manager.

'Wasson,' she says.

'Wasson.'

She nudges my shoulder. 'I must hand it to you, Donna. There've been quite a few murders carried out on that stage over the past few years, but this is one production that will take some beating!'

She jumps down a level to sit next to me. I manage a laugh and shake my head. 'Sorry about this, Louise,' I say. 'That blood is going to be a right pain to shift.'

'It's not your fault,' she says. 'The trustees won't mind because the publicity for the Minack will be brilliant. We'll probably introduce the idea of a ghost.'

'How have the staff taken it?' I ask.

She shrugs. 'No one seems to be too fussed or surprised. I hear there's a brilliant clip on TikTok.'

'Have the police let them all go?'

'Yes, there's only me left from the Minack staff now and I'll stay for the night, just to make sure they don't trash the place, if nothing else.'

We both quieten and watch the stage. Insignificant bits of nothing are being bagged up and labelled.

'Best watch yourself, though,' she says, breaking the silence. 'Word is that you threatened to kill him at the pub… The whole town knows about that little fracas, by the way.'

Great.

'Well… yes, I did say that, but what was I supposed to say when he was trying to turn me into his bloody stooge again – *and* topple me from Penberth?'

'Fair enough. But why did you give him a part in the play?'

'I didn't.'

'Hmm,' she says.

'Hmm,' I confirm.

'You been interviewed yet?' she asks.

'Briefly. Demelza.'

I don't need to turn to see the eyeroll.

'How was she?'

'Too nice. I smell a rat. Have you seen my uncle, by the way? Christ alone knows what's happened to him. I suppose I should look for him, really.'

'Jago?' repeats Louise. 'Oh, he's in the café. I gave him a brandy. The police have just finished interviewing him.'

'Jago?'

'Yes.'

'Shit.'

Louise nudges my arm. 'I was in the back room for the whole interview if you want to know what he told them.'

I do.

'I'm hoping he had a convincing – non-incriminating – reason to explain why Jack Crowlas was found dead in *his* dog suit after playing the part *he* should have been playing, although Jack did go for it particularly convincingly, to be fair.'

Louise pats my hand. 'Jago said he got a note from you saying that one of his piglets had got out and it had been seen down Nanjizal way, that he was to be sure to go and rescue it and not to come to the Minack, and that you'd pick up the suit from his study and get someone to stand in for him.'

'A note,' I say. 'From me?'

She nods.

'Didn't you wonder where he was in the interval?' she asks. 'I thought you'd put a door on the back of the kennel so he could get out?'

'We did. But he said he wanted to be left alone in there because he'd been struggling to get to grips with the real thematic significance of *The Iliad* and that tonight was the perfect opportunity for a bit of a read – he likes to keep up with his old Oxford scholar buddies, you see.'

'Sounds like Jago,' says Louise.

'Doesn't it just,' I agree. 'Oh, I don't know. It's all getting very...'

'Shakespearean?'

'No. Nightshadean.'

Louise laughs, but like a joke at a funeral it rings out uncomfortably around the theatre. Joe's gaze follows the direction of the laughter. Louise stands. 'Anyway, must get on. The coppers want some tea making. Don't sit on the cold stone too long though or you'll get piles.'

I smile up at her. She fishes a hand inside a coat pocket and takes out a set of ear pods.

'Here,' she says. 'Put these in.'

I take the ear pods and look up, confused.

'The stage mic is still live,' she says. 'We've turned off the speakers, but the earphones are still working... Stage manager's perks and all that.' Louise rests a hand on my shoulder. 'If it helps. I'm glad he's dead,' she says. 'We all are.'

Chapter Thirteen

DONNA

Louise drifts away as I slip the ear pods in. The chatter is all a bit benign, so I take out my brand-new Edge of the World Detective Agency notebook and a new easy flow pen I'd bought especially for my detective work. On the first page I write:

Things I noticed at scene of crime (SOC) before the police arrived:

1. *When Pete built the kennel he put the back panel on a latch so Uncle Jago wouldn't have to spend the whole play in there. The panel was Pete's idea.*
2. *When Joe hurriedly tried to release the dog collar that had seemingly strangled Jack, the collar wouldn't unfasten. A knife was called for (Joe said not to remove the one from his neck) and the collar was slit. Attached to the collar inside was exactly the sort of zip tie we put around tree stakes at the manor and once those zip*

ties click into place, there's no unfastening them. Who had access to the collar?

3. *The dog suit dead Jack is wearing is not the dog suit I gave to Uncle Jago. It's the same type, but it's different – Jack's has a patch on the left eye. There are, therefore, two dog suits kicking around and I only bought one – not that I revealed this to the police.*

4. *Perhaps the most important observation I have made and should perhaps have been point number one, is that the knife in his neck is mine and I can't deny it as, when they take it out, they will see that it has my name engraved on the blade – at least I know what happened to it now.*

5. *How did the murderer know that Jack would be in the kennel rather than Jago? Was someone trying to kill Jago?*

6. *There was a smell of burning after the interval. It didn't last long but it was definitely there, and I noticed Joe Enys with his nostrils in the air, too.*

I'm about to write 7 when I hear the DCI say, 'Take a look at this,' through the earphones.

I watch Joe follow Penworthy as they walk to the back of the tent and out of view. They must be looking over the safety barrier down the sheer drop of rocks to the sea below, because she says, 'Do you think someone could scale this without a rope?'

Yes. The answer to that is yes. I know someone who's done it.

'I'll need to have a look in the daylight and from below,' says Joe, 'and get a rock climber in to confirm it, but I shouldn't think so. Put it this way, it's not something that could be done in a hurry, or without a rope.'

'A rope could have been tied to the barrier,' says Penworthy, 'but how would it have been untied, if the murderer left that way?'

Joe doesn't answer straight away, but eventually he says what everyone is thinking.

'It couldn't, which means the murderer never left, or it's a two-man job.'

They reappear. If this had been a play, there would have been far too much action off stage.

'Come on then,' says the DCI, 'what do we know so far? Hit me with it.'

Joe clears his throat. 'We know that Jack Crowlas ran into the kennel at the start of the show, although the man in the dog suit should have been Jago Nightshade. The box has a hinge at the back. Two hours later at the end of the show, Jack was found dead inside the kennel, effectively strangled and stabbed. The postmortem will clarify.'

Come on Joe, you can do better than that. How do you know it was Jack who was wearing the dog suit?

'And how do you know it was Jack who ran into the kennel,' she asks. 'Did you see his face?'

See! (I'm good at this.)

'No.'

Penworthy sighs. Sighing is never good from the boss. 'Did whoever it was that run into the kennel have the same build as Jack?'

'Difficult to say, given the suit and the fact that he—'

'Or she…'

Come on, Joe.

'Or she, was bounding on all fours.'

The DCI sighs again. That's two sighs inside twenty seconds.

'So,' continues Joe, rubbing his forehead, 'a man *or* a woman who may or may not have been Jack Crowlas, entered the kennel at the start of the show. Unless there's been some kind of smoke and mirrors thing going on with a dummy back panel, there was no one else in there at the time.'

'You're certain?'

'I was right in front of it. Not a chance. Donna closed the door on... let's call it "the dog", and we didn't see inside the kennel again until the end of the show.'

'How convenient,' says Penworthy. 'Almost like the play was written that way... And you're certain there couldn't have been a dummy back, where the murderer could have hidden?'

'Looking at the depth of the kennel, it's unlikely. And to move a panel and dispose of it without the audience seeing or hearing would have been difficult.'

'I doubt anyone could see round the back of the kennel from any of the seats, what with the hessian screening,' says Penworthy. 'Get a constable to check that out. I'd say that the play and kennel fit in with the mechanics of the murder quite conveniently. Who wrote it?'

'Donna Nightshade, but to be fair—'

'The ex-con?' interrupts the DCI.

'The reformed teenager who went a bit awry, yes,' confirms Joe.

Fair play, that was nice of him.

'Sergeant Braithwaite interviewed her and she confirmed that Jack had not been given a part in the play, so if it *was* Jack who ran down the steps and play-acted a dying dog at the beginning of the play, Donna has no idea how he would have known what to do or how to act it out.'

'Or so she says. Who should have been in the dog suit?'

'Jago Nightshade. Donna's uncle.'

'Isn't he a bit…?'

'Eccentric? Yes.'

'And why wasn't he in the suit himself?'

Joe refers to his notebook. 'He received a note saying that one of his pigs was missing. And he went to look for it.'

'Wait… pigs? He'd miss a play for a pig?'

'They're like children to him. He does kill them in the end, though.'

'Seems like it's a regular theme in the family. I take it no pig was missing.'

'No. It was a bogus note.'

'Convenient.'

If she says the word convenient again, I'll go down there and throttle her!

'So,' continues Joe, 'either someone sent the note to get Jago out of the way to get their hands on the suit – basically, Jack Crowlas – or Jago is in on it and is lying about the note, or Jack Crowlas wasn't in the suit at all, and he was backstage the whole time and then went into the kennel at the end in a different dog suit.'

Didn't I say there are two dog suits kicking around?

'But then we have the problem of why on earth Jack was

in a dog suit in the first place. I can't see how it was done without at least one of the cast knowing about it – or doing it. What about the Minack staff?'

'They were all front of house and accounted for. Donna never lets anyone backstage other than the players.'

'Again, how very… convenient.'

Right! That's it!

'The zip tie inside the collar was a neat trick,' she says, 'but Jack was a strong fella. Let's say someone had hidden around the back, opened the latch, and gone in to strangle him? He'd have put up a fight, surely?'

'You'd have thought so. But that's when the knife could have gone in.'

'Why go through the rigmarole of the collar if you're going to stab him anyway?'

'It could be an elaborate suicide,' says Joe. 'Designed to frame Donna? They do have history.'

You're just making yourself look like a trainee copper now, Joe…

'Jack Crowlas commit suicide?' she scoffs. 'No way. This is murder, Joe, plain and simple – although maybe not that simple. Handy that you were here… I didn't see you as someone who'd watch something so naff?'

You can really go off a person.

'I was sent a note earlier – a tip-off.'

Joe puts on blue plastic gloves, reaches into his inside jacket pocket, and takes out something that looks like a freezer bag. He removes a piece of paper and starts to read.

'Sir. If you search a certain "animal" at the Minack Theatre on the opening night of the Nightshade play – *after* the play, that is most important – you will find a significant stash of cocaine on that person (or drugs of some description). Can't say more. Anon.'

'How very cute,' says Penworthy. 'Any idea who sent it?'

'Not a clue.'

'I take it the "animal" was Jack?'

'There were no other animals in the play.'

'And there were no drugs on him?'

'Not a sniff.'

'Hmm. Get forensics to check out the suit. Has the place been sniffed out?'

'The dogs are arriving now.'

Penworthy disappears inside the tent. 'And what's with the toy train that was left on his back?' she asks. 'How weird is that? Was it part of the play?'

'Apparently not,' says Joe, 'according to Donna's statement.'

Penworthy sighs. 'The whole play sounds like a completely ridiculous farce. I don't know how you sat through it.'

Joe laughs, but it's a kind laugh, not mocking. 'It wasn't ridiculous. It was... nuanced. But as for the train, it's possibly a reference to the time, years ago, when Jack Crowlas—'

La, la, la, I'm not listening!

'Jesus. Evil bastard,' says Penworthy, once Joe has explained what happened. 'I wouldn't blame her for killing him. If I'd been Donna, I'd have found a way to push him off a cliff years ago. Who knew about it?'

'Very few people. She doesn't know I know.'

I do now.

'Who told you?'

'Her aunt.'

'The nutter or the hippy?'

'The nutter.'

Really...

'What we definitely know is this,' she begins. 'Either Donna did it or was involved in it, or she's been set up by one of her cast who were the only people – other than an expert rock climber – who could have done it.'

She's right, damn her.

'That's my initial summation, yes,' says Joe.

'The toy train could be Donna's calling card,' she says. 'She's obviously the dramatic, batshit crazy type, and the weirdness of the play proves that she has the kind of imagination that could drum up an elaborate thing like this. Maybe she knows we'll catch her? Maybe she just doesn't care about going back to prison and killing him was worth it? Maybe she's the next Cornish serial killer?' Penworthy sniffs. 'Anyway, must be off. I've got a real dog at home crossing his legs. Keep doing the legwork, Joe, and look at the interview statements, start drawing up a hypothesis, and wait for the results of the PM.'

She must mean postmortem.

'I'll get them rushed through for you,' she says. 'By the looks of things, your list of suspects is straightforward. I would expect you to have this cleared up quickly.' She pauses to touch his arm. 'You sure you got this?'

Joe nods a little too vigorously to be convincing, like a

kid persuading his mum that he's ready to walk to school on his own.

She crosses the stage. 'And when you've caught the killer, I want you to get straight back onto finding the drug suppliers. It's coming ashore somewhere on your patch, Joe, and I'm taking all kinds of crap defending you. Latest intel suggests a link to France – I'll send you the file. And as for the murder, I'll give you four days – there's no way it should take longer than that. I'd start with the uncle. My money's on him – at least him being in on it. He was probably doing Donna's bidding, mind you.'

What happened to innocent before proven guilty?

'Well, not necessarily…'

Go on, Joe, tell her!

Penworthy puts up a hand. 'Listen, Donna's got form; she hated Jack, and she had the means, the motive, and the imagination to pull it off. You put her away once, Joe. You can do it again. The woman is clearly unhinged. Occam's razor. Sometimes the most obvious solution is the right one. You said yourself that the answer would be simple. Jago will know something about the whole thing even if he didn't do it. He must do. Thumbscrew it out of him.

'No, the whole thing has Donna Nightshade's name all over it. Maybe the drug dealer you can't find is one and the same person and it's all linked – remember the note? I reckon Donna was in cahoots with Jack with the drugs – it wouldn't be the first time – and she arranged this fiasco to finish him off to get the stash herself and get him out of the way…'

But the rest of the sentence must wait because a man in

white overalls has taken her to one side. There's mumbling that I miss. I tap my ears in case the mics are playing up. Penworthy walks back to Joe.

'The knife has Donna's name on it,' she says. 'Engraved on the blade.'

'Her what?'

I wondered when this would come up.

'Her name. Her actual name. It's engraved on the blade. Job done. Bring her in.'

Joe turns away and puts his hands through his hair. When he turns back, his expression is desperate. Their performance, I admit, is getting better.

'Just give me those four days to investigate it before I bring her in – please. She's got an ankle monitor so she can't go anywhere, and if you knew how hard she's worked to pull it all back together again… I think she's been framed. The family business has been struggling and she's needed to diversify, but—'

'Ha! Exactly!'

'Please?' says Joe.

'Fine. I'll give you four days. But my money's on her.'

'How much money?' he says, his demeanour somewhat coquettish suddenly.

Penworthy takes an astonished step back. Joe's blown it now. Definitely blown it.

'Twenty?'

What the actual f—?

'Make if fifty and you're on!' he says.

It's poor policing, but I can't help but be pleased. Joe's money is on me, which is lovely, actually.

They shake hands just as another man in a white coat approaches.

'You're certain?' she says to him. The man nods. She turns to Joe. 'Well, that's a turn-up. The dogs have sniffed out a Sports Direct bag full of drugs.'

'Where?'

'Stuffed inside a massive rucksack backstage in the dressing room.'

'Whose rucksack?' asks Joe. 'Not Donna's?'

'No, some actress called Gabrielle Jones.'

Never!

Joe's response mirrors my own. 'The vicar?!' he splutters. 'Jesus.'

'Jesus? I don't care if she's the archbishop of bloody Canterbury. Bring her in!'

Penworthy turns away while throwing one last dynamite piece of information his way.

'Oh, and they've found traces of cocaine on the inside of Jack's dog suit.' Penworthy claps her hands like a gleeful child. 'I think a very convenient picture is starting to emerge, DS Enys, don't you? This case is a Piece. Of. Piss.'

Joe sighs the sigh of a very troubled man. 'Maybe it's all a bit too convenient,' he says.

'Nah. A kill's a kill. Pin it on Donna – on the lot of them. And remember,' she says, walking away this time. 'I want the name of that supplier in France, and you've got four days to sort the whole lot out – drugs, murder, everything!'

Joe looks up to the gods, directly at me. He holds my gaze. I'll process that later.

Chapter Fourteen

DONNA

3 am and I'm alone in the glasshouse. Moonlight fills the space with a calming silver light. This building has always been my safe space, but tonight I've locked myself inside, and I can't help but feel like I'm a little fish in a great big bowl, with many unseen sets of eyes bearing down upon me.

Uncle Jago was pretty much useless and shaking like a jelly when I walked him home at midnight. Joe had interviewed him and been gentle from what I could see. The bogus note I supposedly sent him is nonsensical and apparently went along the lines of:

Had a call to say there's a stray piglet with a mark like a cross on its ear down Nanjizal Cove. I reckon it's Banjo. I've got a stand-in for your part if you want to go and look. Hope she's all right. Donna.

Jago never bothered to check if the piglet in question

was missing but dashed straight to Nanjizal and searched for an hour with a flashlight in the dark. Both facts are concerning because it means that whoever left the bogus note knew Jago's whereabouts and was familiar with his personality sufficiently to know that he would behave that way, and they also knew other details including information about the pigs, such as their names and the logistical details of the play. Jago is adamant that his dog suit was stolen, but I'm almost certain that Jack was wearing a different suit. Someone must have ordered a replica suit, but how on earth did Jack know the details of the play and the exact make of the suit? And where is Jago's suit? I make a note to myself to phone the dog suit company in the morning. Someone around here must have ordered another one recently, and I want to know who it was. Detective work is quite simple, really.

I put down my pen and rest my face in my hands, feeling overwhelmed. There are several floral bouquets that need to be put together for delivery by lunchtime tomorrow, which means I must be out in the flower patches and cutting by 6am. (Florist's tip: it's important to cut garden flowers first thing in the morning when the stems are full of water and nice and turgid.)

Anyhow, I reckon Joe Enys will pitch up at around 9am and as I'm the main suspect in this fiasco it's vital that I stay several steps ahead of Joe and work out what the hell to do, what to say, and exactly how to act, because if there's one thing I'm certain of it's this: I've got form, I've got the means and the motive to kill Jack, and twenty quid (or fifty, if you're Joe) says I'm back in cuffs by teatime. So, as the DCI said earlier, what do we know…?

The straightforward solution is that the person in the dog suit who ran through the audience at the beginning of the play was Jack Crowlas and unless one of the players did it, which I doubt, someone must have sailed a boat to the bottom of the cliffs, scaled the cliffs carrying a toy train, jumped over the railings and accessed the kennel via the back panel (the hessian sacking acting as a screen meant no one would see the interloper). This person then stabbed him in the neck (let's ignore the fact for a moment that his neck had swollen inside the dog collar leading to strangulation), slipped out via the back panel, then fled back down the rocks. I know that such a stunt is possible in the time they had without a rope, although one of the players could have been in on it and released the rope (if there had been one) and thrown it down to the sea once the murderer left. But why would Jack have wanted to be in the play in the first place? As a clever way of getting the drugs ashore? Were the drugs in the bag smuggled in by Jack? Most probably. He had been looking for a foolproof place to do a drop last night… But how did he know what to do, or how to act in the performance? I remember what the DCI said about 'the most obvious solution' etc. but the only obvious solution is that Jago and I were in cahoots to kill Jack. The only obvious solution is that I offered him a part in the play, gave him a slow-release drug that made him unconscious shortly after being shut in the kennel and also caused his neck to swell, made sure the collar couldn't untighten because of the zip tie (which I have here at Penberth, clearly), and for good measure, I then thrust my own personal knife in his neck when I was offstage as some kind of revenge calling card and then, as if that wasn't enough, left a toy train on his back because of what he did to my dog – the bastard, the absolute bastard.

Yep, that *is* the obvious solution.

By my reckoning, the murderer would need to have access to the following: slow-release poison (how else would anyone stab Jack without a fight and I've got loads of plants around the place that can act as poison), zip ties (ditto), a means of getting into the back of the kennel during the show (check), an in-depth knowledge of the play (er, hello!), a Thomas the Tank Engine toy train (not difficult to get hold of; I recently gave one away in a box of old toys we donated to the church jumble sale), and a motive (where do I start?).

That's it then. My first crime is solved. *I* did it.

Only, it wasn't me.

But if not me, then who?

Who else had the means and the motive to kill Jack Crowlas? In other words, who set me up?

The motive? Lots of people.

The means? Only those people with an in-depth knowledge of the play and access to the stage and my knife – like, the players.

A flyer for *Sleeping Dogs Lie* sits on the table in front of me. I turn the programme over and glance down the list of performers. In a life-imitating-art kind of a way, I realise that we are all now playing the very same roles, only for real this time.

Weird. Awful. Shocking.
But also, quite exciting!
My phone pings. It's a text from a withheld number.

*Don't you ever worry about sitting alone at night? I'm watching
you.*

Ah.
Not so exciting after all, then.

Chapter Fifteen

Joe Enys is in the station incident room looking as mad as hell.

Three constables and his desk sergeant are sitting across from him.

'I want to know everything about Jack Crowlas and his activity over the past week,' he barks. 'Who he saw, where he went, what he ate, where he stayed, when he had a shit, everything. Every. Single. Detail. Of his sorry, pathetic existence needs to be catalogued and checked. Someone will know something – find that person. Build me a picture. And Demelza?'

She glances up from her notebook and offers Joe an adoring smile.

'Yes, sir?'

'Get a climber on those cliffs at the Minack. I want him—'

'Or her,' says one of the constables.

'Or her, sorry, there today. And I want to know if they're

scalable without a rope. And there's a cave under those cliffs so get them to search the cave, too.' He pauses for dramatic effect. 'Now!'

Joe retires to his office and leans back in his chair, puts his hands behind his head, and allows himself a smile. Jack Crowlas, the bane of his life, is dead. Actually dead! Stiff as a board by now. Even the grotesque memory of his purple, pufferfish face sticking out of that bloody ridiculous dog suit can't dampen Joe's spirits. Some people are born bad and die bad, like the ugly witches in fairy tales, and Jack Crowlas was one of them; he may as well have been wearing sparkly red shoes. Joe considers having a quick celebratory dance around the office while singing 'Ding dong the witch is dead', but there's a window between him and the outer office where Demelza and the rest of the officers sit and, as fragile as it is, he has a reputation to uphold.

In many ways it's a day like any other: his reusable cup is sitting on the desk full of Skinny Pete's excellent coffee, his childhood sweetheart Donna Nightshade is dominating the headlines of the *Penzance Packet*, and he's missed (ignored) ten calls from Bill Smiley. So yes, it's just an ordinary day at the office, except for the fact that Jack Crowlas finally did something good for the world – he removed himself from it.

Joe looks at yet another photo of Donna on the front page of the newspaper. She looks shocked, but also… just a little bit… euphoric? And why shouldn't she? Ding dong, etc. But whether he likes the idea or not, all fingers point in her direction. If only he could bury the whole thing – the witch is dead after all; let him remain so and well done to whomever the murderer was. (Donna, it was Donna). But if only he had the power to decide which crimes were worthy of investigating and which could be thrown into the 'who cares' bin, life would be so much easier. As the play suggested, let sleeping dogs lie – or dead dogs, in this case. But what if... what if... the murderer *wasn't* Donna, and what if whoever stuck the knife in is a nutter on the rampage? What if Joe is about to uncover a whole new underworld of crime? It's possible. After all, someone supplied the drugs...

Now wouldn't that be something? Joe Enys, the new darling of Devon and Cornwall Police? He imagines himself receiving his MBE... He would wear grey wool...

Feeling more elated than he should, Joe drinks his coffee and looks at the paper. He tries to think of scenarios that don't reveal Donna as a murderer until the phone rings. It's DCI Penworthy with the results of the postmortem. ('I only take cash for my winnings, by the way.')

He ends the call and his forehead crashes onto the photo of Donna on the desk because everything – absolutely everything – has just changed.

Chapter Sixteen

Joe hasn't driven down the track to Penberth Manor since he arrested Donna all those years ago, when they were young and more than a bit foolish (well, she was; Joe wasn't). There have been many times when he has wanted to return to Penberth, times when he has driven over from Penzance with every intention of dropping by and suggesting bygones be bygones, but he has never managed to venture beyond the big stone arch that sits at the foot of the drive. Joe Enys was, and forever would be, the turncoat who put Donna in the clink – the man who put the cuffs on when he could have looked the other way. There was no question that he was in her book, and once you were in the Nightshade Book of Ye Deadly Wrecker's Curses, or whatever it was called, there was simply no getting out of it. He was only surprised that he'd lived this long.

And yet here he is, Detective Sergeant Enys, driving an unmarked grey BMW (the whole of Penzance knows it's him) down the pot-holed rickety track that leads to the gothic wonder of Penberth Manor. They would all be there, no doubt: Donna, Kerensa, Uncle Jago, and Lamorna (along with a few more hangers-on than eighteen years ago). A Nightshade had attempted to kill Jack before, of course – that barking mad aunt of hers had got herself banged-up in prison as a result – but please God, he thinks as he grabs his jacket from the back seat and quickly checks out his hair in the wing mirror… this time, let it not be his Donna who stuck the knife in. Please let her be as innocent as the snowdrop posies she delivers for free to the old folks' homes in February, or at least, if not innocent, then twenty-seven steps ahead of him and able to completely cover her tracks.

Joe doesn't bother knocking on the glorious and ancient oak front door to the main house because the only person who ever seemed to spend any time in the big house, he remembers, was Uncle Jago, and although he very much needed to speak with him again, it was Donna who would receive the benefit of his attention today. He heads towards the walled garden – Donna's favourite place – opens the painted wooden door, and there she is, sitting on a swing seat just inside the wall, next to a bed of bright-orange dahlias, looking amazing, wearing shorts, flipflops, a vest top, and a chunky emerald-green cardigan. (Donna didn't really feel the cold until late November, he remembers, before thinking that he really did hold on to too much information about this woman). She's looking at her phone. Her long, shiny hair is loose and curly and pulled around one shoulder. This is the first time they've been alone together in years and if Joe didn't know better, he'd say that she's been waiting for him. He thinks about shaking her hand, but his heart is going like the clappers and his palms are sweaty.

'Nice suit,' she says, looking up from her phone. She stills the swing with her feet. 'Prada?'

Joe laughs, although it's more of an awkward titter, really. 'Something like that,' he says.

'I'm honoured.' She stands and tucks her phone into her left bra cup. 'I hope it's your'—she lowers her voice to a manly tone—'"suit I wear when interviewing murder suspects" suit?'

Joe doesn't respond; he's just amazed that she hasn't ordered him out of the garden. The lack of a prickle is disconcerting, too. She's teasing him, yes, but there's no prickle... and that's not quite right.

'Let's go into the greenhouse,' she says, turning her back to him and walking away. 'We can do the thing properly in there.' She stops and turns to look at him. 'Or are you going straight for the cuffs again?'

There it is.

'No cuffs,' he says, 'just the obvious questions.'

She starts to walk again, while throwing her conversation over her shoulder for Joe to catch. 'Like why was there a dead man on the stage of the Minack with a knife with my name on it stuck in his neck?'

'That kind of thing, yes.'

'The knife has been missing for a few days, although I'm not sure which day I saw it last exactly, before you ask.' She steps into the glasshouse. 'I *have* been interviewed already, and Demelza was pretty thorough, so...'

Joe follows her through the door. 'Some key evidence has come to light,' he says. 'Meaning that we need to speak to everyone again.' He glances around. Absolutely nothing in this place has changed. 'And I'm hoping you'll be able to give me your opinion on something else. Something... plant related.'

'Because they found a poison in his blood?' she asks, deadpan. 'And the poison came from a plant?'

How does she do it? Second guessing him all the damn time? And why incriminate herself by admitting that she knows so much? The woman can never help herself.

'Something like that,' he says.

Donna gestures towards a stool on the other side of the workbench. The scent in the greenhouse has awarded him with the familiar scent of spending warm summer days with Donna here at Penberth – it's the scent of pure teenage contentment. He tries to push a reel of memories from his mind, memories of the two of them laughing, playing, fighting...

'Coffee?'

Donna walks over to a filter coffee jug that's bubbling away while Joe takes a seat on the bench. It's his old seat, where he used to sit and watch her work and try to persuade her to come out on the boat. But coffee? That's unexpected. He starts to relax a little. Could it really be that she's started to forgive him?

'And no, I haven't forgiven you,' she says with her back to him as she pours. 'But we're going to need to get along if the two of us are going to get anywhere with this investigation.' She reaches across the bench and offers him the cup before taking a seat herself.

'The two of us?' he repeats, taking the cup.

'It's my first case, as it happens.'

'Ah, the Edge of the World Detective Agency. I heard about that.'

'Don't be dismissive.'

'I'm not.'

'Yes, you are,' she chides. 'Your mouth always goes into a reluctant twitch when you're amused, Joe Enys. Even so, I must admit that you're the expert and I'd be grateful for a few pointers.'

Joe puts down his cup, noting that she called him by his full name. Hmm.

'Who's paying your investigation fee?' he asks.

'I am. Jack was a relative, of sorts, so I'm putting it down as a business expense.'

Of course she is.

'And let's not forget that a man was found dead – murdered – during the performance of my play, and I'm almost certainly your lead suspect. As far as I'm concerned, I'm entitled to investigate the hell out of it, if only to save myself from the gallows, don't you think?'

Joe wants to say, *don't be silly, you're not a suspect*, but he can't, so he carries on drinking, if only to hide his twitching mouth. But when he takes out his notebook and pen, Joe knows he hasn't felt this happy in a very long time: here they are, the two amigos, back together again. But with the kind of questions he needs to ask, the bonhomie can't last for long.

'Good God!' shouts Donna. 'And all of it cocaine?'

Joe has just admitted to the size of the stash that was hidden inside the vicar's rucksack.

'Yep!'

'That's quite the heist, detective sergeant. You must be chuffed. But poor Gabby. What a shock for her – to have it found in her rucksack like that. I'll pop by and see her later; take her some of Jago's lemon drizzle…'

'She'll need it. She's been with the drug squad all morning.'

'But you can't think Gabby had anything to do with it, Joe? She's a bloody vicar! She's obviously been set up.'

Joe thinks better of saying, *if you're going to be a successful detective, you need to park preconceived ideas at the door*, and instead flicks through a few pages in his notebook before eventually saying, 'Brugmansia.'

'Brugmansia?'

'It's a plant. The pathologist has confirmed that there were traces of it in his blood. Any ideas where someone might find it?'

'Toxic stuff,' she says. 'How much had he been given?'

'A lot.'

'Enough to kill him?'

Joe's phone rings. It's the coroner's office.

'Sorry, I need to take this.' He swipes right. 'DS Enys.

Just wait a moment, please.' Joe nods towards the door. 'Back in a sec.'

When Joe steps back into the glasshouse two minutes later, he knows two important things: the first is that Jack Crowlas was poisoned not once but twice before the knife went in. The first was from a draught of Brugmansia, which had been administered perhaps days before; and as for the second, a tiny pin prick was found up his nose, which is where a second poison was administered just before he died (rooky mistake) and that second poison wasn't brugmansia at all. It was *Atropa Belladonna*... aka deadly nightshade. It was as if the murderer wasn't content with killing him with one attempt, but just kept going and going – fair enough, he was a difficult one to kill, was Jack Crowlas.

'I was wondering if you're familiar with that plant at all, with brugmansia?' says Joe, returning to the stool.

Donna laughs. 'Familiar with it? Come on. Why don't you just ask what you really want to ask.'

Joe's face is impassive. 'Which is?'

'Do I have brugmansia here at Penberth?'

'And do you?'

Donna sits back on her stool and smiles. 'I do, and to coin a pantomime phrase, it's behind you.'

Joe turns around sharply like there's a gunman at his back. Donna laughs, puts on her gardening gloves, and walks around the bench to join him. A flamboyant-looking potted plant sits on the low windowsill. It stands two metres high and unbeknownst to Joe, one of the flower heads has been resting on his shoulder the whole time. A little bit of pollen sits on his shoulder. Donna brushes it off with her glove.

'Say hello to *Brugmansia Feingold*,' she says, assessing the plant with obvious admiration. The leaves are large and the flowers – bright orange – are pendulous. 'It's also known as angel's-trumpet. It's native to South America and as you are obviously aware, it's highly toxic.' She lifts a trumpet and puts her nose to it. 'Want to smell?'

Joe takes a sniff and quickly realises that it's the same scent he's always associated with the big glasshouse at Penberth – and with Donna, come to that. It's lovely... but deadly.

Yep. That would be just about right.

'And you don't mind having it around the place when it's so... toxic?' he asks.

She looks at him squarely. 'Loads of common or garden plants are toxic. And if I didn't have it, how else could I poison people?'

'Donna...'

She drops the flower head. 'All right, keep your knickers on. I have it here because it's beautiful, and also... it's part of the family.'

Joe shakes his head. 'You're related to plants now?'

'Of course I am.'

She's flirting. Definitely flirting, thinks Joe.

'This little beauty is a relation of *Atropa Belladonna*, who I'm named after, as you'll remember.' Donna nods to the tattoo on her leg. 'Otherwise known as deadly nightshade.'

Joe looks at her thigh and glances away while thinking, *great legs. But also, deadly nightshade?*

Donna leans her back against the bench. 'Brugmansia has been quite the naughty little plant then?' Her face hardens. 'Although we should never blame a beautiful plant for the actions of the person who misuses her, should we, Joe?'

Joe hasn't time for her games. He thinks of grabbing Donna's hand and telling her about the deadly nightshade in Jack's bloodstream. Telling her to run away. Run right away.

'But if you really want to know all about it,' she adds, 'you should know that it's used for good purposes, too.'

'Such as?'

'Oh, all kinds of things. For extracting important alkaloids and for lots of other medicinal things that to be honest I have absolutely no idea about.'

'And do you have to import them from South America, these types of plants? Are they tricky to get hold of?'

Donna has begun deadheading a pelargonium at the end of the bench. 'Not particularly. I got this one at the garden centre at Breage five years ago. Honestly, Joe, relax with all the cloak and dagger stuff. It's a perfectly safe plant if you know how to handle it.'

'And what if you don't?'

'Then you could kill someone, or make them feel really poorly, at the very least.'

Joe picks up his coffee cup and stares into it rather than allow her to read his expression or see his twitching lips. What if she's just playing with him? Donna is nothing if not unpredictable. What if it really is Donna who's on a rampage of revenge? What if she killed Jack and now she's out to poison everyone in her book…?

Joe is in her book.

Maybe the coffee is…

She stops deadheading. 'Don't worry. I have no intention of seeking my revenge by poisoning you, if that's what you're thinking.'

Joe forces a smile and knocks back his coffee, which suddenly tastes a little bitter.

'Who else around here would know about the effects of a plant like this?' he asks.

Donna shrugs and picks up a spray bottle. She mists an asparagus fern.

'A plantsman, perhaps? Or anyone with a knowledge of South American cultu—' The bottle spraying stops. Joe hears a cog click into place in Donna's mind.

'You've thought of something,' he says.

She starts to spray again, her back to him. 'It's nothing. I just remembered that brugmansia is used in South America by shamans to alleviate ailments, that's all.'

She's lying. He leaves it. 'And it's used there in a good way, right?'

'That all depends on the shaman. Some shamans are good, some are… not so good.'

'What would a bad shaman do with it?'

She turns to face him, and with the look of someone on the periphery of unhingement says, 'Magic!' She laughs and returns to her stool.

'You're winding me up,' says Joe.

'I'm being perfectly serious. Black magic rituals are still performed in some parts of the world. Mainly by those bad men I was talking about.'

Or women, thinks Joe, having learned this lesson from his constable. 'Why?'

'To bring on hallucinations...' Donna pauses again. There is an idea slowly piecing itself together in her mind, and then Joe remembers that hallucinations are something a previous Nightshade boss lady knew all about – her Aunty Deadly, aka Jack Crowlas's wife, aka the woman who is still in prison for his attempted murder – the woman who suffered terribly from hallucinations. And she suffered all this purely because someone (unproven but, let's face it, it was Jack) had been slowly poisoning her, which is why she got off with a spell in a psychiatric prison.

'And are there any practising shamans around here?' he asks.

She answers him too quickly. 'No.'

'And which bit is the dangerous bit?'

'All of it, but especially the leaves and the seeds.'

'Through ingestion?'

'Yes.'

'And what kinds of symptoms would you get if you ingested it?'

Donna rolls her eyes. 'Jesus. I have no idea, Joe.'

He writes a few notes in his book to give her a moment.

'And who else knows that you have one here?' he asks.

Donna sighs. 'Everyone? No one? I've no idea! And I don't have just one either, so write *that* down in your book. I have three.' She cocks her head and assesses him. 'You know… you could easily have looked up brugmansia on Wikipedia or asked the toxicologist in Truro to give you the rundown.'

'I could,' agrees Joe.

'But you wanted to ask me so you could see if I have it at Penberth?'

'I did.'

'Am I a suspect?'

'Everyone is a suspect.'

'And by everyone, you mean the players.'

What's the point of lying? 'I mean the players.'

'All right. Let's go through them now,' she says.

'Donna…'

'No, you're right. This needs to be done properly or not at all. What was the time of death? What did the coroner say?'

'He died towards the end of the second act, but he could have been poisoned within the half hour before that.'

'I take it his throat swelled as a result of the poison, and then the collar – that he couldn't remove – tightened and strangled him.'

She sooooo did it, thinks Joe.

'You take it correctly.'

'Right. The question is, who had access to the back of the kennel? Let's go through them.'

'I already have,' he says, cutting her off, 'and every single one of them had enough time in the dressing room alone while the others were on stage and could have slipped out the back and done it, including you. Lamorna's silhouette was visible in the music tent the whole time.'

She leans across the table and grabs his empty cup. 'No surprises that I'm suspect number one.' She tips her head to one side and smiles. 'I suppose you've heard by now that I threatened to kill him.'

'I have.'

She slams the cup down. 'And why the hell shouldn't I kill him?' She leans across the table again. Joe would be dizzy if not for her sharp green eyes being fixed like daggers on his. 'But I'll tell you this, Joe Enys: if I *was* going to kill him, I wouldn't have used angel's-trumpet to finish him off, that's for damn sure.'

'Why?'

She smiles, wryly (because there is simply no other way to smile in situations like this). 'Because it's not *quite* deadly enough.' She sniffs, in conclusion. 'There's too much of a margin for error.'

'And which plant – which poison – would you have used instead, seeing as how you're the expert?' He's leading her in the wrong direction; he knows it. Oldest trick in the book, but…

She sits back once more, looking smug.

'To kill Jack Crowlas? What else but the best plant for the job?'

'Which is?'

'Deadly nightshade, obviously.'

There it is.

Donna jumps off the stool, walks to the glasshouse door and opens it. The shrug of the left shoulder is infinitesimal but it's enough to show him that she's ready for him to leave. It's also enough to sober him into some straight-talking. He remains seated. 'And when you say deadly nightshade, are you referring to the plant or to yourself?'

Donna doesn't answer but nods more definitely towards the garden. It's over. He grabs his jacket and walks towards the door.

'Can't you just leave it this time, Joe?' she whispers, placing a hand on his arm. 'No one cares that he's dead. The whole town – the whole county – can relax without him in it. He was bad news. You know he was.'

Joe shakes his head.

'Look, Donna, even if I wanted to…'

She rips her hand away.

'What's the matter, Joe?' she spits. 'Frightened you'll lose the bet? Same old Joe Enys. You're not a person anymore, you're just a machine, spouting out regulations and rules and restrictions. No thoughts, no feelings. And if you want to know how I know about the bet between you and Penworthy, I'll tell you! I was listening in to your cosy summation at the Minack – I had ear buds in.'

'I know,' he says. 'Who do you think asked Louise to give them to you?'

The pause between them is cavernous.

'Even so,' says Donna, clearly flustered.

'Look,' begins Joe. 'The moment a policeman even thinks about going rogue, the rule of law is over. I can't cherry-pick my cases. I can't bury a murder case just because the man was the devil and Donna Nightshade has asked me to…'

He puts on his jacket and turns to leave, but ten paces down the gravel path his heart fills with… what? Rage? No.

Indignation? Yes, definitely indignation. He marches back to the glasshouse door. She's returned to her stool. Her elbows are on the table and her head is in her hands.

'You want my help?' he says. 'Then think about this: a man was found murdered on stage while performing in a play you wrote. He had large quantities of brugmansia in his blood, which is a plant you have on the premises. He also – and I shouldn't tell you this but what the hell – had a further poison in his system, which – can you guess what it was? – none other than our old friend *Atropa Belladonna*, deadly nightshade. Oh, yes, you might look at me now but I'm not quite finished. The dog collar around his neck – put there by you as far as I can deduce, bearing in mind you wrote the bloody play and issued the costume – was impossible to release once the neck expanded from the effect of the poison. Not everyone would react in this way, but Jack would because he had allergies and, as a member of the family, by God, I bet you knew it.'

He steps closer.

'You were seen talking to him at The Star two nights ago. Why?'

'He wanted to see me.'

'Why?'

'To catch up.'

'Bullshit. What did you talk about?'

'The weather.'

'And that induced you to threaten to kill him, did it?'

'The weather can be quite an emotive subject,' she says, using her finger to draw imaginary circles on the table.

Joe stops his pounce and looks at her in the way

eighteen-year-old Joe would have looked at eighteen-year-old Donna – well, not quite the same way, but close.

'Just stop for a moment, and think,' he says. 'Don't keep incriminating yourself like it's some kind of amusing game. For the last time, what did Jack Crowlas talk to you about at the pub?'

Donna's whole frame sinks. 'He wanted me to let him do a drugs drop at Penberth, which he said was his right because he's still married to Aunty Donna. They never divorced. He wanted to move back in and take over... Wanted to get the old gang back together.'

'And why did you threaten to kill him?'

'Seriously? You really need to ask me that question?'

Joe closes his eyes and pinches the space between his eyebrows. She's not lying; he knows that much. Truly, he can't blame her for anything she might have done – even killing him.

'Are we done?' she asks. 'Because I've got a business to run.'

Joe rests a hand on her arm. She doesn't wrench it away. 'I'll be working my way through all the players, and I suggest you do that by yourself, quietly and carefully – and don't rule anyone out, even the vicar, because if *you* didn't kill Jack, then someone close to you did. If you don't tell me exactly what you know or who you suspect – and I know you suspect someone – then I can't help you or any of your friends who were clearly in the best position to do the job. You don't trust me. I get it. You hate me. I get it. The whole thing is totally bonkers – Jesus, even the audience laughed when they saw him lying there dead. But no matter what we thought of him, just to be perfectly clear, a man that you are known to despise – no, stop it, Donna, you hated him – was found dead on your turf with two drugs in his body that you have knowledge of and can easily access, not to mention the knife in his neck with your name on it. When I arrived here you already knew they'd found poison in his blood. How? How did you know?'

'A lucky guess.'

He grabs her arm tighter.

'Stop it right now and tell me!'

'All right, I'll bloody tell you! It was obvious from the swelling around his neck and, as you said, I knew Jack carried an EpiPen in case of wasp stings and that kind of thing. We'd always joked that Aunty Donna should have just hidden his pen and shoved him into a wasps' nest. If you poison him then you don't have to use your hands or even be there when he's strangled. Also, he came to me for help because he was frightened... well, annoyed. He was sure someone was trying to do him in.'

'When?'

'Two days ago, the morning of the day I saw him in The Star.'

'Where?'

'Here. He came to Penberth. He said he'd picked up one of my private detective cards at the pub and wanted me to do some digging around.'

'And why did he need help, exactly?' asks Joe, who is not just frustrated, he's apoplectic.

'Because someone had been sending him hate mail through the post, threatening letters, that type of thing.'

'To his mother's old place in Newlyn?'

'Yes.'

'Did he have any idea who was doing it?'

'Possibly a one-handed man with an eye patch.'

'Donna…'

'What? I'm being serious. That's what he said. He told me in the pub that a one-handed man with an eye patch would be doing the next drop.'

Joe's done. He takes out a card from his wallet and puts it on the bench in front of her. 'My private number,' he says. 'Just in case you need it. Any time.'

Donna looks at the card and nods.

Joe takes a deep breath. 'I'll leave you to your day,' he says. 'You've been very helpful Ms Nightshade and I thank you for your time. And if you could pin down the last time you had the knife in your possession, that would be beneficial to us both.'

He doesn't hesitate to dash away this time, and when he jumps in the car and starts the engine, the classic song, 'She' is playing on Pirate FM. Joe can't help but pause a moment to remember a teenage girl laughing up at him from the deck of a boat on a glorious summer's day. He shouldn't be leaving. He should be marching Donna to the station along with all the others, especially Jago. But some deep instinct warns Joe to go slowly-slowly this time. There's no hurry. Donna's right – who cares who killed Jack Crowlas, really?

Penworthy. DCI Penworthy does.

Chapter Seventeen

DONNA

It's official: Joe Enys is still the sexiest man in Cornwall. But I haven't got time to think about that now because the vicar has just walked in dressed for work. Jesus, she looks rough. Time to cheer her up.

'Well, if it isn't the pusher of Penzance!' I say. 'Got any skunk for me this morning?'

She starts to cry – wail, even.

'Too early for humour?' I ask.

She flops onto Joe's stool. 'I'll never laugh again,' she says.

Half an hour, two coffees, and a whole packet of Jaffa Cakes later, and I'm fully up to date with the past twelve hours of Gabby's life, which has been…

'Awful, Donna. Just awful. You have no idea how bad it is in a police station.' (Er, hello!) 'All those *questions*, and that Demelza woman is such a bitch! I never knew how different it would be to be *in* a cell, rather than visiting one.'

'It must have been awful for you,' I say. (My words are sympathetic, but my tone says, 'Dry your eyes, buttercup, and buck up!')

'Where is everyone?' she asks, glancing around.

That is a particularly good question.

'I'd guess that Jago is moping around with his pigs and Lamorna said she wanted to go for a walk to reset her balance, so I'll be lucky to see her this side of next Wednesday. They all seem to forget that I'm trying to run a business here and I haven't filled the roadside cart with any flower bunches for three days, so that's at least fifty quid a day I'm losing out on. I'll be honest with you, Gabby, we're borrowing from Peter to pay Paul now and I'm not sure how much longer we can go on.'

'What about Kerensa? Can't she help today?'

I shake my head. 'She's gone to see Aunty Donna, to break the news about Jack.'

'Why?'

My answer is deadpan. 'He was her husband.'

'Oh, yes. Of course. Upsetting for her.'

'Upsetting? They'll both be doing cartwheels across the prison lawns all afternoon. It'll be the best day of Aunty Donna's life!'

Gabby loosens her dog collar. She's been loosening her dog collar a lot lately.

I open a fresh bag of coffee while she chatters on. Eventually she gets to the point.

'The police were only concerned with asking me about

the drug stash, but have they…? I mean, do they…? Do they think it was suicide, or was it…?'

'It was good old-fashioned murder, Gabby.' I grab her cup to refill it once again and use it to gesticulate. 'And here's something else you might want to pray about the next time you're cosying up to that Lord of yours. Joe Enys—'

'*Your* Joe Enys?' she asks. 'The policeman?'

'He's not mine, but yes, Joe the copper, has come to the – quite correct – conclusion that the murderer must have had in-depth knowledge of my play, my plants, the Minack, the fact that I had form with Jack Crowlas and issue over what happened with my dog—'

'Why, what happened with your dog?'

'Doesn't matter.'

'Which means?' she says.

I faff about making coffee before answering, because in truth, I don't want to answer that question. I don't want to say, *it means that I'm murder suspect number one. And as I'm pretty certain that I didn't do it, then one of you lot did*, but that's what I do eventually say as I hand her the cup.

'One of *us*?!' Gabby's eyes are finally open. She crosses herself. 'May the Lord in heaven preserve their soul. But why on earth?'

'Because he was a dreadful man, Gabby! Dig deep enough and I guarantee that the others will all have had some kind of dodgy dealings with Jack Crowlas. Who was it that put the drugs in your bag? Have you asked yourself that?'

'Oh, I have,' she says. 'But surely, you would have known if one of us had wanted him dead?' she says.

'Everyone has secrets, even you, I should think.'

Is that a blush?

'No, mark my words. There will be plenty of shenanigans that have gone down over the years that I'm not privy to.' I grab a bucket of flowers that I'm prepping for a wedding florist that's made up mainly of dahlia 'café au lait' (heavenly). I take one out and strip surplus leaves from a stem. 'You know what they say, Gab. Keep your enemies close but your friends closer...'

She stops drinking. 'It's the other way around.'

I look at her over the top of imaginary glasses. 'Not in this case. No, there's nothing else for it. I'm going to have to dig the dirt on my mates and my family and find out which one of them slotted Jack Crowlas and also, who slid the drugs into your rucksack, and before Joe Enys beats me to it – or worse, before he pins the whole thing on me. Out of interest, why did you have a big, presumably empty rucksack with you anyway?'

'It wasn't empty when I arrived,' she said. 'It had the after-party pastries and nibbles in from Lidl. I'd taken them out and put them on the trestle table.'

That's right. She had.

Her hands rush to her face. 'But Lord Almighty, Donna! What if you *do* find out that it was one of us that did it? Could be tricky for you... awkward, you know?' She starts to play with an ear. 'I mean, would you grass them up, or...?'

'To the police? You've got to be kidding! No Nightshade

would ever do that!' I pop the dahlia back in the bucket and grab a folder containing today's order invoices. 'You wouldn't do me a favour and write out message cards for me, would you?' I ask. 'For the bouquet orders?'

'Of course.' She relaxes into a smile and removes her dog collar completely. 'You wouldn't believe how uncomfortable this thing gets,' she says.

'Just ask Jack!' I say, laughing out loud for the first time in what seems like ages. My joke goes down like a lead balloon, so I spin the invoice folder across the table. 'There you go,' I say, leaning backwards on the stool to grab a flowerpot full of message cards and pens from the back dresser. 'If you open the file, you'll see page dividers for each day of the month. Just open today's date and you'll find messages printed out at the bottom of each invoice. It'll take your mind off things. All you need to do is copy the message onto the card – best handwriting please!'

Gabby gets herself organised and with pen in hand, reads out the first message. *'You are the sexiest woman on earth. I'm desperate for you. We'll be together one day, won't we?'* She glances up. Her eyes are certainly open now. 'Bloody Nora!' she says, scanning the invoice. 'Who sent that?'

Ah. *That* message.

'My lips are sealed, I'm afraid,' I say with a wink. 'After all, confidentiality is the…' I begin to make a hand-tied bouquet. 'Sixth, no, seventh rule of floristry.'

She laughs. 'Really? What are the first six?'

I add a second stem. 'Proportion, scale, harmony, rhythm, a nice bit of balance, and finally, unity.'

Gabby laughs. 'It sounds like a catechism.'

'It is, in a way. Now get on with your writing.'

She works through the invoices while I begin putting together the 'sexy woman' bouquet (from old man Bosullow again) until I sense that she's stopped writing.

'You don't want to see this message,' she says, looking up from the folder.

'Don't be silly, of course I do. Pass it over.'

There are tears in her eyes as she hands me the folder. A handwritten note has been stapled to the order. It reads:

Please deliver a funeral-style bouquet to Jack Crowlas in Newlyn.

> *Card reads: In memory of Jack Crowlas. An absolute cock.*
> *Cash enclosed.*

'He really did have someone out to get him, then?' I murmur, rereading the message. My eyes search the invoice for details of the sender but there's no email address, no telephone number, nothing. Someone (Kerensa?) has created an order slip and written, *received in the post with £100 cash*, on the invoice. Gabby is crying again. She dabs her misty eyes with her sleeve and pulls herself together.

'Sorry,' she says. 'I'm tired, that's all. It's been so awful and now you're in a position where you're forced to suspect all your friends.'

'Hmm,' I murmur, not really listening. 'Yes, I suppose I am. This order must have arrived yesterday, or maybe the day before.' The cogs of my brain begin to clank a few facts into place uncomfortably. 'Which was…'

'Before Jack was killed,' she says.

'Mark my words,' I say, in my firm don't-argue-with-me voice. 'I reckon these flowers were sent from whoever it was that was trying to put the frighteners on him – and probably killed him – but at least it means that I've got one less order to do and got paid for it, so it's a win-win really.'

'Frighteners?' she asks.

'Yes. Some poor sod had obviously come a cropper with Jack and decided to take their revenge by sending him threatening notes; that's what he said, anyhow. Jack wanted me to find out who it was. Too late now, though, eh?'

She nods regretfully. 'Yes,' she sighs. 'Too late now. Will you tell the police about it?'

'About this? A dodgy message someone attached to a funeral flower order, an order that was placed before he was dead?' I scrunch my nose. 'Nah. I mean, clearly I should. But I probably won't. No, I'll keep this little nugget to myself for now. Like I said, I want to stay one step ahead of Joe Enys, if I can.'

I take the invoice out of the file and put it in an envelope inside the drawer I keep locked at the far end of the greenhouse. Returning to the bench, I continue to put together an arrangement for a man who's having an affair with an ex-mayor's wife. Gabby lets out a long, relaxing sigh. 'Well,' she says, knocking back the dregs and putting down the pen (with several message cards left unwritten). 'Must get on.'

She's halfway to the door before I can say, 'Hey, slacker, you haven't finished your job.' She laughs, shrugs, and carries on walking. 'Oh, and Gabby?' She turns around. 'You forgot your dog collar.'

That got her attention. She glances towards the stiff white collar on the table, looking at it oddly for a moment, like it's something alien and unpleasant. I pick it up to hand it to her and see that a zip tie – to be fair, it's an unfastenable one – has been glued to the inside of the collar. Many words go unspoken.

'Catch you later, yeah?' I say as she snatches the collar and stuffs it in her pocket.

'Yeah, later,' she says absently, and I hear a 'God bless' thrown across the garden in my direction as she hurries away.

Hmm.

I close my eyes and take a long breath in through my nose and let it out through my mouth, like Kerensa once taught me to do. My mind is a blank page with nothing but question marks written all over it. When I focus I realise that I've been staring at the brugmansia and remember my conversation with Joe. There is a bookshelf at the far end of the glasshouse that requires my immediate attention. I run an eye along a line of mainly gardening books until I spot the one I'm looking for: *An Encyclopaedia of Shamanism* by Christina Pratt. A quick flick down the index leads me to the brugmansia page and I see that someone has written:

Need to break the soul-tie!

in the margin. After speed reading the etymology and toxicology of the plant, I read:

'Brugmansia *induces a powerful trance with violent and unpleasant effects, sickening after-effects, and at times temporary insanity… disconnection from reality (psychosis) and amnesia of episode, such as one example reported in* Psychiatry and Clinical Neuroscience, *of a young man who amputated his own penis and tongue after drinking only one cup of brugmansia tea…*'

Another note in the margin reads:

This will be perfect!

Ah.

I close the book and tap my fingers on the cover before absently opening the cover again where a handwritten dedication on the opening leaf reads:

To Ms Nightshade, the most talented and fascinating student I ever met. From, Shaman Paulo.

My phone pings.
Unknown number.

Cosying up to the police now? Keep your nose out, Nightshade. Or else!

Chapter Eighteen

Lamorna is sitting with her arms wrapped tightly around her legs on a seat high up in the gods at the top of the Minack theatre. She's in her dungarees as usual but is wearing a chunky sky-blue Argyle jumper over the top of them, to guard against the strengthening westerly wind no doubt. Joe notices her the moment he steps on the top terrace, not because he's familiar with the back of Lamorna's head, but because of the bird of paradise sitting on her shoulder. After a quick wave to the constable guarding the stage, Joe stands at the end of a line of grass-covered stone seats and coughs.

'Oh, hello, inspector.' Lamorna glances up. 'I've been waiting for you. The constable down there said you'd be back before too long, so I thought it best to wait.'

Joe edges his way down the narrow aisle and is about to take a seat next to her when Lamorna cries out, 'Wait!' His arse shoots upwards like he's just sat on hot coals. 'The grass is damp,' she says, 'and that's a nice suit.' She grabs her raincoat and lays it out for him to sit on. 'There you go; that should keep you nice and presentable.'

'Thanks,' says Joe, sitting down. 'Now then, how can I help? Although, you should know that I'm not an inspector. The real inspector was here last night.'

'Gone back to Truro, has she?' asks Lamorna.

'Gone back to Truro. Would you rather speak to her?'

Ruby fluffs her feathers and sticks her beak in Joe's ear.

'Ruby!' chides Lamorna. 'Be good or go home!' Ruby walks around Lamorna's back and sits on the other shoulder, looking away. 'No, it's you that I want to speak to,' she says. 'I thought it probably best to speak to you straight away because I suppose you'll have worked it all out by now?'

Joe shakes his head. 'Not yet, no. A few ideas have come to mind, but nothing concrete. What about you? Any ideas?'

Lamorna, who is looking out to sea and seems like an otherworldly character from Tolkien – possibly Elvish – says, 'Perhaps,' and after a good minute of them both sitting there staring at the troubled ocean, she adds, 'You haven't brought the cuffs, then?'

Joe laughs. What is it about the Nightshades and handcuffs?

'They're in the car,' he says. 'No, I've just come for another look around and to check on my constable down there.' He nods towards the stage.

'In that case,' she says while standing up (and after a dramatic slap of the legs), 'I'd better save you all lots of bother – wasting police time and all that – and just confess.'

She holds out her wrists. 'Slap 'em on, inspector. I'm the chap you're looking for!'

Joe does not like the sound of this.

'Confess to what?' he asks, trying to maintain an air of light conversation, as if it would be simply impossible for Lamorna Nightshade – ethereal, beautiful, childlike Lamorna Nightshade – to ever confess to—

'Murder, of course,' she says, looking at him as if he's not quite the full shilling. 'What else?'

Chapter Nineteen

DONNA

With the flower orders completed for the day (they're not my best to be honest; some of the colours clash and the filler is a bit shabby) I fly around town for an hour delivering to my customers as discretely as possible. Neither ambition is realised because absolutely everyone in Penzance knows that Jack Crowlas is dead and absolutely everyone thinks I did it. The pats on the back and offers of free drinks have been endless. I return to my swing seat in the walled garden with my investigator's notebook and best pen in hand, but where to start? I make a mind map of everything Joe said (well, not everything; the man went on a bit) but cover the pertinent points, and draw a circle around an offshoot that reads, *'Tip-off note to Joe?'*. A line leads to another bubble that reads, *'Tone is familiar'* and from that another line leads directly to, *'Uncle Jago?'* Did Jago send the tip-off note to Joe stating that Jack would have drugs on him last night? If so, how did he know? I smile to myself. It's obvious really. Jago may love music and pigs, but his first love is the pub. The Admiral Benbow, The Turks Head, The Star, The Yacht – they're all his haunts, and he could easily have got wind of something that was going down last night. He *was* skulking in a corner of The Star with a pint of Spingo in hand on the night I met Jack, come to think of it…

I draw another line on my mind map that reads, '*Jack's dog suit? Who ordered it?*'. I grab my phone and search the internet to find the telephone number of the dog-suit company, Fancy Pants, which is just up the road in Redruth. A young male voice answers.

'Fancy Pants.' His voice does not convey enthusiasm for his job. I'm going to need to lie.

'Hi, yes. I want to order a dog suit from you, but—'

He interrupts me with: 'Jack Russell, Dalmatian, or Mongrel of Indeterminate Breeding?'

'What?'

'That's all we've got left. There's been a rush on Pugs.'

'That's fine, it's the mongrel I'm after, but I just want to check in case one of my employees has ordered one already. Can you check for me please?'

'Postcode?'

Tricky. What I want him to check is if a suit was sent to the Penzance region lately and I only know one postcode by heart – my own.

After a little tapping, he comes back with, 'Someone ordered a Mongrel of Indeterminate Breeding (short man size) online, to be delivered to that address by same day express delivery. There's a note with the order saying to leave the parcel in the recycling box in the first stable on the left with the blue door. It was delivered yesterday afternoon. Says here it was hand-delivered and signed for.'

'By whom?' I ask.

'Some fella called Nightshade. Is he one of yours?'

He certainly is.

Oh, Jago.

———

Uncle Jago is standing by the fire in his study when I go in. Jago always has a fire on the go, even in midsummer, which costs me a fortune in kiln-dried logs, but he says he needs a fire on account of the study's small north-facing window, thick walls, and (as he claims) 'the thin blood of the Nightshade male line'. It will be my first proper interview in my new role as a private investigator. It's exciting, really. I'll start by asking him about the other note, the one saying the pig was missing.

'And what did the note say, exactly?' I ask, taking a seat in a high-backed leather armchair in front of the fire. Jago takes a seat opposite me. His identical chair is more comfortable than mine, having had more use.

'Note?' he says.

'Yes, Uncle, the note. The one you said you received last evening telling you one of the piglets was missing.'

Jago bristles at this. 'I didn't *say* I received it; I *did* receive it. It was from you – at least, that's what I thought at the time.'

A bit defensive for Jago. I let it go.

'And where is it now?'

'What?'

Jesus.

'The note.'

'I don't have it.'

'You didn't keep it?'

'No.'

God give me strength.

'It was evidence, Uncle. You should have kept it.'

'Ah, but remember, I didn't know that it was evidence at the time. I thought it was nothing more than a quick missive from you... so I disposed of it.'

'Disposed of it?'

He looks at the fire. 'Is that a problem?'

I sigh, but thinking about it, if the note was written by one of our own – if one of the players did indeed kill Jack – then it's probably best that the note is gone. Uncle may have helped, dear man. Still, there's something about Jago that seems shifty today, and the whole situation with the dog suit doesn't add up. He may be a sweet chap who wants to do nothing more than spend his days listening to Radio 3, reading literature, playing the violin, and tending to his pigs, but the man knows something important about last night, or else why order another dog suit? I stand and open the window – it's like the Gobi Desert in here – and remember something I read during my 'how to become a detective' research. It was all about how an interviewer should allow the interviewee to ramble on because they will eventually give something away through the desire to fill the ensuing awkward gaps in conversation. I don't think Uncle Jago will fall into that category of interviewee. He's picked up his pipe already and a copy of the *New Scientist* and is at his absolute happiest when sitting in front of the fire with a loved one close by while maintaining absolute silence. He wouldn't care a stuff if we didn't talk all day.

'What puzzles me,' I say, 'is how the person in the dog suit—'

'Jack,' he states, not looking up from his magazine.

'Not necessarily, not at the beginning. The police say that we should not necessarily assume that.'

He looks up. 'Rubbish! Of course it was Jack.'

'Right. But what I was saying was, how did the person – whoever it was – get their hands on a dog suit that you had here, in your study?'

He turns back to the *New Scientist*. 'I have no idea.'

'Did you notice it had gone?'

'No.'

Time to go in for the kill.

'So why did you order another dog suit to be delivered to this address on the day of the play?' I go back to my chair, sit, and wait for an answer. One comes, eventually, served with a side order of sheepish expression.

'Ah, well, you see... I didn't want to tell you – I know how worried you get about money – but I... well, I'm ashamed to say that I lost the last one. That's right. I remember now. I noticed it was gone and didn't want to give you extra work to do so I ordered another one.'

'You lost it? Where?'

He smiles. 'If I knew that, it wouldn't be lost.'

'Uncle.'

'I took it to the pub.'

'What for?'

'To give the chaps a laugh.'

'Why order the replacement in short man size? You're over six feet tall.'

'I wasn't aware that I had.'

'But regarding the new suit. Jack must have been wearing it. When did you notice that it had gone missing?'

Jago shrugs, all innocence. 'It was still here when I checked at around six. The blighter must have been watching my movements, broken in, and taken it once I had run off to find the pig!'

'Broken in? Any sign of forced entry?'

'I left the door unlocked.'

This, I decide, is impossible.

Chapter Twenty

The last thing Joe Enys wants to do is arrest another Nightshade, especially Donna's younger sister, which is why he doesn't bundle Lamorna into the car and blue light her straight off to the station. Working on nothing more than a gut feeling that the girl with the Titian hair is probably protecting someone (her sister, she's protecting her sister) he suggests that they adjourn to the empty theatre café and informs Donna's mate Louise (who is haranguing Joe to confirm a date when the police will bugger off and allow the theatre to reopen) that they are not to be disturbed.

'And can we have two coffees, please?' he shouts after her. 'And perhaps a biscuit or two?' Louise pauses with her back to him for a moment, before walking away. Joe whispers to Lamorna not to spout forth with her confession until after the coffees have arrived, and all possible prying ears have retreated behind a closed door, which is why they spend a rather surreal ten minutes talking about birds of paradise, including details about the moulting habits of macaws. Ruby, Lamorna explains, is moulting now and it's making her moody as all hell. She also explains how macaw feathers are as individual as human fingerprints.

'That's so interesting,' he says as the coffees arrive. 'Sugar?' He opens a second sachet for himself (it's a sugary kind of a day).

Lamorna smiles. 'Two, thank you.'

'She's pretty fond of you,' says Joe, nodding towards Ruby who's having a bit of a bounce around the café.

Lamorna looks at him straight and says with complete clarity, as if it's the most important thing in the world, 'She *never* leaves my side, inspector. Never. Except occasionally to sit with Kerensa, and sometimes she goes to Donna, but that depends on both their moods. They're *very* similar, you see.'

'Donna and Kerensa?' he asks.

'Donna and Ruby. They're both Virgos.' Lamorna eyes him knowingly before taking a sip of coffee and adding, 'Anyhow, I'll cut to the chase: I killed Jack, well, partly… probably… possibly.'

Joe sips on his coffee. It's too hot. He puts the mug down.

Lamorna's brow furrows. 'You haven't taken out your notebook. Aren't you going to write any of this down?'

'Not for now. You haven't told me how you did it yet. Why don't you start at the beginning and tell me exactly what happened?'

Lamorna takes a deep breath. 'Well, for a start I know that they found a drug in him, correct?'

Damn.

'Correct. How do you know?'

'Because it was me that administered it.'

'And what kind of poison was it?' he asks, dreading the answer.

'Brugmansia.'

Shit.

'And how did you do it?'

'I put it in a pasty.'

'Cornish?'

'Of course.'

'When?'

'The day before the play. I went to see him in the afternoon.'

'Where?'

'At his place in Newlyn, but he wasn't in. I knew he wasn't in; that's why I went.'

Joe considers taking out his notebook. This is not good. 'Go on.'

'I left the pasty in the house with a note – we have a spare key as it's actually our house, you see.'

Another damn note.

'A note?'

'Yes, instructing him to meet me at Logan Rock later that evening.' She nods through the wall-to-wall café windows towards a rocky headland about a quarter of a mile away further along the coast. 'I said in the note that I'd got something he wanted – something he'd always wanted – and he could have it if he left Donna alone.'

'And what was that?'

'The Nightshade ruby. It's worth a mint.'

Joe's never heard of such a thing. 'You've got to be kidding.'

Lamorna looked at him as if she had no idea what the word *kidding* meant.

'I'm perfectly serious. It was stolen from the *Savage Princess* – that was a ship, not a real princess – by the fourth Donna Nightshade. Aunty Donna could tell you the exact details if you needed to know. Perhaps you could pop to see her in prison. My sister wouldn't know anything about it, really, because she's too busy dashing about scratching a few pennies together to get into the detail of legends as laid out in the old Nightshade diaries.'

'Right. And how did Jack know about it? The ruby.'

'Because he was married to Aunty Donna.'

'And it's valuable, you say?'

'It *would* be priceless... if only we could find the thing. Aunty Donna's mum (dead now) hid it somewhere and then she forgot where – dementia. Anyhow, the ruby was all that Jack ever really wanted, which is why I made out that I'd found it and he could have it.'

'And why would he think you'd do that?'

'Because I wanted him to leave Donna alone. He came to see us, you see. He walked straight into the glasshouse the day before the play and said he'd got a few jobs for Donna to be getting on with – dodgy, criminal jobs, you know, and if she didn't carry out his bidding, well... "woof, woof", which is a reference I know you'll understand.'

'And how did Donna react to this?'

'She was quiet, mainly – stoic, obviously – but I think...

well, I think deep down she was petrified.' Lamorna narrows her eyes, knowingly. 'Most people don't tend to think my sister can fear anything, but I know that she feared Jack. He wasn't a nice man, you see, Insp— What do I call you, if not inspector?'

'Joe is fine.'

'Joe,' she repeats softly, as if it's the nicest name in the world. 'Anyhow, he met her in The Star that night and I was worried.'

'Worried?'

'Worried she might get back in with him, to protect us. I made my mind up to kill him later that evening. It really was the only way out of it and it's what Nightshades tend to do when they find themselves in a spot of bother or backed into a corner, you know?'

Lamorna pauses to allow Joe to speak, but he doesn't. He simply folds his hands around his coffee and waits.

'Aaand then, I realised that he might not take the letter – the one telling him to meet me at Logan Rock – seriously, and that he might not eat the pasty either. It was a flawed plan, in retrospect; there were too many variables that might go wrong. Donna would be ever so cross if she knew.'

'Knew that you'd been to his house?'

'No, that I'd come up with a flawed plan.'

'I see.'

'I went to The Star a couple of hours after I'd dropped off the pasty…'

'To talk to Jack?'

'Yes – he was *bound* to be there because he was meeting

Donna later, unless, of course, he'd eaten the pasty already – but he *was* there and Uncle Jago was already talking to him, so I waited for Uncle to depart.'

'How long were they talking?'

'Quite a while. Half an hour?'

'Did Jago see you?'

'No, I hid in the back. Uncle left eventually, and I went straight to Jack, who laughed in my face about the pasty and the letter. I asked him if he was coming to meet me at Logan Rock and, well, the long and short of it is that he said he'd only come if I gave him something else, too – I don't think he believed me about the ruby.'

'And what was that?'

'Me.'

'You? What do you mean, you?'

'I believe he wanted to have sexual intercourse with me.'

Joe shakes his head.

'So I said yes, anything to save my sister, and he confirmed that he would leave her alone if I let him have his way (*and* give him the ruby) and we shook on it and he got up to go to the loo, which was when I slipped more brugmansia into his pint – I'd made rather a big batch and had some left over.'

'Clever. And did he come to the rock?'

'Yes, a couple of hours or so later. I was already in position on top of the rock when he started clambering up, and it was obvious the brugmansia had taken effect – he'd possibly eaten the pasty, too, by then, so he'd had a double dose. I wasn't nervous because I'd taken Kerensa's stop sign with me as a weapon, so I knew I was safe.'

'Stop sign?'

'She's a lollipop lady at Mousehole School.'

'Right.'

Lamorna stands to act out the scenario. 'And when he'd almost reached me on top of the rock, I grabbed the stop sign and I whacked him with it! He fell quite a good way into the sea – it was quite a splash. The sign is dented in the shape of his head, if you want to check it... It'll probably have his DNA on it too, a hair follicle or something...'

Joe can't help but smile.

'And how did he end up in a dog suit on the stage at the Minack a day later?'

Lamorna shakes her head. 'I have absolutely no idea. He should have been dead already after that fall... and the poisoning, of course.'

Thank. God.

'So why do you think it was you who killed him?'

'Isn't it obvious? It was me who drugged him, and even if he survived the fall—'

'Which he did. Jack Crowlas died during the performance.'

'Even so, can't you see? What must have happened is that the brugmansia must have had some kind of delayed swelling process in him – I knew he'd swell up, you see, what with the EpiPen I saw sticking out of his jeans pocket when he came to Penberth – which is why the dog collar got too tight and subsequently why he died. No, it wasn't quite in the neat way I'd hoped, with the body swallowed up by the sea, but... them's the breaks.' She holds out her wrists. 'Cuff me up, Joe, I reckon I'll get ten years for attempted murder, but I'm not too bothered as I'll be out in four. If my sister and my aunty can do time, so can I.'

Joe rubs his forehead. 'There will be no cuffs today, Lamorna.'

'Really?' she asks. 'Why?'

'Jack Crowlas did die of poisoning and subsequent strangulation by the dog collar, but the poison that finished him off – well, almost finished him off – was not brugmansia.'

'And, you know that for sure?' She doesn't look relieved. She looks... nervous.

'One hundred per cent positive.'

She sits back in her chair, looking a little like the wind has been taken out of her sails. Joe lets her have a moment. She doesn't need one. She rallies.

'Well, I for one am glad he's dead. At least Donna is free now.'

And now it all makes sense. 'Is that why you did it? To free her?' he asks.

Her left shoulder shrugs. 'Of course. It frees her to love again.'

There's a silence. A moment of peace.

She tips her head to one side and smiles.

'You and Donna were once madly in love, weren't you?' she says. 'Like that film with Bing Crosby and Grace Kelly... *High Society*. Donna loves that film, especially the bit when they're on the boat, in love and happy, just like when the two of you used to go out on your boat.'

Joe narrows his eyes. 'Did Donna tell you that?'

Lamorna shakes her head. 'She didn't need to. It's all in her diary.'

'Ah, yes,' he says, 'the infamous Belladonna Nightshade diaries. I'm not so sure Donna would have said that we were *desperately* in love though…'

He's fishing, clearly.

'She did. Cross my heart. But for your part? Were you desperately in love?'

Why lie? 'For my part, yes, I loved her.'

'Desperately?'

'Desperately.'

Ruby lands on Lamorna's shoulder and nuzzles into her neck. A feather drops onto the table.

'I wish… I do so wish that you and Donna could make up,' says Lamorna.

Joe picks up the feather. 'I think you're forgetting something,' he says. 'I'm in her book.'

Ruby squawks and Lamorna shakes her head. 'No, you aren't.'

Interesting.

'How do you know?'

'Oh, Joe. For a police officer, you're not so bright. I've read *all* of them.'

'All of them? The diaries? How many has she written?'

'Not just my sister's diaries. I mean, I've read *all* the Belladonna Nightshade diaries. They're supposed to be written in pirate-speak, which makes them a little difficult to translate sometimes, but somebody had to read them. They go back for hundreds of years. Donna makes out that she's read them too, but I know she hasn't; she's too impatient to sit and read shelf after shelf of books, so I thought I'd better read them, just in case there was something important inside.'

'And was there?'

Lamorna winks. 'Oh, yes. Definitely.'

Joe looks at Lamorna with a new respect. Maybe she's not quite so… naïve.

'I remember the day you were born,' he says. 'Donna… she was inconsolable at the loss of her mother – your mother – but delighted to meet you at the same time.'

'And then you arrested her,' states Lamorna.

Will he ever be free of it?

'Not on that day, but yes, shortly afterwards I arrested her.'

'But you did it because you loved her,' she says, placing a soft, cold hand on his. 'To get her away from Uncle Jack, didn't you? You wanted to help her towards a new life, even though in doing so you knew you were losing the love of your life forever. I think it was utterly selfless of you. Only a man truly in love would do such a selfless thing.'

Joe glances down at the hand. 'I doubt your sister would agree.'

'She doesn't.'

That's that then.

It's time to wrap this up, thinks Joe.

'Whatever happened, he's gone now,' says Joe.

Lamorna smiles her brightest smile. She holds up a hand for a high five. 'He certainly has!'

Joe laughs and high fives her back.

'Better not tell the inspector I did that,' he says.

She shakes her head. 'Your secret is safe with me. Are you at least going to arrest me for attempted murder? I did *try* to kill him, and I did poison him and batter him off a precipice with a stop sign.'

For the very first time in his career, Joe realises with a flash of, if not horror then sad inevitability, that he has no intention of going by the book this time. Yes, he really should take Lamorna straight down to the station to at least make a statement, but really, how can he? The poor kid lost her mother at birth, was raised by wolves, (well, a hippie and an eccentric uncle while Donna was in prison, and then by Donna when she got out, so it amounts to the same thing) and has had to live with the fact that her other aunt is in the clink for attempted murder. No, he can't do it; he can't arrest this young woman, a young woman who is clearly very different, clearly very gifted, and clearly very special. (And Donna would never forgive him, either).

'I'm not going to arrest you, Lamorna.'

'But...'

'I've made no notes, there's no recording of our chat, so, if you don't tell anyone – including Donna – nor will I.'

'You're doing this for her, aren't you?' she says.

Joe is saved by the bell when his phone pings. It's a message from Demelza.

The climber reckons that the cliffs CAN'T be scaled without a rope anymore because a ledge came loose last year. Oh, and forensics have found a teeny tiny bit of bird's feather (red in colour) between Thomas and the track...

He turns away and texts back.

Thomas? Who's Thomas?

The reply comes a few seconds later.

The Tank Engine – the one found on Jack in the kennel. The train and the track were glued together.

Joe puts his phone away and swishes his jacket off the back of the chair. He's still holding the feather.

'Just promise me you won't go around plotting any more murders, eh?'

Lamorna laughs. It's a lovely, wild, free, joyful laugh. 'Scout's honour,' she says. 'I'll even shake on it.'

Joe walks to the door. He pauses and glances back as he slips his arms through the jacket sleeves. Lamorna and Ruby are watching him.

'Thanks for the feather!' he says, giving it a flourish. 'And just to confirm... you've never seen my name in Donna's book?' He turns the handle to the café's door. 'There's no red line through my name anywhere in there?'

Lamorna smiles and shakes her head. 'No one by the name of Joe Enys has ever been cursed in the Nightshade Book of Ye Deadly Wrecker's Curses. Jack was. He was cursed by Aunty Donna *and* by my sister *and* Aunt Kerensa. Uncle Jago even squeezed a curse in there, so Jack didn't stand a chance, really. And that new chap, Jase Clarkson, has been cursed. But not you. There *was* a Joseph Pitt-Enys back in 1782... an ancestor of yours, I believe, but that's not you, unless you're a time traveller, which would be cool and if you are you *must* tell me because I'd be happy to be your sidekick, no question!'

Joe smiles. He is so happy right now. Jase Clarkson is in Donna's book!

'I'm not a time traveller, I'm afraid,' he says. 'Sorry.'

'Pity. But if you were, would I be the perfect person to travel with you?'

'You'd be the first person I'd ask,' he says, and somehow means it. 'Goodbye, Lamorna. And goodbye, Ruby,' he adds as Lamorna waves goodbye. Despite everything he's just heard, as Joe walks out of the door he's not entirely sure that he's any further forward than when he walked in.

Chapter Twenty-One

DONNA

It's 2pm and I'm back in the glasshouse at Penberth, which is becoming less of a flower farm and more of a detective agency HQ. Be careful what you wish for, isn't that what they say? Jack Crowlas has been dead less than twenty-four hours and I'm up to my eyeballs in suspects – the most obvious one being myself.

I tap my fingers on the table and wonder if this detective malarkey might not be so simple after all. The worst thing about this whole business – because to be clear, I'm thrilled to bits that Jack is dead – is that I'm beginning to wonder if I know my friends and family at all. Uncle Jago has lied to me, and Lamorna and Kerensa aren't home yet, which is strange, especially as Kerensa hasn't popped in to collect her lollipop lady garb and school is out in less than an hour. None of my family owns a mobile phone (they see phones as nothing but a tether) and if Kerensa isn't back by 3pm I'm going to have to don a lollipop lady jacket sharpish and hotfoot it to the local school. I'm also going to have to declare both of them AWOL and mark them down in my Special Detective Notepad as 'suspects'. (The margin note in the shaman book is a little disquieting as, come on, it *must* have been Kerensa who wrote it, and if I'm honest with myself, even Lamorna has a 'look' sometimes that might be construed as a little... edgy, unpredictable, marginally unhinged?)

As for the others – my players – any one of them could have got their hands on *Atropa Belladonna*, which grows like wildfire at Penberth, and a vial of lethal poison could easily have been put together via means of instructions on the internet.

The door goes. It's Pete, and he's brought coffee.

I close the laptop lid.

'Wasson.'

'Wasson.'

He sits on Joe's stool and passes the coffee across the table.

'Thought you might need one of these today,' he says. 'It's a double shot.'

When he sits back down on the stool, I swear the brugmansia reaches out a stem and brushes his shoulder – that plant does have a way of wanting to leave its mark on people. I look into the cup to see a flat white with a heart motif on top.

'How come it's so hot?' I ask.

'I'm just up the road today,' he says. 'I parked the van outside the Minack to cash in on the action. Thought there'd be lots of people heading up that way today for a goof, you know.'

'And are there?'

'Tons. No one's allowed in though. The police are still crawling all over the place.'

I think of Joe. Sitting there. On the same stool. Just a few hours ago. Looking gorgeous.

'That journalist fella is up there too,' says Pete.

I inform my hackles to calm down. 'Jase Clarkson?'

'Yep.'

Pete unfastens his tatty army-style jacket (it's one he's had for years and if I ever saw him wear anything else I'm not sure I'd cope). 'He bought coffee for all the coppers and even dug deep for an almond croissant for them all. Not complaining, though. He cleared me out.'

'Did you see the article?' I ask. 'The one about me?'

Pete nods. 'I'd watch your step with him, if I were you.'

'Why, what do you know?'

'Just rumours, people chatting by the wagon, that kind of thing. Let's just say he's the sort of man to have quite a few fingers in quite a few pies, and not all of them legit. He might see you as a threat.'

I laugh. 'Me? Why?'

'Because you're the queen of Cornwall, obviously.'

Nah. Surely not. (Nice idea, though.)

'Me? Don't be daft.'

'No, seriously, you are, for this part of Cornwall at any rate. And if someone new rocks up and wants to be king...'

'They'd need to topple the queen, first...' I say.

'You'll be on your guard then, yeah?' he says.

I blow out a sigh. 'As the prime suspect for Jack's murder, I'm already doing that.'

'We're all suspects, Donna. But here's a titbit for you.' Pete leans forward. 'Jase Clarkson was there last night, in the audience, and he came to the dressing room about halfway through the second half.'

Did he, now?

'How did he get past the Minack staff?'

'He used his press pass. Told them you'd agreed he could have a quick chat with us for a piece he was doing for the *Packet*.'

'I never agreed to that. What an arsehole. What happened?'

Pete laughs. 'Gabby told him to get lost. She can be quite feisty when her dander's up.'

'She's spent too much time with the rougher side of society,' I say. 'It's rubbed off a bit. Did you see him leave?'

Pete shakes his head. 'I went on the stage to do my next bit and I left him in there.'

'Who with?'

'Gabby and Cat.'

'Did you tell the police?'

'No way.'

Well, that's one more suspect to add to the list. A thought crosses my mind...

'Pete... at the rehearsal the other day, Cat wanted to see you about something. Was anything wrong? Only, she seemed a bit...'

He closes his eyes and shakes his head. 'It was nothing. Cat can be a pain in the arse. Forget it. Come on then. How was it done do you think? You must have come up with something by now.'

'I have indeed. The how, at least, if not the by whom or the why. First, he was poisoned—'

'Poisoned?' repeats Pete, who's gone a lighter shade of pale. 'What kind of poison? Did they say?'

Hmm. *How much shall I tell him?* I wonder. *Everything. He's a mate.*

'Brugmansia, which I have here, obviously, and also deadly nightshade.'

If Pete was pale before, he's translucent now. 'Deadly… what did you say?'

'Deadly nightshade – you know, the plant. Then he was strangled by the dog collar and stabbed for good measure. It's so elaborate. Why not just kill him quickly with the knife?'

'I'll tell you why,' he says, and I sense his leg start to shake under the table. Pete does this when he's nervous. 'It's because out of all of us, except for Jase Clarkson, I'm the only one who had access to the stage who would be strong enough to get away with attacking him with a knife if he wasn't already drugged…'

'And did you?' The words are out before I can haul them back in.

We hear the door go.

Pete looks at me and it's a look of absolute disappointment. I feel ashamed.

Kerensa slides in and cuts through the moment.

'You're back!' I say, my voice overly enthusiastic. 'Thank goodness. I was getting worried.'

She grabs her lollipop lady coat and slips it on over Kate Hudson yoga gear. That's new – and expensive.

'Oh, hello, Pete,' she says. 'Lovely to see you.' She flicks her long mane out of the coat and over her shoulder. 'You were worried about me? But why? I only went to the prison to give Aunty Donna the good news. I'm sure I told you.'

She did. But paranoia is my new best friend.

'You did. Sorry. It's been an odd day.'

She kisses me on the head. 'I'll cleanse your chakras later – that'll make you feel better. Have you seen the nail scissors, by the way?'

I'm just about to say, *Do tell me about the margin notes in this book...* when she grabs a pair of nail scissors from the drawer and floats out of the door. Which is when Lamorna and Ruby float in.

Buses.

I try to learn from my previous error of paranoia-fed worry and say not a word, although, *And where the hell have you been all day?* is hovering on the end of my tongue.

'Good day?' I ask.

I'm given a bear hug in answer and a kiss on the cheek before Lamorna skips off to collect her ukulele from the far end of the glasshouse.

'I'd better be off,' says Pete, standing. He looks gutted. I'm such an idiot. 'But you'll remember what I said about Jase Clarkson,' he says. 'Yeah?'

'Of course.'

'And about Cat...' he says. 'Do you think she'll be staying on, after?'

'As one of the players, you mean?'

He shrugs.

'Why?' I ask.

157

'No reason, except... I might call it a day myself this year. I'm not much of an actor.'

Hmm.

He turns to walk away.

I shout after him. 'Pete! You're coming to my birthday party next week, yeah?'

He shrugs. 'Should think so,' he says, and turns to walk away again. The man can't get out quickly enough.

'Oh, and Pete...' He stops again and sighs. 'Lots of people come here for a coffee,' I say, 'which I love, but it does end up feeling like I run a café sometimes. You're the only person to ever bring one to me, and I don't deserve it.'

His head drops. 'Don't apologise,' he says. 'Just... don't.' And then he dashes away, leaving the door open behind him.

Lamorna takes his seat – Joe's seat – and nods to Pete's jacket, which he's left on the table. I grab it and dart out, but as I head out of the walled garden and towards the driveway, I see Uncle Jago rushing towards Pete from the house, and something in Jago's anxious expression tells me to stop and watch. They talk in hushed, urgent voices. Pete runs a hand through his hair and says, 'I knew I should never have got involved! I'll go down for this, Jago! It's only a matter of time before they trace it all back to me!' Jago grabs Pete's arm, not a little aggressively, and says, 'Just hold your nerve, lad.' Pete shrugs him off. Jago puts his face in his hands and Pete walks away down the drive.

Interesting.

I look down at Pete's coat in my hands. A quick rifle through the pockets wouldn't harm anyone, would it?

I go to my swing seat and start the search. Army jackets have a lot of pockets.

Here's what I've found: the article about me in the newspaper, folded into four (I don't want to think about why that's there right now), half a packet of chewing gum, a betting slip (slippery slope, Pete), a receipt from Lidl for cider... oh, and a Wikipedia page about *Atropa Belladonna*.

Jesus Christ.

I make sure to put everything back in the pocket it came out of and wander back into the glasshouse. Lamorna is channelling Joni Mitchell – 'Both Sides Now'.

So... there are two essential things in life that go hand in hand with Joni Mitchell – booze and cigarettes – and there has been a packet of untouched Marlborough Lights and a lighter in the back of the odds and ends drawer for over a year. I put Pete's coat on the bench exactly as he left it and decide that perhaps today is the one day I could forgive myself for having a bit of a smoke. There's also a rather fine bottle of Merlot hidden away in Kerensa's secret stash of booze at the back of the raffia, ribbons, and bows cupboard. I get the wine first and pour a glass, then go for the Marlboroughs. The drawer isn't one we often use, and it's stuck. I open the cupboard that sits underneath the drawer and feel upwards blindly to see if I can release the drawer from underneath. There's something fixed to the underside of the drawer. I grab a torch and my pruning knife – not the one used to stab Jack in the neck, the police have kept that – get on my back, and edge into the cupboard, looking up. What I find does not lighten my mood. The torch illuminates a plastic bag of industrial zip ties which have been taped to the underside of the drawer. I cut away the tape and put the zip ties on the table next to the wine glass. Lamorna glances up from the guitar, frowns, then returns to the music. I light a cigarette, rest my right elbow on the table, rest my temple on the heel of my hand, and allow the smoke to drift around the room, while wondering if the zip ties were planted to stitch me up.

This is getting out of control – *I'm* getting out of control. I need help, and there's only one person I can turn to now. Only one person I can trust. And that's really bloody annoying.

I fire out a text.

I'm out of my depth and think I'm being set up. Will you help me?

Less than a minute goes by before my phone pings.

Meet me at Jack's house in Newlyn at 7.30pm tonight

I analyse the text. Joe hasn't said that he'll help, but then he hasn't said that he won't. I've got nothing to lose and reply:

See you there. PS Jase Clarkson was backstage during the second half of the play.

I feel Lamorna's eyes on me. I don't look up. She ups the tempo and changes the words of the song slightly.

'*Tears and fears and feeling proud, just say I love you, right out loud.*'

I stub out the cigarette and pour the wine back into the bottle.

'I can't do that, Lamorna,' I say, just as Pete rushes in and grabs his coat off the bench. 'I just can't do that.'

Chapter Twenty-Two

DONNA

Once Kerensa's lollipop lady duties are done for the day I gather my family together in the Manor's kitchen. It's a fabulous, almost baronial room, full of free-standing oak units, hanging copper pans, fresh herbs, spices, and recipe books. Meat hooks are secured into beams where old retainers would have hung game to cure, and where, according to her diary and therefore according to Lamorna, Great-Great-Great-Granny Nightshade strung up a rival pirate and watched on as the last putrid breath spilled out of his windpipe. I'd write it off as fiction, but if you look hard enough there's still the blood stain on the slate floor beneath the beam: we don't hang a pan on that meat hook.

So yes, the kitchen is untouched by time, except for the four oven Aga and the east-facing French doors that Aunty Donna put in, which was a great decision. They fill the room with much-needed light and warmth, particularly in the morning, when we sit and have breakfast and chew over the jobs for the day. Other than the walled garden, the kitchen is my favourite space here, but it's pretty much Uncle Jago's domain as he's the chef of the family. And here he is now, serving up a late afternoon tea of griddled Irish scones, cheese, and homemade chutney. I glance around – Lamorna, Kerensa, Ruby, and Jago are all gathered around the table, happily chatting away and tucking into high tea. You'd think Uncle Jack had never returned, let alone been slotted last night, and all credit to us, we're quite a practical family and there's no point faking grief. We hated him. He's gone. We're delighted. Nevertheless, I put down my scone. It's best to get straight to the point.

'The thing is, we need to quickly explain to each other exactly – and truthfully – what we each of us were doing yesterday during the play so that we know we're in the clear, and if anyone asks—'

'Anyone? Like, the police, you mean.' This, from Jago.

'Well, yes, the police… but as I was saying, if anyone asks, we know that we'll be giving a unified response. If you're guilty, just tell me. I'll understand and we'll deal with it.'

No one responds. Everyone looks down at the table (stripped pine). Jago is the first to break the silence by standing and heading to the Aga to take the whistling kettle off the heat. His tone surprises me when he speaks. He's not himself today. His hand starts to shake as he pours the water into the teapot.

'Donna Nightshade,' he begins. 'If you want to know if

one of us killed Jack Crowlas then I wish you'd just jolly well come out with it and ask us.'

Wasn't that what I just did?

'All right, I'll say it plainly. Did anyone around this table murder Jack Crowlas?'

Two pairs of eyes head to the table again. Murmured denials escape from Lamorna and Kerensa.

Jago is indignant as he pours the tea. 'All I shall say is this'—he says, and I know full well that it certainly will not be *all* that he says—'...whoever did it deserves a medal.'

Well, this is more awkward than I'd imagined. I'm going to have to be frank.

'Look, I've been talking to Joe Enys...' I begin.

Knowing glances are handed around and picked up like dealt cards.

'I thought he was in your book?' says Kerensa.

I *knew* that would come up.

'He isn't,' says Lamorna.

'And the harsh fact is that the person most likely to have the means of accessing the stage and killing him was one of us...'

'Persons,' corrects Lamorna.

'What?'

'You're assuming that just one person is involved. There might have been several.'

She's got a point.

'All right, the fact is that the person – or *persons* – most likely to have done it was one – or more – of us, and by "us" I mean the family and the players. Like it or not, we're all murder suspects. And Jase Clarkson, too.'

'The bounder?' asks Jago.

'The bounder,' I confirm.

'*I'm* not a suspect!' pipes up Kerensa. 'I wasn't even there. I was teaching my Zoom yoga class back here.'

'Can you prove it?' I ask, taking out my notebook.

'Of course I can. Just ask any of my clients.'

'And how long did the yoga classes last for?'

'From seven in the evening until midnight.'

'Midnight?'

'Australian clients,' she explains.

At least that's one ticked off. 'Great!' I say.

'So, how, er, was it actually done?' asks Kerensa. 'Was it wonderfully gruesome?'

I take a bite of my scone before answering. Jago's baking gets better and better. I really ought to put him up for *Bake Off* because he'd win, no question. And the subsequent book and TV deals would be lucrative...

I wipe my mouth with the back of my hand. Jago offers me a napkin with an associated tut.

'It's looking like he was drugged twice, then strangled by the dog collar, presumably by the swelling of his neck because of the reaction to the poison. I don't think he was dead before the knife – my knife, by the way – went in.'

Kerensa's face is pure confusion. 'But wait a minute, he was drugged twice, you say?'

'And by two different types of drugs?' dibs in Lamorna.

'Yes, as I said, drugged twice but not necessarily both times in the kennel. And both drugs were extracted from plants that can be found here at Penberth. *Brugmansia* and *Atropa Belladonna*.'

'Our calling cards,' says Uncle Jago.

'Exactly,' I say. 'It's so odd.'

'Not really,' says Lamorna who, having polished off her scone, pops some crumbs on the table for Ruby to eat and, dabbing her mouth, says, 'Not when you consider the fact that *I* administered the brugmansia.'

There is a moment during which speech is beyond me. Eventually, I turn to her.

'What? Why? Why would you do that?'

She shrugs. 'To frighten him? To kill him? Who can really tell what one's motives are in these situations? Murder is easy. Isn't that what Agatha Christie said? And if she didn't, it's exactly the sort of thing she would have said, so the quote stands.'

I look at the others. They are open-mouthed. I think she's joking, but to my horror I realise that she isn't.

Words need to form. I begin with: 'Why didn't you tell me this when I asked you about your actions five minutes ago?'

'Because you asked if any of us had killed him,' she answers, looking far too relaxed. 'If you had asked if I'd tried to poison him the day before he died, I would have said yes.' She nods towards Kerensa. 'It was all Aunt Kerensa's idea. Wasn't it, Aunt Kerensa?'

Kerensa, her mouth still gaping open, glances from me to Lamorna several times before she says, 'Well, yes.'

Lamorna goes on to explain how, after a bizarre ceremony on Logan Rock, Jack (having been drugged with brugmansia that was both hidden inside a pasty and administered to a pint at The Star) was lured there with offers of sex and jewels, attacked with the lollipop lady sign and sent off to a watery grave.

'I'm sorry to admit it,' she says, 'but the plan was flawed. He only fell a few feet before he hit the water. We forgot about the tide issue, you see. We just wanted to show him that he couldn't start messing about with the Nightshades... didn't we, Kerensa? *Suum cuique* you said, and all that.'

Kerensa nods her agreement reluctantly, looking awkward. As well she might.

Lamorna turns to me. 'And anyway, didn't you always say that if he ever came back, we'd kill him?'

I did say that, yes.

Jago pipes up, scratching his head: 'He must have thought it was someone else on the rock, though. Or surely, he would have come straight here to string us all up!'

Good point.

'Oh, but I would have been ready for him if he had, never you fear,' says Lamorna.

'Is that why you carried the cutlass all day,' I ask.

'That's why I carried a cutlass all day,' she confirms.

I. Can't. Speak.

'Anyhow, there's nothing to worry about now...' adds Lamorna.

'Oh, really? How so, little sister?'

She shrugs, her face pure innocence. 'Because I told that nice police chap, Joe Enys, all about it, and he said that I wasn't to worry.'

'WHAT?!' shouts Kerensa.

'Don't worry. I didn't tell Joe about you being there, too.' Lamorna laughs. 'There was no need for both of us to be sent down! I simply told him about my part in it.'

'Why on earth would you do that?' I ask.

'I suppose I just felt that it was best to come clean. I wouldn't have gone to prison for long… and Aunty Donna would have looked after me; stopped me from becoming some other woman's bitch or something.'

Jago gets a bottle of brandy from the baking cupboard and pours a measure into my tea. I need to gather my wits.

'And Joe knows all of this already?' I ask.

She nods the affirmation of a child who is confirming that they have been good. 'I gave him my full confession this morning.'

'This morning?'

'I waited for him at the Minack.'

I look at Kerensa. She's gone deathly pale, and her expression is utterly unfathomable. I turn to Lamorna. At least she's still got her wits about her – well, kind of.

'And?'

'He was very good about it, actually.'

I have entered a surreal dream. I'll wake up in a minute.

'He *did* say that it would probably be a good idea if I didn't go around drugging people as a matter of course, and then hitting them with lollipop stop signs, although it was Kerensa who did the actual hitting… oh, and she wore the cape.'

I put my head in my hands. It's all my fault. I've brought her up like a feral cat.

'You should have told me,' I murmur into my hands. 'I would never have let you go…'

Lamorna stands, walks round the table, and puts her arms around me.

'Donna, my wonderful sister, you are not responsible for my – or anyone else's – actions.' She nods towards Kerensa. 'We are all free spirits allowed to make our own choices and our own mistakes, aren't we, Aunty?'

Kerensa is still mute.

'But… why?' I ask. '*Why* did you do it?'

Again, Lamorna simply shrugs. 'To be perfectly honest, I just didn't like him.'

Twenty minutes later and I've gathered myself together enough to make sure that my family's alibis are watertight. Kerensa was giving yoga classes from the turret room here at Penberth on Zoom (I checked with legit clients in Australia). It's a very distinctive room so that's that sorted. Lamorna was in the music tent all night and her silhouette could be seen by the audience throughout the performance, and as for Jago, well, he was chasing down a piglet at Nanjizal Cove, although no one saw him there and the story of his expedition is becoming more and more embroidered every time he tells it. I simply don't believe him. He starts to clear the plates. I stand.

'Where are you going now?' asks Jago.

This could be tricky. Should I lie, or…?

'I've got some pricking out to do in the big polytunnel,' I say.

'The hardy annuals?' asks Kerensa. 'That's a big job. I'll help you.'

Hmm.

'And then I'm off to Newlyn... to meet Joe.'

'Enys?' say Jago and Kerensa at the same time, both looking... disappointed.

I head towards the door and throw a 'Yeeesss,' over my shoulder.

Kerensa sighs. 'You do know that Aunty Donna would not approve of you knocking about with that policeman,' she says. (Her free spirit Buddhist tiara is definitely slipping).

'That's all right,' I say, 'because Aunty Donna's not here, is she?' I turn to face them at the door. '*I'm* the queen of the castle now. And if you all keep your mouths shut about it, she'll never know!'

Kerensa looks at Jago. Jago looks at Kerensa. And Lamorna? Well, she just smiles her wonderful smile and says, 'We'll not wait up!' which should be the final word, except that the final word is usually reserved for Ruby and today is no exception. She takes flight, heads towards me like a peregrine falcon jumping off a cliff with eyes only for its prey, and with a handbrake-turn landing on my shoulder she says, 'Donna did it! Donna did it!'

Despite it clearly being a mad joke on Ruby's behalf (she's like that, is Ruby – a sick sense of humour), they all throw their best knowing glances in my direction.

'What? You can't really think...?'

Jago turns his back to me. 'We'd be lying if we didn't admit that it hadn't crossed our minds,' he murmurs.

'And that's all of you, is it?' I ask, glancing around.

They all shrug.

For Christ's sake, Ruby.

That's all I need!

Chapter Twenty-Three

It's early evening and Detective Sergeant Joe Enys, who doesn't realise he's smiling to himself, cuts a pace through the Cornish countryside as he heads towards Newlyn and his rendezvous with Donna Nightshade. The hours that have passed since leaving Lamorna at the Minack Theatre have not been without productivity. He caught a couple of pollock off Sennen, and Demelza has come up trumps with background information on Jack – namely, where he's been hiding these past few years. It seems he's been living in Lithuania, and for some of the time was banged up in prison. Poor Lithuania.

The story from Demelza goes along the lines of Jack getting himself a nice little racket going until ultimately – inevitably – Interpol got wind of it. He was chased across Europe by various police forces and yet it wasn't his smuggling (drugs and humans) that got him arrested in the end, but a simple case of dangerous driving. The details were unclear, but Joe suspected that the old copper's trick of, *if you can't get them for one thing then get them on another (tenuous) one* had perhaps come in to play. But for all that, the Lithuania link might prove fruitful. Joe had no idea why or how right now, but he had his best man (who happened to be a woman) all over it.

Jack's house is a mid-terrace fisherman's cottage halfway up Bowjey Hill, Newlyn. Joe stands outside the front door with a key in his hand and *shithole* is the first word that comes to mind. It's Jack's mother's old place and was used as a squat by all and sundry during the long years while Jack was absent (while the cat's away, etc.). It was let to his mother on a long-term rent-free basis by Donna's Aunty Deadly, and then Donna the Younger didn't have the heart to kick out the squatters. Jack, on his return, had kicked them out (literally, using his size nines) without a moment's hesitation. Two of Joe's team have already done a search of the house, looking for Jack's mobile phone primarily, which to everyone's surprise was not tucked down his underpants in the dog suit. One of his constables put police tape across the cottage and closed and locked the door this morning to stop any prying eyes – or feet – from entering. As for inviting Donna to the scene… well, what's a man to do?

Put the cuffs on, Joe, that's what a man has to do!

When he arrives, he sees that the tape has been broken, a light is on downstairs, and the front door is ajar. He steps one foot inside the cottage and his Fitbit watch beeps to tell Joe that his heart is going a bit too fast, which is strange considering that he's not exercising, and he feels no apprehension going into the house of a dead man.

'I'm through here!' shouts Donna. Joe pokes his head around the lounge door. Donna is rifling through a sideboard. At least she's wearing gloves – gardening, but it's better than nothing.

The cottage has two rooms downstairs: a lounge and a kitchen. Neither has had a clean-up since it was a squat, although maybe it was clean as a whistle as a squat, and this was how Jack lived in the brief time he was back. Joe crosses the room to join Donna. She doesn't look up.

'How long have you been here?' he asks, noting that most of the drawers are open and Donna has a pile of papers in her hand.

'About an hour.'

For Christ's sake.

'Donna! Jesus! I said—'

'What? I just wanted to get ahead of the game, that's all. And I took all the right precautions, so don't worry. Look, I'm even wearing gloves.' She shakes jazz hands in his direction. 'Your own guys have made a right pig's ear of the place already so no one will have any idea that I was here.'

'At least tell me the door was open and you didn't break in…'

Donna puts the pile of papers down on the sideboard and faces him somewhat defiantly, if a little flirtatiously.

Don't buckle to it Joe. Just don't buckle.

'Break in?' she repeats. 'Not at all, officer.' She reaches into a pocket. 'This house is a Penberth Estate cottage, and I still have the spare key.' She holds it up to show him. 'That old door hasn't been changed in eighty years.' She returns to her occupation of searching through the detritus of Jack's sideboard. 'Anyway, Uncle Jack was one of the family and this place belongs to us.'

He glances around. It really is a shithole, but in Newlyn, it will probably be worth a mint.

'What will you do with it?' he asks.

Donna shrugs. 'Tidy it up and rent it out to a local.'

Joe remembers what Bill Smiley said about Donna being strapped for cash. 'Or you could sell it for a packet. Newlyn is quite the des res these days.'

Donna stops rifling and gives Joe her hard stare. 'You mean flog it off as a second home to some rich tosser who'll rock up in his Range Rover once in a blue moon, not pay a penny in council tax then get bored of it and sell it on for a massive profit? Never!' She picks up the pile of papers from the sideboard. 'Let's go into the garden,' she says. 'I want to show you something. And, the smell in here is making me want to barf!'

'What do you think the numbers mean?' asks Donna, who's looking over Joe's shoulder as they sit together on a low stone wall in the back yard.

'No idea,' says Joe, who is flicking through a pile of handwritten notes Donna found in the sideboard. Each piece of paper (Basildon Bond good quality letter paper, deduces Donna, holding one up to the light to see the watermark) has nothing more than numbers on it.

'And there were no envelopes with them?'

Donna shakes her head. 'Nope. Maybe it's some kind of code, or coordinates for a drop or something?'

'Possibly,' agrees Joe, a little absently. He takes a plastic evidence bag out of his jacket pocket and bags up the notes. 'I'll get the team on it and have them checked for prints; see what that brings up.'

Donna rolls her eyes. 'Nothing. That's what checking them for prints will bring up. As if the sender would have been that daft!'

'You'd be surprised how stupid people can be,' says Joe. 'What were you looking for, anyway?'

'Looking for?'

'Yes, Donna. Looking for. And don't start playing games again. I thought we were working on this together?'

'All right, all right. I was looking for evidence of threats.'

'Threats?'

'I told you. Jack came to me and said someone had been sending him death threats and he wanted me to find out who it was. I thought I might find blackmail letters in here, or something like that.'

Joe smiles. He tries desperately not to patronise her, but...

'Donna, if Jack was being blackmailed it would have been done on the phone – by text from a pay as you go number, most likely.'

'Do you know that for sure?'

'No. His phone is missing. All we know was that he had the latest model of iPhone on a contract with EE.'

Donna sighs. 'Basically we're looking for someone who had access to the stage, who hated Jack, has a taste for brewing up poison and who is waltzing around Cornwall with a new iPhone in their pocket.'

'Pretty much. Although I doubt they'd keep the phone.'

'Why?'

'Too risky. It's probably sitting at the bottom of the ocean by now.'

There's a moment's silence, which is too difficult for Joe to bear, so he stands up and says, 'Come on, Sherlock, lots to do. Let's have another gander around the place.'

The gander proves fruitless. Turning over the house simply proves what they already know: Jack Crowlas was a gluttonous slob who liked to partake in a line of coke and was best mates with the local bookmaker. There's no laptop, no notebook, nothing at all other than empty pizza boxes, beer cans, and those peculiar pieces of paper with the numbers on. All his dodgy dealings were obviously kept in his head and on his phone.

The streetlights are on by the time they step outside. Donna locks the door while Joe fiddles with his tie, wondering how to end the rendezvous. Should he invite her to the pub? Nah, too public. Should he invite her back to his place? God, no; she'd laugh in his face. Should he—

'Fancy a walk along the prom towards town?' she says, putting the key in her pocket and looking up at him warmly. 'I could buy you some chips?'

They head down the hill towards Newlyn Harbour. 'Only, I wanted to say thanks...' She glances around. 'For Lamorna,' she whispers. 'For letting her off the hook, you know, what with her... well, her attempt to murder Jack...'

Joe coughs nervously. 'She told you about that, then,' he

says, while thinking, *shit, I should never have been so lax*. 'She wasn't supposed to tell you.'

'Don't worry,' says Donna, who has begun walking again. 'Your secret's safe with me. But I can't believe she did it. It honestly doesn't compute in my brain. And the whole thing has got me thinking... that perhaps I don't know the people around me as much as I thought I did.'

As they walk past the harbour a man is preparing a small yacht for departure. It's that damn Jase Clarkson, off to do some night fishing, no doubt. Donna hasn't seen Jase and is still talking. '...Which is a tricky thing to come to terms with, you know, not really knowing the reality behind the people you thought you knew – thought you knew like the back of your hand. But then, who really knows the back of their hand? You could show me ten pictures of the backs of hands and I bet I wouldn't know which one was mine.'

'Yes, exactly,' murmurs Joe, hurrying his steps and trying to walk in a way that hides Donna from line of sight with Jase.

They arrive at the chippy.

'Closed,' says Joe.

Donna turns to him. 'You know, Joe, I've got a sinking feeling that whoever it was that killed Jack, did it for me.'

'Donna...'

'No, hear me out. Just look at what Lamorna tried to do to him... simply to protect me.'

'I think you're barking up the wrong tree,' he says, instantly regretting the doggie metaphor. 'It's not a strong enough motive. They all love you dearly, but trust me, if one of your friends or family killed him, it wasn't for you. No one is that nice. It was for themselves.'

'Unless... someone was trying to kill Uncle Jago, and accidentally killed Jack instead?'

Joe shakes his head again. 'I thought of that. But when they went into the kennel, they would have seen that it was Jack, not Jago – he had the hood off. Whoever murdered Jack pulled the dog suit down and stabbed him up the nose with a needle. Pretty hard to get the wrong man.'

They stand and stare at the closed chip shop.

'No chips,' says Joe.

'No chips,' repeats Donna. She turns to face him. 'It's a matter of trust,' she says, her eyes misty.

'Trust no one,' he says as they begin to walk again.

'Not even you?' she asks.

'Since when did you trust me?'

Donna doesn't answer.

They retrace their steps and stroll towards the harbour in silence. He's never seen Donna looking this way. *What way?* he asks himself. *Vulnerable*, he replies. His phone pings. It's Demelza. She's sent him a photo and a text.

Got this from Scotland Yard. Taken in Lithuania a couple of years ago by Interpol. Recognise anyone?

Joe stops walking and zooms in to assess the photo. Gabby – Donna's vicar friend, the woman who denied any knowledge of how a stash of drugs found its way into her rucksack – is front and centre in the scene. She's wearing a thick coat and a bobble hat but it's definitely her. She's talking to Jack Crowlas – arguing with him by the looks of the hand gestures and they're standing outside what looks like a bar.

'Is it about Jack?' asks Donna, nodding towards his phone.

There is no way Joe can show her this photo – for so many reasons, not least because he's a police officer and she isn't.

'Yes, but only that he's been traced to a Lithuanian prison.'

They reach the harbour wall and the surprises just keep coming. The yacht is leaving. Jase Clarkson is at the tiller, which isn't surprising, but what *is* surprising is that Donna's friend and Minack player, Cat, is with him. She pops her head out of the cabin and cranes her neck to kiss him – passionately.

Joe turns towards Donna. It's too late. She's seen them. Her face gives nothing away.

'Did you know she was involved with him?' he asks.

Donna shakes her head. 'No, but I'm not her keeper.'

'How well do you know her?' asks Joe.

'I don't know her at all, I suppose,' admits Donna. 'Actually, Joe, I think it's probably time to go home.'

Joe nods, relieved. As much as spending time with Donna is a wonderful gift, he really – *really* – should not be doing this.

'Where are you parked?' he asks.

'On the prom.'

'I'll drive you.'

She shakes her head as the yacht, its sails down, its

engine on, navigation light shining out into the darkness, passes between the harbour walls and chugs its way towards the open sea.

'I'll walk,' she says brusquely, the old Donna returning. But then she smiles. 'There's nothing quite like a walk along the prom in the evening to clear the head. It'll help me sleep. I'm in a precarious position, Joe, and I've a feeling someone wants to keep it that way.'

Joe runs a hand through his hair. It's the only thing left to do.

'Listen, Donna. Personally, I don't give a damn about Jack. I'm glad he's dead. It's what he was involved in that I want to get to the bottom of.'

'What does it matter now?' she says, her voice betraying her tiredness and bordering on irritated. 'He's dead. You have some of the drugs. Anything he was involved in will die away with him, surely?'

Joe shakes his head. 'I doubt it. I have a feeling that Jack was just one cog in a big wheel. And what if that's what this is all about? Not setting you up or seeking revenge for past crimes, but a very real and very nasty present day crime racket involving extremely undesirable people. People we absolutely don't want hanging around Penzance.'

'I don't remember Jack ever working for anyone else,' says Donna. 'It wasn't his style. Did I tell you that he wanted me to run his next drop for him? Not the drop he wanted at Penberth, but another one?'

Of course she hadn't.

'Did he give you any details?'

'I was supposed to go with him to Porthleven tomorrow

afternoon and meet some geezer – Aeolus Jones, which must be a made-up name – who's coming in on a cruiser from France. Something like that, anyway.'

Joe simply cannot believe his ears. 'Why didn't you tell me before?'

Donna takes a deep breath. She stops walking and turns to face him. 'I did. I distinctly remember telling you about the one-handed man with an eye patch.'

'Donna!'

'All right... I didn't tell you the *whole* detail, because deep, deep down, I simply don't – didn't – trust you completely and I wanted to work as much out for myself as possible to save my own skin.'

Joe stares out to the blackness of the sea in a silent trance. Donna tugs at his sleeve.

'Hey, come on. Moody doesn't suit you,' she says. 'It never has. Say something, even if it's to tell me to sod off.'

'Just shush a moment,' he says. 'I'm thinking.'

Donna folds her arms and sighs.

'What if...' says Joe, turning to face her suddenly, his pulse almost at a level his Fitbit would record as decent exercise, 'what if... you still go?'

'Go?'

'To Porthleven.'

'Me? Why on earth would I do that? Everyone knows Jack's dead. And how would I know who this Aeolus is, even if he is there, which he won't be?'

'It'll be obvious,' says Joe.

'Will it? Why?'

Joe fixes a stare. 'How many one-handed men with an eye patch do you know in Porthleven?'

He doesn't wait for an answer, because Joe is becoming excited now. 'And I guarantee there will only be one cruiser that's not registered in Cornwall alongside in Porthleven tomorrow night. I've got loads of fishing mates and they know every boat and every skipper. They'll be able to tell me who this Aeolus is, no question. All you must do is get there early and wait. You would be wired up, obviously...'

'Wired up? No way!'

'And I'll be on the dockside watching. Come on, Donna, just pretend you want a piece of whatever they've got on offer and see what turns up.'

Donna lets out a low grumble, but Joe doesn't give in.

'My DCI wants me to pull you in if I don't have another lead in three days' time,' he says quietly.

'Tell me something I don't know.'

'Ok, I will. They found a trace of a red feather stuck between the train and the track. All forensics have to do is match the feather to one of Ruby's and you're even further in the dwang.'

Donna drops her head. A breeze cosies up to her from the incoming tide. It's Donna's turn to think. He waits in silence, something he learned to do many years ago, when they were sixteen and in love and...

'All right,' she says, 'I'll do it. But just so you know, I want to say now and for the record that it's a complete waste of time. Without Jack there, this French fella – if he is even French which I doubt with a name like Aeolus Jones –

will smell a rat for sure, especially when I explain that Jack is dead – and not just dead but murdered.'

'Then don't tell him.'

She raises a finger. 'And I won't wear a wire, either.'

The woman is insufferable.

'OK, no wire.'

She is so having a wire.

'And if I find you your drugs den, I want my ankle monitor removed as a reward.'

'It's a deal,' he says, not that Joe has that kind of authority.

Donna turns to walk away. 'I'll phone you tomorrow,' she says. 'And you'll let me know if you find anything out about those notes, yeah?'

She looks so alone, so lost, so vulnerable. He wants to reach out to her, to tell her that she's not alone and that everything will be all right.

'I'll let you know as soon as I hear anything,' he says.

She nods curtly. The softness is gone. He calls after her.

'Donna!'

She turns back.

'About Gabby and Cat... They aren't any less of a friend for having secrets, you know that.'

She nods again, gently this time. Then, quick as a flash, says, 'Gabby? Why Gabby? What secrets does Gabby have?'

Shit.

'Sorry, I meant Cat. Just Cat. I'm tired, that's all.'

Donna smiles the smile of the resigned, and if Joe isn't mistaken, a stray tear falls just as she turns away. She wipes her face quickly and disappears down the prom.

Chapter Twenty-Four

DONNA

I'm back in the glasshouse and I'll admit that it was nice to see Joe. Tinged with melancholy, yes. But nice.

What do I know? It seems that Gabby has a secret that Joe's in on (I thought that dog collar/zip tie thing was a bit dodgy) and Cat is shagging Jase Clarkson. She must be nuts. He's a complete player. It's bound to end in tears. Pound to a pinch of salt that Cat will be sitting in this glasshouse sobbing her heart out inside a month – mark me! Anyhow, it's 10pm and I'm trying to catch up on a whole heap of jobs so that my business doesn't go under. Also, there's no getting away from it: Joe Enys is still the loveliest man in the county, and I need to wash him from my mind before I go to bed. What's a girl to do?

Forget him. That's what.

My phone pings. Ah, lovely. My stalker/chief threatener is back. Let's see what delights he's got for me this time... Ooh, it starts with a quote:

"But sometimes I think sailors have an extra sense that tells them when they are in danger. Sometimes I think evil is a tangible thing...with wave lengths, just as sound and light have." Author – Richard Connell. Book – The Most Dangerous Game. *Character – General Zaroff*

BEWARE, DONNA NIGHTSHADE. EVIL IS CLOSER THAN YOU THINK. BACK OFF, OR ELSE.

Well, that's interesting. A threatening note, the author of which has the good manners of crediting the author of the used quote. I'll file that little nugget in the 'weird and insignificant' part of my brain while I pull on a thick fisherman's jumper and slide an iPhone out of my left bra cup. The phone's not mine; it's Jack's.

What was it Joe said about trust, again?

Trust no one.

Exactly.

Sorry, Joe.

Chapter Twenty-Five

DONNA

The following morning, with a sunrise swim and several flower farmer jobs in the bag, I return to the forensic examination of Jack's phone. As Jack's mother's old cottage is a Penberth Estate cottage, I was already aware of the loose stone behind the old bread oven that has, for generations of fishermen, acted as a safe. I knew that if Jack had anything to hide it would most likely be stashed in there. That's where the weird notes were hidden too, not in the drawer. No, sometimes you hit the jackpot and sometimes you don't, and speaking of jackpot, when I tried to turn the phone on last night it flashed up! It was password protected, of course, with a six-digit code, leading me to wonder what number sequence Jack Crowlas would use as a password. The man might have been successful in his ill-gotten adventures over the years, but he only got away with his evil shenanigans because he was a psychopathic bully. 'Strong of arm, thick of head', that's what Jago always said of him because, make no mistake, there are amoeba at the bottom of the Amazon basin that have more intellectual prowess than Jack Crowlas. I reckoned he would want to be able to type something easily onto the screen when driving, so I went for the obvious and typed the numbers one to six in sequence. It didn't work, so I reversed it...

6 5 4 3 2 1

Bingo!

What an absolute idiot.

The contacts in his phone are not listed with real names as it seems he assigned an animal to each contact. I cross reference my own number from my contact card to see if it's in there and find that I'm referred to as 'Dog'. (Well, *that* came back to bite him on the arse, didn't it?!) There are all kinds of other animals listed in there too, and I'm guessing that the actual humans they represent must hold a passing resemblance to the animal that represents them. There is a skunk (smelly? Stripy?), a beaver (big teeth?), a lizard (long tongue, perhaps?), a baboon (which I'm guessing is a man who may or may not have a very sore bottom), and a cuckoo (no idea).

There's little else stored on the phone. Jack was clearly a man who deleted his text and WhatsApp messages after reading them, which is always a sign of a guilty party. There are no social media accounts associated with him either; no photos, no notes, no diary entries, nothing. There *is* one text message from a contact that was classified as a fish – a herring, of all things. The message reads:

St Malo are good to go. Porthleven Harbour. 4pm at The Mussel Shoal.

It's not particularly ground-breaking as it's almost certainly the meeting Jack wanted me to go to, but at least it's a definite place, which is handy. I look at the clock. It's 10am. There are six hours until I need to be in Porthleven, five if I factor in meeting up with Joe for a quick chat beforehand. But first, there are a few people I want to catch up with today, namely, Cat, Gabby, and Pete. No wonder Cat was off with me at rehearsal – she'd probably read the flirtatious piece Jase wrote about me in the *Packet*. I think of Pete shaking off Jago's arm after their barny, and Lamorna and Kerensa turning into night-rampaging poisoners, and I can't help but feel lonely. Except that I'm not lonely, am I? I still have Aunty Donna. She might be banged up and certified insane, but she's still there for me. I must go and see her tomorrow. She'll know what to do.

I grab the keys to the camper just as Lamorna comes in. She walks straight over and puts her arms around me.

'Don't worry,' she sings into my ear, 'about a thing. 'Cause every little thing is gonna be alright.'

I kiss her on the head.

'I hope so, baby,' I say. 'I hope so.'

Chapter Twenty-Six

The morning service at Penberth church is at ten. Joe sits in the car in the lane outside the church at 9.50am and watches two spritely octogenarian women walk inside. One of them is wearing a multi-coloured pillbox hat.

Joe has been sitting in the car waiting for an opportune moment to enter the church while staring at his phone at the photo of Gabby and Jack. There's anger in her eyes, yes, but there's something else there, too. Passion? Frustration? Love? He's looking at the photo partly to stop himself thinking about Donna, who has kind of double-crossed him. At 10.30pm he got a phone call from Demelza – truly the hardest working sergeant he has ever known; the woman is never off duty – to say that a phone company had reported that Jack's phone had been turned on and that they had traced it to – Joe should have guessed – Penberth Manor.

He should have sent the blues and twos straight down there to haul her lying arse straight into the station, but he had held off, and he mainly held off because the bottom line is that he needs her – or more specifically, he needs to *use* her, as bait, and he couldn't do that if she was getting the third degree from Penworthy. Also, Jack Crowlas got what he deserved, and if Joe never caught the man (or woman) who did it, frankly, he didn't care, but what Joe did care about was getting to the bottom of a smuggling and pirating cartel working out of local harbours and coves that he damn well knew existed. The cartels had been one step ahead of him for far too long, and his old pirate friend, Donna Nightshade, whether she liked it or not, was going to be his key to finding the treasure, and the fact that she was in possession of a murdered man's mobile phone would provide him with just the leverage he needed to make her dance to his tune.

But Donna Nightshade will have to wait for now because Joe's got a vicar to interrogate. He jumps out of the car, grabs his jacket, tiptoes into church, and after taking a seat in a rear pew, picks up a Bible and waits for the service to begin. He opens a page at random and reads the passage:

John 8:32 Then you will know the truth, and the truth will set you free.

'Apt,' he says under his breath, just as the vicar begins her sermon, which builds into a frenzy that is all hellfire and brimstone until, taking a gentler turn, Gabby smiles sweetly and ends the service with a hymn – 'Lord of the Dance'. When the two women he saw earlier exit a pew and

turn to leave, Joe expects them to look like they've been put
through the ringer, what with all the fire and brimstone, but
they don't. If anything, they look... enlivened, with one of
them saying to the other as they saunter down the aisle (the
one with the hat), 'I reckon the vicar has heard about you
carrying on with old man Bosullow, Irene. I told you to be
more careful!'

———————

'I never had the pleasure of meeting Mr Crowlas,' says
Gabby, having led Joe through to the vestry and gestured
towards a chair. 'And there's little to tell you other than
what I told your sergeant already – over several hours of
questioning, I might add.'

Gabby begins to disrobe.

'Which is?'

'That I know nothing about the drugs you found in my
rucksack and what I saw when the kennel door opened...'

'Which was?'

She swallows. 'A dead man in a dog suit.' She removes
her cross and places it on the table. 'God rest his soul.'

Joe takes out his notebook. 'I see. And just to confirm'—
he clicks the top of his biro— 'you never met Jack Crowlas
before?'

'No, never.'

'Not even through the church – through your job?'

Gabby shakes her head and takes a seat next to him. 'I'm
sorry, I know it doesn't help, but no.'

'And you've been here how long?'

'In Cornwall? Three years, give or take.'

Joe glances around the damp vestry. 'And what a lovely place to be,' he says, smiling.

'Yes, I'm very lucky. Penberth is a wonderful place. So peaceful.'

'Very different to where you were before, I should imagine,' he says, his expression kind. 'I saw from your statement that you were a prison chaplain. I think I'm right in saying that's where you met Donna Nightshade – in prison.'

Gabby nods warmly but offers only a limited 'Yes.'

'And where were you stationed before that, if *stationed* is the correct term?'

'Me?'

Joe doesn't answer, and he's stopped smiling.

'I, er, I was in Europe.'

'That's rather a large area to be in all at one time.'

'I was in Estonia, and later in Lithuania.'

'Why?'

Gabby smiles the smile of the righteous. 'Pilgrimage. I wanted to spread the word of our Lord.'

Joe takes a moment to consider which way to go with this. Should he go around the mountains and let her drag herself further and further into the mire, or get straight to the point? He decides to go with the latter. She is a vicar after all, and God might be watching.

Without explanation, he takes his phone out of his pocket, selects the photo of Gabby and Jack together, and zooms in. He slides the phone across the table to Gabby. It's a good job she's sitting down.

'Jesus Christ,' she says.

Gabby puts a hand to her throat and hooks out a smaller cross on a chain from beneath the neck of her sweater. Words are running rampantly in her head; eventually, she pins a few down.

'I honestly didn't know that Jack Crowlas and the man I knew in Europe were one and the same person... not until I saw him dead on the stage floor and someone said what his name was.'

Likely story.

'I knew him by another name completely, in fact.'

'Which was?'

'Simon Curtis.'

Joe writes the name down. It will be easy enough to check.

'And what was your relationship with Simon Curtis?'

Gabby drops the cross and looks at Joe.

'Relationship?' she repeats, shaking her head in regret, her face the picture of a broken woman. 'There was no relationship.'

'Really? You look close in the photo,' he says.

'Photos lie. I met him when I was doing some pastoral work at a prison over there. We became friends, of sorts.'

'You became friends with an inmate?'

'Yes.'

'You seem to make a habit of that.'

She glances down at the table. 'We're all God's children.'

'But this photo was not taken inside a prison,' says Joe.

'No.'

'Where was it taken?'

'In Budapest.'

'Budapest is not in Lithuania.'

'I bumped into him there.'

'Small world,' says Joe.

'It is,' says Gabby.

Every pore of her face tells Joe that she's in deeper than she's letting on. That she's... embarrassed? Ashamed? This is the moment where Joe should really step up the pace – lean in, physically and metaphorically, rip her story apart and grind her to the bone until she's a quivering, truth-spilling mess.

Instead, on the instinct of a copper who has learned to bide his time, he jumps to his feet and says, 'Thank you for your time, Reverend.'

Gabby watches him walk to the vestry door.

'How... how did you get the photo?' she asks.

'It was on file,' he says, 'with the Lithuanian police. There are lots of photos of Jack Crowlas on file, in all kinds of places with all kinds of people. We're putting together quite a backstory.'

Gabby's expression is the picture of innocence. 'I thought I could help him. I really did.' She drops her head, and the tears begin to fall. 'Too late now.'

Joe opens the vestry door. He's used to tears, albeit never from a vicar.

'Is that it?' she asks, surprised, wiping her nose with her sleeve.

'For now.'

'May I leave the area? Only, there's an ecclesiastical conference...'

'It wouldn't be wise to leave,' he says. 'And perhaps, the next time you're interviewed, you might try to remember John 8:32?'

'And you will know the truth,' says Gabby.

'And the truth will set you free.'

Chapter Twenty-Seven

DONNA

I'm standing outside the Old Stables Café, sipping on a coffee at a place called the Penrose Estate. It's a National Trust affair consisting of stately grounds, a big lake, and lots of retired folk wandering around in cut-off walking trousers and waterproof jackets bought from Mountain Warehouse.

Joe has arranged to meet me here for a little chat before I head down to Porthleven Harbour to sell my soul to a drugs cartel. He reckons a National Trust café is not the kind of place where drug barons usually hang out, so we should be able to converse unrecognised. I've seen six people I know already.

Arriving early gives me the opportunity to take out my investigator's notebook and mull over the details of the day, which aren't amounting to much given that I have managed to interview no one since leaving Penberth this morning. I'm beginning to wonder if this private investigator malarkey isn't just a bit tedious. I'd give up on the whole thing if I weren't desperately trying to save myself from the ire of Penworthy (and if I hadn't just spent forty quid having business cards for my new detective agency made up). I *did* find Uncle Jago eventually because he was, predictably as ever, spending time with his pigs, but he says that he has no intention of speaking to me – or anyone else who pitches up brandishing a notebook and a supercilious grin – unless in the presence of a lawyer. Kerensa has gone off on a peace march of some description and Lamorna, who is supposed to be checking the accounts for rent arrears, has her nose in a book and it's not an accounting one. Pete is serving coffee from his horse box, Gabby is being a vicar, and Cat… well, Cat is nowhere to be found, but I'm guessing she's tickling Jase Clarkson's tonsils, so I'll give her a wide berth.

But it hasn't been a total waste of a morning – quite the opposite. As neither Gabby nor Cat were at home, I took the opportunity to have a bit of a snoop around their houses (let's face it, I broke in) and in the process uncovered a couple of interesting (OK, perturbing) finds. Firstly, in Cat's knickers and bras drawer I found not only a brochure for honeymoon hotels in Bora Bora, but also the passport for a woman called Susan Jones… a woman who bears a striking resemblance to Cat in the photo.

(Note: hiding high-risk personal items in your knicker drawer is like using your dog's name as your online banking password – pointless. It's the first place a burglar will look.)

The passport doesn't necessarily spark any concern because if I were called Susan, I'd probably change my name to the more modern 'Cat' too… but on closer inspection, the multitude of Eastern European, South American, and African stamps in her passport are interesting. I also note that her passport expires next month, so that'll bugger up the Bora Bora holiday quite nicely!

But yes, that's quite a lot of overseas travel for someone who pitched up at Penberth as a homeless vagrant in need of a bed, a job, and a hot meal.

I'm also beginning to think that I don't know Gabby quite as well as I ought to…

The vicarage revealed nothing of importance. Gabby is very tidy and owns little in her own right, not even a telly. I think she sits by the fire in the evenings, listening to the radio while beavering away at a little needlework on an embroidery ring. She really is a tireless devotee to the pared-down life, that one. I've long since thought that what she needs is a nice bit of romance in her life – passion, even. Are vicars allowed to be passionate? Even if they aren't, would anyone ever know?

God. God would know.

So no, my search of the vicarage proved fruitless, but when nipping into the church afterwards I happened to peer into the Nightshade family crypt to say a quick hello to relatives past (and, OK, say a little prayer for help and guidance) I found something stashed inside the crypt that really should belong elsewhere… namely, three advertising-type banners of the pop-up variety.

Interesting, I thought to myself. *Interesting*.

But back to the Penrose Estate and my meeting with Joe, who's just arrived.

I stuff the notebook into my bag and watch Joe as he

walks the last couple of hundred yards down the path towards me. He's opted for a more casual outfit today. If I didn't know better, I'd say he's made an effort. I've decided to tell him about Jack's phone. And I've bought him a coffee… as a softener.

He's here. No smile.

'Your favourite,' I say, flashing my most radiant smile and handing over a cardboard cup.

'Let's walk,' he says, or bristles, rather.

This'll be fun.

We walk down a woodland path that hugs the lake and leads to Loe Bar, which is an impressive half-mile shingle bank that separates Loe Pool (the estate's lake) from the sea. Joe whitters on about the ins and outs of undercover work until I remind him that I am, in fact, an ex-con and therefore know perfectly well how to 'play-it right' with the Porthleven crew. We stand on the coastal path and look down the length of the bar. Joe's mood has meandered down awkward street.

'I wish you'd just say what's wrong, Joe,' I say. 'You've been spiky ever since you arrived, which is a bit unfair, considering that I've agreed to be your stooge for the day.'

'I know you've got Jack's phone,' he says, before turning away and heading back towards the café.

I run to catch up.

'Now, you're never going to believe this and it's the funniest thing, but I was going to tell you about the phone today – give it to you, in a minute in fact, on the walk back, but… no flies on you – you've beaten me to it.'

'Of course you were,' he says, walking.

I tug on his jumper.

'Joe, please, just stop a moment and see it from my point of view.' He stops. His face is pure stone. He's waiting for me to explain. Right. Here goes. 'To start from the beginning, and bear with me here… You were kind enough to point out last night that your boss wants to lock me up and throw away the key, and we both know that at some point very soon a snippet of evidence will be found pinning the whole thing on me – the feather will be Ruby's feather and my fingerprints will be on it and then I'll be back in the clink before you can say *miscarriage of justice*. I think it's perfectly understandable that I would want to check out his phone for myself before the police get involved and use something nebulous to pin the whole thing on me. I *am* investigating this thing myself; you remember.'

He scoffs, commits to a full eyeroll, and carries on walking. I pull him up again just as a dog runs towards us from the opposite direction. Joe opens his mouth to speak but a woman is only a few paces behind the dog. We both begin to walk more naturally and smile at her. Appearances are everything.

The woman disappears. I hand over Jack's phone.

'I've put it in a freezer bag and everything,' I say.

'Have you deleted anything?' he asks, turning it over in his hand.

'No.'

'Donna?'

'I swear to you.'

'Where was it?'

'In the bread oven behind the fireplace. Those weird notes were there too, not in the sideboard. To be honest, I think your guys did a poor job. If I were you, I'd—'

He stops walking.

Right. Tender spot. I feel a lecture coming on.

'The only thing I *should* be doing right now, Donna Nightshade, is dragging your lying arse into the station.'

'What? Why?'

(*I know why, really, but let's play the game.*)

'Jesus, where to start! Only last night we both said that the person most likely to have Jack's phone in their possession was the murderer. And hey, what a coincidence, it turns out that *you* of all people, have Jack's phone, the very person who has the means and best motive – in the history of motives – to have killed him. And now your prints are all over the damn thing.' He waves the phone about. 'Why couldn't you just for once in your life play with a straight bat!'

'To be fair, my prints aren't—'

He starts walking again but... it's cool. I remember Joe like this. The anger won't last. He can't keep it up. Me, I can keep a rage on for hours, but Joe, he just doesn't have the stamina. Best not to argue and let it pass, except that I can't help but say, 'Fair enough, but it works both ways, and do please remember that I didn't get all pissy about the text message.'

'What text message?' Give him a second... 'Oh, right, last night. That wasn't about this.'

'Yes, it was. Your left cheek blotches up ever so slightly when you lie, and it blotched up last night.'

He knows I'm right. His shoulders drop. That's a start.

'Look, just accept that I couldn't tell you about the text,' he says. 'The information I received was too sensitive... for a whole load of reasons. I just couldn't show it to you. I couldn't.'

'I guessed that,' I say, softly. 'Which is why I didn't give you a hard time about it. Unlike you, who, just because I keep something to myself for less than twenty-four hours...'

He throws up his arms. 'But *I'm* not a suspect in a murder inquiry!'

'Let me finish,' I add, calmly. 'Can't you see that I need to protect my friends and family. You can understand that, can't you?' A memory of Joe putting the cuffs on me all those years ago runs – no, gallops – across my mind. 'Or maybe you can't.'

He harrumphs and carries on walking, which is progress. Harrumphs are good. He stops again. His face is softer, a bit contorted perhaps, but softer.

'About your friends,' he says.

'What about them?'

He takes a deep breath.

'How would you feel if I told you that Gabby knew Jack?'

'When?'

'Before she lived here. A few years ago.'

'Where?'

'Europe. Lithuania.'

'How do you know?'

'The text last night was a photo of the two of them together – looking cosy.'

'She told me she never met the man,' I say.

'That might not have been an absolute lie. She said she knew him when he went under a different name – Simon Curtis. Although that could be bullshit. She said she hadn't put the two aliases together, until she saw him dead on the stage. I think… I think she loved him.'

I pick my jaw up from the floor. 'What? Gabby the vicar loved Jack Crowlas the psychopath?'

'It seems so.'

'And she had no idea that her Simon was our Jack?'

'As ridiculous as that seems, I don't think so. But she could be lying her arse off.'

My brain flick-flacks itself into oblivion as we continue to wander down the path. I try to bring some kind of order to my thoughts about Gabby and her possible motives for murder, but then remember that Joe's boss has only given him a few days to prove me innocent (so much for innocent until proven guilty) and, oh yes, I'm about to meet some drug barons, so decide that it's probably best to file Gabby under *my brain can't compute that now so I'll pretend I don't know about it* and focus on the job in hand.

Joe, who has allowed me the quiet space to have a moment's thought, seems to have thawed a little with the phone thing.

I nudge his arm and say, 'About Jack's phone… don't you want me to tell you what's on it? Go on, I know you do…'

I'm playing it soft – cajoling.

He lets out a laugh and shakes his head. It's a friendly, *what on earth am I going to do with you, Donna Nightshade*, type of a shake. He realises his mistake and tries to recover by playing it straight again.

Too late, Joe.

'I'll take a look at it at the station,' he says.

'OK, but I'll help you out by explaining that he listed his contacts by their animal doppelgangers.'

He stops walking. 'Their what?'

'Doppelganger. That's someone's double. Only this case, an animal double. I'm a dog.'

His face is contorted into bewildered confusion. 'A dog? Wait, *you* were in his contacts?' He throws his hands up and starts walking again.

'What's wrong this time?!' I shout. 'He must have saved my number to his phone when he picked up my card…'

Joe stops walking again. 'What card?'

'Hello? For my investigation business? I told you; he picked it up at the pub. There's a skunk, a beaver, a lizard, a baboon and a cuckoo in his contacts, but the only message he left on there was from a herring, and that was to say that the RV was still on.' I tug his sleeve gently. 'Want me to tell you the phone's password?'

Joe stops walking (it's a stop-start kind of a day).

'Firstly, Donna…' He scratches his scull with both hands in a gesture of frustration. 'How will I ever know that you haven't deleted important messages and that you weren't in cahoots with Jack?'

'You won't. Sorry. I didn't think of that. And can I just say, before the moment passes and as a complete aside just to help you out... if you want to come across as a hard nut copper, don't say "cahoots".'

More eyerolling.

'You guessed the password?' he says, looking dubious.

'I told you I'd be good at this detective malarkey.'

He frowns. 'Rubbish. How did you crack it?'

'Oh, ask me no secrets...' I say. 'I have my ways.'

'You mean you guessed an obvious password and then changed it to something else...'

Ah.

'Anyway, in the spirit of cooperation and openness,' I say, 'I think that you and I should declare an *entente cordiale* and go through what we know. I've picked up a few clues you might be interested in.'

We take a seat at a convenient bench. 'OK, but *you* should know that if you want to be taken seriously in this detective malarkey, no one says "clues" anymore.'

I bow my touché, but Joe has more to add.

'Hold on a minute,' he begins, 'less than twenty-four hours ago you swore to me that you'd told me everything you knew.'

'Twenty-four hours is a long time in this game, Joe.'

He looks at his watch. 'Quickly then. Tell me what you have.'

I flip closed my trusty investigator's notepad and sigh. I simply couldn't tell him about Gabby's dog collar, or Pete's Wikipedia page about deadly nightshade. I did mention the funeral wreath and the religious message in the flower farm order book ('something about the devil' I say), but there's no way I'm telling him about the margin notes in the shaman book, or Jago's new dog suit, which still doesn't sit right, or the pop-up banners I found in the Nightshade crypt. Family is family, after all.

'And that's all I've got,' I conclude. 'Thoughts?'

'Thoughts?' he repeats, laughing. 'I thought you'd got something decent to tell me! The funeral wreath is a non-starter, but what really confuses me is why forensics found no traces of Jago in the dog suit – Jago must have tried it on before, surely? Had he worn it during rehearsal?'

I'd better tell him about the second dog suit.

'Ah, well, I can solve that little mystery for you,' I say. 'There were two suits. The suit Jack was wearing was a brand-new suit. Jago lost the other one down the pub – he wore it to the Admiral Benbow to give the old duffers a laugh – but he lost it; either that or it was nicked, so he ordered another one. The one Jack wore, no doubt stolen from Jago's study, had not been taken out of the bag before the performance, I believe.'

Joe puts his face in his hands and shakes his head, murmuring something like, 'Your bloody family!' and 'God, give me strength!'. I give him a moment before nudging him.

'Admit it…' I say.

He drops his hands. 'Admit what?'

'That I've been very helpful, and you're impressed.'

His lips twitch – almost into a smile.

'You *have* been helpful,' he says, standing suddenly and

holding out his hands to help me up. (Joe hasn't realised that he's behaving like the old days. He'll kick himself in a minute.)

We start to meander down the lane.

'My conclusion is that you're a lucky amateur,' he says, before nudging me again. That's a good sign. Nudges are good; nudges are friendly. 'But let's not forget that you concealed vital evidence from the police...' His face clouds over. 'Which you *must* stop doing, Donna!'

(There's the kick).

We walk on. The pace quickens. We reach the car park. Joe takes a deep breath.

'We'll drive there separately,' he says.

Hello? Obviously.

'I've got a couple of my guys there already, and I'll be hidden in the—'

'Bushes? Shadows?'

'Café.'

'Right.'

We stop at his BMW. He opens the passenger door and pulls something out of a backpack. It's a wire. He's got to be joking.

'No way, José!' I say. (Kerensa is right – it *is* a name to be shouted!) I back away like a frightened puppy.

'Well, you can't do it *without* one,' he says, edging forwards.

'Hello? I absolutely cannot do it *with* one, either!'

I glance around. There are *way* too many people in this car park for this conversation. I step in closer.

'Listen. I *know* these kinds of people. The first thing they'll do is search me for a wire,' I whisper. 'Trust me.'

'In the open? In Porthleven?!'

I turn to walk away.

'Donna!'

He walks after me.

'Do you want to catch these scumbags or not?' I ask, still walking.

'I do, but not by putting you at risk. I'd never forgive—'

We stop. I face him. For both our sakes it's best he doesn't finish that sentence. I might have to like him, or forgive him, or both.

I turn towards the van again.

'Just remember,' I say, suddenly giving the naughty devil that sits pretty much permanently on my left shoulder a leg up by allowing her to take over my speech processes for a moment. 'If I get nobbled – or killed – this was all your idea, and all because you wanted to be awarded copper of the month.'

His nostrils flare. I wink and sashay to my van. I shouldn't sashay for Joe, but hey, what's a girl to do?

'See you on the flipside,' I shout, before pressing play on some funky Viking rock music and wheel spinning my way out of the carpark, which isn't that easy in a VW camper, but I just about manage it all the same.

Chapter Twenty-Eight

A mile or so down the road in the picturesque harbour town of Porthleven, Joe takes his seat by the window in a restaurant called Amélie's. It's a waterside spot serving locally caught fish/shellfish, plus burgers and grills from a wood-fired oven, not to mention the mouth-watering fritto misto, which is seasoned fried fish, whole tiger prawns, squid, sweet chilli mayonnaise and seasoned fries – Joe's absolute favourite. It's usually impossible to get a window seat at such short notice, especially on such a beautiful September evening, when the upcountry townies are still lingering in droves and posting pictures of meals on Instagram, but he goes night-fishing with the manager so that sorted that out.

Joe settles himself in, smiles at the waitress as she pours his glass of sparkling water and settles down to keep his eye on the rendezvous spot, which is The Mussel Shoal, an absolute gem of a licenced café-cum-kiosk on the quay serving mainly seafood. Donna has rocked up at The Mussel Shoal and Joe's eyes have nearly burst out of his head. She's a couple of hundred yards away, but even so, Joe can tell that the woman looks *amazing*! She's let her hair down and has put on the sexiest short shorts he's ever seen. (Kickboxing and teaching the tango on a Thursday night down the town hall has not done Donna Nightshade any harm.) A leather jacket sits over a vest top and her footwear of choice is the Ugg boot (to cover the ankle monitor, no doubt). Expensive-looking sunglasses that Joe knows will be rip-offs from Skinny Pete finish the look. Joe finds himself feeling proud of her – jealous too – but proud, definitely proud.

Donna chats with a waiter for a while before taking a beer from the counter. She finds a seat on the decking area by the water's edge and looks directly at Joe, raising her glass. So much for hiding in the shadows.

Twenty minutes pass by. Nothing.

Just as Joe pops into his mouth the last morsel of his starter of warm artisanal bread dipped in olive oil (probably from the local baker, Baker Tom) a tall, gangly man wearing a white and blue striped T-shirt, shorts, and deck shoes taps Donna on the shoulder. Feeling the tap, she turns around on her stool, stands, and they kiss on both cheeks. Conversing happens. Donna looks happy enough – content. She even shows him her ankle monitor and Joe is halfway through his fritto misto when another man pitches up. He looks like a total thug and if there had been a British Bulldog listed on Jack's phone then this would have been him. The original man gestures towards a boat moored by the far harbour wall. Donna nods her approval, and they stand. The man pays her bill and without a side glance towards Joe, Donna leaves The Mussel Shoal just as Joe's phone pings. It's one of his PCs. He was sitting at the table next to Donna at The Mussel Shoal and he's looking to Joe for direction.

Joe stands and grabs his jumper off the back of his chair. He strains to watch Donna as she edges further away around the harbour. The restaurant manager appears by his side.

'Perhaps you would like me to keep this warm for you, sir?' he offers, his voice hushed. (He knows there's only one reason a casually dressed DS Joe Enys would be dining alone at Amélie's while keeping a beady eye on the harbour.)

'That would be great,' says Joe, stepping away from the table, distracted. 'Back in a tick.'

The restaurant door slams behind him and he starts to walk around the harbour, past The Mussel Shoal and towards the Harbour Inn. It's not that he doesn't trust the constable to do a good job, but he doesn't trust the constable to do a good job. This is Donna. And she's doing this because he asked her to, and there can be absolutely no messing it up this time. Also, his boss doesn't know that this is going down and she's going to be pissed as all hell if he messes it up.

The beer garden at the Harbour Inn sits nicely above the harbour, providing a decent view of the cruiser, which isn't French, according to his second constable who's already in the beer garden, but registered in South Africa. Joe gives up trying to appear nonchalant and hangs over the harbour wall, ogling the boat. Where's Donna? Why can't he see Donna? His phone pings. It's a text from his constable who's had 'eyes on' the whole time from the road above the village (good man that one; one to watch). The text explains that Donna was frisked, albeit in the guise of being hugged, but it was definitely a frisk ('for a wire', is the constable's guess) before being invited below.

Joe starts to feel a bit sick. He doesn't like this. He doesn't like this one bit.

The engine is flashed up and, with the bulldog at the helm, the boat very quickly edges away from the harbour wall.

Shit.

The fenders are brought in quickly (by the herring, Joe surmises) and both men stay on deck while the boat edges between the harbour walls and disappears out of view. Joe gets eyes on his constable, who shrugs and makes an 'eek' face.

Eek indeed.

He's just about to step inside the restaurant to settle his bill when his phone pings. It's a text from Donna:

Off to the Isles of Scilly. Back tomorrow. Don't text me, don't phone me, don't come for me. Let it run. Tell my family I'm OK (and to get the rest of the daffs planted in). PS Aeolus Jones is here, and I think I've met the baboon! Adios amigo

Joe's head drops. Even if Donna survives to tell the tale and he manages to keep the whole sorry mess from his boss, he'll still have to explain why Donna's ankle monitor has alerted the authorities to say that she's left the area.

Ankle monitor?

That's actually a blessing.

He pays his bill, is handed the remnants of his meal in a cardboard container (no plastic here), dashes to his car, and takes the road that runs up and out of the village and round to a headland west of Porthleven. He jumps out of the car and dashes up the coastal path to get a good view of the cruiser while texting Demelza to tell her to run background checks on the boat. Eventually he starts to eat, calming down a little now that he's remembered Donna's ankle monitor, and starts to think that perhaps there might be a handy flipside to her disappearance. With Donna out of the picture he can really go to town on her relatives and friends – Jago, Pete, Cat, and yes, even the vicar. If the murderer isn't Jase Clarkson, and if no one shimmied up the cliffs and back down again, then one of them is guilty, unless... unless Donna is playing a mean game of double bluff, and she's actually in cahoots with the guys she's just sailed off with, and is stringing Joe along?

She's right about one thing though, thinks Joe. He really does need to stop using the word, *cahoots*.

His phone pings. It's a message from DCI Penworthy.

You've 48hrs left to find someone to nail it on or I'll come down and bring that Nightshade woman in myself!

He's about to text back when his phone pings again. It's Demelza with a string of informative text messages:

TEXT 1: *The feather is a direct match with the Nightshade macaw. Bring her in? (The sister not the bird)*

TEXT 2: *Been having a dig around the notes for the old Donna Nightshade case (the mad aunty). We took copies of her diaries. Been reading them… interesting. Have left copies on your desk and highlighted pertinent stuff.*

TEXT 3: *You're never going to believe it, but Jack Crowlas married a woman called Susan Jones at Penzance town hall last week. Susan Jones is Cat's real name. I know! Bonkers! A man called Adam Stewart was the witness. And Donna Nightshade's ankle monitor is showing her in the sea just off Porthleven.*

TEXT 4: *Also, and you're gonna love this, we've had confirmation that the note telling you about the drugs stash was definitely written by Jago Nightshade, who just phoned the station wondering if you can pop round to see him tomorrow (he's playing cards at the Turk's Head tonight, but he wants to confess something to you and only to you). Confess to murder, with any luck!*

Joe thinks he really must have a word with Demelza about linking her messages, or maybe even phoning, before letting out a silent scream to the universe. He types out a text:

Fantastic work. Get me a full rundown on Susan Jones. I'm coming in to read the diaries. See you in half an hour or so.

Closing the lid on the food – he's not hungry after all – Joe wanders back to the car in the knowledge that tonight is going to be a long, troublesome night.

Chapter Twenty-Nine

DONNA

It's 7.30pm and I'm on a nice little cruiser about a mile off the Cornish coast sharing a bottle of Chianti with Aeolus Jones. He's of Greek/Welsh heritage – I saw that coming – and he's informed me (because, of course, I asked) that his first name is taken from the Greek god of winds. And then he farted and laughed. Tidy.

I've had to navigate my way through the choppy waters of being the only person on board who knows that Jack is dead, and I know this for a fact because at The Mussel Shoal Skunk's opening line was, 'Where's Jack?' (Or words to that effect).

Despite our initial joviality on the quay, once below, the niceties ended, and I was subjected to the ninth degree as we pootled out of Porthleven Harbour. I wasn't grabbed by the throat until I squealed, nor made to walk the plank, but Aeolus looked pretty pissed off that I was there without Jack, and an annoyed scowl is pretty disconcerting coming from a one-handed man with a cleft lip and a glass eye.

As an excuse I said that Jack had been rushed to the hospital with a gastric issue (which isn't a lie – his stomach must have hurt like hell when the deadly nightshade hit him) but he had given instructions that they are to negotiate with me – take it or leave it. After my second glass of cheap Chianti, I said that they were better off dealing with me anyhow as *I'm* the woman who owns Penberth and explained that Jack is seen locally as becoming more and more delusional and off his game these days. I said that I, Donna Nightshade, of the infamous Nightshade pirate family, was the only woman they needed for all their business needs in Cornwall (nod, nod, wink, wink and all that).

And as easy as that, they believed me. We sailed past Penzance Harbour heading west and the Champagne came out (cheap, but better than the Chianti) and we've been on the piss ever since. I've also discovered that they've been negotiating with the 'French connection' on Jack's behalf, which I'm guessing isn't the popular, if over-priced, clothing store. And so, I have the distinct impression that this bunch of reprobates are the unimportant middlemen who transport the shipment (I'm guessing drugs or people) between whoever their contact is in Europe and Jack.

I've played along, saying that future drops can happen at Penberth Cove, and thereafter stashed at my manor as per Jack's original plan. They seemed happy with this and by five o'clock the whole shooting match – the transportation of shipments from St Malo in France to Penberth, camouflaged by hiding the drugs inside gouged-out melons and other large fruits and vegetables, and sent on from Penberth smuggled up-country in Ocado delivery vans – has been organised. But in the meantime, for tonight's pick-up, we're off to Wolf Rock, which is a slab of granite a considerable number of miles out in the Atlantic and has a massive, unmanned lighthouse perched on top of it. These guys will take control of the shipment there and then sit off Scilly until morning to RV with another boat. This shipment isn't coming ashore at Penberth. It appears there has been some last-minute reorganisation, all of which hurriedly took place while we were still close enough to landfall for a phone signal but out of my earshot. (I've suggested to them that they really ought to invest in satellite phones if they're going to be taken seriously as a drug cartel.) Nevertheless, it's a slick affair, which means it's not likely that these monkeys (sorry, these miscellaneous animals of indeterminate breed) are the masterminds behind the operation. So, who is?

This is the question I'm asking myself on deck as we chug along in the twilight, having been left alone with the baboon, who can't stop ogling my legs. After two glasses of Chianti and half a magnum of Champagne, I have enough Dutch courage to simply ask him outright who's really in charge.

'The cuckoo,' he said.

(Sometimes all you have to do with this investigation malarky is ask.)

Baboon has never met Cuckoo – none of these guys have – because Jack was the go-between, but the head honcho is apparently going to be there at the big RV. Conveniently, the baboon nips below deck and leaves me with my thoughts.

It seems I won't have long to find out who the infamous cuckoo is because we're going to RV with their boat – a nice little yacht, apparently – off one of the uninhabited Scilly Isles tomorrow morning, at which point we'll hash out the final details of future drops and I'll meet them face to face (they don't do WhatsApp or Zoom, apparently). All of which means that I'm getting close to solving this whole thing – all of it, I can feel it – the murder *and* the drugs cartel. To be honest, I'm pretty sure I cracked the murder once I'd been inside the crypt, and I don't think the drugs and the murder are linked, but we'll see. So yes, there's lots to be pleased about, namely that my first case will be done and dusted inside just a few days, along with the pleasure of beating Joe Enys to the solution in the process. (At least he'll be able to seek solace in claiming fifty quid from Penworthy.)

I take a moment to think of the message Joe pinged back to me from the harbourside (now deleted) before the herring took my phone from me for 'safekeeping':

I knew I should never have let you go...

No. He shouldn't. But that's a different story.

Chapter Thirty

The note that Demelza stuck to the buff file she deposited on Joe's desk before she left the office for the evening reads as follows:

Boss. Here are passages I found in the 'Aunty Donna' diaries that I thought you might find interesting. She always titled her entries, which was helpful. See you tomorrow. (I'll leave the work mobile on all night just in case you need me.)

'Tireless, that one,' murmurs Joe, picturing Demelza in ten years' time as Chief Constable of Devon and Cornwall Police. 'Tireless.'

Joe takes a seat at his desk and, with a degree of apprehension, opens the file.

'Right then, Donna Nightshade XII,' he says. 'Let's see what we can find out from you...'

. . .

EXHIBIT 1

Diary entry date: 17 June 1983

Title: I did it!

It was my fifth attempt but finally – finally – I cracked it! Yes, I defeated the naysayers and scaled the cliffs at the Minack. There was quite a crowd waiting for me at the top, I can tell you, and I've earned Jago £50 in the sweepstake he had running at the Admiral Benbow, so that's all very nice. I found a new way up this time, thank God, because at one point I really did think I was going to fall, but those sticky boots Kerensa bought me really made a difference. (She's a lifesaver, that twin of mine.) But despite showing Nature who's master on the cliffs, life isn't sweet completely, because Sam Enys has thrown me over – and for good this time. I will declare it now – right here on these, the most important of pages – that I, Donna Nightshade XII do love Samuel Joseph Enys, and I know that I will never love anyone else in the same way again. It seems that he has fallen in love with some hag from St Agnes, and it also seems that even the charms of Donna Nightshade cannot persuade him otherwise. Should I curse her and send her the way of all vagabonds and traitors? Yes, I should. But – and it's an unusual course of action for me – I simply want him to be happy. Which is why I send him on his way with a heavy heart, but I swear to God Almighty that neither he, nor his wife-to-be, nor future offspring, will darken my door again; it would simply be too painful.

Anyhow, Kerensa has brought home several waifs and strays for a party this weekend, and one of their number (a certain Jack Crowlas) seems to be giving me the eye. He's no Sam, of course, but there is, perhaps, a certain something quite intriguing about him that might tempt me towards a little dalliance? Rebound men are never a clever idea, but really, what harm can it do? I'll get rid of him next week.

Suum Ciuque, *and all that.*

Donna

EXHIBIT 2

Diary entry date: 5 February 1987

Title: My World Here Hath Ended

My younger sister, the beautiful, gentle Lilias, has returned from her sojourn in Botswana and has confessed to being 'with child'. I am happy for her, and yet it is nothing but a knife to my heart when we all know how much I long for a child of my own. The father, I am told, is 'one of three wonderful men' and she intends to raise the child here, at Penberth. But how shall I bear it?

Bravely, and with dignity, clearly.

There is a silver lining, however. If the child is a woman, then I shall at least have an heir to the throne, so perhaps it is all for the best. Jago says that it's time to accept that I am a pod without seed and to embrace this good fortune as a blessing for the family.

'Many births of a woman make her old, as many crops make the earth barren,' he said, quoting Jonson to make me feel better. Kerensa could not care in the least that our younger sister has beaten us to the finish line. Because that's what giving birth would be to me – a finish line, a completion of myself as a being, as a wholly fulfilled human soul.

Ah, well.

Suum Cuique *and all that,*

Donna

PS I do not like the way Jack looks at Lilias.

EXHIBIT 3

Diary entry date: 20 September 1987

Title: It's a girl!

She has come! And I have asked Lilias to name her Belladonna, for what other name could we possibly give the sweet child? No, she is not the spawn of my own loins, but it is the closest possible thing, and I would not want to conceive a child with Jack now, even if I were able to. But black words about Jack are for another day, because the baby is here, and we all adore her. And Jago was right all along because the child is indeed a blessing and with me barren and Kerensa voluntarily sterile, this is, it seems, our only chance for an heir apparent. Poor Lilias suffered terribly during both labour and the birth. Indeed, it was touch and go whether we would have either sister or baby with us today, and she has been told never to commit to pregnancy again as it would no doubt kill her. All of which makes the child even more special, even more loved and even more adorable.

I swear to you now, to all the Donna Nightshades dead and gone, that I will protect my niece to the ends of the earth – and to the death, if necessary.

EXHIBIT 4

Diary entry date: 16 September 2003

Title: Sam's Son

Donna denies it, but I can tell that she's obsessed with that damn tyke who's always knocking about here. His name is Joe Enys, also known as 'Sam's son'. (And yes, by 'Sam' I mean the Sam, my Sam, the one that got away.) Which is more annoying, the fact that he is a living reminder of the love I lost, that he is the daughter of a hag I should have hexed (I still could?), or that he is a policeman? I have told Donna that I can no longer have him on the estate because of Jack, whose dealings become deeper and darker and more unwise by the day. And so, Donna spends more and more time away from the house, walking the cliffs and moors with the dog, and has said that she would rather give up Penberth than give up Joe. But mark me... if Jack (who has become obsessed with looking for that damn family ruby that I doubt now even exists) is to have his way, then surely she will have to give up both...

Over my dead body, I tell you (or his, more likely).

As for Jago? He hides away increasingly in his study, and when I visit him for guidance all he can say is, 'All shall be well, Sister. All shall be well.' But I cannot help but sense catastrophe ahead. I can taste it, smell it, breathe it. Dark times are upon us, and I am certain that 'something wicked this way comes'. Yes, something very wicked surely bears down upon us. As sure as night follows day, I know it.

Suum Cuique

Donna

EXHIBIT 5

Diary entry date: October 2004 (abridged)

Title: She is pregnant.

My sister, Lilias, is pregnant again. I have begged her to abort but she will not and so I have spoken to Shaman Paulo, and he suggests adding Queen Anne's Lace to her breakfast but I have not the heart to harm my sister in the process of disposing of the foetus, for that is all the thing is right now – a foetus. And yet it will grow, and grow and grow, until it is no longer a baby but a killing machine. Has Jack done this to her? My sister surely would not bear it, would not entertain it, and yet she will not tell me who the father is. The bruising around her eye and jaw last month spoke words that none of us can bear to say. I must find a way to end all this madness. I must, I must find a way.

Suum Cuique

Donna

EXHIBIT 6

Diary entry date: July 2005 (abridged)

Title: The dog is dead.

Donna is bereft. He did it. I know he did. She has thrown over her young man – I know it will have been to protect him – and the girl has gone to the bad, perhaps for ever now, and we are all prostrate in our uselessness. I am ashamed, but I will find a way out of this. Help me, ancestral Donnas of old. Please, for the love of God, help me.

Suum cuique

Donna

EXHIBIT 7

Diary entry date: October 2005

Title: My sister is dead

The baby has come and Lilias, my dear, sweet Lilias, is dead. And all the while she, the one who brought this upon us yet cannot eat and cannot sleep, wanders in delirium.

'Stars, hide your fires; Let not light see my black and deep desires.'

I curse thee, Jack Crowlas. I curse thee with all the might and power of the Nightshades. For as God is my witness, I will kill you if no one else does. Yes, as God is my witness, I will kill you.

Washed through with sadness (and gratitude that Aunty Donna never got round to cursing his mum), Joe closes the file and whispers, 'Something wicked this way comes.'

Because just like Aunty Donna all those years before, Joe can feel it now, too.

Chapter Thirty-One

As sure as day follows night, the next morning dawns on Cornwall in its usual bright and breezy manner, and Joe, having slept little and fitfully, is on his way to Penberth to cobble at least one of the Nightshades. En route, and on a whim, he parks his BMW outside the church to take a quick snoop around. He awoke at 4am thinking about the diary entries and wondering if Donna was OK (all right, alive) and considered which Nightshade to pull in first – Jago or Lamorna. Neither interview was going to be easy, and all he could do was thank his lucky stars that Donna was out of the picture today, because once she knew he'd given her nearest and dearest a grilling while she was doing his bidding, she'd have his balls for earrings. Perhaps she'd think she'd been duped by being purposefully put onto the trail of the potential drug dealers while he was left on the mainland to round up her family? Who was he kidding? Of course she'd think she'd been duped. (And hadn't she, really? A little bit?)

Joe doesn't answer that question but gets out of the car thinking that Gabrielle Jones may be a woman of the cloth, but she has secrets – oh, boy, does she have secrets. The church door slams behind him as he steps, with reverent, silent strides, towards the altar. The familiar smell of damp walls and wood polish takes him straight back to Sunday school with Donna, except that without any congregation to liven the mood of the place, the old church feels spooky as hell. He pauses a moment at the top of the nave just as the sun, which is only just getting around to scratching its balls and having a morning stretch, decides to shine a light through the huge stained-glass window at the far end of the church (Joe knows it has a special name but can't for the life of him remember what it is) and suddenly the great Almighty is smiling down at him and beckoning him deeper into the church. Other men have found faith for less and Joe takes it as a sign – a sign to get a grip of his emotions and search the place before Gabby pitches up. He tries the vestry door – it's open.

As vestries go it's sparse, and mould is creeping unchecked over the whitewash. A filthy window lets in enough light for Joe to notice the vicar's robes hanging from a tall cupboard on the wall opposite the door, and a large pile of hymn books on the table in the middle of the room, as though someone is expecting – hoping – the congregation numbers to pick up (either that or someone has booked a wedding... or a funeral).

An arched oak door with *PRIVATE* written on it sits in the centre of the far wall. He tries the handle, but it's locked, which has never stopped Joe Enys before and it won't, frankly, stop him now. He takes a card out of his wallet and fiddles with the thing until it gives way and the door creaks open, revealing a dank cupboard lined with shelves which are almost empty, except for a Bible (flagged in several places), a large cross on a chain, a dog collar (vicar's) and an envelope with Boots the Chemist written on it.

He takes a seat at the table and opens the envelope. Joe didn't think anyone bothered to get photos printed these days, but this person obviously has. He takes out the only photograph in the packet.

Well, well, well.

Gabrielle Jones, you little tinker!

The photo shows a near-naked Gabby in a photoshoot pose, her cross and fancy vicar's scarf draped between her breasts in a seductive manner. By the looks of things, she was shut inside a prison cell when it was taken. She's biting her moist lower lip. He turns the photo over. Someone has written:

Remember this? Do as you're told and keep your gob shut or else!

Blackmailed, then? And probably by Jack, which gives Joe a motive for murder for someone other than a Nightshade – what a result! Yes, the day is getting better and better and Joe can't help but award himself a little titter. That fifty quid is looking vaguely promising for the first time since the murder inquiry began. He opens the Bible at the first flag. A passage has been highlighted.

1 Peter: 5:8 Your adversary the devil prowls around like a roaring lion, seeking someone to devour

Well, well, well.

He turns to the next flag, and then the next, which is when a thought hits him; Demelza would call it a real *lightbulb* moment. He takes out his notebook and flicks to the page where he copied down the numbers written on the notes Donna found in Jack's house, and then cross references them to the flags and, what do you know, they all tally. Someone (and it's not too much of a leap of the imagination to assume it was the vicar) was threatening Jack with aggressive hellfire and damnation passages from the Bible, knowing that he would understand the references due to his religious upbringing.

Oh, Gabby.

And then he looks at the dog collar.

Oh dear, oh dear.

The inside of the collar is lined with a strip of horticultural fastener – the kind that was glued into Jack's collar (dog's not vicar's).

He shakes his head while taking photos of the evidence. He texts his sergeant:

Bring Gabrielle Jones in on suspicion of the murder of Jack Crowlas. I'll interview her at 2pm.

Demelza texts back within a minute.

Will do. Also, the Lidl store manager has some interesting CCTV footage from the morning of the play. In the footage, Skinny Pete clearly takes a package out of his jacket pocket and stuffs it in a slipper in one of the deep tubs in the middle aisle. He looked very cagey. And guess who went looking in the same bin half an hour later? Cat! Probably just drugs, but worth mentioning.

Joe puts his phone away and after exiting the vestry sharpish, he marches down the aisle, stopping briefly to have a last look up at God, who doesn't seem quite so pleased with Joe as He was twenty minutes ago. Nevertheless, Joe allows himself a moment of bittersweet melancholy. He remembers standing in this very spot once, with Donna, when they were fourteen. They had been pratting about in the graveyard and had run inside the church when it started to rain. Joe had taken her damp hand in his and said, 'We'll get married here one day, Donna Nightshade. You just see if we don't.' And she'd slapped him on the backside, laughed, and legged it outside while shouting, 'Bollocks to that!'

Happy times.

And with a spring in his step, Joe Enys leaves the church a happier man than when he walked in – which he supposes is the point of churches – but then remembers the inconvenient detail of the macaw feather, and Jago, and the note, and it dawns on him as he opens the car door that this thing might not be quite so cut and dried after all.

Chapter Thirty-Two

S	*he never leaves my side... Never!*
These are the words ringing in Joe's ears as he walks towards the front door at Penberth Manor, words that have been running amok in the far reaches of his mind since his impromptu meeting with Lamorna at the Minack. Because if Ruby never leaves Lamorna's side, then bearing in mind one of Ruby's feathers was glued between the Thomas train and his track, then Lamorna must have had contact with the train... mustn't she? If not, then someone else who was physically close to Lamorna must have had the train with them at the time, and recently, what with the moulting issue. Could Lamorna be double bluffing him? Are *all* the Nightshade's double bluffing him? Could she have admitted to the brugmansia poisoning and the whack around the head with the lollipop lady stick just to give him a stiff enough nudge to steer him in a different direction?

Of course she could. She's a Nightshade.

But if that were the case, why tell him that macaw

feathers were like fingerprints? Surely she would keep that nugget to herself? Except... she wouldn't have known that the trace of a feather was going to be found on Thomas.

Mad.

He is going barking mad!

He knocks on the door at Penberth. If he were playing it straight, Joe would have dispatched a constable to Penberth once Ruby's feather had come up as a match, with the instruction to bundle both Lamorna *and* Jago Nightshade into a panda car and blue light them to the station. But he didn't do that because – and he has no choice but to face it – he isn't playing it straight this time... and all because he doesn't want to upset Donna again, and because nothing can ever be straight or easy or simple when the Nightshades are involved. Instead, he follows a visibly shaky Jago into the kitchen and smiles up at Lamorna who drifts in from the garden *without* Ruby on her shoulder.

She never leaves my side. Never.

'Tea, inspector?' asks Jago, trying too hard to look relaxed while walking backwards towards the Aga.

'He's not an inspector; he's a detective sergeant,' corrects Lamorna. She flashes Joe a thousand-watt smile. 'But to us, he's just Joe.'

'Where's Ruby?' asks Joe.

'She's with Aunt Kerensa in the big field putting the daffodil bulbs in, so Donna won't feel overwhelmed when she gets back.'

Shit! He was supposed to tell them about Donna.

He coughs. 'Ah, about Donna...'

'She's away for a couple of days or so,' says Jago,

looking shadier by the minute and arriving with the tea tray. 'A little trip out on a boat. Cat told us. Said you'd given the green light for her to go.' He picks up his cup and murmurs, 'What with the ankle monitor, and everything.'

'Yes. That's right. I did,' says Joe. 'Did she phone you at all?'

'Us?' asks Jago.

'Yes.'

'No. Cat phoned us on the real phone,' explains Lamorna.

'We don't have mobiles, you see,' adds Jago.

'*Cat* told you?' says Joe, thinking, *weird...*

'Yes. Donna must have told Cat about it, or texted her or something,' confirms Lamorna. 'She said that we were not to worry and absolutely not to inform the police that she's gone away, which was an odd thing to say, come to think of it, bearing in mind you gave her permission to go. She'll be back either tomorrow or sometime in the next week.'

Tea is poured.

Cake is cut.

Eyes are averted.

Joe, who is already confused, and he's only been in the place a minute, returns to his original point, which is quite important. He takes out his notebook to indicate that this is official.

'Now, Lamorna,' he begins. 'You said that Ruby never leaves your side?'

Lamorna swallows a piece of cake and looks up at Jago, who grabs a tea towel, heads to the sink, and starts to dry a saucer.

'Yes, I did say that didn't I?'

'And as a rule, she doesn't,' chips in Jago from the sink.

'Except when she's with Kerensa,' finishes Lamorna. 'But only sometimes.'

Why – *why* – are things that should be so straightforward always turned into a complicated mess by the Nightshades?

'So... just to confirm,' begins Joe, his hands stretched out as if he's patting the air, 'and this is very important... Ruby the macaw *does* leave your side... sometimes?'

Lamorna holds Joe's gaze while awarding this question some serious thought. Eventually, she nods.

'Yes, she does. But not very often, and usually with Aunt Kerensa, and even then, it depends on her mood because sometimes she's foul with her. Ruby can be a bit...'

'Hormonal,' shouts Jago, still at the sink.

'Well, yes,' agrees Lamorna. 'But also, there's the crow issue.'

'Crow issue?'

'Take today for example,' explains Lamorna. 'Ruby absolutely did not want to go outside with Aunt Kerensa – she was having a right peck at her ear on the way out – but Kerensa is planting daffodils and so it's Ruby's job to shoo the crows off. They like to peck out the newly planted bulbs, you see.'

'The crows?'

'Yes.'

'We've trained Ruby as a scarecrow – an attack macaw, if you like. She's not with *any* of us then, when she's shooing the crows.'

'One sniff of a crow and, poof! A red flash and she's gone – out of the window,' confirms Jago.

'I see.' Joe sits back in his chair and eats cake. His mind is addled.

If Ruby spends time with Kerensa, then Kerensa is in the loop. Kerensa. The only person with a rock-solid alibi who was teaching yoga the night of the murder, which he would think a likely story if it hadn't been checked out by Demelza as being watertight. All of which takes him full circle back to Lamorna again. Jago is still drying that saucer.

'Mr Nightshade,' begins Joe again, turning in his chair to look at Jago. 'You wanted to see me about something. Something to do with Jack Crowlas?'

Jago puts down the very dry saucer and brings the tatty tea towel (Royal Wedding of some description) back with him to the table. He sits down and runs the damp towel through his shaking fingers.

'Yes. You see the thing is, I'd very much like to... well, I'd like to...'

Joe puts his hand up.

'Perhaps it would be best if Lamorna...?'

'Leaves? That won't be necessary.' He makes a swashbuckling gesture. 'One for all and all for one, eh, honeybunch?'

Lamorna winks. 'Hundred percent, Uncle.'

Joe offers Jago a fixed stare.

Jago coughs. 'The thing is, I wanted to clarify something about the night of the... er...'

'Murder?' says Lamorna, helping.

'Yes. Quite. Exactly. Murder. The thing is... about the note...'

'Which one?' asks Joe, deciding to go straight for the kill, because there is absolutely no point letting the old boy get himself into deeper water. 'The one telling you the pig had gone missing or the one *you* wrote telling me to frisk an animal after the performance?'

Jago's face is a picture of wretchedness. He looks at Lamorna, who doesn't appear in the least surprised by Joe's statement but simply shrugs as if to say, *I got nothing*.

'Did the note have his dabs on it?' asks Lamorna, who's beginning to enjoy this, clearly.

Jago's face is ashen. 'Dabs? But I... I...'

'Your uncle writes up the minutes at the bowling club,' explains Joe. 'A handwriting expert confirmed the note as being written by the same hand.'

'Ooh, clever,' says Lamorna. 'There really are such people then? Handwriting experts? Do they get paid much because I would be good at that, and we could do with some extra cash?'

Jago puts his head in his hands and lets out a low moan while Lamorna pulls her harp towards her and starts playing the slow and haunting 'Clair de Lune' very quietly.

Jago eventually looks up.

'In that case, I suppose there's nothing for it but to confess to everything.'

The harp stops.

'Confess?' repeats Joe.

No, no no! He's got a vicar who's about to do that.

Jago takes a blue handkerchief out of his trouser pocket and flicks it open. He blows his nose.

'I mean, I didn't actually tighten the collar around his neck,' pleads Jago, 'or drug him, but I *did* put him in the kennel, yes, I certainly did that, and I also put the zip tie in the dog collar – but that was only because the other one kept slipping, not to kill the man. By the looks of things, I almost certainly played a part in the poor chap's demise. Most unfortunate, most unfortunate.'

Lamorna reaches a hand across the table. 'Don't worry, Uncle. For a start, the man was a psychopath, not a poor chap, and second... Joe doesn't usually carry cuffs with him, so you won't be humiliated when he takes you in.' She pats his hand.

Joe clicks the top of his biro and prays to God that he can get Jago out of whatever mess he's got himself into.

'Just tell me what happened,' he says.

'From the beginning is usually best,' says Lamorna, winking at Joe.

'I wouldn't know where to start,' says Jago. 'And Donna... she's going to be so disappointed in me when she finds out.'

'Because you got involved with Jack?' asks Joe, his tone gentle, consolatory.

Jago, in a moment of clarity, looks over his spectacles as if Joe is speaking a different language.

'No. Because I didn't cover my tracks properly. First rule of the Nightshades: always cover your tracks properly.' He looks at Lamorna. 'I'm afraid I never was quite as clever as the rest of you.'

Lamorna nods in agreement.

'Perhaps you could begin with the note you sent to the police station, Mr Nightshade.'

'Jago, please.'

'And then perhaps tell us about the dog suit. Donna said you ordered a new one because you lost the old one at the pub, but I'm guessing you ordered it for Jack. Is that correct?'

Jago nods. 'It was all such a very strange turn of events really, and it all happened so quickly – too quickly – just in a day. And I had absolutely no idea that it would come to this. No idea at all…'

His hands start to shake again.

'Perhaps a whisky?' says Joe.

'I'm on it.' Lamorna jumps up to do the honours.

'From the beginning then, sir. When you're ready…'

Jago dabs his eyes with the tea towel and clears his throat. 'I was in The Star, enjoying a pint of that nice crisp Polgoon cider – they're doing ever so well down there nowadays, you know.'

'That is such great stuff,' says Lamorna.

'It is. It is.'

Joe coughs.

'Yes, right. Well. I was sitting in one of the booths at the back of the pub doing the *Daily Mail* crossword…'

Lamorna lets out a groan.

'I know, I know, but I'd done *The Times* already and I fancied a quickie, when Donna appeared. I was about to shout out to her when Crowlas walked in and, to my horror, sat down at a table with her.'

'I can corroborate all of this,' says Lamorna with great sincerity. 'I was there, too.'

'That won't be necessary,' says Joe. 'Go on, Jago.'

'I moved booths to hear what they were talking about – I'll confess that I was worried he was trying to involve her in his nefarious ways again.'

'Which he was,' adds Lamorna.

'Which he was,' agrees Jago. 'And that ankle monitor she has is not a good look on her; I'm hoping she can get it removed sooner rather than later.'

That'll be a dig in Joe's direction.

'When I heard what he wanted…'

'Which was?'

'Oh, the usual – alibi, drugs drop and a whole host of nonsense to do with taking control of our home. I thought, this man is never going to let my poor Donna go. He's going to ruin our lives forever if we let him carry on this way, and I thought… well, as the man of the family who hasn't been very good at being the man of the family…'

'Oh, Uncle, you have. You *are*—'

'No, hear me out. I thought, really, I must do something about this. But then, poor Donna, she suddenly jumped up and screamed out that she'd kill him, and then I thought… I've already lost enough family members to this man; I'm going to sort this blighter out once and for all. So, when she left, I sidled up next to him with a pint of cider in my hand and told him I'd help even if Donna wouldn't, with the drop and the alibi – I said I'd even give him one of those houses we own at Sennen; they're worth a pretty bob or two, done up – just so long as he left us alone. And right then and there I came up with, if I say so myself, quite an ingenious location for him to drop his stash *and* the perfect alibi.'

'Which was?'

'At the Minack, during the play. We worked the whole thing out in the booth at the pub.'

'And what was the plan?' asks Joe.

'For a start, it wasn't Jack who ran onto the stage at the beginning of the performance, it was me.'

Pah! Penworthy was right, thinks Joe. *Damn her.*

'What about the missing piglet?' asks Lamorna.

'Oh, I sent that note to myself.'

'Which is why you burnt it,' confirms Lamorna.

'Burnt it? It never existed outside my imagination. I'd already been to the Minack while Donna and the cast were having dinner in the dressing room and hid a substantial length of rope behind the hessian. I knew that the back of the kennel was on a hinge so, once the door to the audience closed on me and I'd done my actor bit, I secured the rope to the safety rail at the cliff edge behind the kennel – I knew the audience wouldn't see me on account of the hessian screens – and dropped it down. Did you know there's a cave below the Minack cliffs?'

'We searched it the following day,' says Joe. 'Nothing there.'

'Right. Jack, for his part, had already got himself there – at the cave – by the beginning of the play, carrying his stash of drugs, of course. It wasn't what you might call a substantial stash, but he was creaming some off the top, you see, bit by bit. He knew that you – the police – were watching all the harbours and coves, so he was edgy. I explained that all he had to do was look out for the rope after eight o'clock, put on the dog suit I'd lowered down – that is, over the top of the drugs that were strapped to him – and climb up the rope. I had remembered that Jack was always a bloody good climber.'

'And what happened then?'

'Well. What was *supposed* to happen was that *you*, Joe Enys, having received my note, were supposed to search him after the show and put him away for life for smuggling drugs. My dabs weren't in Jack's dog suit because I'd used gloves to attach the collar – didn't want any trace of myself inside that particular suit for when you arrested him, you see.'

'Why did you care about the collar slipping?'

'Dear chap… Because I wasn't prepared to ruin Donna's show with a sloppy costume for the finale, was I? Those suits were shoddily made, and the collar kept coming loose. Anyhow, I might say that the plan was failproof, yes, completely failproof, if it hadn't been for the fact that, you know…'

'He was murdered,' says Lamorna, helping.

'Yes,' says Jago. 'Murdered.'

'To confirm,' says Joe, rubbing his forehead. 'You were in the kennel to start with, and Jack came in through the back panel later.'

'Yes.'

'What time was that?'

'Just after the interval. He still had the hood of the suit down and looked frightfully ill, I have to say.'

'That was probably my fault,' says Lamorna. 'What with giving him the poison the previous day.'

'But how could you tell he looked ill?' asks Joe. 'Wasn't it dark in the kennel?'

'Pete had set me up a little light. We traded places and I shimmied down the rope. He untied the rope and threw it down. Presumably he then dashed back into the kennel, and I rowed off. To be fair, I didn't lie *completely* about the fact that I wasn't there. There was just no pig with me.'

'A minor, inconsequential detail,' says Lamorna, helping again.

'I did row round to Nanjizal, where there were no policemen waiting, so he might just as well have come ashore there and not got himself embroiled in my elaborate plan. I dashed up the road to the Minack and waited in the shadows for the play to end. Oh dear, oh dear. I told him it would be the easiest performance of his life because all he had to do was play dead. Oh, the irony. It's dreadful, really.' Jago returns to his occupation of burying his face in his hands.

'And if he hadn't died for real, what was supposed to happen next?' asks Joe.

Jago rubs his face and looks up. 'He was supposed to take his bow, leaving the dog suit hood up of course, make a sharp exit out of the Minack and escape with the drugs.' Jago taps his nose. 'But I'd tipped off the police to arrest him, hadn't I, young man, so that was never going to happen. I believe it's called a "double cross". I suppose the question is,' went on Jago, reading Joe's mind and cutting everyone a second piece of cake, 'what on earth happened in the space of that hour, give or take, while he was waiting in the kennel? Basically, who put the knife in? And how on earth did the drugs travel from inside Jack's dog suit to the inside of Gabby's rucksack in the dressing room?'

'And who injected him with deadly nightshade?' asks Lamorna, which provokes a bit of a stare from Jago, Joe notices.

This takes some digesting.

They eat more cake.

'Just to confirm… again,' says Joe, 'it was you who glued the zip tie to the inside of the dog suit's collar?'

'Me? Yes. It was Gabby's idea. The original one was too slack, you see, and it kept coming undone during the performance meaning that the hood fell. So I reasoned that the same thing would happen to the new one and give the game away. Gabby has the same problem with her vicar's collar, so she suggested I use a zip tie – for my own costume, of course. She didn't know about the double cross, oh my word no. That would never do for a vicar. She even gave me a packet of them – the zip ties. But then, when I heard it was the zip tie that had strangled him, I panicked and hid the rest of the ties in Donna's greenhouse.'

'Why didn't you just throw them all away?'

'Throw them away?' repeated Jago, his brow furrowed into disbelief. 'My dear, dear chap, we don't throw away plastic at Penberth. It's bad enough that those wraps are single use! Also,' adds Jago, his memory miraculously returning, 'you might want to know that when I left The Star pub that night, Jase Clarkson walked in. I had forgotten my spectacles and went back inside, and Jase and Jack were already heading upstairs.'

'Lovers!' declares Lamorna.

'Partners in crime,' I believe,' offers Jago. 'Although "lovers" is equally plausible,' he adds with a shrug.

'And did anyone else know of your plan?' asks Joe.

'No one,' says Jago.

'I did,' says Lamorna. 'I heard you talking…'

'Don't tell me, at The Star,' says Joe.

'Well, yes, but I also heard Jago telling the whole plan to Skinny Pete. And Kerensa knew, too.'

It's Joe's turn for his head to fall into his hands.

'I'm sorry I didn't tell you everything before, Joe,' adds Lamorna, 'but as you know, the Nightshades never grass up their own.'

Jesus help me, thinks Joe.

Chapter Thirty-Three

Once Jago starts to talk, the flood gates open, and Joe soon discovers that Pete and Jago have got themselves involved in a dodgy financial pyramid scheme – not that they knew it was a pyramid scheme at the time; they thought it was a failproof investment portfolio that increased its revenue with every new member they attracted.

'Poor, naïve Uncle,' says Lamorna.

You complete idiot, thinks Joe.

'And who was it that sold you the scheme, Mr Nightshade?' asks Joe.

Jago looks at his hands, which have become fascinating. 'Cat, Donna's friend. She said she'd been given an insider tip by one of the panellists on *The Apprentice* when they popped into Lidl for pastries; they're incredibly good value for money, you see.'

'But why did you want the money, Uncle?' asks

Lamorna, the harp having been silent for quite some time now.

Jago shrugs. 'Why else? To help the family. To help Donna. And poor Pete just wanted to save up to get married.'

'Married?' repeats Joe, who has never, in the many mornings he's chatted away with Skinny Pete while waiting for his coffee to be made, gleaned any inkling of a love interest on the scene.

'Married to whom?' asks Lamorna, her eyes narrowing.

Jago shrugs. 'Well, to Donna, obviously. He's crazy about her.'

Joe takes a deep breath and visualises putting the cuffs on Pete.

'But to return to the original point,' says Joe, because he hadn't necessarily meant for Jago to tell him about his dealings with Skinny Pete – that was just a bonus. 'Why did you tell Pete about your plan to double cross Jack Crowlas?'

Jago falters and shrugs. 'I'm not sure, exactly. Just to show that we would have our revenge, I suppose. He's a very close friend, and it's nice to run through a plan with someone else, don't you think?'

Hmm.

'And, of course, I knew Pete wouldn't grass me up because he'd do absolutely anything to help Donna.'

'Does Donna know all of this?' asks Joe.

'About the pyramid scheme? Dear me, no.'

Lamorna straightens her harp. 'He means, is she aware that Pete loves her, Uncle. Joe has a personal interest in that issue, you see.'

Joe flushes but looks at Jago for an answer, nevertheless.

'She possibly may have guessed,' says Jago. 'But I don't think she'd ever entertain the concept. Tell me, young man, did we'—a look towards Lamorna—'kill him? Did the fact that Lamorna issued the brugmansia and *I* secured the zip tie to the collar in the afternoon – not knowing, of course that she was doing this – actually, and inadvertently, lead to his death? Basically, are we murderers?'

'We are not,' says Lamorna. 'Are we, Joe?'

Joe takes a moment to digest both the information and his last bite of lemon drizzle. He swallows. The pathologist said that on their own the brugmansia didn't kill him, the collar didn't kill him, and even the deadly nightshade didn't kill him, but should he reveal this to the Nightshades? Why not?

'What did kill him then?' asks Jago, having had confirmation about the deadly nightshade.

'That would be the knife,' says Kerensa, gliding in with Ruby on her shoulder.

'Oh, hello, Sis,' says Jago, jumping off his chair and heading to the Aga. 'This is Detective Sergeant Joseph Enys. He's just popped round to ask a few questions. I can't remember, have you two met before?'

Kerensa slides onto a chair next to Joe while Ruby decamps to Lamorna's shoulder.

'We have indeed. It was a very memorable day.'

'You mean, the day he locked up Donna,' says Lamorna.

'Yes,' purrs Kerensa, her voice pure gravel.

Great, another woman who hates me, thinks Joe. He looks down at his notepad as a distraction but mainly to try and make sense of the diatribe of information Jago has just released. He sees a note he made earlier:

Macaw feather is a match – grill Lamorna.

'Lamorna, I was asking you about Ruby—'

'I'm not under arrest, then?' pipes up Jago from the Aga.

'Not today, sir, no,' says Joe.

Jago starts to hum 'Sweet Caroline'.

Joe turns to Lamorna. 'Where was Ruby during the performance? Was she with you at the Minack, or…?'

'She was with me in the music tent.'

'For the whole evening?'

'Most of it. She popped out during the 'Adagio'.'

'Why, does she not like Italian music?' Joe's joke falls flat.

'She loves it, but I play it on the violin, which is kind of hard with a macaw on your shoulder, so she went off to find somewhere else to perch. She probably popped outside.'

'Why are you interested in Ruby, Mr Enys?' asks Kerensa.

Joe considers this. Should he tell them the truth about the toy train and the feather? He remembers that they are Nightshades so, no, he definitely should not tell them.

Kerensa moves on anyhow. 'She's nearly thirty years old, you know. Aren't you, poppet?'

'Wow!' says Joe. 'And how old is that in parrot years?'

Kerensa raises an eyebrow. 'Thirty. And she's a macaw.'

'Right.' Joe closes his notebook. He needs to get away from this madhouse and have a think – assess what he's learned so far: Jago lured Jack into the kennel – which means the question of the drugs and why Jack was there is taken care of – but there's still the question of the feather, and also Skinny Pete, who is now very truly in the frame; except Joe's already got his man (woman) – the vicar... or has he? He changes his mind about holding back. Sometimes shock and awe is the best option. He stands and heads towards the door.

'Thank you for your time,' says, Joe, 'and for the tea, Mr Nightshade. There is just one last thing...' He turns towards Kerensa. 'You asked why Ruby is important to the investigation.'

'Did I? Oh, yes. And?'

'You're aware that a toy train and track were found with Jack inside the kennel?'

'I was.'

'And that the train wasn't part of the play – it was placed on him deliberately, after he died.'

'Was it? I wasn't aware.'

'What's interesting is that we've found a fragment of one of Ruby's feathers between the train and the track, which were glued together.'

'Goodness,' says Jago.

'My, my,' says Lamorna.

'Bullshit,' says Kerensa. 'How do you know it's Ruby's feather?'

'Macaw feathers are the same as fingerprints,' offers Lamorna. 'I helped you with that, didn't I, Joe?'

'You certainly did, Lamorna, thank you. And if Ruby only ever spends time with the two of you...'

'Then one of them must be the murderer!' shouts Jago, thrilled to have solved the crime. He coughs. 'Although that can't be correct, clearly.'

'No, it can't,' says Kerensa, who's looking a little too much like a diva for a woman who's a yogi and a Buddhist.

'Why can't it?' asks Joe, not a little mischievously.

'Because neither one of us, you'll remember, could have possibly gone into that kennel! I was giving yoga classes all night from here, and Lamorna was stuck in the music tent. You saw her there yourself.'

'The silhouette of her, yes,' he says.

'But that could have been someone else entirely – another musician,' says Lamorna, clearly excited at the prospect of getting stuck into the minutiae.

'Not with a bloody parrot on their shoulder,' says Kerensa.

'Macaw,' corrects Lamorna.

Circles. That's what Joe is going around in. Circles.

'How old was the feather?' asks Jago. 'Did they say?'

Shit. That's a good point. Joe must remember to ask.

'They didn't say.'

'Because that feather could have got caught on the track years and years ago,' explains Jago, clearly desperate to get the two women off the hook. 'Out of interest, did the train have a little bit missing out of the chimney? Dog chew marks on one of the wheels?'

'It did,' confirms Joe.

Jago turns to Kerensa. 'When did we buy Donna that train set? Thirty or so years ago?'

Three pairs of eyes fix on Jago. He doesn't notice; he's gone way too far down memory lane to stop now.

'Oh, she loved that train,' he says. 'Poor old Schooner – our dog – chewed on it like a bone when he was a puppy. Donna didn't mind. I thought that old train set was in the attic with all the other train memorabilia? Fat controller costume, whistle – she had the lot. I bet you didn't know she went through a train spotter phase...'

Joe didn't, and he can't decide which bit of the sentence is the most illuminating.

'Could we have it back, do you think, after the investigation?' asks Jago. 'Only, it's of great sentimental value...'

Joe sits back down. He opens his notebook. 'You believe that the train found next to Jack's body belonged to Donna?'

'I don't *believe* so, young man, I know so, if the chimney is dog-chewed' The penny starts to drop. Jago blushes.

'Where was the train kept?' asks Joe, while thinking, *shit, I've put a ruthless murderer on a boat with a bunch of drug dealers. She'll be laughing all the way to the bank.* He's also annoyed that he's probably lost fifty quid.

'In the church hall,' states Kerensa, who gets up and opens the kitchen door, encouraging Joe to leave. 'It *was* in the attic, but Donna gave all her old toys, and some of Lamorna's, to the vicar a couple of weeks ago, so that the local mother and toddler group could entertain their kiddies while they sit around gossiping. Anyone could have got their hands on that train, Joseph Enys. Anyone.'

Particularly someone who knew Donna well and was trying to stitch her up, thinks Joe, grateful to have that fifty quid back in his pocket.

Joe closes his notebook with a snap and steps through the kitchen door.

'Don't leave the county, Mr Nightshade.' He throws a hard stare in the direction of all of them. 'Or any of you, in fact.'

'Leave Cornwall?' exclaims Jago. 'Why on earth would I want to do that, young man? I never venture east of Penzance!'

Chapter Thirty-Four

J oe enters the interview room at the station with one hell of a headache, purely because of the conversation he's just had with the Nightshades. Even worse, on his way back to Penzance he detoured to the promenade to question Skinny Pete, who was serving coffee from his van, which hasn't helped the headache. After a long, drawn-out discussion involving a great deal of lying and then lamenting on Pete's behalf, Joe has concluded that although Pete's a first-class idiot, he's probably not a murderer, although Pete did hurry to get off the phone when Joe arrived, and it was likely a call from Jago Nightshade, because their stories matched up a little too perfectly for Joe's liking. When asked what he knew about the effects of deadly nightshade if ingested, he took a piece of paper out his jacket pocket and handed it to Joe.

'It's all in there,' he said, pulling the shutter down on the coffee wagon and gesturing to Joe to join him around the back. 'I looked it up on the internet after I read the article about Donna; the one written by that Jase arsehole.' He pauses. 'It might sound odd, but it spurred me on to... well, I've made her a tiny vial of poison – deadly nightshade – and hung it on a necklace. It's a cut-glass vial so it's classy.'

Joe doubts it.

'Only, it's her birthday coming up and Donna loves that kind of thing – she sees herself as a bit of a pirate, you see.'

Odd? Thinks Joe. *It's Weird! Totally weird.*

'You love Donna,' said Joe.

'I love Donna,' said Pete.

'What was in the package you stuffed into the slipper at Lidl?'

Pete gulped.

'You left it there for Cat, didn't you.'

'What can I say, Joe? I... don't remember...'

'You were caught on the store CCTV, Pete.'

Pete's head drops into submission. 'It was a vial of deadly nightshade. Cat knew I was making up a batch for Donna and she wanted a bit.'

Joe was going to miss Pete's speciality coffee every morning and was considering getting the cuffs from the car when Pete said, 'But honest to God, Joe, she told me it was for her asthma – low doses can actually help with breathing apparently.'

And Pete had more...

'Please Joe!' he pleaded. 'I'm innocent!' He took out his phone and thrust it towards Joe. 'Google it and you'll see that it really can help with asthma, I swear to God.'

Joe batted the phone away. 'Has Cat ever said to you that she suffered from asthma before?'

Pete stuffed his phone in his pocket and scratched his ear. 'No, but she said the cold weather brought it on.'

'In September?'

'She was getting ahead of the game.'

Of course she was.

'And you didn't think it was weird – a bit, you know, clandestine – that she asked you to leave it in a slipper in the middle aisle at Lidl?'

Pete shrugged. 'She works there, and I thought it was probably illegal to deal in unregistered poisons, so...'

Joe told the man not to leave the area.

———

Back in the interview room, a red-eyed vicar is sitting with a police constable in the interview room waiting for Joe to start the interrogation – no more Mr Nice Guy. Ten minutes in, he's disappointed to find that, if she is to be believed, Gabrielle Jones is more sinned against than sinner – just about.

Joe says: 'I am showing Reverend Jones several pieces of paper with numbers written on them. The numbers are references to religious passages. Do you recognise these pieces of paper, Reverend Jones?'

Gabby closes her eyes and says, barely audibly, 'I do.'

'And was it you who sent them to the deceased, Jack Crowlas?'

'I did.'

'When?'

'Over the course of the past week or so.'

'Why?'

'I wanted to remind him of the ways of our Lord and to encourage him to walk a more enlightened path.'

'Right. And did he know they were sent by you?'

'I have no idea.'

'You used religion to put the frighteners on him.'

She doesn't answer but is aware enough to look contrite.

'And why would you think Jack Crowlas would know what the references meant?'

Gabby's expression lightens. This is easier territory. 'Jack's father, who he lived with when he was young, was a religious man – abusive too, which is why Jack turned away from religion. It was a tragic story... such children often travel down a non-conformist path when they're older. I was just trying to help him find his way home. In Lithuania, he began embracing Christ, often attending church...'

'Interesting,' Joe says, glancing up at the constable with a bit of an eyeroll, 'especially as Jack Crowlas's dad died in a road accident in Camborne when Jack was a toddler. And as far as I know, his mum – who admittedly was a devoutly Christian woman – never took up with anyone again.'

'But... I thought it was his father...' Gabby's face is pure confusion.

'I think you've been strung along with a nice little sob story, Vicar,' says Joe. 'Either that or you're lying to me.'

'I assure you; I am not.'

Joe takes a deep breath and examines his hands before asking, 'Did Jack know you're the vicar at Penberth?'

'No. At least, I don't think so.'

'And when did you last see Jack – to speak to?'

'October 11th 2018. In Lithuania.'

'And when did you discover that Jack had returned to Cornwall?'

'A week or so ago. I was having coffee at an outside table at the Duke Street Café in Newlyn, and I saw him walking down the road.'

'And how did you get the notes to the deceased?' he asks.

'Through his letter box.'

'That's a lot of notes to send inside a few days.'

'It was,' she admits. 'Several per day. I was hoping to saturate him in the word of the Lord.'

'And how did you know where he lived?'

'I asked around.'

'About Jack Crowlas?'

'Yes.'

'But you thought he was called Simon Curtis.'

Gabby didn't hesitate. 'Yes, it was a shock to find out his real name when I pointed him out to a waitress at the café, and the link with Donna was clearly shocking.'

'But you ploughed on anyway. And you lied to me.'

'I'm afraid so.'

'Why didn't you just say hello and, I don't know, talk to him.'

'I didn't want to see him.'

'Why?'

'It felt... awkward.'

Gabby sighs. Joe knows what this is really all about.

259

'Because you fell in love with him in Lithuania,' says Joe.

'Yes.'

'When you were a prison padre, and he was an inmate.' Joe hates to be ruthless with a vicar but the thing needed to be said.

Gabby glances up. Her eyes flash. 'Yes, yes, yes! I'm a human being, for goodness' sake, not a nun.'

'How long did the relationship last?'

Gabby lets out a deep sigh. 'For a month or so after he was released.'

'Why did it end?'

'He left.'

'Did he tell you he was leaving?'

'No.'

'You were humiliated, then?'

'A little.'

'Angry?'

'Yes.'

'What do you know about Jack's history with the Nightshade family?' asks Joe.

'Only what Donna told me, but you must try to remember that when Donna told me about this man, Jack Crowlas, I had no idea at all that I knew him – that my Simon and her Jack were the same man.'

Joe takes out his phone and shows Gabby the photo he retrieved (stole) from the vestry cupboard this morning – the photo of her in the compromising pose. He says what he has done for the purpose of the police recording and waits for a response, which is:

'You had no right! No right at all!'

He swipes right to show her the photograph of the writing on the back of the photo:

Remember this? Do as you're told and keep your gob shut, or else!

'You were being blackmailed,' he says.

Gabby, having realised the futility of her rant, closes her eyes.

'Blackmailed by Jack Crowlas,' adds Joe. 'What did he want you to do, Reverend Jones? Hide his drugs inside the church kneelers? Kinky sex? What?'

Gabby invokes her right to remain silent.

Joe leans forward. A wild stab of an idea of what's happened is forming in his mind. He decides to throw it out there to gauge her reaction.

'Here's what I think happened,' he says. 'I think Jack Crowlas saw you that day in Newlyn. We already know he was looking for henchmen, for fall guys, for alibis. He wanted you to lie and cheat for him, to be one of the gang – and what better than to enrol a vicar to lie for you. When you said no, he upped the ante and sent you the photo – to blackmail you into being part of his crooked gang. But Gabby Jones – the do-good vicar who's chosen to spend most of her career around thieves and murderers – couldn't have that. You set it all up very nicely. You murdered Jack and framed Donna in the process...'

She shakes her head.

'It wasn't like that,' she murmurs, her head bowed. 'It wasn't like that at all.'

Joe stands. 'You're lying! It was *you* who stole Donna's knife!' he shouts. 'It was *you* who snuck around the back of the kennel in the second half and poisoned Jack Crowlas then stabbed him for good measure! *You* who took the drugs from the body of a dead man and stashed them in your bag. *You* who stitched up Donna by taking the toy train from the box of donated toys and sticking a macaw feather on the track!'

'No,' she screams. 'I would never do that to Donna. Never!'

He takes an evidence bag out of his inside jacket pocket and hands it to Gabby.

'I have handed Reverend Jones a bag containing a vicar's collar.' Gabby takes the collar out of the bag, her expression that of utter confusion. 'Do you recognise the collar?' he asks.

'Of course. It's mine, but—'

'Did you glue the zip tie to the inside?'

'Well, yes.'

'Why?'

'To make it tight. The Velcro tends to slip. But I can't see what this has to do with anything…'

Joe knows that Gabby didn't attach the zip tie to the dog suit collar – Jago did – but she was the one who suggested it, and this might just be enough to get a confession out of her. He signals to the constable to pass him another piece of evidence. This time it's a photo of Jack's face. His dead face, lying on the stage of the Minack. Jago's dog suit collar is next to the face and held open to show the zip tie glued to the inside of the collar.

Gabby finally looks directly at Joe. She has nothing. She closes her eyes, and a sea of big fat tears begins to fall.

Time to go in for the kill.

'Gabrielle Jones I am arresting you on suspicion of the murder of Jack Crowlas. You have the right to remain silent. Anything you say can be—'

'It wasn't Jack Crowlas!' she shouts, halting Joe in midflow. He smiles to himself. It works every time – well, almost every time – and it never fails to amaze Joe what titbit suspects will finally admit to once the classic words, *I'm arresting you on suspicion etc.*, start to flow.

'The person who was – is – blackmailing me wasn't Jack; it's someone else. Someone more terrible than Jack.'

'Who?'

'If I told you that I'd be dead before the end of the week.'

'If you don't, you'll be sent down for murder. Your call. How did this other guy get his hands on the photo?'

Gabby's head drops. 'He must have taken it from Jack.'

'Where? When?' he presses.

'Back in Lithuania. This other man was part of Jack's – Simon's – gang. I'm pretty sure that the reason Jack left me was to get away from this man, all those years ago.'

Joe holds his tongue. The woman is beyond naïve.

'And do you think it's a coincidence that both men took up residence in Penzance?' he asks.

'No. I think the man followed Jack here.'

'Like you did…'

'I came to Penberth a long time before Jack came home.'

'But you knew he'd come home one day, which was why you wheedled your way into the Penberth Church gig.'

Gabby's nostrils are flaring good and proper now. 'All right, damn you!' she shouts. 'I admit it!'

'You *did* know Jack's real name?'

'Yes.'

'And you put two and two together when you met Donna?'

'Yes.'

'And you persuaded her to get you a position here.'

'Yes.'

'Jack must be quite the Lothario…'

She shakes her head. 'Jack was a very sensuous man. None of you really knew him.'

Obsessed, blinded women – Joe saw them all the time. Bonkers.

'And why was this other man blackmailing you?' he asks.

'When he realised I was here in Cornwall, that photo pitched up in the vestry. I suppose he wanted to make sure I didn't tell anyone about his background, that he's a liar and a crook. He's pretending to be straight as a die now. Wandering around the community like a saint, thinking he owns the place.'

Joe takes a deep breath. The woman is wrung out. He decides to take a softer approach.

'You're going to have to give me his name.'

'I can't. If he finds out it was me who told you about him, my life won't be worth living, if I even had a life at the end of it. Better to put me in the cells and be done with it.'

'And that's your final answer.'

'I'm sorry but it has to be.'

Joe nods to the constable to take Gabby to a cell.

When she reaches the door, and with the interview recording switched off, Joe says, 'Do you know where Donna is right now?'

Gabby shakes her head.

'She's on a boat – spending time with the crime ring that Jack was doing business with. She's trying to get to the bottom of what's been going on so that she can clear her name, and hopefully stop more drugs coming ashore.'

Gabby's face turns ashen. 'Why would you let her do that?' she asks. 'These people... this man, if he's involved, he makes Jack Crowlas look like a pussycat. Trust me. If they find out what she's up to, Donna Nightshade is a dead woman.'

'Tell me his name,' he says softly. 'Just tell me.'

Gabby puts her head in her hands and sobs. Two little words eek out from under the hands.

'Jase Clarkson,' she says.

'Say that again.'

Gabby glances up. 'Jason Clarkson.'

'The journalist?' asks Joe, his hands rushing to his temples while he tries to take it in.

'That man is no journalist,' says Gabby. 'That's just his cover. He's a monster. He gets away with it because he's a decent writer, but he's the type to fake references and qualifications, although he did go to a good university – he did a law degree – although… hello!? That was most probably a lie, too. I may have been quite gullible with Jason and Jack, come to think of it.'

Joe closes his eyes.

'Take her away.'

Chapter Thirty-Five

'And you're sure it was Jase Clarkson who sent you the note?'

Joe has resumed his interrogation of Gabby after a brief break for her to think things through, although 'interrogation' is a bit of an exaggeration. He's asking her polite questions, really.

'Yes.'

'Not Jack, who would also presumably not want you talking to people about him or his dealings in Lithuania?'

'Jack wouldn't do that to me. He's quite a nice man, deep down.'

Joe allows himself the indulgence of an eyeroll.

Gabby puts her head in her hands. A guttural wail comes through her fingers. She glances up, bereft. 'I thought I'd made a real difference in his life, I did, truly. But when he left Lithuania, I found out what he'd been up to all along.'

'Which was?'

'Supplying drugs, and also...' She shakes her head in shame. 'Human trafficking. Girls from the Eastern bloc being shipped over here.' Her eyes brighten with tears. 'Although Jack told me that those girls wanted to come to the UK... for hotel work and everything... so he was doing them a favour really... we're all God's children in the end. Even Jase Clarkson.'

Joe can't take much more of this naivety. Is she kidding or what?

'Right. And what else do you know about him, Jase Clarkson – this child of God?'

'Jack called him the cuckoo. Well, that's not quite correct; he called the person pulling the strings the cuckoo, and I assumed that was Jase... until I had a little think about what a cuckoo is and how the drugs pitched up in my bag.'

'In what sense?' asks Joe.

'A cuckoo is a brood parasite. Cuckoos don't bother to build their own nests from scratch but lay their chick in another bird's nest. That chick will hatch first and then throw out the unhatched eggs and then take everything from the mother bird for itself, and that reminded me of someone else – one of the few people who could have stitched me up with the drugs at the Minack.'

'And who is that?'

'Cat.'

Several things run through Joe's mind – mainly the sight of Cat licking Jase's tonsils when they were cosying up on the yacht. Gabby breaks Joe's train of thought (a runaway train by this point) by adding, 'Jack always thought Jase was working for someone else, you know.'

'Really? Seems unlikely,' says Joe.

'No, it's true.' She smiles, remembering. 'Jack had a sixth sense for things like this... It's one of the things that drew me to him...'

'Right, Gabby, listen because this is so, so important. When – how – did Donna meet Cat? Do you know?'

She does.

'Through me.'

This vicar is an absolute menace.

'It was odd, really, come to think of it. I got chatting to her in Lidl last... May, I think it was. She saw my dog collar and asked for help. She said she'd run away from an abusive home a few years ago, only later to have run away from an abusive boyfriend. She jumped on the train in London and stayed on until it came to a final stop and found herself in Penzance – lots of people have ended up in Penzance that way. Anyhow, she was homeless and jobless and wondered if I could suggest anywhere she might doss down for a few weeks till she got her bearings. I thought of Donna straight away, obviously. She's *so* generous. I went straight to Penberth – taking Cat with me – but Donna said she was stretched to the bone and couldn't help, so I took Cat home with me until we could figure something out, but an hour later Lamorna pitched up and said that she'd persuaded Donna to let Cat set herself up in the room above the stables until she'd found somewhere to live. (I think Cat realised that Lamorna fancied her and played on it – flirted with her, you know.) They all became mates very quickly – Cat helped with the flower farm and so on and Donna got her mate at Lidl to give her a job – and eventually Donna found an estate house for her to live in.'

'And did you know that she'd become intimately involved with Jase Clarkson?' he asks.

Gabby's eyes pop out on storks.

Obviously not.

Joe turns to his constable. 'Ask Sergeant Braithwaite if she's got that rundown on Cat – real name Susan Jones – I asked her for. *And* for Jason Clarkson. Relationship history, jobs, criminal record, everything. And I want it yesterday.'

'If you're doing that then you'll need his real name,' says Gabby.

Joe swings around. 'What?'

'He wasn't going by the name Jase Clarkson in Lithuania.'

'Go on?'

'If I tell you, will you let me go?'

And from a vicar, too.

Joe leans in. 'Let me explain something to you. This'— he flaps his hand to and fro between the two of them— 'doesn't work that way. And what you've just hinted at is bribery. I suggest you retract that last remark, especially given that you're on very thin ice and, oh yes, let's not forget that you're a vicar who's under suspicion for murder.'

'Adam Stewart.'

Adam Stewart? Joe's heard that name before... something to do with a witness at a wedding. Jack's wedding!

Shit.

'Thank you.' He stands in the doorway and jerks his head towards the corridor.

'Am I free to go?' she asks, her drained but hopeful face staring up at him.

Balls to it. What harm can she do?

'Yes. For now. Just don't leave the area, and maybe be careful who you fall in love with next time... and keep away from any prisons!'

Gabby doesn't need telling twice. She darts to the door, pausing in front of Joe.

'There's something else... and I know you're going to be pretty cross that I didn't tell you earlier, but I didn't want to get her into trouble...'

These people!

'Go on.'

'On the night of the show, I came off stage and went into the dressing room not long into the second half. Cat should have been there, in the dressing room, but she wasn't. Five minutes later she came in from the back. She said she'd nipped out for a cigarette. After Jack's body was found she said not to mention that I'd seen her nip out of the back of the dressing room. That it might look suspicious. She's quite a heavy smoker so I didn't think anything of it, but now...'

Idiots. All of them.

Joe remembers that it was Cat who had told Lamorna that Donna had gone off on a trip and not to worry or to inform the police. *Jesus.* He takes out his phone and starts to write a WhatsApp message to Donna:

Get yourself off that boat and home – now. And phone me.

The message is undelivered.

His phone pings with another message from his sergeant, Demelza.

A motorised mannequin has washed up at Nanjizal cove. I've got a wild idea I want to share with you. And Donna Nightshade's ankle monitor is showing her bobbing about off Scilly. Shall I send a team in?

Oh, Donna, thinks Joe, now running along the station corridors to see what else Demelza has unearthed. *What the hell have I done to you this time?*

Chapter Thirty-Six

DONNA

I t's a gorgeous day for September and I'm sitting on a RIB being ferried across the glistening waters of a shallow sea that has been blessed by the tender kisses of the Atlantic... which is a more genteel way of saying that I'm being ferried across the wet stuff to meet my new partner in crime, 'Cuckoo'. We weighed anchor at dawn a hundred yards or so from a beach that is so golden and so beautiful that we could almost imagine we'd sailed the seven seas and run ashore in the Caribbean; only this isn't Barbados, this is the island of Samson, which is one of the one-hundred and forty islands, mainly uninhabited, that make up the Isles of Scilly archipelago. My menagerie has more or less sobered up after a quick nap, and as for me... I've drunk so much rum I've no idea if I'm sober or paralytic, but a bit of Dutch courage in this kind of situation never hurt anyone.

As 'deserted islands suitable for a clandestine rendezvous' go it's pretty much perfect, although I'm slightly disappointed that the drug baron I'm meeting hasn't moored up in a superyacht, but then I suppose that's why this lot haven't been caught yet; they've kept a low profile to keep the police away from their door, or out of their hull, more precisely.

As we approach Cuckoo's yacht, I feel that there's something familiar about it but haven't time to consider why because one of the menagerie nods upwards and says, 'Go on then', meaning that I'm to transfer to the other boat and enter the lion's den – or the cuckoo's nest, more appropriately. Not that cuckoos build their own nests, but I'll stick with the imagery for now.

Stepping on board I notice that there's no one on deck so the drug barons must be waiting for me below (to keep up the image of their dominance, no doubt). Even so, all I need to do for the next few hours is pull off pretending to be 'someone who's happy to be a criminal in return for a tidy cut of the profits' and I'll be back at Penberth eating hot buttered toast by teatime. Job's a good 'un. Also, I'm not as nervous as I should be because they will notice that I've got an ankle monitor (if I happen to conveniently remove my Ugg boot) so I should imagine that I'm probably more of a worry to them than they are to me. No, I'm as safe as houses. These people don't know me from Adam.

A head pops out from the cabin below.

It's Jase Clarkson.

Bollocks.

Chapter Thirty-Seven

Absolutely every piece of hardware Cornwall has to offer, which isn't much, has been mobilised towards the Isles of Scilly, mainly because Joe has told DCI Penworthy that the biggest drug haul the UK has ever seen is in his grasp. This is a lie, clearly, as he's no idea if Donna's boat is full of bananas or bullshit, but Penworthy doesn't know that. The coastguard helicopter is not coming, unfortunately, as it has another job off the Lizard peninsula rescuing a sailor who is clinging onto the underbelly of a capsized dinghy (the currents off the Lizard can be quite tricky to navigate, to be fair), and the Isles of Scilly lifeboat is having its rudder fixed having been on a difficult shout last week; but the Sennen Cove lifeboat has been launched, although it will take some time to get there. Nevertheless, by a stroke of great good luck, HMS *Westminster* is carrying out manoeuvres with a Dutch destroyer of some description in the Southwest Approaches, and she's been retasked to power towards the Scilly Isles under their remit of tackling pirating, and the Royal Navy have a helicopter on board to help if things get tricky.

Proper job!

Of course, Joe has no idea if Donna *is* holed up with drug runners – they could all just be an eccentric group of Jack's weird mates that happen to look like animals – but he doubts it. He desperately wants to save Donna Nightshade's arse this time, and this is the only way he knows how... by asking the Royal Navy to turn hard to port and have them steam towards her at a fair old lick. *Not a bad bit of support whistled up on a whim by a local copper*, thinks Joe, who's just shown his warrant to a confused but happy-to-help pilot at Land's End aerodrome. The pilot was just jumping into his Cherokee for a flight around the Cornish coast when Joe rocked up and commandeered both aircraft and pilot. The captain – Wing Commander Ted Hargreaves (retired) – quickly explained that he's been paid to tow a banner behind the aircraft advertising Flambards theme park all day and it would be a right faff to uncouple the banner now.

'The banner can come,' says Joe, adding, 'Can this thing shift?'

It can, kind of, according to the wing commander.

As they take off in the direction of the Scilly Isles, Joe puts on a pair of headphones with accompanying microphone and says, 'You'll get a citizen's commendation for this.'

'No need, old chap. I'm already a DSO,' says Ted, who's thrashing the life out of the poor Cherokee. 'I'm an ex-bomber pilot, so I'm used to this kind of fracas! A woman involved, is there?' asks Ted after Joe has explained the basics of the situation.

Joe laughs. 'How did you know?'

Ted shrugs. 'There usually is, old chap. There usually is.'

Once the wing commander has landed his 'kite' at St Mary's airport (more of a minor aerodrome, really) Joe goes to the incident room at the police station to muster his team. St Mary's is the largest and most populated of the islands so it's a good place to set up a forward incident room and conscript any available workforce from the local constabulary. The resident sergeant, a young, enthusiastic chap called Caden who last saw Joe at a policeman's piss-up in Mousehole two months ago, is in attendance and is happy (ecstatic) to be on board with the job. He can't offer the assistance of his two constables as they're both doing a spot of decorating at a mate's house on Tresco, which is a slightly smaller but ridiculously expensive island across the water from St Mary's, but he's more than pleased to jump on board with whatever Joe needs by himself.

Unperturbed, Joe arranges for the Cherokee to be refuelled and tasks the wing commander with the especially important job of being his eyes in the sky – banner and all if he can't detach it in time. He hands Ted a radio and sends him on his way with express instructions to report back any sighting of possible drug dealers who may be in the process of murdering 'the best-looking woman in Cornwall.'

'Will they be on a superyacht?' asks Ted.

'Nah,' says Joe. 'Just look for a little sailing boat – or couple of boats, most likely – and report back. We'll be in the police RIB searching the western islands and waiting for news.'

'Righty-ho,' says Ted.

Ten minutes later, Joe, dressed in proper police clothing for once, and the overly excited sergeant, are on a very fast RIB and headed to the outer isles. Ted does a low flyby of the RIB just as Joe glances up at the banner to read the words, 'Flambards. Best day of the week!'

Joe smiles, but at the same time feels more than a little bit sick. It's all getting far too real.

Chapter Thirty-Eight

DONNA

It's been a funny last half hour or so. Not funny-ha-ha, just funny.

I'm back on the boat with the menagerie and have the distinct feeling that something rather unpleasant is about to happen to me because, to recap...

When Jase Clarkson ordered me below, it took a while to find my voice because my jaw fell to the floor when I discovered Cat sitting cross-legged on a bunk, filing her nails and looking smug. At first, I thought, *poor Cat, she's been blinded by his ripped abs* (they're honestly not that great), *his perfect teeth and his smooth, calculating words*. But then I saw the 'Ah, Ms Nightshade, I've been expecting you' look on her face and thought to myself... *Hmm, I may have misjudged this woman*. And I have. Cat and Jase Clarkson are Cornwall's very own Bonnie and Clyde. Who saw that coming?

You know? Maybe I did?

Over a bacon sandwich and a cuppa made by Jase on

the cabin's gas hob (as drug barons go, they are at least hospitable), Cat slowly (smugly) revealed her cunning plan – she's Cuckoo, by the way. It went something like this:

Cat, Jase, and Jack knew each other in Lithuania. Jase and Cat played Jack along to get the drugs ashore at Penberth.

'But how did you know he'd be in the kennel?' I asked, thinking, *I bet it was Jago...*

'Jack told me, and because of Jago, too,' she said. 'We all set up the drop together – with your uncle helping out, of all people, so put that in your pipe and smoke it.' (Super villains just can't get the lingo right, these days.) 'I nipped into the kennel in the second half to get the stash from Jack, just in case Jago was double crossing him, and that's when I stuck the needle in.'

'Needle in? It was *you* who gave Jack the deadly nightshade in the kennel!' My powers of deduction were at their peak of astuteness.

'Absolutely,' admitted Cat. 'Easy as pie. He thought I'd snuck in there for a bit of a snog – I mean, as if!'

As if, indeed. The man was a beast.

'I thought Gabby might have an inkling that I'd done it,' she went on, 'but I soon sorted that out.'

'By stuffing the drugs that Jack gave you in her bag?' I surmised.

'Not at first,' she said. 'Jase was supposed to take them from me and hotfoot it out of Dodge, but that damn vicar kept getting in the way.'

'Ah,' I said, 'the classic foiled plan. What a shame. I

suppose once Jack's body was found and the police rocked up and started searching the place, you had to ditch it all.'

'Exactly,' she said, grabbing the nail file from the table and starting on her left hand. 'I had my sights set on you, but I couldn't find your bag in time. Shame to lose it all, though. Jack'd got his hands on some good quality stuff.'

Made sense. But I was confused. She was going to have to elaborate.

'Wait a minute,' I said. 'For some bizarre reason, you arranged a drug drop with Jack at the Minack, but then when you went backstage and let yourself in the kennel, you shoved a needle of poison up his nose with the express purpose of killing him?'

'Exactly,' she said. 'Ten out of ten. Top of the class.'

'It's an old-fashioned kind of a question but... why?'

'Oh, a few reasons,' she said, winking at Jase.

'But why stab him as well?' I asked, thinking, *who is this woman? Could she be any smuggler?* 'Were you worried he'd run out onto the stage once he was poisoned, or...?'

Cat throws her head back and laughs. 'Stab him?' she says. 'Not my style. No. That was a convenient – if dramatic – coincidence. Thanks for that, Donna. You took the heat right off me!'

'Me? What? I didn't kill Jack!'

'Yeah. Right. The whole thing has literally got your name all over it. If I felt any guilt about stitching you up by shoving deadly nightshade up his nose – my genius stroke by the way – I certainly don't now. Don't sweat it though; you'll be shark food before the police nab you. Cut the tag, Adam, let's give the police a nice little trail to follow.'

'Adam?' I said, looking at Jase, who was sitting next to Cat like a bored politician lounging on a bench at the House of Commons. 'I thought his name was Jase? But then, you're not called Cat either... are you, Susan!'

I expected a reaction, something like, 'What?! You had absolutely no right to be snooping around my house, you bitch!' but she just laughed, annoyingly.

'But why on earth did you want to kill Jack if you were all in cahoots together?' (That bloody word is catching!)

Cat started to laugh. It was an evil villain laugh – *mwah ha ha ha ha* – and she was very good at it (not as good as Aunty Donna when she's on a roll, but good).

'Say hello to the widow of Jack Crowlas,' she said, thrusting her wedding finger into my face. 'Who is soon to be heir of Penberth and all that goes with it. We were married last week – sorry I didn't invite you, but it was close friends only.'

'*You* married *Jack*?' I said. 'Never.'

'You'd better believe it,' she sneered. 'Remember last year when you – very benevolently – let me have a house and said, "Me casa es su casa"? You had no idea how right you'd become!'

What. A. Bitch.

'Originally, I only intended to set Jack up as the fall guy for the drugs, you know, to use Penberth as a base, but then when I realised that I could easily get Penberth for myself by other means, well, I knew that the night of your ridiculous play would make the perfect opportunity to "do him in", as they say. Murder really is incredibly easy when you just go for it. Hand over the keys, bitch, because the manor is mine now. All mine!'

Lose Penberth to Mrs Jack? OK. I admit it, I *didn't* see that coming. Except... how to tell her this...

'The Queen is dead. Long live the Queen!' I said. (My deadpan tone and raised eyebrows should have given her ample warning that something was amiss.)

'Exactly.'

'Except, the queen isn't dead, not the original one,' I said, adopting my own resting smug face. 'Here's a little something to pee on your parade... Susan. My aunty, Jack's real wife, is very much alive and is still the legal owner of Penberth.'

'He told me they were divorced,' she said, more to Jase than to me. Jase, for his part, is beginning to look uncomfortable.

'And you believed him?' I scoff. 'You believed Jack?! That marriage certificate of yours will mean absolutely nothing in a court of law. I don't know what his motive was for marrying you, but it was probably as simple as having sex on tap. I suppose he got your knickers off by telling you that you'd be Queen of Penberth, did he?' I laughed my best scornful, pitying laugh. 'You fell for that one, good and proper! What. An. Idiot.'

Her face was a picture of furious realisation. A disgusting thought crossed my mind.

'Urgh... Sex with Jack! Stale fags and Paco Rabanne. Disgusting!'

'It's irrelevant,' she snarled. 'Once word gets out that you killed Jack and then, funny old thing, have done a bunk, the police will close the case thinking that Donna Nightshade was once again up to no good with Jack Crowlas then murdered him when he threatened to take her beloved Penberth, and ran off to Europe with some cocaine smugglers.'

'And what about the real Donna Nightshade?' I asked. 'What are you going to do with me? Because you'll be shitting unicorn bricks before I ever let you get your hands on Penberth.'

She shook her head and smiled. 'Oh, Donna. Always the optimist. We're in the middle of nowhere and absolutely no one knows you're here.'

'Except the tag monitoring people,' I said, adding a shrug. 'They'll have noticed that I've left my inclusion zone by now. They'll know I'm here.'

'Here? Where's here?' she said. 'You sailed off with a bunch of crooks and carried out your deal before moving on to France – which is where I'll be taking the tag by the way. And what with that uncle of yours having been well and truly embroiled in the whole thing, once I pitch up at the manor and you're gone, he'll soon see that he has no choice but to hand over control of Penberth to me. No, I'm afraid the reign of Donna Nightshade – sorry, *Deadly* Nightshade – is over. Not that you've got any idea what being "deadly" really is. You're an amateur, Donna. A fake. The boys will enjoy dealing with you.'

'You haven't the balls to take me on yourself then?' I asked, squaring up as best I could in the tiny cabin.

She sneered. 'Why have a dog and bark yourself?'

An uncomfortable pause in conversation ensued because

we all looked at my ankle monitor which was still in place – it was the elephant in the room, you might say.

Jase (aka Adam, but let's stick with Jase for now), obviously anxious to do Cat's bidding and cut off my tag, told Cat to budge up a bit so he could grab a toolbox from under the bench. It was a tiny cabin and the awkward moving of the cushions to facilitate the lifting of the bench didn't exactly fit with Cat's act. He'll cop it later for making her look like an amateur, that's for sure.

I threw my leg onto the table so that he could assess the ankle monitor – and to piss off Cat. Jase was frowning while assessing the tag (hello! they're not supposed to be easily removed) and with the box on the table he had a rummage around for a suitable tool. I knew Cat would *hate* me flashing my leg at him because her own pins are average to be honest and he did, after all, tell the whole of the *Penzance Packet* readership that I have great legs.

'Kick boxing,' I said to Cat, throwing in a wink.

Bolt cutters appeared, but they were too thick to get under the tag, and then a whole raft of other tools one by one were discounted as they failed to make their mark. Planning was not this couple's forte.

'Things not quite going to plan?' I said, just as Jase threw wire snips onto the table after yet another attempt failed, which riled Cat (ha!) and she shoved my leg off the table in a huff.

'For Christ's sake! Just get me the damn hacksaw, Adam!' shouted Cat. 'I'll do it myself!'

Unhinged. Totally unhinged.

Not wishing to have my leg sawn off and taking

matters into my own hands, I grabbed the cutters and started on the tag because, unlike Cat, I *had* Googled how to get rid of an ankle monitor (many times), and it turned out to be quite straightforward if you knew exactly where to cut, and I did. I'm pretty sure I saw Jase hide a bit of a smile.

With nothing to lose, I turned to him. 'Here's the thing, Jase – sorry, Adam. Cat thinks you're a complete cock and treats you like a piece of crap, so this is the point where you turn around and say, "Not so fast, Susan," because that's her real name by the way, and then you show her your Interpol badge and arrest her – instead of killing me. And then we can all go home and laugh about it.'

Jase flopped down on the bench next to Cat and took her hand, eying her lovingly. 'Interpol?' he scoffed. 'They couldn't pay me enough. How much did our last drop make us, hun? Two-fifty? Three hundred?'

Cat looked up at me with an uncomfortable glance. I knew immediately that she was skimming some profits off the top.

'Well, as lovely as it's been to catch up, my dear friend,' said Cat, heading to the ladder. 'I'm afraid it's time to say our farewells.'

'Not *au revoir*?' I asked, standing.

'Definitely not that.' She turned to Jase. 'Best get moving with the load… and get rid of this one while you're at it. The boys will know what to do.' Jase stood up. 'But first, kiss me, babe,' said Cat, grabbing Jase by the T-shirt. Honestly, it was like watching a pike gobble a haddock.

Jase released himself from her suckers and gestured that

I should climb the ladder. I put a foot on the first rung, but I'd got two little titbits to offer as a parting gift.

'By the way, Jase,' I began. 'She's cheating on you – Cat is. Not with men – at least not that I know of – but with money, creaming quite a bit off the top.' He doesn't respond, which is disappointing. 'And Cat? Don't feel too bad, because he's been cheating on you too.' I lean into him. 'We had quite the session after my interview at Jubilee Pool, didn't we, Jase? Not a bad body, but if I could just give you a quick tip? Remember that it's not the size of the vessel a woman cares about but the motion of the ocean.'

Cat is standing at the bottom of the ladder with her mouth open, but Jase just laughs. And although I have no way of knowing if she is cheating him and I absolutely did not sleep with the damn man after our meeting at the pool (ripped or not), she'll never know for sure now, will she?

'Just get rid of the bitch!' said Cat. 'And make sure it hurts.'

Me and my big mouth.

That was all twenty minutes ago. I'm now back on the deck of the boat I sailed in on, waiting for Jase Clarkson to come aboard. (I can't get used to calling him Adam.)

I've gleaned that they're shortly to head back to France to meet the head honcho of the whole operation. (They really are far too loose with how much information they allow me to hear, this crowd.) A considerable number of Sports Direct bags (filled with 'melons') have been transferred from Cat's yacht to this boat, adding to the not insignificant stash we already picked up at Wolf Rock, and I can see from my vantage point on deck that she's preparing to up anchor and set sail. A piece of two-by-four has been attached to the side of my cruiser. The menagerie grin at me like hyenas (more animals!) and Lizard prods me with a grappling hook while they all chant, 'Walk the plank! Walk the plank! Make her, make her walk the plank!'

Now, there's a certain satisfying symmetry to knowing that I'm going to meet my maker in a way befitting a descendent of pirates, but balls to that. I'm not ready to go just yet. Even so, I simply cannot see a way out of this.

Chapter Thirty-Nine

Meanwhile, Joe and Caden are racing across the tropical-looking but rather chilly azure-blue waters west of the island of St Mary's. Demelza caught them on the radio with news of a tip-off (from a most unexpected source) to say that Donna was being taken to the islands known as the Western Rocks, for 'immediate and untraceable disposal'. Demelza also informed him that the Royal Navy was on their way to help as the lifeboat was a good hour away, so in terms of feet on the ground, it's just Joe and his excitable sergeant.

Joe, who was quick to kick Caden out of the driving seat, is thrashing the police RIB to within an inch of its life. Caden has spent the crossing so far appraising Joe on how he's been desperate for a proper 'cops and robbers' chase in the RIB for 'bloody ages' and here he is now, skimming the tops of waves with the Penzance DS, just like those two coppers in that police drama he watched as a nipper set in Miami that he can't remember the name of.

'This is bloody brilliant, Joe!' shouts Caden, straining to be heard above the roar of the engine and the bang, bang, bang of the RIB as it bounces from wave to wave. But Joe doesn't think any of this mess is particularly brilliant. Firstly, this is dangerous work and he's not sure Caden quite realises what trouble they are in – chasing towards a desolated island, unarmed, in pursuit of bad-arse criminals who are prepared to kill. And secondly, all he can see in his mind's eye is Donna's face as she glanced his way at Porthleven Harbour, when he should have run after her – swum if he had to – and kept her safe, just like he should have done so many times before.

What the hell have I done? he asks himself as the motor powered on?

What the hell have I done?

Chapter Forty

DONNA

While Baboon arses about trying to re-attach the plank to the side of the boat (it fell off as soon as I stepped on it), I take a moment to think to myself, *what would the Donna Nightshade's of old do to get out of this situation?*

If only I'd read all those diaries of theirs, I might have known.

Nevertheless, when I cry out, 'What should I do Great-Great-Great-Great-Grandma Donna? I'm completely in the shit here!' I swear I hear a small yet booming voice answer back within my head saying, '*Bribe them, me hearty! (And then kick the shit out of that Cat woman!)*' Or words to that effect.

Taking the opportunity to enter negotiations with the menagerie while Jase returns to the yacht (to grab the next batch of Sports Direct bags), I take it upon myself to bribe them by offering a greater percentage of the cut if they mutiny and join forces with me. And the bribe has almost worked. I am getting somewhere with that Aeolus fella, because the deal I offer is based on the fact that most people (men) are pretty malleable (aka easily bought) and, as I remind them, we had all got along really quite well over the past twelve or so hours, what with the drinking, the smoking, the dancing and the playing of cards etc. It was as if I was in their gang already. And then Cat makes the mistake of humiliating Aeolus Jones, the ringleader, by shouting across the watery void from her boat to ours, 'Just kill the bitch already, you one-eyed one-handed freak!'

A look of something very interesting passes between us, Aeolus and me. It is a look that speaks of the early whisperings of a mutiny. Fabulous!

All of that happened two minutes ago.

The gang mutinied.

Hurray!

I am now their leader.

Except, I'm kind of not, because Jase has jumped on board carrying a rather big knife and now no one will look me in the eye.

Which is why I need a Plan B, because Jase Clarkson has lashed the plank to the boat correctly this time and is now holding my hands behind my back and pushing me towards the edge, so if I'm going to think of something to save my skin it needs to come to me pretty damn quickly. Aeolus Jones passes him a rope and has the courtesy to shrug his apologies in my direction. Jase begins to tie my wrists together. I'm quite nervous now. Cat flashes the engine up and reappears on the side of the deck.

'Just push her off, you absolute bunch of complete arse-wipes!' she shouts.

Truly. Who is this strange woman I see before me?

I am just about to ask Jase that very question (and then turn around and knee him in the balls, grab his knife, and run it through his throat) when he leans forward and whispers in my ear, 'Grab the knot to keep it secure. It's not fastened. Take a deep breath and when you go in, flounder a bit, go under this boat, and then get yourself ashore staying underwater as much as you can. I've seen you swim. You're amazing.'

Well, well, well.

And like a sharp dart of female perfection, I'm pushed in.

Chapter Forty-One

D S Enys is beyond dismayed for two reasons. The first: according to Demelza, who's radioed in, that damn Jase Clarkson is the 'unexpected source' who tipped off the police regarding Donna's whereabouts; he even gave her their position using the very useful app What Three Words, which Demelza has handily configured into geographical coordinates. All of which means that Jase bloody Clarkson has turned out to be some kind of hybrid between an Interpol copper and an MI6 agent, which also means that if Donna survives this thing, she will see him as a hero: Joe hates Jase even more now.

And the second: he's remembered that the archipelago of the Scilly Isles covers a ridiculously vast area, which is why the police RIB, with Caden now at the helm, is bouncing around between the remote western islands looking for a needle in a haystack – or a Donna in a cruiser, more precisely. Joe has no idea where to start looking because he's now lost communications with Demelza, which means he's lost contact with the ankle tag monitoring people; in fact, he's lost communication with just about everyone, including Ted, the pilot in the Cherokee. Caden is still wetting himself with excitement, while Joe, drenched from the sea spray, is slowly starting to think he might be too late to save Donna, and if he is, he might as well throw himself into the ocean too.

They say you don't know how much someone means to you until they're gone, and never was a truer word spoken, thinks Joe, just as the little Cherokee aircraft, trailing its banner, appears over the brow of an island in front of them.

Joe transmits to Ted, hoping to receive a sitrep, but the aircraft merely waggles its wings before heading off into the distance. Waggles its wings…?

It's a sign! thinks Joe.

'Follow that banner!' shouts Joe, pointing needlessly towards the aircraft.

'Shall I open her up?' asks Caden, pushing the throttle forwards.

'Caden. It's time to give me everything she's got!'

Chapter Forty-Two

DONNA

That was close.

I've clambered onto a rocky outcrop and can see the cruiser and the yacht heading away at a pace, so I think I'm probably OK... except for being wet, very cold, and barefoot. My Ugg boots were weighing me down so much I had to abandon them to the bottom of the sea, which is a shame because I loved those boots.

Bearing in mind my ankle monitor is presently en route to France with Cat, it's doubtful anyone will look for me here... Unless, of course, Jase Clarkson is a good guy after all (Met police? Celestial angel?) in which case, presumably at some point he'll let someone know my whereabouts... except I'm starting to shiver, having spent the past fifteen minutes swimming mainly underwater and only popping up for a breath of air when necessary.

Sitting like a lonely, orphaned child in a cold assembly room, I wrap my arms around my bare legs and realise that I really should listen to my sister more. It turns out that

Lamorna was right about Jase Clarkson being an OK kind of a guy and I'm regretting putting him in my book now, because something very bad is bound to happen to him soon. (Although my book doesn't offer an actual timeline on 'the wrecker's curse', so maybe has a little while yet.)

My thoughts turn to Joe, and I force out a teeth-chattering sigh.

Oh, Joe. Where did it all go wrong?

(Sending me to prison, that's where it all went wrong, but let's not dwell on that right now.)

Let's also not dwell on the fact that he persuaded me to go deep undercover with a gang of miscreants and murderers, placing me in grave danger, which can only mean that he's not in love with me anymore (come on, Donna, he's not in love with you anymore), although the expression on his face as I sailed off into the sunset out of Porthleven Harbour was one of grave concern, and if I ever see him again, fifty quid says he gives me a right dressing down for allowing myself to get into this little kettle of fish. He probably can't even be bothered to waste police resources coming to find me, but I'd really love it if he did... In fact, I'd give anything to be rescued by Joe Enys more than anyone else. I swear, if he were to pitch up right now, I'd fling my arms around him and give him the biggest, most amazing passionate kiss the world has ever seen.

But he's not here, the horizon is empty, and I have to face the fact that when it comes to my childhood sweetheart, it's all over between us, and it's sad, so sad – *'it's a sad, sad situation'* – and it really is getting more and more absurd, because an aircraft has just flown over me waggling its wings while announcing that Flambards is the 'best day of the week' (as if I didn't know – I just love the Victorian village). And when I turn around to look west, it might be my imagination, but isn't that... a power boat heading towards my little rock at great speed? And I can't be sure, but there seems to be a man standing on the bow, and he's smiling a full-beamer and waving his arms at me frantically.

It's Joe Enys!

He has come!

I bloody well knew he would.

I just knew it.

Chapter Forty-Three

DONNA

'Oh my God! That's *so* romantic!' exclaims Lamorna, hanging off my every word while Jago places a buttered crumpet and a pot of tea on the kitchen table in front of me. Kerensa is cleansing my chakras and Ruby is sitting on the meat hook pretending not to be interested. 'And what happened then?! Did you kiss him?'

I take a bite of crumpet before bursting Lamorna's bubble by saying, 'When the first words out of your rescuer's mouth are, "Have you actually lost the brains you were born with, you complete imbecilic idiot?!" you kind of know that it's perhaps not best to grab him by the balls and force a tonsil tickle down his throat.'

'No kissing the copper then?' asks Kerensa. 'Just to be sure.'

I shake my head and offer a *c'est la vie* kind of a shrug.

'Oh, that's such bad luck,' says Lamorna.

'For the best,' says Jago.

'Thank God for that,' says Kerensa, while pressing a cold blue stone to my forehead.

'And after he rescued you,' continues Lamorna – a dog with a bone – reaching across the table to grab herself a crumpet, 'what happened then?'

I take a deep breath. *What happened then?* she asks. This is going to take some explaining. Well, what happened was ...

———

Joe's smile faded at the moment the young copper at the helm (Caden, nice guy, a bit keen) handbrake-turned the RIB up against my little island. Once it had been loosely tethered to an obligingly jagged rock, the pair stepped off and when Joe realised that I was perfectly fine (hello, what about the hypothermia?), the dressing-down followed, which was a bit shouty for Joe. (Fifty quid to me, I think.)

'Well, hello to you too, Joe Enys!' I shouted back through chattering teeth. 'How's about a bit of a "thank you, Donna", bearing in mind that I've uncovered a massive stash of cocaine *and* I know who the local drug baron is – no, really, don't think of thanking me.'

'Wow!' says Caden.

'Stop being dramatic,' said Joe.

'It's my ex-mate, Cat, by the way,' I went on, 'the drug dealer is. Oh, and she's the murderer – Jack's murderer.' (That bit might be somewhat of an exaggeration as I genuinely don't think she put the knife in but let her take the whole rap anyway.) 'And Jase Clarkson saved my life; I think he's some kind of cool spy. I bet you didn't see any of *that* coming, did you, DS Nobody of Nowhere!'

Joe shrugged as if he had seen it all coming, which was more than a little annoying.

Caden, noticing my blue lips, wrapped his police jacket around my shoulders.

'Not to worry, my lovely,' soothed Caden. 'We'll soon get you back to the station and get a nice warm drink down you.'

I looked at him like he was speaking the rare, complex language of an undiscovered Amazonian tribe.

'Back to the station?!' I repeated. 'Are you a man or a mouse?'

He didn't answer so I harnessed my inner Kiera Knightly from *Pirates of the Caribbean*, jumped on the RIB, whose engine was idling, untethered the rope, and began to rev her up.

Joe was shaking now too, but from annoyance most likely. How to explain this to the police...?

'Look. A so-called friend of mine just tried to kill me and steal my home,' I said. 'And if you think for one second that I'm going to let that daft bitch get one over on me then you have absolutely no idea what it is to be descended from pirates – or just basically Cornish! Call yourselves coppers? You are literally within spitting distance of the biggest drug haul Cornwall has ever seen. Are you coming or not?'

I threw Joe my best *I dare you* stare – it always worked when we were kids.

'Too right I am,' said Caden, jumping aboard.

'Just get off the boat, Donna,' said Joe.

I revved the engine again and tried another tack.

'Do you want that fifty quid from Penworthy, or not?'

Joe's lips flickered into an involuntary twitch and I knew I'd got him. He ran a hand through his sexy, salt-thickened hair and turned to Caden.

'You up for another high-speed chase?'

Caden's salivating lips were the only answer Joe needed.

'Viva Kernow!' I shouted as Caden throttled it.

'Viva Kernow!' Caden screamed back at me.

'Just watch where you're going,' said Joe.

God, it really was so good to be alive.

'Wow! Just like a proper pirate!' says Lamorna. 'But how did you get the black eye? And that neck brace looks *so* nasty…'

'Well, that's when things got hairy,' I explain.

'What? Hairier than when you walked the plank?' scoffs Jago.

I throw him a hard stare. 'Yes, Uncle. Even hairier than that.'

Jago takes the teapot to the Aga to refill it.

'Never mind him,' says Lamorna. 'He's just jealous because you're the only true pirate in the family. Go on, Donna. What happened then?'

Chapter Forty-Four

As the police boat approaches Cat's yacht at great speed, Joe can't help but come to a couple of conclusions: firstly, he doesn't reckon they have the fuel to go the distance; and secondly, Donna might not be so optimistic about the outcome of the high-speed chase if she knew that their only back-up until the Royal Navy finally pitch up is an ageing Royal Air Force veteran who's flying circles of the islands while advertising for a local amusement park. Nevertheless, having come to the conclusion that Jase Clarkson must be trustworthy after all (despite the bizarre story about Jase being the 'beast of Lithuania' from the vicar) and that he must be an agent that's so deeply undercover that even the local plod haven't been trusted to know about him, Joe decides to leave the menagerie and the best drugs haul in history to 'that Clarkson knob' and chase after the ring leader instead.

'Don't worry, I don't think she's armed,' shouts Donna

as the RIB comes up fast on Cat's yacht. A shot rings out. They all hit the deck. 'Ah. Maybe she is.'

Regaining a little of the sense he was born with, Joe relieves Caden of his duties at the helm and powers the engine back to idle. If he is going to stand any chance of keeping the three of them alive, he needs to have a bit of a think, which is difficult to do when all he can hear in the background is Donna Nightshade shouting, 'Fire it up, you muppet! She's getting away!'

No, he is going to have to think of something clever – cunning even – if he's going to keep the rogue, wild-eyed Donna out of the clink and keep Caden alive while at the same time trapping Cat.

'Ha! She's luffed up!' says Donna, giving Joe information he is perfectly capable of deducing for himself. 'There's never going to be a better time to reel her in! Come on!'

Joe assesses the scene. Jase Clarkson's boat is headed away at ninety degrees to Cat's yacht – he'll deal with that later (or, rather, the Royal Navy will, because if Joe isn't mistaken, he can see the massive hulk of a warship powering towards him from the south). But for now, assessing his assets, he's not entirely sure that he can catch, let alone net, this fish. The radio crackles into life.

'Pilot calling policeman. Pilot calling policeman. Is that damn blighter shooting at you? Want me to buzz her a bit, scare her off? Over.'

Joe checks the fuel gauge. It's nearly out, which means he hasn't the gas to follow Cat much further, and there's no way he's risking anyone getting shot by attempting to board the yacht. Cat fires out a couple more shots, as if to simply remind Joe that he's not out of the woods – or to sink the RIB, more likely.

'Pilot calling policeman, over. Any instructions? You chaps all right down there?'

Joe looks up. The Cherokee is approaching at no more than three hundred feet above the sea and the banner is flying as straight as a die behind it.

The banner…

A flash of genius crosses Joe's mind.

'Hi Ted, it's Joe here. Are you receiving me, over?'

'Loud and clear, old boy. Loud and clear.'

Joe feels he really ought to get on board with the fighter ace lingo by starting his next transmission with something like, 'I say, old chap, it would be bally good of you if you could…' But goes with, 'Does that banner of yours disconnect mid-flight?'

'It certainly does. I see where you're going with this. Want me to drop it on the blighter, over?'

Joe takes a moment to think. Those banners are lined with thick wire and are bloody heavy; it could kill Cat if it landed badly, and it's more than a long shot that Ted can manage it… An image of Barns Wallace and the bouncing bomb crosses his mind. Surely, if anyone can manage this, Ted can…

Another shot fires out.

Sod it, he'll claim self-defence.

'Yes, Ted. Drop the banner on the yacht. Not on the cruiser. I repeat, not on the cruiser.'

'Wilko,' crackles Ted. 'Over and out.'

Joe turns around to appraise his crew, but where once there was a pirate and a policeman, only Caden's shoes and a bright yellow policeman's jacket remain behind.

'Shit,' shouts Joe, raising his head above the parapet to check the water for bodies. It doesn't take a rocket scientist (or a detective sergeant) to know where Donna (that sharp dart of feline perfection) and Caden (Devon and Cornwall Police open water swimming champion two years in a row) have gone.

There's no sign of Cat on the deck of the yacht, so he scans the couple of hundred metres of water between the RIB and the yacht.

Nothing.

He scans again and notices a head pop up for air, then another, before both, like seals, disappear beneath the waves again. Joe decides that if Donna doesn't die in this fracas, *he'll* bloody well kill her. Another thought hits him. Joe grabs the radio. He needs to stop Ted and 'Operation Drop the Banner' before he has a blood bath on his hands.

'Ted, this is Joe. Friendly forces approaching the yacht. Do not drop the banner. I repeat, do not drop the banner, over...'

Nothing.

'Pilot Ted from Joe the policeman, are you receiving me, over?'

Nothing.

'Pilot Ted, if you're receiving me waggle your wings, over.'

Nothing.

He looks up. The Cherokee is downwind and will be

shortly making its final turn inbound for an approach on the yacht, a yacht that Donna has now reached and is beginning to clamber onto via a rope ladder attached to the hull.

Dear God, thinks Joe. This is turning into even more of a nightmare than before. An image of Penworthy waggling a pig's ear in his face and scowling at him comes to mind.

Chapter Forty-Five

DONNA

'That was so brave, Donna!' says Lamorna.

'But rather reckless,' says Jago, who is at least paying attention now. 'You could have been shot, and where would that have left us, eh?

'With Lamorna in charge,' says Kerensa. 'Because honestly, I'm not up to it.'

'Ooh, that would be rather fun,' says Lamorna. 'And as my first act as queen I'd give all the cottages to the poor, and then—'

I need to grab this.

'Are you listening to my story or not?' I say.

'Of course. Sorry.'

I turn to address Jago. 'But to return to your point, Uncle, I absolutely could not have been killed because the chances of her hitting either of us with a shot were pretty slim. Pistols are not accurate weapons, you know; other than at close range, they're absolute rubbish. *And*, I'd counted the shots – at least, I thought I had, although Caden

thought he'd only heard five, but I was certain I'd heard six
– so I knew she was out of ammo, and having seen Cat dash
below deck after the last shot (while Joe was babbling some
nonsense on the radio to the pilot guy) I quickly persuaded
Caden to swim out to the yacht with me. As I said, he's a
super-keen copper and a champion swimmer. How
convenient was that?'

'You might say unbelievably so,' mutters Jago, before
adding, 'And did you swim with a knife between your
teeth, like a proper pirate?'

Hmm.

'I'm sensing a twang of disbelief from you, Uncle
dearest, which is harsh considering you expected us all to
believe that ridiculous yarn about your pig being on the
rampage at Nanjizal.'

Jago heads towards the dresser muttering something
about getting something stronger to add to his tea.

'Anyhow,' I continue, 'you're not far from the truth
about the knife because – even better – I had already taken
Caden's police-issue nunchuck out of his jacket pocket and
put my gnashers around that—'

'She was wearing it, you remember... his jacket,'
interrupts Lamorna, looking pointedly at Kerensa and
Ruby, just in case they aren't keeping up.

'That's right,' I say. 'When we reached the yacht, the
ladder hanging down the hull was this rope-type affair—'

'Wait a minute. A ladder?' says Jago, returning with a
bottle of rum. He unscrews the lid. 'You're saying she'd left
the ladder down, even though she'd set sail? What kind of
mariner *is* she?'

'A poor one, clearly,' offers Kerensa.

I turn towards Lamorna, the only one genuinely interested in my story as Kerensa is now examining her nails and Ruby is inspecting her feathers with her beak. 'So anyway, once I got on board, that's when we had *the big fight*!'

'Fight! Fight!' squawks Ruby, glancing up.

'I thought that word might pique your interest, Ruby,' I say. 'Exactly. A fight!'

'And did you whack her with the nunchuck or... wait! Even better. Did you go all-out bare-knuckle fighting?' asks Lamorna.

(I'm slightly concerned that Lamorna is showing a darker side than I've seen before. She's practically salivating.)

'Whatever happened,' begins Jago, 'Donna didn't come out of it well, did she? Just look at the state of her!'

They all nod and offer me sympathetic glances.

'Wait. What?! This wasn't Cat's doing! You really believe that that skinny cow would get the better of *me* in a fight!'

'Well, if *she* didn't, who did?' asks Kerensa.

'The banner, obviously!'

The penny drops. 'Oh...' they all say in unison.

'But that was after Jase Clarkson shot her.'

'Does anyone else feel like they've turned over two pages at once?' asks Kerensa.

'Right, yes. To rewind a bit. Having noticed that Cat had started to fire shots at the RIB, Jase turned the cruiser around and headed back towards the yacht.'

'Good chap that,' says Jago. 'Always liked the man.'

'And he managed to get close enough to see what happened next, you know, after we boarded the yacht.'

'Which was?' asks Jago.

'Cat shooting Caden.'

'And she killed him!' screams Lamorna, delighted.

'No, she caught him in the arm,' I said. 'I told you they aren't accurate weapons – and then, oh yeah, check this out, she put the gun to *my* head.'

'How inconvenient,' says Kerensa.

'I thought you said she'd run out of ammo,' says Jago.

I shrug. 'Caden must have been right after all that there had only been five shots.'

'C'est la vie,' says Lamorna.

'Sadly ironic,' says Kerensa.

'Improbable,' says Jago.

'Did you whack her one at that point?' asks Lamorna, standing up and moving her arms around like Kung Fu Panda. 'I mean, you knew all the shots had definitely been fired by then, so…'

'Well, that's the thing. I was about to say something really cool to Cat – although to be fair, cool things to say turn out to be quite hard to think of in the spur of the moment – and then nunchuck the shit out of her, but I didn't get the chance because that's when *she* got shot, too.'

'Jesus Christ!' says Jago.

'No, but close,' I say. 'Jase Clarkson. He must have had a gun on him too, because he simply pulled up alongside in the yacht and shot her in the head.'

'Dead?' asks Jago.

'As a doornail,' I confirm. 'Most of the blood on me isn't

mine…' I glance down at my blood-spattered top. 'In fact, I think this bit of mush on my shoulder is possibly a tiny bit of her brain.'

'I'm going to be sick,' says Kerensa.

'But you were saying about the banner?' says Jago, who is more interested in the story now that the action has perked up a bit.

'Ah, yes. The thing you must remember is that this all happened very quickly, and so when the pilot – Ted, I think he was called – completed his run-in and dropped the banner, he hit his target all right, but he couldn't really hit one boat without hitting the other, so just after Jase shot Cat, we all copped for it. Poor Caden was just applying a tourniquet to his arm using the handle of a Sports Direct bag when he got flattened, and the blow knocked me down the cabin steps and that's how I got the whiplash and the black eye.'

'Wow. And what about Jase?' asks Lamorna. 'Did he cop it too?'

'Brain injury,' I say with a shrug. 'The boat took the brunt of the banner, and it was the banner cable that hit him.'

'Ouch,' says Lamorna, putting a hand to her head.

'He's having a bleed on his brain drained in Truro Hospital as we speak,' I add. 'Perhaps, with hindsight, I was a little rash putting him in my book.'

Glances are exchanged.

'But wait a minute, guys, I'll take the rap for Jase,' I say, 'but I can't be blamed for Cat's demise, can I? I never put Cat in my book!'

'No, but I did,' says Kerensa, nonplussed.

'What? When?'

'Oh, I put her in there ages ago,' she says, returning to the examination of her nails. 'I gave her the wrecker's curse good and proper, and unlike you, Donna Nightshade,' she adds, looking up, 'I used my own blood!'

Even Ruby does a double take. The only response is...

'Why?'

Kerensa is all innocence. 'I caught her with her hands in the petty cash, so I hid her name between that internet scammer who fiddled Jago out of his beer money and that weird peeping Tom we had as a window cleaner, God rest his soul. I always felt her aura was too out of kilter to ever be trusted, and I was right.'

No words. Simply no words.

Jago has moved on. 'And what about the other blighters?' he says. (I don't believe he has taken in the true gravitas of the fact that Cat is dead; nor has Lamorna, who is still practising kung fu moves.) 'What did you call them? The menagerie?

'I couldn't say exactly,' I say, 'but Aeolus Jones was whipped by the cable and may lose a leg.'

'An eye, a hand, a cleft lip, and now a leg...' says Kerensa. 'That man just doesn't get a break, does he?'

'So just to confirm...' begins Jago, who has begun to find the crumbs on his plate tremendously interesting. 'Did we ever actually find out who it was that killed Jack? Was it, you know, Cat?'

'Good point,' says Lamorna, taking a seat. 'Although what I think he means is, are we in the clear?'

Shall I toy with them? I wonder. *No, I can't do it.*

'I think so. Once the Royal Navy finally pitched up and removed the banner and arrested the drug den menagerie – oh and winched up Jase and Caden into the helicopter to offer lifesaving first aid – Jase managed to get a message to Joe via the winchman – before he passed out, obviously – that Cat had confessed to Jack's murder.'

'We're in the clear, then?' says Jago, who is looking decidedly chirpier suddenly.

'It would seem so...' I say. 'Except that he's wrong, isn't he?'

'Wrong?' they all say together.

'Cat didn't do it,' I say. 'She told me everything when she thought I was going to be killed. She drugged him, yes, but she didn't stick the knife in, and as we're all painfully aware, it was the knife that killed him. I've no idea why Jase said she's the murderer to the police, but so long as Joe Enys believes him, who cares?'

'If you don't think it was Cat, who *do* you think it was?' asks Lamorna, taking up a guitar that had been resting against the table.

'OK, here goes. I think it was—'

Jago coughs, jumps up, and starts clearing away the tea things.

'Best not to answer that question right now, eh?' he says, shuffling towards the sink. 'Let sleeping dogs lie, don't you think?'

I take a good look at each of them in turn. Only Ruby will look me in the eye.

Kerensa eventually says, 'Agreed. Let sleeping dogs lie.

But what I want to know is, what was DS Enys doing when all this was going on? It sounds to me like he was a bit of a wimp.'

I frown. 'He's not a wimp. He's just careful – thorough. Once he saw that I was on the yacht, he powered up the RIB and headed towards us. But then he ran out of fuel so he ended up being stranded a few yards from the yacht, which was blooming lucky because it meant there was someone who wasn't injured who could sort the whole thing out. It was a bloodbath out there, really it was.' I sigh with the relief of it all being over.

'Great news for Flambards though,' says Jago. 'That kind of publicity is priceless.'

Kerensa rests a comforting hand on mine. 'Banners? Dead and mutilated villains? Aren't you embroidering the story, darling, just a tad?'

'Embroidering?' repeats Jago. 'She could have darned a whole new tapestry with that tall tale by now!'

'Ignore them, Donna,' offers Lamorna. '*I* believe you. Nightshades never lie to each other, do we? It's our code!'

All eyes other than Lamorna's head to the table. After an appropriate pause, Kerensa jumps up. 'Well, that all seems very tidy,' she says. 'But I think we should draw a line under the whole sorry business now and move on.'

'You're right,' I say, placing my hands on the table and pushing my tired and aching body to my feet. A foil blanket that Joe draped around my shoulders in A&E falls to the floor.

'And at least you know who the murderer was, even though we don't, so that's a relief,' says Lamorna.

I place an arm around her shoulders, rip off the neck collar and head to the door; neck injury or not, there's someone I really do need to see tonight, and Ruby is coming with me. With my ankle monitor missing in action, Joe and Penworthy will never know where on earth I am.

Chapter Forty-Six

DONNA

Aunty Donna's prison on Bodmin Moor is a relatively relaxed place, with most of the inmates being seen as delusional women who went a bit awry during the menopause rather than cold-blooded murderers, which is why they've allowed me to bring Ruby with me this evening (they often have 'bring a pet' days so it's no big deal). Aunty Donna and I have been allowed to come out to the garden grounds, even though it's late in the day. Ruby is being remarkably well-behaved. She's standing on a perch in her cage, watching a guard patrol the perimeter.

I retell the story and Aunty Donna throws up her arms in delight.

'How exciting for you! And to think that you caught – well, kind of *killed* – a gangster and captured her mob, as well as leading the police to a massive drugs haul! Of course, you were never in any real danger, none at all.'

'How so?'

'Darling! All the ancestral Belladonnas would have been

watching over you from the great celestial plane and urging you on, acting as illuminating beacons to show you the way. They would never have let anything bad happen to you!' she says. 'Never!'

Aunty Donna takes a seat on a bench as I rest Ruby's cage on the grass. 'Tell me,' she says. 'Have you cracked your first case yet? Have you worked out how it was done?'

'You mean Jack's murder?' I say. 'I think so.'

I'm unable to hide the smug smile that's leaking across my face.

She pats the bench. 'Well sit down then and tell me all about it… from the beginning!'

From the beginning? I scratch my head. Where to start?

'After a little confusion early on regarding Jack's final hour on stage in the kennel – what with the administering of two different poisons and a strangulation with a zip tie – we figured out that, when it came down to it, the case of who was the murderer all boiled down to one question…'

'Ooh. Brilliantly gruesome. Which was?'

'Who stuck the knife in? Jack didn't die until he was stabbed, you see. The poison probably wouldn't have polished him off by itself.'

'Of course it wouldn't,' she says, shaking her head and sighing. 'But I'm confused… what do you mean, *we*?'

Ah.

'Oh, right,' I begin. 'That would be myself and Joe Enys, the detective sergeant on the case. We decided to work on it together.' Her expression blackens. 'Well, when I say "together" I mean, sort of, kind of, a little bit, hardly at all, really.'

'Do you mean *the* Joe Enys... the young buck you used to play with at school? The police person chappy who sent you to prison?' There is a venomous edge to her pronunciation of *police person*.

'Yes, I suppose I do.'

'Hmm.'

'But moving on... because you must be wondering why on earth Jack was in the kennel in the first place...'

'I am, rather,' she says, perking up. 'Odd place for a brute like Jack to find himself.' She shudders at the thought of him.

'That was all Jago's fault.'

I explain that Uncle Jago had overheard me threaten to kill Jack in the pub etc. and go on to describe how Jago came up with a cunning plan of pretending to help Jack with the drug running, but with the intention of dobbing him into the police in the process.

'A cunning plan?' she says. 'Orchestrated by Jago? Oh dear. He's far too innocent to be coming up with any kind of a plan, let alone a cunning one.'

I must agree. 'Although, to be fair, despite a random story about rogue pigs giving him away, his plan kind of worked, except for the fact that Jack was murdered rather than arrested.'

'And hurrah to that!' she says, punching the air. 'In that case, despite not thinking out his plan properly, about which I will have words with him, give my brother a medal. What *was* his plan, exactly?'

'Right. According to Joe, who Jago confessed to, to start with, he told Jack to row to the cave at the bottom of the

Minack, you know, the one at the bottom of the cliffs behind the stage?'

'I know it well, go on...'

'There was a panel that opened at the back of the kennel that the audience couldn't see, so once Jago ran in and closed the door behind himself at the beginning of the play, he quickly dashed out of the back – actually, he might have dashed out after the interval – and dropped a rope down to the cave so that Jack could shimmy up.'

'And where did he hide the rope?'

Hmm.

'I'm not sure. Joe didn't say. In his own dog suit? Or maybe he positioned it there beforehand... one or the other.'

Aunty Donna sighs out her disappointment in my lack of clarity.

'Anyhow, Jack shimmied up the rope and took Jago's place in the kennel, wearing a different dog suit and with the drugs hidden around his body on the inside – the police were watching all the ports, you see.'

'And did he shimmy up while wearing the dog suit, because that would be difficult, especially while carrying all those drugs?'

She's right. It would. Except...

'The drugs were strapped to his body, and I think, perhaps, Jago had hidden the suit in or behind the kennel when he prepared the rope,' I say.

'Where exactly?'

Hmm.

'Again, not too sure on that one.'

Another sigh. *I need to grab this.*

'And where did Jago go once Jack was in the kennel?' she asks.

'He shimmied down the rope.'

'But didn't you all wonder where Jago was during the performance? After all, if the latch was put on there for the sole reason of giving Jago a break from the kennel, didn't anyone think to go and look for him?'

'No, because the cunning crow told us that he'd changed his mind about coming backstage and was going to take the opportunity to finish his book – some classic tragedy that he'd got into a heated discussion about with one of his academia friends. He didn't want to be disturbed, he said.'

'And none of you thought that was a little odd?'

'Odd?' Aunty Donna has been away from her family for far too long. 'This is Jago we're talking about. Hiding away in the kennel while reading is *exactly* what I would expect him to want to do.'

'Well, true,' she agrees. 'But back to the murder.'

'Ah, yes. Jack, you see, was already feeling a little dodgy on account of being drugged – well, poisoned – by Lamorna.'

Aunty Donna begins to positively beam with delight.

'That's my girl!' she says. 'But how? Why?'

'I believe that—'

'You *believe*, or you know?' she interjects.

This could be going better.

'I *know*, well, as certain as I can be with my sister, that she took it upon herself to kill Jack once she knew he was back in town – to protect me and the family, you see.'

'Of course she did. Wonderful creature.'

'So, she got Kerensa in on the act…' I say.

'Kerensa?' Aunty Donna lets out a cackle. 'My, my. Her tiara really is slipping…'

'Well, quite, and they decided to drug him with brugmansia by lacing a pasty the night before the play, and then they lured him onto the rocks and pushed him off. Basically, they tried to kill him.'

'Using brugmansia?' her tone is one of disparagement.

'I'm afraid so. He obviously survived that attack.'

'Of course he did. It was the wrong poison for a thick-set man like Jack.'

'They realise that now,' I say, 'but the point is, the autopsy found traces of brugmansia in his system, which is why Lamorna confessed to Joe.'

'Please refer to him as DS Enys, darling. I really don't approve of the familiarity you've developed with this man.'

'Fine, so anyway, *DS Enys*, decided not to prosecute her because…' (I almost say, 'because he's nice like that' but correct myself) 'because it wasn't the brugmansia that killed Jack.'

'Clearly. And yet Jack died on the stage at the Minack. How?'

'This is the thing… Quite by chance, several people intended to do Jack harm that evening, and it all kind of came together in one very big and very convenient crime – although the zip tie was quite coincidental.'

I wait for a comment. None comes.

'So… the next person to want Jack dead after Lamorna, was my friend Cat.'

'The drug dealer? The dead woman?'

'Yes,' I say, my thunder stolen. 'How do you know about that?'

'Kerensa telephoned and told me all about it,' she says, throwing a glance at Ruby, who is being *unbelievably* quiet.

'Telephoned? Since when were you allowed telephone calls at any hour of the day?'

'Since I found out that the Senior Officer is having a fling with one of the inmates.'

'Right. So anyway, Cat and Jack were running drugs together and she had recently married Jack with the intention of killing him to get her hands on Penberth.'

'Over my dead body!' says Aunty Deadly.

'That's what I said. But Cat, once she knew about the plan for the Minack from Jack, decided it would give her the perfect opportunity to do a bit of poisoning herself – and set me up in the process. And that's where the deadly nightshade came in. In the second half, she nipped into the back, pretended to smooch with him, what with being his wife – albeit a bigamist because of you – shoved a hypodermic needle full of deadly nightshade up his nose, and retreated to the dressing room expecting Jack to die.'

'But the new poison didn't kill him?'

'Not according to the pathologist.'

'Oh. Did he have his EpiPen on him?' she asks.

Why has no one asked this question before? I wonder.

'I don't believe so, no.'

'Strange,' says Aunty Donna. 'He usually did. Although it does sound as though this Cat person had the foresight to glue the zip tie to the inside of the collar, so we should give her a little credit for knowing the side-effects of the poison.'

'Ah, but that was a complete coincidence.'

'Another one?'

'Another one. Jago, having worn his own suit a few times down the pub for a laugh and in rehearsal, knew that the dog collar was too loose and got the idea from my friend Gabby, the vicar, to glue a zip tie inside it to keep it tight.'

'Bloody idiot,' says Aunty. 'Although, as you say, coincidentally effective.'

'But even the second lot of poison, and the partial strangulation by the zip tie once his neck became swollen, didn't kill him,' I say.

'That husband of mine really was a complete pig to kill...' she says, throwing out a laugh. 'I mean, I wouldn't be in here if he wasn't, would I? Tell me this, Donna Nightshade: despite all the shenanigans early on, who finally killed him?'

Right, here we go.

I take Ruby out of her cage and place her onto Aunty Donna's shoulder. She flaps and squawks and swears like a dockyard brawler on payday – Ruby, not Aunty – but it doesn't matter because the final piece of the puzzle is solved. I return Ruby to the cage.

'That would be you, Aunty Donna. You killed Jack.'

Chapter Forty-Seven

DONNA

'Oh, darling, your imagination really has started to get the better of you,' says Aunty Donna as I struggle to force Ruby back in her cage. Once her dander's up she's a nightmare to manhandle. 'I blame the internet,' says Aunty.

'Blame whatever you like, Aunty, but we both know it's the truth.'

Her expression darkens, just a tad, but enough to put me on edge. Aunty Donna wasn't known as the Nutter of Newlyn for nothing.

'And you might say that it's an interesting conclusion to reach,' she says, 'bearing in mind that I'm in here,' she nods towards an uninterested guard, 'spending time at His Majesty's pleasure.'

It's not easy to stand up to Aunty Donna – some things simply aren't done – but still, cometh the hour, cometh the man...

'Even so,' I say, 'there are a number of clues leading to only one conclusion...'

'A number,' she repeats, looking more than a little tired with the conversation's direction of travel. 'Be more specific, Donna. How many?' (Seriously, my aunty could give Penworthy a lesson in pedantry.)

'OK, three.'

'And the first?'

'Everyone assumed that one of the players must have done it – put the knife in – because it's regarded as simply not possible to scale the cliffs behind the Minack stage without the aid of a rope, but there is one person who has proven it *is* possible to climb up those cliffs – who knows a secret way up – and that person is you, Aunty Donna. It says so quite clearly in one of your diaries.'

'Oh, you've read them then?' she says, sarcasm dripping off each word like treacle edging its way off a spoon. 'Lamorna suggested that you hadn't.'

'Oh, yes, I've read them,' I say, thinking that I must have a word with Lamorna about sisterly confidentiality.

'It proves nothing,' she says, and bats a dismissive hand in my direction. 'Just because I *can* do something doesn't mean I *did*, and anyway, those old diaries are full of nothing but gossip and lies.'

'So how do you explain the pop-up banners I found hidden in the family crypt?' This is my trump card and I think she's starting to look a little concerned.

'I don't follow you,' she says.

She does and she bloody well knows it.

'You'll not be surprised to hear that I found pop-up murals that slot together quite nicely depicting the backdrop of Kerensa's yoga studio at the manor – you know, the stone wall, the mullion window…'

She waves a dismissive hand. 'So what? That could be a picture of any manor house in England – they all look the same.'

'Do they?' I scoff, gaining confidence. 'And do they all have a stuffed fox head hanging on the wall, too? The one we call Brian? The one with Jago's tricorn captain's hat hanging off its ear… Oh, and the picture of our family is hanging on the wall, too.'

Aunty Deadly rolls her eyes. Kerensa is going to cop it for that.

'And then, of course, we have Ruby.'

A nod towards the cage. 'That damn bird?' says Aunty Donna.

'Absolutely. That damn bird has been nothing but odd with Kerensa lately – one minute happy to sit on her shoulder, one minute not… and that's because she was the only one of us who guessed what's been going on.'

'Which is?' she asks.

'That you and Kerensa have been swapping places with each other! How long has it been going on, Aunty? Weeks? Months? Years?'

She turns away. 'Oh, Donna, that imagination of yours!'

'Is wild, yes, but this time I'm bang on the money. Face it, Aunty: you and Kerensa dreamed up this whole thing together. Once Jago told her about his plan – and he was bound to have told her, or Lamorna did, because neither one of them can hold their own water. I think you'll find that Aunt

Kerensa came to this prison on the eve of the play, swapped places with you without the guards noticing – or, now I know that you've got the governor by the balls, probably *with* the guards noticing – put the banners up in your cell faking her location, logged into the Wi-Fi – this prison really is too soft – and she carried on with her online yoga classes all night from your cosy cell, thereby placing her at Penberth and giving you a solid alibi as being safely tucked up here. Meanwhile, *you* took the car back to Penberth, rowed round to the Minack (no doubt with my knife and my old Thomas train), scaled the cliffs, let yourself into the back of the kennel, and not knowing that Cat had already been in and poisoned him, or knowing that he was slowly suffocating from the tight collar over his swelling neck, you stabbed him in the neck with my knife, let him fall to the ground, and then put the train on top – pointing the finger more than aptly in my direction, I might add. And the only person who witnessed all of that wasn't a person at all, but a bloody bird – Ruby! She's been trying to tell me for days who the murderer was, but when she squawked, "Donna did it," I thought she meant me.'

'Are you finished?' she asks.

Am I? Yes.

'That's my summation complete. Oh, except for the Kate Hudson yoga gear you were wearing that day in the glasshouse, meaning that you stayed on at Penberth for a day or so. Kerensa, of course, would never wear anything that isn't certified Fair Trade, nor would she put pastel-coloured sweet peas in with orange dahlias, although that happened before Jack died, so I'm a little bit confused now as to the actual timing of the swap, but I stick by my summation.'

Her expression darkens even more for a few moments, before she throws her arms around me and shouts, 'Bravo, Belladonna! I knew you'd get there in the end! And to put you out of your confusion, I'd already been at the house for a week before Jack arrived. It was me that lured him up Logan Rock with Lamorna, not Kerensa. As if Kerensa would ever do such a thing!'

I wriggle out of her grasp.

'But... why set me up to look like the murderer?' I ask, the tears welling on my lower lids. 'I nearly ended up in the clink! It's only because I chased after the drug pushers and because Jase Clarkson lied for me that Penworthy hasn't sent me down!'

She looks at me like I've gone bonkers. 'Set you up? Of course, we didn't set you up, darling. Why on earth would you say that we did? I made it obvious to you – to everyone – that it was me who did it... *my* knife, and the revenge symbolism of the train, the—'

'*Your* knife? But you gave that knife to *me*, Aunty.'

Her eyes flash. 'Yes, I did. And on that note, Donna Nightshade, I'm not happy that you left it lying around! Honestly, anyone could have stolen it!'

'But *I'm* known as Deadly Nightshade now, so when you used the knife, it all pointed to the *new* Donna, not the old one!'

She shakes her head. 'Don't be silly. As if anyone would believe that you would use your own knife, with your own name on it, to kill someone. That calling card was purely from me to you. You must admit,' she says, 'it was a superb double bluff!'

I sit back on the bench, arms folded, frowning.

'Please don't be cross,' she says, sidling up and stroking my hair. 'I thought you'd love the hilariousness of it all once you worked it out. I mean, come on, you must have twigged that we were playing out the evil twin thing? And what about the deadly message I asked to be written on the card for the bouquet? The one I ordered to be sent directly to Jack in funeral colours? It was so obviously me! And, well...' She pats me on the knee. 'I wanted you to have a *really* successful first case – set your business off with a massive bang! Killing Jack in the process was simply the icing on the cake, and Ruby hating me was such a bonus. We really did think you'd guess ages ago that we were trading places. We've been doing it for years! I still have absolutely no idea how to clean your chakras, no idea at all, but I do try!'

'But...'

Aunty Donna starts fiddling with the hem of her prison-issue smock. 'Lamorna guessed straight away, of course. Dear girl. She's extra special, that one – celestial. And Jago guessed a year or so ago when I had an arm wrestle with one of his friends in the pub. What japes! Kerensa already had the banner, you see, from all the other times she's stood in for me at the old homestead.'

Prison. She means at the prison.

She's not finished. 'I'll admit, I had to have a bit of a rethink as the thing played out. Jack was supposed to die on Logan Rock because I decided as soon as Jack pitched up at

Penberth that it was time to finish him off once and for all, and there's no time like the present, as they say. You can't know how ashamed I am that the first attempt failed, but all I can say is, it was a rushed plan.'

The penny finally drops.

'It was *you* who wrote the margin note in the shaman book!'

'Of course – that was a lovely little clue I set up for you, wasn't it? I did have fun doing that.'

'And Shaman Paulo?'

'An old boyfriend. It was Paulo who introduced me to José.'

No words. Truly.

'And then... well, when that crazed drug-pushing friend of yours started having a pop at him, too... that was pure coincidence. Bonkers really, but he truly was a dreadful man. I'm surprised no one managed to pop him off years ago, although maybe they tried and failed because, as I said, the man was a real pig to kill.'

I drum my fingers on the bench. 'Let me get this right, the whole family knew about your antics except for me – even Ruby knew?'

She cocks her head, thinking. 'Yes, everyone. I had absolutely no idea I'd glued a bit of Ruby's feather onto Thomas's track, but Ruby kept flapping around, shooing me off, and a bit of feather must have fallen off when I batted her away. Brilliant piece of luck though... I bet it got the police really scratching their heads!'

'It led them in my direction, actually, but—'

'Ooh, and how did you like the threatening texts I sent you?'

That's that mystery sorted.

'Didn't they add *exactly* the perfect touch of drama that was kind of missing from the whole thing? A gentle touch of menace? I just knew you'd be hiding away in that glasshouse of yours when I sent them.'

'But you don't own a—' I stop speaking, because of course she owns a mobile phone. She's got the top prison officer tightly by the balls, so to speak.

'Well, that all makes me feel like an absolute chump,' I say. 'I'm clearly an outsider not to be trusted in my own family. It's awful.'

Aunty Donna places a consolatory arm around my shoulder. 'But only because you've got enough to think about… and we wanted to give you an actual case to solve, to give you a bit of a boost, you know?' She cups her hands on my cheeks, quite tenderly for Aunty Donna. 'And, let's face it, it doesn't matter if the police find out about me; I mean to say, what would they do, lock me up? The brilliance of that terrible beast of a friend of yours – Cat, was it? – by taking the rap for me and dying in the process? Well, that's all just icing on the cake, really.'

She throws her head back. Her laughter is straight out of a play about a madhouse.

Lie down.

I need to lie down.

Chapter Forty-Eight

It's been an odd forty-eight hours for Joe Enys who, despite having won fifty quid from Penworthy, and despite having been put up for the 'Copper of the Year' award, is feeling quite put out.

Jase Clarkson didn't die from his injuries (*more's the pity*, thinks Joe) and Caden has been stitched back together at the hospital and has returned to Scilly as a local hero. But all Joe can think is, *why, why, why did it have to be that absolute tit Jase Clarkson who saved Donna's life?* And fancy even Penworthy not knowing that he was Interpol.

Or did she?

Joe had to face it; he'd been made to look like an absolute amateur – Bill Smiley had said as much when he bumped into him outside the pasty shop this morning.

If only Ted had dropped the banner from a few feet higher, the crack on his head would have been even harder and Jase Clarkson would be dead. But then Donna would probably be dead, too, and that would have been the end of the world as Joe knew it. But she wasn't dead, and Joe was left feeling like everyone else was a daring hero with wounds to prove it – Jase, Donna, Caden, even Ted, had been heroes – all except Joe, who had stayed on the boat and ran out of fuel, like the sensible copper he was born to be.

Demelza had tried to comfort him. 'But it was *you* who arranged the drop of the banner,' she said. 'It was *you* who commandeered the aircraft and legged it, unarmed, and mobilised the Navy. If you hadn't done all those things then Jase Clarkson would still be deep undercover headed to France, about to go even deeper undercover, and a load of Cornish teenagers would be off their faces on crack! You did well, Joe. I mean, so what if Jase has a gun and a great body? The world needs the normal guys as well as the James Bonds you know!'

Brilliant. Just brilliant.

Chapter Forty-Nine

And now, as the sun goes down on Penzance a couple of days later, Joe is sitting at an outdoor table at the café at Jubilee Pool, which is kind of where it all started, waiting for Donna to arrive.

He glances up from his pint of locally brewed ale because here she is now, wearing jeans and a baggy jumper and a happy smile. (She wore shorts and a vest top for Jase, he seems to remember.)

'Wasson?' she says, taking a seat opposite.

'Wasson,' Joe replies.

An hour or so later and it's Joe's turn to drum his fingers on the table.

Donna has been regaling him with the most fanciful story about how it was actually Aunty Donna who murdered Jack Crowlas, but has asked if he could possibly let the world keep believing that it was Cat who did it all – the poison, the zip tie, the stabbing – because, after all, 'Aunty Donna is already in prison and Cat is dead so what harm can it do?'

One question races through Joe's mind, though: why did Jase Clarkson make a statement that Cat murdered Jack – knife and all – if he knew all along that she hadn't finished him off?

'I think he wanted to save my skin,' says Donna. 'I'm not sure why though,' she adds, coquettishly.

Jesus, thinks Joe, *could this guy possibly be any more transparent? More annoying?* He was clearly just trying to get into her—

'Pants,' says Donna. (His eyes really do give away far too much.)

'What?'

'The word you're looking for is *pants*.' She jumps up to take the seat directly next to Joe and elbows him in the ribs. 'Did I tell you I put Jase in my book?'

She didn't. His mouth twitches into a smile.

'You mean you subjected the man who saved your life to the plight of the wrecker's curse?'

'I certainly did.'

Joe knew this already of course, but he could dance right now.

'Shame on you, Donna Nightshade,' he says, taking a sip of ale. 'The whole of Penzance is talking about it by the way... the curse, I mean.'

Donna throws him a questioning glance.

'Jago was showing off down the pub last night,' he explains, 'about how effective the Nightshade curse is.'

'It's always best to keep people on their toes,' says Donna. 'And it just goes to show that a curse from a Nightshade is not something to be thrown out lightly, especially considering what happened to Cat...'

'Meaning...?'

'Kerensa cursed her a while back. Or it might have been Aunty Donna who did it – who knows these days?'

'Who indeed?' thinks Joe.

Donna turns her gaze towards the pool. The geothermal spa is busy today.

'*You know I never cursed you, right?*' she says, then looks at him and shrugs. 'I was going to, but then I just couldn't do it.'

Joe smiles, and it's a big, finally-let-out-your-breath kind of a smile.

'You always did know what I was thinking,' he says.

'Which is why I know that you don't believe me about Aunty Donna killing Jack – perhaps you don't want to admit that I cracked the case?'

Does she really think that? Yes, she does. Joe glances down at his pint, which is nearly empty.

'Perhaps, just a tiny bit,' he says. 'Although maybe you're mistaking disbelief for shock. I thought the Nightshades never confessed to the police. One for all and all for one. That's what Lamorna said.'

'Well, yes.' Donna rests a hand on his arm. There's a bit of a jolt. Was that... a tiny spark of electricity they just created, or is this shirt polyester? 'It's not a big issue, is it?' she asks, pretending not to have noticed the spark.

Despite the hand, and the electricity, Joe decides to play it straight, for now.

'It is if I decide to act on the information. Kerensa and Jago will go down as accessories.' Donna removes her hand. 'And even Lamorna will be up for attempted murder, what with the brugmansia issue.'

Donna takes a deep breath and looks Joe straight in the eye. 'Look. I've told you the whole truth because this time I want you to know that I'm straight – even to the extent of grassing up my family. No secrets, no lies anymore between the two of us. It's important to me that you know that.'

There's a pause. It's cavernous.

'And also... I think you're a different person now,' she says, 'and I think you're very happy that Jack is dead, and it's my hunch that you'll let... well, as Uncle Jago said – and pardon the pun – you'll let sleeping dogs lie.'

Joe picks up his glass and begins to swish the dregs of his ale around the bottom.

Donna nudges him again. 'Shall we bury that hatchet, Joe, once and for all?'

'Hmm,' says Joe, thinking, because there's something niggling at him that simply doesn't ring true. Isn't it all a bit too... convenient? Could Aunty Donna really have escaped from prison, shimmied up a cliff face carrying a toy train and a knife, nipped in the back of the kennel, and slotted Jack in the neck? No, Joe doesn't believe that she could. In fact, he'd already discounted that option when he read the diaries for himself and saw that good old Donna

Nightshade Senior boasted that she'd scaled the cliffs at the Minack in 1983. He'd taken this idea seriously until the police climber said that they were unscalable, and when he read on and saw that she had also written that she'd shimmied up the Leaning Tower of Pisa (the side with the lean) in 1982 wearing nothing but an enigmatic smile, he realised that this was a woman who was not necessarily on speaking terms with the truth, so...

His phone pings, breaking the moment. Joe ignores it. Donna grabs his pint glass and stands.

'I'll get another one in and give you a moment to have a think and make a decision.' She edges away from the table. 'It's a lot to take in,' she says, smiling as if they're having a normal evening out, and she hasn't just told him that her whole family have been embroiled in murder (and asked him to cover it up for her). 'Same again?' she asks.

Joe nods, waits for her to disappear, then looks at his phone. It's a text from Demelza.

Regarding my theory on the mannequin and Lamorna – we've got a fingerprint match. Hurrah! Send out the lads?

Joe knows that the answer to this text will shape the rest of his life.

Let sleeping dogs lie

he types, while visualising that hatchet (the one Donna just offered him) being buried so deep that not even the most inquisitive, shitbag of a terrier could unearth it.

Chapter Fifty

Nevertheless, Joe is simply too much of a 'dot the i's and cross the t's' kind of a guy not to take the case to its conclusion, which is why, having spent the whole night trawling through even more of Aunty Donna Nightshade's diaries, he is back at Jubilee Pool, waiting for his two invitees to appear. He's bought three coffees and asked for extra sugar.

Lamorna is the first to arrive. Joe notices that she hasn't brought the macaw today. He bloody knew that the ruse about Ruby never leaving her side was nothing but hogwash.

She takes a seat and nods towards the coffee with a smile.

'You worked it all out then?' she says.

Psychic. The girl is definitely psychic.

Joe considers saying, *I think so*, but there really is no room for doubt in his mind and so goes with a definite, 'Yes,

I have. I'm afraid I didn't buy the evil twin story that was sold to Donna. Sorry.'

Lamorna laughs. 'What? Even after Aunty Deadly and I went to all the trouble to train Ruby to say, "Donna did it" as a kind of double bluff thing?'

'Even then I didn't buy it.'

Lamorna sighs a deep sigh reflecting the inevitability of her acceptance. 'S'ok. I don't mind,' she says. 'Not really. Donna fell for it, and that's all that matters.' She brightens. 'It was a fab ruse though, don't you think? And good of Aunty Donna to be prepared to take the rap for... well, murder. She's such a good egg, that aunty of mine.'

'Indeed, she is,' says Joe, sipping on hot coffee.

'And it's great that Donna has the confidence to think she can actually do detective work now,' adds Lamorna, 'even though she's a bit crap at it.'

Joe bites his bottom lip. 'I really couldn't comment,' he says.

'And what was it that sealed it for you, in the end?' asks Lamorna. 'I take it you found Jane?'

'Jane?'

'That's the name of the mannequin – Jane,' she explains.

'Ah. Right. She didn't seal it, but she helped. She washed up at Nanjizal Cove, on the beach there.'

Lamorna nods her understanding. 'And did you like the mechanics I added,' she asks, 'or maybe they've been washed away? I'm not very good at soldering, I'm afraid.' She shakes her head in wonder. 'Honestly, Joe, you have no idea how difficult it is to motorise a mannequin – to get the arm moving with the bow at exactly the correct angle was an absolute pain, and I only had a few hours to do it, but I managed it in the end. *Suum cuique*, and all that.'

Suum cuique, and all that? Joe has heard – in fact, read – those words before, in Aunty Donna's diary. (Like aunty, like niece, clearly.)

Joe pretends to agree that the mechanics were indeed impressive, given the time constraint (whereas they were absolute rubbish).

'I'm guessing the idea was to have the mannequin positioned inside the music tent,' says Joe, 'showing your silhouette playing the violin to the audience on the outside, while you put on a recording of the music and snuck around the back of the hessian screening to access the kennel from the back and ultimately kill Jack?'

'Exactly that,' she says. 'Clever, wasn't it?' Lamorna holds out her wrists. 'It's a bit of a déjà vu moment, Joe, but put the cuffs on. It's a fair cop, as they say.'

Joe nods towards the coffee. 'Just give me a minute. I've got my coffee to drink yet. And, I won't be "putting the cuffs on" as you aren't the murderer, are you, Lamorna? This is simply you finding another way – yet again – to cover up for the actual murderer.'

Lamorna scoffs, shaking her head as if an irritating fly has landed on her nose. 'Of course I am. Who else could it possibly be? You said yourself that you found the mannequin – a mannequin that *I* threw into the sea after the performance. I'm not worried about prison, you know, because I'll plead insanity – say it runs in the family. Thirty quid says I'm out within the year.'

Joe shakes his head. 'Nah. That's a load of rubbish.'

'But—'

'Oh, I agree, you did have the *intention* of murdering Jack that night, especially after your attempt at Logan Rock failed, but as you're now keenly aware, more than one person tried to kill Jack Crowlas at the Minack while he was whiling the time away in the kennel, but only one person managed it – and that person wasn't you. The mannequin idea was quite decent, if a little predictable: you gave yourself the alibi of having been in the music tent all night because your silhouette and the music would prove it, while you nipped round the back and killed him. But we've had forensics look over the mannequin and the motor would never have been strong enough to move the bow up and down for more than a minute without burning out – certainly not long enough for you to murder Jack. I think you set the mannequin in motion after the interval, but the motor burnt out and that was that. I remember the definite scent of burning in the air. You must have laid the mannequin on the floor during a subsequent break in the music. You also no doubt threw the dummy into the sea just at the moment the kennel door opened at the end of the play?'

She considers arguing her case for a moment, and she certainly could, because Joe knows that all he's got here is conjecture, but Lamorna scrunches up her face to show that she's beaten, which is such a relief because he made the whole thing up about having forensics look over the motor.

'I was so disappointed when Jane started to smoke,' she admits. Then she laughs. 'Sorry, I just got an image of a mannequin lighting up a cigarette! I obviously mean that the motor started to smoke.'

'You see, I wasn't prepared to slot him without a watertight alibi. But to be honest, I'm not sure I had the bottle to kill him in the way I'd planned it anyhow, so I doubt I would have gone through with it, even if the motor *had* been up to the job.'

'And out of interest'—Joe can't help himself—'how *did* you plan to do it this time?'

Lamorna makes an 'eek' face. 'Trust me, Joe, you don't want to know, but let's just say that I'd taken a pair of castrating irons out of the old cattle shed at Penberth. I threw those in the sea, too.'

She's quite correct; Joe absolutely does not want to know.

Lamorna sighs. 'To be clear, if you don't think it was Aunty Donna, and you don't think it was me...'

'Who *do* I think it was?' asks Joe. 'As I said, I didn't buy the evil twin ruse for a moment. There's no way Donna Senior could have scaled those cliffs.'

'How do you know?'

'Because we've had the best climber in the southwest try to scale them, and it's simply not possible. Apparently there used to be a protruding ledge that made a climb just about possible, but that ledge crumbled away in the storms last winter, leaving those cliffs unquestionably impossible to scale.'

'It wasn't Aunty Donna, then?'

'No, but you know that already, don't you?'

Lamorna shrugs. 'How did you work it all out?'

It's Joe's turn to shrug. 'Oh, I suppose it was DCI Penworthy who helped me out in the end, more's the pity.'

This clearly does not impress Lamorna, who says, 'That old crow bag? Never.'

'I'm afraid so,' confirms Joe. 'It was something she said about the obvious answer being the correct one – and the fact that there really was only one sensible answer in the end. The truth is – as you're well aware – that the person who killed Jack Crowlas was the same person who made sure that Cat had a stash of deadly nightshade to hand (thanks to embroiling Pete), and it was also the same person who knew what the consequences would be in terms of the swelling of the neck, which was the same person who had easy access to the dog suit and had the idea of gluing a zip tie to the inside of the dog collar. In fact, using the principle of Occam's razor, the murderer was the only person who had clear and easy access to the kennel and that person hid in your music tent, which is why I know that you know who the murderer is, as does the rest of your family... except for Donna.

'It was the person'—Joe is building up to a big reveal moment and he's too committed now to simply *say* the name of the murderer—'that you would all protect even more fiercely than you would protect Donna, or yourselves, which is why you and your Aunty Donna decided to take the rap for that individual, rather than allow them to go to prison. The murderer, I'm afraid to say, is—'

A shadow appears behind Joe.

'Me. You did your best, honeybunch,' says Jago. 'But the caper's up.'

'Run for it, Uncle!' shouts Lamorna, jumping up and grabbing Joe by the arm. 'Run for it and head to the hills! I'll hold him down!'

Jago takes a seat. 'My dear girl, I haven't the energy for any running today. I'm glad to be free of the pretence of it all. All this "covering one's tracks" business was becoming rather tiresome.'

Joe pushes the extra cup of coffee towards Jago, who inhales the kind of very deep breath befitting the build-up to a confession of murder. He glances around to make sure the people on the next table aren't listening and leans in.

'It all started down at the pub a week and a half ago when Jack walked in, bold as brass, calling the shots and saying he wanted to get the gang back together and that we were to hand the keys to Penberth over to him.'

'A week and a half ago?' says Joe. 'But during our last conversation, Mr Nightshade, you told me that you only discovered that Jack was back when he came into the pub the night before the play.'

Jago looks at Joe over the top of his glasses. 'I was clearly lying to you, young man. This, now, is my actual confession.'

'Right, of course,' says Joe, feeling a bit daft.

'I thought I'd keep an eye on the bounder and an ear to the ground to see what I could pick up. I even pretended to befriend him, just to see if I could infiltrate whatever dealings he was involved with… It was me who gave him Donna's card.'

'Like a self-made secret agent,' says Lamorna.

'I suppose so, yes,' agrees Jago.

'Cool,' offers Lamorna. 'That'll stand you in good stead with the judge, won't it, Joe?'

Joe declines to comment.

'It was obvious that he was twitched about something,' continues Jago. 'And obvious that he had returned to his nefarious ways. I got in with him and slowly but surely, I worked out a plan... not that Jack had the least idea that he was being played. He was a clueless idiot rather than a first-rate criminal, really.'

'Go on...'

'I learned from Jack that Gabby had had an affair with him in Lithuania – she was crazy about him, truly crazy – but he kept shooing her off once he bumped into her in Penzance, and he really didn't want her telling anyone that she knew him from Lithuania either – something about Interpol being on his case. He told me to leave an envelope at the vicarage... Inside was a photograph. Oh, dear me, yes, it was quite a photograph.'

'Bloody hell!' says Lamorna. 'Gabby and Jack were lovers?! Who'd have thought it? We'll see her in a totally different way now in church, won't we?'

Well, quite, thinks Joe.

'The one person I didn't get the measure of was that Jase Clarkson fella – superb operator. Fabulous body, too.'

Joe holds back an eyeroll.

'No, the only way to get rid of Jack, I realised, was to set him up with a higher force altogether...'

'Donna?' asks Joe, leading Lamorna to laugh out loud.

'*You*, of course,' says Jago, throwing Joe a disparaging glance.

'Well, yes,' says Joe.

'Hence, the note to the police,' says Lamorna.

'Which said to search *an animal* at the Minack... meaning the dog, obviously, although I admit that my plan was flawed, because you could have searched Cat – oh, the irony if you had! You see, I didn't know that Cat was the cuckoo, but it's clear now that Jack told Cat, his accomplice, about the drop and arranged for her to come backstage to relieve him of the stash.'

'Which is when she made her move to kill him with the deadly nightshade,' says Lamorna. 'And stitch Donna up like a kipper in the process.'

'Exactly right,' agrees Jago. 'And I would like to reiterate, officer, that you will see during the course of my confession that I truly did not intend to kill the man, merely set him up like, well, a kipper, as Lamorna said...'

'I'll keep an open mind,' says Joe.

'Very good. So, on the night of the play, I donned my own dog suit, which I *hadn't* lost at the pub – that was a lie – and bounded down onto the stage – a superb performance; one of my best – before getting shut in the kennel for the first half and settling down to read my book with my headtorch. All went to plan, and I even spent the interval in the kennel, too – having told everyone not to disturb me...'

'Except for me,' said Lamorna. 'I brought you a drink, didn't I, Uncle?'

'You did indeed, sweetheart. Thank you for that.'

Lamorna turns to Joe. 'Aunty Donna told me to keep that little snippet to myself, obviously, when she came up with her plan.'

'Plan?' repeats Joe.

'The cover-up plan,' explains Lamorna. 'We came up with it in the kitchen after the show, at about one in the morning when Donna had gone to bed – or she may have been in the greenhouse, I can't remember. Aunty Donna was still pretending to be Kerensa, you see.'

'I see,' says Joe. 'Kind of.'

'Once the second half kicked off,' continues Jago, 'I nipped out of the back of the kennel behind the hessian screen, secured the rope – which I'd positioned earlier – and dropped it down to Jack, who was waiting at the bottom. I gave him the second dog suit which I'd also hidden in preparation, and we swapped places and he dashed into the kennel. Getting the dog suit delivered on time was touch and go, I tell you. Anyhoo, it turned out that Jack told Cat to come and get the drug stash halfway through the second half, and that's when she stuck the poison up his nose with the intention of killing him because – as we now know – she wanted her hands on Penberth and wasn't prepared to share. Of course, I had no idea that she was going to stick poison up his nostrils. I've no idea where she got the deadly nightshade from.'

'She got it from Pete who left it in a slipper at Lidl,' says Joe. 'As you well know.'

'Ah, you know about that,' says Jago.

'CCTV,' says Joe.

Jago and Lamorna exchange eyerolls. 'Goodness knows why they handed the thing over in such a clandestine manner,' says Jago, shaking his head. 'If he'd simply met her on the prom and handed it over, no one would have been any the wiser. Such are the mistakes of amateur criminals, I suppose.

'Cat had persuaded Pete to make up another vial by saying that she needed it for her arthritis. When he questioned the fact that she'd never complained of arthritis before, she said that if he didn't do it, she'd tell the police about his involvement in a money laundering financial pyramid scheme – which *she* bloody well sold him, I might add!'

'It's all very complicated,' adds Lamorna.

'It wasn't supposed to be,' says Jago, 'but other people kept getting in the way.'

'Hmm,' says Joe, rubbing his temples, while wondering if he'll have any skin left by the end of the confession. 'Even so, sir, it seems to me that you always intended to kill Jack... hence the knife. You had set the whole thing up so perfectly, and yet you say you didn't plan to. How so?'

'Well, that's my point – my point about other people messing up the plan. I was supposed to shimmy down the rope and Lamorna – who I must confess to having embroiled in the scheme – was supposed to release it and throw it down immediately after the performance. I'd then row away in the boat Jack rowed in on, but blow me, when I reached the bottom of the rope, there was Kerensa, bold as brass, rowing into the cave in some boat she'd purloined! Only it wasn't Kerensa; it was my other sister, Donna!'

What? Wait a minute! Joe's brain is about to explode because he had completely discounted the mad aunt. And yet here she is again, the proverbial bad penny.

'Go on...' he says.

'Well,' continues Jago, 'you can imagine the laugh we had about the fact that we'd *both* decided to take it upon ourselves to sort out Jack, but when I told her what I'd done, she said that I was a blithering idiot and that I needed to *kill* him, not imprison him, or else the blighter (she used another word) would simply keep rolling up at Penberth – remember that neither of us had any idea that Cat was in the process of poisoning him while we were having this conversation. She said something along the lines off, "Jesus Christ! If you want a job doing, do it yourself," and started to shimmy up the rope, but she'd grown her nails, pretending to be Kerensa—'

'Who has beautiful nails,' chips in Lamorna.'

'She really does,' agrees Jago, 'and she's simply not as young or as fit as she used to be (which really gripped her shit, I can tell you). After three failed attempts and in desperate need of a manicure, she insisted that *I* take her knife (that she'd stolen from Donna earlier while pretending to be Kerensa) and she sent *me* up the rope to finish off the job. My mother used to make us shimmy up ropes quite regularly, you see; we Nightshades have never forgotten our pirating roots.'

'And Uncle is very fit for his age, aren't you, Uncle?' explains Lamorna, who, once again, is filling in the gaps quite nicely. 'He does a Joe Wicks workout every single day!'

'And what happened then, Mr Nightshade?' asks Joe, who's supposed to be doing a spot of night-fishing later and who wanted to get this whole confession thing in the bag much quicker.

'We argued while standing in the cave for a while because, according to my sister – who would know – Jack Crowlas "is an absolute pig" to kill – a phrase I didn't approve of, by the way. But in the end, I had no choice but to get my backside up there and finish the job, and sharpish, because my sister can be very persuasive, especially when she's holding a knife.'

'I can imagine,' says Joe, remembering that fateful day years ago when Aunty Donna was arrested. She had threatened to cut off Joe's testicles. He crosses his legs.

'Anyhoo,' says Jago. 'Handily, this was all happening – the conversation with my sister Donna – during Lamorna's rousing rendition of "Libertango"—'

'Ooh, how *perfect*!' says Lamorna.

'Yes, I thought so myself at the time,' agrees Jago. 'And when I snuck back into the kennel – just as the fireworks started going off – to my horror I saw that Jack's neck was swollen inside the collar, that his face was blue, and that he was flailing around the kennel like a... well, like someone who was being strangled. My reaction, of course, was to help the poor chap – when you come face to face with someone who's dying, your first reaction is to help them out, obviously.'

'Ooh, this is the best bit! You'll never believe it, Joe!' says Lamorna, her sparkling eyes urging Jago on.

Joe is pretty certain he probably won't.

'I raised the knife to cut the zip tie,' explains Jago. 'But Jack started to really flail at that point and rather than let me help him, bugger me if he didn't put his hands around my own neck and start to squeeze, so I stabbed him in the neck, and he fell to the floor. Blood everywhere! It's a miracle we didn't fall out of the kennel and onto the stage.'

'I told you it was good!' says Lamorna.

'And the train?' says Joe.

'Ah, yes. My sister had stuffed the train in the pocket of my dog suit, instructing me to leave it on the body – she's dramatic that way, and of course, it was a macabre, somewhat comic, reference to what Jack did to Donna's dog – so I thought, *well, in for a penny, in for a pound. He's almost certainly dead now.* I placed it on his back and that was that job done... I didn't think to remove the knife, which was very remiss, considering that it was Donna's – my sister was less than pleased with that faux pas, I can tell you. But anyhow, quick as a flash, I stripped off the dog suit, which was covered with Jack's blood, tied it to the rope and dropped the rope down for Donna to catch—'

'That's *Aunty* Donna,' Lamorna stresses, leading Joe to offer her a reassuring pat on the hand to show that he really does understand that Donna Junior was not involved in any way.

'Then, I waited in the shadows – well, in the back of Lamorna's music tent – until the play ended. I was quite shaken, what with having just killed someone. My sister had already told me to nip around the back of the theatre once the body was discovered and what to say for an alibi – about the missing pig etc.'

'She's such a quick thinker, is Aunty Donna,' explains Lamorna.

'And then? Well, all hell broke loose, as you know,' continues Jago. 'Which meant that no one noticed me dashing up the steps from around the back of the stage – no one except Louise, Donna's friend. She winked at me and tapped her nose, and we left it at that. Do you know, the dear girl has known all along who the murderer was and never said a peep. That's a true Cornish woman for you!'

'Good egg, that,' says Lamorna.

'And what did your sister do with the blood-splattered dog suit?' asks Joe, who is beginning to believe that Jago is probably telling the truth about it being an accident – or, if not an accident, not premeditated either... although, not premeditated by Jago but it *was* premeditated by Aunty Donna, who didn't put the knife in. He smiles, thinking, *unpick that, judge!*

'Do you know, young man, I have no idea what she did with the damn thing. But if I know my sister, no blighter will ever find it.'

Lamorna turns to Joe, taking up the narrative. 'And that's when Aunty Donna – who was still pretending to be Kerensa and had rowed back round to Penberth – held the emergency meeting I was telling you about, and we all came up with other, what we thought were plausible, means of having killed Jack, just in case you were on to Jago. Aunty Donna always intended to take the rap if necessary, but I decided on my own account to try to put the blame on me. No judge would give someone with my angelic face too long a stretch, and it was better than Aunty Donna being re-convicted. She's out in a couple of years, you know – if she's certified sane. It was generally agreed amongst myself, Uncle Jago, Aunty Donna, oh, and Aunt Kerensa, who was both thrilled and mortified when we went to the prison to tell her, that Uncle Jago would *never* survive in prison!'

Jago slaps his thighs and takes a long nasal breath. 'Anyhow, I think it's time to wrap things up. You know now how I did it, but I don't want all the others to be in trouble. *I* want to take the rap for the whole bally lot of it! Best to limit the damage, as t'were.'

'But you haven't finished the whole story yet, Uncle,' says Lamorna, taking his hand. 'What about the *why*?' says Lamorna.

'Why?' repeats Jago.

Lamorna shrugs. 'Motive is everything in cases like this, and Joe will certainly want to know *why* you murdered him, so—'

'It was self-defence, I tell you!' pleads Jago.

'Not entirely,' murmurs Lamorna, who is suddenly finding the dregs of her coffee quite interesting.

But Joe already knows why Jago wanted Jack to disappear on a permanent basis. After all, he's read the diaries. Or at least Demelza has and pointed out the pertinent bits so it's the same thing.

'We have all your Aunty Donna's diaries on file,' says Joe. 'We made copies when she was convicted, and I think the motive has something to do with Jack's involvement with Lamorna's mother.' Joe glances at Lamorna and begins to feel quite uncomfortable.

'Don't worry, she knows already,' says Jago.

'That Jack raped my mother and is subsequently not only my father but also basically my mother's killer because she had a rare condition meaning that, although she survived giving birth to Donna, just about, she was told that she'd likely die in childbirth if she tried it again?' says Lamorna. 'I've known about that for years.'

'Is that why you tried to kill him, too?' says Joe to Lamorna.

'Not really. He may have been my biological father, but he had absolutely nothing to do with my upbringing. When I read that part of the diary for the first time I was quite put out, but then Aunt Kerensa taught me all about tabula rasa, so I don't worry about any inconsequential stuff like that anymore.'

'Tabula rasa?' repeats Joe.

'A clean slate. It's the idea that we're born with no built-in ideas. I don't fear the fact that Jack is my father because he's never been around to influence my thoughts. Even the absence of him hasn't influenced me. I want the same thing for Donna.'

'What do you mean?' asks Joe.

'How to explain…' Lamorna stares at the swimming pool for an uncomfortable amount of time before saying, 'Think back to the Romans. They had these tabula slates – writing tablets, I suppose we'd call them now.'

'Like a very early iPad,' explains Jago.

'Exactly. To reuse them they heated wax and smoothed the wax over the tablet – hence the phrase, blank slate. I'm hoping that the ending of Jack will lead to tabula rasa for Donna – the blanking and smoothing of her mind, the wiping out of past horrors…'

Joe thinks of the diary entries he read and doubts that

anyone can ever wipe Donna's mind clean, or Aunty Donna's. 'Did you ever tell Donna about Jack?' he asks.

'Being my dad? No. I thought she might look at me differently if she knew. Which is why I destroyed our copy of the entry that pointed us in that direction, although she could have read it before then, but I doubt it, what with her being in prison. Donna can't be bothered to read the diaries, like I said. Which is a relief, really. I know Aunty Donna will never tell her, either.'

'Why?' asks Joe.

'Because I asked her not to. But how did you know for certain that it was my uncle who put the knife in?' she asks.

Joe shrugs. 'I'm afraid I didn't. Not completely. It was more a case of ruling everyone else out. I suspected him once I knew that Donna Senior's last diary entry was written by Jago.' Joe turns to face him. 'My sergeant noticed the slight difference in style, and then our handwriting expert confirmed it.'

'Using the note I sent to the police station, I suppose,' says Jago.

'I'm afraid so,' says Joe. 'It was a promise to a dead sister that you would one day avenge her death, wasn't it?'

'A curse written in red,' says Lamorna.

'But I never would have had the courage to actually do it,' says Jago, hanging his head in shame. 'Not if he hadn't had his hands around my neck.'

Lamorna stands suddenly and rushes round the table, throwing herself on her knees and grabbing Joe's hands. 'Please, Joe. I'm begging you!' she wails (albeit quietly as they don't want the whole café to hear). 'Don't send him down. It was self-defence! You know it was! You've just been lucky guessing it was Jago because of the other bits of detail, and that's not fair. If he hadn't confessed, you couldn't have proved a thing! Let dead Cat take the rap, like ripped Jase wants her to. She's dead anyway and she was bad news – bad. A total drug dealer. You must see that we'd all be completely lost without him...'

'He's your rock,' says Joe, finally understanding the true dynamic of the Nightshade family.

Lamorna considers this. 'Well, yes. But also, not one of the Nightshade women can cook. We would honestly starve if he left us!'

Joe's phone pings. It's Demelza.

'Just a minute, guys,' he says, turning away.

DEMELZA: *Old Man Bosullow is dead – heart attack while shagging. They found brugmansia in his bloodstream. Nightshades again? Shall I send a car?*

JOE: *FFS*

Demelza: I'm guessing you want me to bury it again?

JOE: *Errr...*

DEMELZA: *OK, but that's two dates you owe me. Oh, and I've given the vicar that photo back (the racy one). She wants to keep it as a memento. (Yuck!)*

JOE: *Make sure she knows that it was Jack who sent her the photo, not Jase. Hopefully it will help her to get over him. She's bloody delusional.*

DEMELZA: *You're far too soft, Joe Enys, but will do. PS Delete these messages or we're screwed [winky face emoji]*

• • •

Jago holds out his wrists.

'Cuff me up, Joe,' he says. 'It's time to go the way of all true Nightshades – to the clink. I'm just ashamed it's taken me this long to get there.'

Decision time again, thinks Joe, looking down at a prostrate Lamorna who has put her hands into the prayer position. She's attracting far too much attention for Joe's liking. He stands, forcing Lamorna to stand also, and puts his phone in his pocket.

'Thank you for answering my questions, Mr Nightshade,' he says, grabbing his jacket. 'You're free to go, sir.'

'Free to go? But…'

Lamorna throws her arms around Joe. 'Oh, I just knew you were a good egg! I knew it! Wait till I tell my aunties! They're bound to let you marry Donna after this!'

Joe buttons in a smile. These Nightshades will be the death of him one day, he just knows it. He turns to walk away, but then reconsiders the text from Demelza.

'Oh, just one more thing. Unrelated. Has Old Man Bosullow been round your way recently? Asking for any help with his health, perhaps?'

Jago shakes his head. 'I don't think so, old chap.'

Lamorna, however, begins to nod. 'Oh, yes, he has, Uncle,' she says. 'Don't you remember? Kerensa – or was it Aunty Donna? It's hard to know these days – gave him that herbal remedy to help him with his… well, you know,' she leans in and whispers, 'lack of ability to carry out any bedroom antics. He came back for another dose just last week. I was a bit worried because obviously Aunty Donna has been standing in for Kerensa, so I'm not entirely sure she got the dose right, but she found this book in the glasshouse that was all about shamanism and potions and she got a recipe for Mr Bosullow out of that. He's not come back to us to complain so it must have worked out. He ordered flowers, too. Old as the hills he is, but he's quite the earner for us, so who are we to question his antics?' She stands behind Jago and puts a hand on his shoulder. 'Why? Is it important?'

Joe can't help himself.

'He's dead – brugmansia poisoning, apparently.'

'Shit,' says Lamorna.

'Crikey,' says Jago.

'Those sleeping dogs really are starting to pile up,' says Joe, rubbing his forehead and turning to leave.

Chapter Fifty-One

DONNA

I t's my birthday today! We're a week on from the night of the murder and somehow Jago was right: all is well. It's a lovely, sunny September afternoon and I'm in my beloved glasshouse listening to Pirate FM and sowing hardy annuals for next year's crop (*Cerinthe*, candytuft, and *Ammi Majus*) into half-seed trays.

(Flower farmer tip from Georgie Newbery's *The Flower Farmer's Year*: it's always better to sow one variety of seeds into a half-seed tray rather than scatter a whole packet into a big one. No one – not even a flower farmer – needs *that* number of seedlings to prick out.)

The final preparations for my birthday tea are underway in the kitchen which is why I'm keeping out of the way. It's a shame that Aunty Donna can't be here, but if I'm uncertain as to which of my aunties is hanging around Penberth at any time again, all I must do is pop Ruby on her shoulder to find out which witch is which.

Job's a good 'un.

So yes, all in all I'm feeling pretty contented at the moment (OK, smug) because now that my first case is done and dusted, and Jack's gone, and Cat's dead, and I didn't end up convicted as a murderer, I can conclude that this private investigator malarkey is much easier than I thought it would be and not tedious at all; except, I'm not getting quite as many clients pass through the door as I'd hoped. Perhaps I'll get a few more seeking out my services once word gets around that I'm not, in fact, a psychotic murderer.

I've been told to report to the courtyard outside the kitchen at 3pm and not a minute before. The usual crowd will be there, no doubt – my family, Gabby, and Pete, Louise from the Minack, and a few other mates from Newlyn. It still amazes me that Gabby was in love with Jack for years and years and befriended me just to get close to him. She's terribly contrite about it all, of course, but I've forgiven her, and we'll never mention another word about it again – not this week, anyway. As for Pete… I'm ashamed now that I thought he was embroiled in the murder because it's all become clear why he had the Wikipedia page on him. He made me a vial of poison for my birthday, dear man. I opened his present this morning. How cool (and a bit weird) was that? And how coincidental!? He really is a great guy – not fanciable – but great. Most of all though, it's telling that, considering Cat was one of the players, no one seems to care in the least that she's dead. It's not even been talked about very much. We humans really are a fickle bunch.

There is one person who probably won't be at my party

who will, I admit, be missed: Joe Enys. I've not seen him since the day I told him that Aunty Donna was the murderer, but it is most pleasing to know that when it came to the crunch, he was on my side, what with not grassing up Aunty Donna and letting dead Cat carry the can for the murder. I wonder why Jase Clarkson said it was Cat who put the knife in, when he absolutely knew that she'd said it wasn't her? Lamorna says it's because he fancies me and is bound to show up at Penberth once his head is out of the metal brace and she may be correct, but when it comes down to it, although Jase saved my life, he's just not Joe and no one ever will be. Also, I stand by the fact that I simply could not scream out the name 'Jase' in bed.

So is life.

'Hi, you...'

I turn around to see someone standing at the door. *Shit.* It's Joe Enys, and he's looking... delicious. Nice clothes, tanned face, just enough stubble on his perfectly shaped jaw to add interest...

He looks relaxed. Happy. Content.

'A little birdie told me it was your birthday,' he says, hovering at the door. (That will probably be Ruby. She's such a gossip).

'Did Lamorna invite you?' I ask.

He shakes his head. 'No. To be honest, I already knew the date of your birthday. You drummed it into me often enough in the old days.'

I laugh, but it sounds tinny and forced. *Get a grip, Donna!*

'Anyway, I came to tell you that DCI Penworthy has managed to get you released permanently from wearing an ankle monitor. She figured correctly that nabbing a drugs ring was probably just about enough of a public service to get you off.'

My eyes swell with tears. 'Thank you, Joe,' I say, my voice breaking. 'It means a lot.'

'And also... I went out on a limb and got you an actual present that... well, let's just say, you may or may not be happy with...'

I jump off my stool and rush to the door, more flustered than I would like to be at such a momentous occasion between us. My boob crack is sweating like I'm back on the boat with a gun to my head, but...

'A present? For me? From you?'

He puts up a hand to stop me stepping any closer towards him.

'Just wait there a minute,' he says. 'I've left it around the corner. Just a mo...' He glances back, smiling. 'Don't. Move. A muscle!'

'I won't!' I laugh. (God, life really is good now.)

He reappears, and his present is... a puppy.

A puppy?

To be precise, it's a little black puppy wearing a neckerchief with skull and crossbones on it.

On the one hand... a puppy! Adorable!

But on the other hand... no, no, no, no, no. We have a rule here at Penberth – absolutely no pets! I fast forward fourteen or so years to my inevitable broken heart and freeze on the spot. How the hell should I react to this? It's such an irresponsible present – the RSPCA would not approve. *A dog is for life* and all that.

Joe steps forwards with the nuzzling puppy in his arms.

'He's called Lysander,' says Joe, kissing the puppy on the nose. 'Which is a fantastic name for a pirate dog, don't you think? It means, "liberator".'

He offers the puppy for me to hold. I step backward.

'It really is good of you, Joe,' I say, 'but…'

He scrunches his face. 'The thing is – old man Bosullow has died…'

'I heard. Poor man. Heart attack?'

'Something like that. Only, his dog, Jess, the Border Terrier, just had a litter. They think she had a bit of hanky panky with that black mongrel that roams round Porthcurno shagging everything in sight. Anyway, they've rehomed the mother, but as for the six puppies…'

'They need homes,' I say.

Joe sets his face into a frown. 'And the good news is that they've all been rehomed, all except… well, nobody wanted poor Lysander here, on account of the underbite. But I thought, if anyone could love a runt…'

'Joe, I just…'

'I know what you're going to say but just hear me out because I thought now that Jack's dead, you'd be free to, you know…' He steps forward and looks me straight in the eye, saying softly, 'Love again? Perhaps you could just have a cuddle and see how you feel about it?'

I bloody could, Joe. But not with a dog!

I nod, take Lysander in my arms, and Jesus, I start to cry. Great big, golf ball tears stream down my face and land on the puppy, messing up his fur a bit. I nuzzle into him and there it is… The irresistible aroma of 'baby dog'. Is there anything on this earth more soothing, more perfectly wonderful, than puppy smell?

Joe takes a handkerchief out of his pocket (he's so organised, that man) and silently dabs my tears.

I smile.

Joe smiles.

Even Lysander smiles (although that might be the underbite).

'I see they're setting up a party for you,' says Joe as we turn to walk out of the door. 'Bunting, cake, karaoke, the lot!'

Say it, Donna. Just say it!

'You should stay,' I say.

Joe steps closer.

He's going to kiss me. He's actually going to *kiss* me! Shall I let him get a lip lock in, or…?

Too right I shall!

The gate to the walled garden clicks open. Bloody hell! We both turn around to see a bizarre metal frame edge its way into the garden. Within the frame is the battered and bruised head of Jase Clarkson.

'Ah,' I say.

Joe's phone pings. He opens a text as Jase approaches. Jase is carrying a wrapped present and trying to smile (which is difficult with a smashed-up face). I take a sneaky glance down at Joe's phone (so does Lysander, who's still in my arms. Nice one, Lysander!). The text is from Demelza. Joe selects it.

About that date? Free tonight?

Joe rushes his phone to his pocket.

Jase approaches and shakes Joe's hand.

'Good to see you, mate,' says Jase.

Joe hates being called *mate* and his nostrils flare a bit.

'You too. Sorry about the banner landing on your head,' says Joe.

Jase shrugs. 'Goes with the territory. I'll be OK once they unscrew the clamps.'

Joe turns to me, kisses me on the cheek (but doesn't linger), gives Lysander a quick pat and says, 'I'll be off, then. Be a good boy, Lysander, and remember to look after Donna for me.' Before I can say anything, he shakes Jase's hand and turns to leave.

And then he's gone.

He's gone.

Jase puts the present down on my workbench.

'A little bird told me it's your birthday,' he says. (Bloody Ruby again!) He turns towards the space that Joe vacated by the door. 'Did I interrupt something, or…?'

Did he interrupt something?

Truth is, I have no idea. No idea at all.

'Not really.' He hands me the present. 'Shall I open it now, or…?'

'It's as good a time as any,' he says. 'I guessed the size.'

Jase looks on anxiously as I rip the wrapping paper apart.

'Ugg boots?' I glance up at him, confused and yet delighted because they're the real deal and not knockoffs like my old ones.

'I guessed that your last ones must have been ruined

when I pushed you into the sea, so I thought it the gentlemanly thing to do to replace them. Try them on!'

I slip off my flipflops and pull on the boots.

'They fit,' I say.

'Just like Cinderella,' says Jase, beaming.

Ah. Perhaps Lamorna was correct. *Sharp dart of feline perfection*, and all that…

'Would you like some cake?' I ask, nestling my nose into Lysander's fur again.

'I'd love some,' he says, a little nervously. I notice his forehead is sweaty – although that could be the brace.

I put Lysander on the floor, and as the three of us saunter out of the walled garden, I know that if I don't ask him one question now, I will have missed my moment forever.

'About Cat's confession…' I begin. 'For the murder… You told Joe that Cat did it but if you remember, she said—'

He stops walking and puts a finger to my lips. 'Look. I think you're amazing and I didn't want you to go to prison, not for that arsehole.' He laughs then. 'You did the world a favour getting rid of him, and it was a brilliant way to do it, in a play. I couldn't resist the slow hand clap at the end of the show – sorry about that, but it was Just. So. Funny.'

Ah. Right. Except for the fact that…

'Wait! Jase! *I* didn't do it!'

He looks at me like, *yeah, good one*. We walk again and I continue to plead my innocence, which he's refusing to believe as we head towards the house. We're laughing and, OK, being flirtatious, and that's when I look up and see Joe's car parked on the drive. Many knowing glances are thrown around as we join the party – that is, until my friends and family see the puppy, and then the fact that the birthday girl has arrived goes completely out of the window because they all want to cuddle Lysander, and I can't blame them. I'm not paying much attention though because I'm still watching Joe's car, which is still there. Waiting. My phone pings. It's a text. From Joe.

I'm glad we're friends again.

I swallow back fresh tears and type:

So am I. I wish you'd stay.

Which I then delete, letter by letter, because, well, it's complicated. The car is still sitting at the end of the drive. He's waiting for my reply. Eventually, I go with:

Do you mind if I change his name? Lysander is a bit of a mouthful. I think I'll call him Patch.

He replies:

Not at all

and as I hear Joe's car head away down the gravel drive, another car comes into view and does a handbrake turn into the courtyard. A woman literally falls out of the driver's door and runs over to me. Her face is a claggy stream of running mascara. She's holding my business card.

'Is this the Edge of the World Detective Agency?' she asks.

I glance at the others, who shrug.

'It certainly is,' I answer, smiling.

'Someone get this woman a chair,' says Lamorna.

'And a drink,' says Jago.

She grabs my arms. 'How are you with murder?' she asks, her eyes the embodiment of 'wild psychopath'.

'Committing or solving?' asks Lamorna, stepping forward and offering up her own glass of cider until Jago returns. 'Only, the fees vary.'

The woman takes the glass. 'I'm not exactly sure yet,' she says. 'Life has gone a bit bonkers lately.'

She starts to cry.

I place an arm around her.

'Then have a drink and a slice of cake, Ms...?'

'Jacobs. Jessie Jacobs.'

'Ms Jacobs, because bonkers is what we Nightshades do best.'

Acknowledgments

As ever, a huge thank you to my editor, Charlotte Ledger, and my agent, Hannah Todd. Thank you to Rachael at *Edge of the World Bookshop* in Penzance for her enduring support, and to Adrian and Emily Clark (they know why). And of course, the biggest great big sloppy thank you of all goes to my husband and son, who I love with all of my heart.